NOT QUITE DEAD

ALSO BY John MacLachlan Gray

The Fiend in Human
White Stone Day

John MacLachlan Gray

NOT QUITE DEAD

St. Martin's Minotaur NEW YORK

NOT QUITE DEAD. Copyright © 2007 by John MacLachlan Gray. All rights reserved. Printed in the United States of America. No part of this book may be used or reproduced in any manner whatsoever without written permission except in the case of brief quotations embodied in critical articles or reviews. For information, address St. Martin's Press, 175 Fifth Avenue, New York, N.Y. 10010.

www.minotaurbooks.com

Library of Congress Cataloging-in-Publication Data

Gray, John, 1946–
    Not quite dead / John MacLachlan Gray. — 1st St. Martin's Minotaur ed.
        p.   cm.
    ISBN-13: 978-0-312-37471-6
    ISBN-10: 0-312-37471-2
    1. Poe, Edgar Allan, 1809-1849—Fiction.   2. Dickens, Charles, 1812–1870—Fiction.   I. Title.

PR9199.3.G753N68   2007
813'.54—dc22
                                                                          2007024873

First Edition: November 2007

10 9 8 7 6 5 4 3 2 1

Not Quite Dead is founded, to the point of collaboration, on the life and work and sensibilities of Edgar Allan Poe and Charles Dickens.

Put in theatrical terms, I have cast these men as actors in a drama of my own imagining. They lived at one time, but now they exist only in the mind, and the mind can mix things up.

> *Remember that what you are told is really threefold: shaped by the teller, reshaped by the listener, and concealed from both by the dead man of the tale.*
>
> ——VLADIMIR NABAKOV

NOT QUITE DEAD

There is no greater human hazard than a defeated Irishman abroad. If you had played a part in the New Ireland rebellion of 1848 on the confederate side, and harbored no wish for hanging and no faith in the good will of your countrymen (whose tepid support for the movement produced its own bitter memory), there were two places you might escape: to France or the United States of America.

France was close by and Catholic, to be certain.

Having chosen that country, however, an Irishman quickly discovered that one Catholic is not like another, that God and the Savior and the Holy Mother and the Universal Church would not remove the stigma of a foreign accent and name. That to be wholly human in France, you had to be wholly French.

For an Irishman to mingle on a daily basis with persons who regarded him as subhuman was a situation demanding a violent response. Finn Devlin would as soon stay home and hang there.

Therefore, like the destitute Irish who came before and after him, he turned to America, where he would be likewise regarded as a sort of elevated ape.

For such humiliation, he might just as well have fled to France.

And once in America, there was no returning home.

FOR TRANSPORTATION TO the New World, the law-abiding Irishman engaged an agent in London or Liverpool, who lied freely since all tickets were one way. They lied about everything: about conditions and provisions on board, the length of crossing, how close Quebec and St. John were to the United States, and how an Irishman could expect to be treated upon his arrival.

Few who could pay the fare were rejected for their own good. Ship's doctors inspected and passed passengers who could barely walk with infirmity and disease. For even the healthiest, already damaged by starvation, a bout of dysentery was enough to do the job.

Over the next six to ten weeks (and six weeks more in quarantine), the Irishman would inhabit the hold of an unseaworthy rust bucket in company with up to five hundred others, in a windowless crawl space between decks, with no toilet facilities and eighteen inches of allotted space apiece. Ship's fever would reap a glorious harvest. The daily splashes of shot-weighted cadavers would multiply. By sight of land, half the ship's human cargo would be consigned to the depths of the sea.

Welcome to the New World.

It was a normal occurrence for a lone survivor of a family of ten to step ashore, bewildered and heartbroken, only to be met on the wharf by yet another "agent"—who, for the price of all he had left, would direct him to a fictional place of employment.

Finn Devlin did not endure all that he had suffered in Ireland, only to fall victim to the imperial beast in another locale.

BY THE ABOVE process of elimination, Devlin stowed away on the cargo vessel *Medium*, a three-masted bark of eight hundred and sixteen tons out of Liverpool. This he accomplished with the assistance of a team of Irish stevedores prepared to look the other way for a leader of New Ireland—especially when the boat was about to transport him far away from home.

In assessing Devlin's chances—alone, friendless, living off the fat of his gut with naught to eat or drink but his own urine and the occasional rat—one might expect that the *Medium* would become for him an even crueler sort of coffin ship. However, such a prospect did not apply in his case.

Given sufficient hardship or grievance, a man can transform into a quite different species—animal or vegetable. During the potato famine, many Irishmen became potatoes themselves, rotting in the ground. Others turned into slugs, slipping by unnoticed. Others became pets for their English masters, Poodle Irishmen, prepared to sit and lie down on command.

A few Irishmen survived by paring their lives down to two overwhelming objectives—independence for Ireland and revenge for themselves—with such hot intensity that the two objects melded into one. Not Poodle Irishmen but quite another sort of dog.

As for the voyage, there is no situation that cannot be turned to your advantage if you are young enough, and single-minded enough, and the possessor of a strong stomach.

Devlin's opportunity occurred one starless night, with the Irish Sea barely behind them and the ship idle. The favorable breeze had forsaken her with little progress to be made by tacking. Already famished and thirsty, Devlin risked a furtive scuttle across the main deck and all but collided with the second mate, on watch beneath the square-rigged foremast, a sailor by the name of Mumford.

After some conversation, the truth of it is that Finn Devlin agreed to commit an unnatural act in return for food and tobacco. This act they performed behind the coiled line by the taffrail, and Devlin so hungry he could have eaten the tar that coated Mumford's hands, themselves the size and texture of pork hocks.

Over the following days and weeks the act was repeated, by which means Devlin avoided exposure and execution, and would live another day to secure independence for Ireland, and to feed his bottomless craving for retaliation.

Devlin endured what took place between them for the rest of the voyage; this he was able to stomach with the assistance of Mumford's tattoos.

As an experienced hand steeped in the ways of seamen, Mumford's tattoos made a visual record of his thoughts and beliefs: eyes on the pectorals for alertness on a long voyage; a rooster for protection from drowning; hinges to add strength to the joints. As well—fortunate Finn Devlin!—there were breasts on Mumford's shoulder blades, and a simulation of a woman's most private part, strategically placed to distract another man from the horror of the act.

In return for his mortal sin, as the weather grew colder Devlin was permitted to share Mumford's bed and blankets. Having charge of the bosun's locker, the second mate provided his altar boy with a reefer jacket against the bone-crushing North Atlantic cold.

For in truth Devlin was an uncommonly handsome young man and Mumford was in love—if the term can be properly applied to such a monstrous association.

Some nine weeks into the voyage, Devlin drove a marlin spike into Mumford's mouth. The eyes on his chest looked not a bit surprised; the eyes on his face, decidedly so. Devlin was not certain why he had done this, whether he hated Mumford more as a defiler, or as a Protestant.

No matter. Overboard went the second mate, down to the bottom of the oily black sea, fodder for toothy fish with glowing yellow eyes and squid with tentacles a fathom long. As the bubbles dispersed on the water's surface leaving only congealed droplets of tar, so disappeared all that had passed between them, though it would fester in Devlin's mind for life, and in the sight of the Virgin who watches over us all.

Crouched in the hold of a between deck, the boots of the crew thumping inches above his head while they underwent a two-day search (second mates were, in general, not highly regarded), Devlin killed and ate a rat, then drank his own urine, to remind himself of what he had avoided.

A week later, on another dark night, huddled against the bollards of the foredeck in Mumford's reefer jacket, Devlin discerned an oncoming vessel—a sloop with a blunt prow like the nose of a whale, a mast well forward for balance and sails the color of tea.

As the sloop approached he could discern the name on her bow— the *Scamp*. Presently the two vessels were at close quarters, their boards touching. The sloop's crew of three held lines steady while her skipper received from the captain of the *Medium* a rectangular package wrapped in heavy paper.

Only the most cursory exchange took place between the two captains—a sure sign that something illicit was taking place.

Sensing an opportunity, Devlin decided to join the possessors of the object, and by the time the *Scamp* was under way he was in hiding beneath the tarpaulins that covered the high coamings over the hold. There he waited until the crew became unwary, and before dawn once again Mumford's marlin spike was put to quiet use, and one by one the captain and crew of the *Scamp* joined the second mate at the bottom of the sea.

In first light, the Pennsylvania coast now visible, Devlin guided the sloop into a small cove, its water like mercury in the gray light of morning. After dropping anchor he searched below for the precious thing, which he eventually located in the captain's quarters, still in its heavy paper wrapping and inscribed with an address: *Topham & Lea Publishing Company, Philadelphia.*

He held the package gently in his fingers—by the weight he no longer expected gold or jewels, yet banknotes or stock certificates remained a tempting possibility.

When he tore open the package, he was utterly unprepared for what he saw.

Devlin stared fixedly at the object for what could have been moments or hours—a piece of time in which everything became, or seemed to become, dreadfully, perfectly clear.

With a sudden motion and a cry that could have been mistaken for the shriek of a gannet, he cast the object overboard with all the force at his command. The vile thing fluttered through the air like a bird, to disappear into the sea with barely a dull splash:

DAVID COPPERFIELD

FINAL FOUR NUMBERS LXI–LXIV

BY

CHARLES DICKENS

"GHOST SHIP" CONFOUNDS LOCAL POPULATION

by James Preston Wilcox, *The Philadelphia Inquirer*

Wednesday, March 14, 1849

Fishermen off the coast of Mystic Island made a significant catch yesterday morning in the form of a sloop, the *Scamp*, drifting smartly in the direction of New York City with no hands on board.

The vessel's registered owner, Mr. Henry Topham, the publisher, reports the theft of "An object of considerable value," and offers a substantial reward for its return, but declines to identify the object, as a protection against fraud.

In the meanwhile, lacking an immediate explanation as to the whereabouts of the *Scamp*'s captain and crew, residents refer darkly to the "ghost ship of Mystic Island," and will no doubt suffer considerable distress when this quartet of scamps are plucked from some squalid hideout on charges of theft.

CHAPTER ONE

History, *n.* An account mostly false, of events mostly
unimportant, brought about by knaves, and fools.
—Ambrose Bierce

*H*ere begin the memoirs of Dr. William Chivers, not to be read until
the author's demise.

I DO NOT expect that my tale will enhance my reputation. I can but
trust the fair-minded reader to take into account my years of service and my spotless moral character, up until the events of which
I write.

Perhaps you have already grasped the fact that, as you read this,
I myself am dead. While I cannot personally affirm this, the manuscript in your hand was secured in a sealed envelope, care of the
lawyer Carville D. Bendix of Richmond, with clear instructions that
it remain so until my death. Only if he followed my instructions to
the letter was he to receive the balance of his fee. (Ordinarily, lawyers
are paid to circumvent the law, but not in this case.)

In reporting the following I harbor two objects:

My first aim, and a public-spirited one, is to shed light on the lingering mystery over the death of Edgar Allan Poe—the author, critic,
and essayist, whose fame and notoriety will resound long after my
death, and yours too, dear reader, I dare say.

My second purpose is to attain an understanding for myself of the
events to follow, and to place them in the context of natural law.

Since Eddie's catastrophic reappearance in my life, one question
has nettled my mind by the day, the hour, the minute: *By what cause-
and-effect sequence of natural events did this happen?*

I say "natural" because many would resort to a metaphysical explanation, which is how the ignorant deal with the unknown. Here in the New World, a plenitude of spooks have immigrated from Europe and Africa on the backs of their believers—not to mention the all-embracing Christian hobgoblin of Original Sin, pounded into us every Sunday morning.

Having eschewed the supernatural, and having found no explanation through ratiocination, I write the following in the hope that a trickle of enlightenment might escape through the nib of my pen onto the paper before me. I write to inform myself; to notice what I see; to enlighten the part of me that thinks it thinks.

At the end of it I hope to put a period to my tale, in mind and on paper, and to lock it away like a tiresome volume of verse—penned, no doubt, by Edgar Allan Poe.

Though my name appears on the title page it seems apt that I identify myself fully. My name is (or from the reader's point of view, *was*) Dr. William John Chivers. I served as resident physician at Washington College Hospital until my resignation (which occurred shortly before its bankruptcy, though I was in no way responsible), and I am an alumnus of the college as well. Putting aside my service in the Mexican War, the hospital was my life—and my home, since my wife's passing, when I took rooms on the top floor.

Though as mentioned I am far from superstitious, as happens with anyone whose life takes an unexpected direction, looking back I am surprised by the absence of anything like a premonition. Seated in my armchair, smoking my pipe, scowling at the latest issue of the *Scientific American,* from my point of view there was nothing unusual whatsoever about the arrival of an emergency patient.

It was Election Day in Baltimore, when white male citizens over the age of twenty-one exercised their franchise with their fists. Inevitably, injuries accrued.

As well, city hospitals such as ours were almost always located in the poor neighborhoods near the docks, whose residents occupy the underside of the city—creatures of sea and land, creatures with claws and teeth. From Washington College Hospital, a short stroll down the hill brought you to Lombard Street, an area notorious for beatings, knifings, garroting, and other popular pastimes of inner-city life.

Therefore, it was scarcely an unusual occurrence that, by mid-afternoon on Election Day, a citizen might find himself transported to Washington College Hospital with a concussion, *sans* his money and watch. In this context, the carriage was spot on schedule, and as I watched the vehicle ascend Washington Hill in a steady grist of rain I actually laughed to myself—snorted rather—as though someone had just told me an old, tired joke.

Whoever the patient was, he was hard up and without family or friends, otherwise he would surely have been nursed at home. Nobody went to Washington College Hospital willingly. Once you encounter the term *hospital gangrene,* by mouth or in print, it tends to stay with you.

In all fairness to my institution, the patient would have been no better off at home. It was the state of medical care that, whichever building you occupied, if you broke a leg and it festered, you would probably die. If you contracted a bad cold or a kidney stone, you might well die. If you were pregnant, there was an excellent chance that you, the child, or both of you would die.

Or more often than not, a person would die with no warning at all: your aunt might experience an earache one evening while at her knitting, and by morning would be discovered dead, having slept late.

People died all the time. In the streets, taverns, and gambling halls, it was not a rare thing for a man, in mid-stride or mid-shout or mid-piss, to drop dead in his tracks. From an early age, pedestrians were taught to distinguish between a sleeping man and a dead man in the street (the sleeping man will cross his ankles).

In short, death was easier to achieve than life, and in America that was enough for devout Protestants to apply the work ethic. Your aunt did not become sick, she began *to fail.* Death was capitulation, and thoughts of death self-defeating, like the expectation of losing at a sport. Though the popular veneration of death approached obscenity in its public expression, the dead themselves were privately despised. People approached hospitals as they might a house filled with vampires, and I have seen even Baptists cross themselves upon entering.

Doctors, on the other hand, tend to view death as akin to the force of gravity: to be resisted or delayed wherever possible, but sooner or later, everyone fails.

> . . . the mad race run
> Up to the end, the golden goal
> Attained and found to be a hole!—Ambrose Bierce

As RESIDENT PHYSICIAN, my private rooms were situated on the top floor of the right tower, its pointed roof directly over my head like a dunce's cap. It made for a tiresome stair-climb but afforded a majestic view of the landmarks of the city—General Washington, Nelson-like on his sixty-foot column; the towers of the great Catholic church; the masts of clippers in the harbor.

Perhaps I relit my pipe, or stoked my blazing fire against what would surely be a cold, dank evening—unseasonably so for October, unhealthily wet, the barometer falling and a squall on the way.

Having painted this cozy domestic picture of myself, it seems odd to disclose that for some time I had been thinking about taking my own life. By mentioning this I do not wish to cast myself in a tragic light. I was not in a state of romantic mourning, nor did I despair for the human race. I swear that the incentive arose from pure laziness, the urge to be done with the tiresome work of breathing.

When it came to the *act* of suicide, however, my deep laziness proved also a blessing, for if I lacked the motive to live, neither was I prepared to take the initiative and bring about my death.

As a consequence, I adopted a pattern of behavior in which I took a detached, scientific interest in life, almost to the exclusion of any other sensation. This disposition made for a conscientious physician, which is to say that I killed fewer patients than did my colleagues. As well, I had compiled a thick portfolio of scientific articles that will surely be of interest one day, or perhaps not.

For probably the fifth time that day, I descended the spiral staircase like an insect going down a drain, entering the great hall just in time to watch the patient carried to the south end of the building—a wing reserved for the Agitated Insane—and ensconced in a private room. Who is paying? I wondered. A close relative, probably—though not so close as to nurse the patient himself. Not an unusual occurrence when it came to the Agitated Insane—defined as patients whose words and behavior had become an embarrassment to the family.

Unlike other sections of the hospital, the wing distinguished itself not by sight or smell, but by sound—an aggregate of confused desperation; a chattering fugue in which occasionally recognizable words could be discerned: *"Jesus! . . . Mother! . . . Snakes!"*

In the room next door to the patient, like a soloist at the opera, a gentleman intoned a litany that might have been said by an especially repentant priest: *"O wretch that I am behold my degradation and ruin what I have suffered and lost and the sorrow and misery I have brought upon others I could sink through this bed into the lowermost abyss forsaken by God, O God . . ."*

According to Nurse Slatin, the new arrival had been lying in the gutter on Light Street outside Gunner's Hall with his head on his valise since early dawn. A compositor with the *Baltimore Sun* happened to notice a crowd collecting and recognized the fellow as somebody famous. After calling for an ambulance, the compositor even went so far as to place a note in the man's coat pocket:

> *Dear Sir or Madam—*
> *This gentleman was found rather the worse for wear near 4th ward polls. He goes under the cognomen Edgar Allan Poe & appears in great distress & says he is acquainted with you & is in need of immediate assistance. I was told to inform Mr. Neilson Poe and will do so.*
>
> *Yours in haste,*
> *Jos. W. Walker*

A Christian gentleman, I thought, and a charitable one. A rare combination in Baltimore on Election Day.

The patient was indeed in a bad way. It required the strength of two additional nurses to put him to bed. Delirious, drenched in sweat, with a violent tremor of the limbs, staring wildly at the ceiling, he kept repeating a name I heard clearly as *Riley*—but which could have been the Queen of Sheba for all it meant.

After ordering Nurse Slatin and her assistant to prepare plasters, I began the examination . . . and abruptly stopped cold.

Well, bless me, if it isn't Eddie Poe.

His medical condition did not at all surprise me, yet his appearance certainly did, as it would anyone who had ever known him.

Even when addled and penniless, Poe's deportment remained smart and orderly, with a well-trimmed mustache, artfully coifed hair, and impeccable linen. By contrast, the gentleman on the bed lay vestless and tieless, in ill-fitting, filthy trousers and a crumpled, yellowed shirt. A stained, faded old bombazine coat had been spread across the foot of the cot. A cheap, greasy palm-leaf hat lay beside his pillow.

The nurses undressed and bathed the patient, then applied the plasters to his feet, thighs, and abdomen, whereupon he began to writhe violently. Color rose to his face and the vessels became swollen at the temples. I ordered ice to be applied to his head and heat to his extremities. The nurses carried this out, to a mournful accompaniment from the gentleman next door:

> *He who arches the heavens and upholds the universe has His decrees written upon the frontlet of every human being and upon demons incarnate!*

Despite my efforts, the muscular twitching and jerking did not subside but grew more violent. At last, however, he began to grow tired, and after a general tremor, fell into a stupor.

For an emergency physician, the first step in treating a new patient is to determine what happened to him. This would lead, one hoped, to either a cure or an explanation. In the absence of a cure, the victory lay in diagnoses: though the patient died, at least you knew why.

Had he fallen in with Election Day rowdies who plied him with drink and robbed him? Had he suffered a contusion to the head and succumbed to swelling of the brain?

I surveyed his personal effects, stacked in the corner of the room, and was satisfied that he had not been robbed. No assailant would leave his victim with a walking stick and a leather valise—both of which I recognized from our time together at West Point.

As I observed the prone figure before me, his eyes opened slightly. Though I detected no sign of recognition, he seemed to calm somewhat on seeing me, and fell into a jittery doze.

By now the assistant nurse had left for other duties and the admitting nurse was impatient for her cup of tea. I gave the dismissal, Nurse Slatin trundled resentfully out of sight, and the door closed, and now I stood alone with the wretched figure of my oldest acquaintance in the world. I would not go so far as to call him a friend.

As noted, to anyone with even a vague familiarity with his reputation it could hardly come as a shock that Eddie Poe had fallen into such a state. Nor did his presence in Baltimore seem odd; although identified with Richmond and Philadelphia, generations of Poes had hailed from Baltimore, and the family plot was situated there.

At some point during his admission, Nurse Slatin informed me that a Baltimore cousin by the name of Neilson had paid for his private room. This fitted with what I knew of Eddie: no doubt he had visited his relations in Baltimore to borrow money, with which to drink and medicate himself to oblivion.

Down the hall, the wretched babble continued as the gentleman in the next room segued to a nautical theme:

Where is the gulf beyond the stream where is the buoy lifeboat ship of fire sea of brass, test, test, shore no more!

I examined the patient's pulse: One hundred and twenty beats to the minute, feeble, sharp, and irregular. As a treatment I considered a febrifuge mixture and a nerve stimulant. (I did not probe nor palpitate so as not to disturb him.) Oddly, I detected no smell of alcohol, only a sour, metallic odor common to inhalers of arsenic, cocaine, and codeine—sometimes used as additives in snuff mixtures. Obviously, the absence of alcohol did not mean that no other medicament or poison had been consumed, and in quantity.

In my preliminary judgment, Poe's condition represented a latter stage of a well-documented general deterioration, a brain poisoned by morbidity, excitability, medicaments, and drink. The only mystifying circumstance was that, by fate or by fluke, he should find himself with me as his attending physician—at my mercy, so to speak. I could have smothered him with a pillow and none would be the wiser . . .

"*O God, is there no ransom for the deathless spirit?*" cried the patient next door.

As my mind turned to unhealthy speculation I became immersed in the wallpaper—an ornate floral pattern once arrayed in patriotic colors, now a blotched greenish-gray and emitting a musty sweetness.

Is there no ransom for the deathless spirit?

BOTH THEORETICAL STUDY (Brewster, '35) and my own observations (*Scientific American* declined to publish, citing a lack of "procedural clarity") suggest that, due to trauma, substance, or pathology, the imagination can break free of the constraints of the conscious will. When such a disconnection occurs, the imagination becomes a sort of free-floating demon, independent of, and even opposed to, the will of its host.

The pathological result of an untamed imagination could find no more fitting embodiment than the figure on the cot before me.

Poe and I spent our boyhood together in Richmond, Virginia, during which time he was my best . . . No. It would be a cruel travesty to call him my best friend, or any friend at all.

He took an indecent pleasure in telling tales that proved to be untrue, and was given to the most intemperate bluffing—recruiting a companion to take part in some risky activity, pretending to know what would happen when in truth he just wanted to *see* what would happen.

Still, at school and church it was agreed that he was a future leader of men (*mis*-leader of men I should say now), with an almost mesmeric ability to persuade.

When I first encountered Eddie Poe, he was the undisputed leader of a gang of local toughs known as the Butcher Cats.

Thanks to Eddie's influence my presence was tolerated. While the gang sat around doing nothing in a menacing kind of a way, Eddie and I played marbles and mumblety-peg, and he dreamed up trouble.

"Old Man Foster, over by Bleaker's Dam?" Eddie asked me on one occasion.

"What of him?" Old Man Foster had two long yellow teeth and threatened with a hatchet anyone who strayed onto his property.

"They say he has a passel of money from grave-robbing. Bam Johnson watched him through the window one night, saw the kitchen table piled with gold coins."

"So why does he live like that if he has that much money?"

"Because he's crazy, is why. But crafty too. Keeps his doors locked day and night. Never does nothing 'cept counts his money. Never goes out 'cept feeds the chickens."

I had nothing to add to this, because I didn't really believe it, so Eddie continued.

"While he's feeding the chickens, you can sneak in through the window."

"The mischief I will!" The thought of it made me sick with fear.

"You're the only one small enough. We'll watch out and warn you, Willie. Honor bright."

Of course eventually I gave in rather than risk being left out, and of course Old Man Foster collared me halfway through the window and threatened to have me jailed and kicked me in the pants, and Eddie and the Butcher Cats were nowhere to be seen.

Later, Eddie presented the incident as a test of my loyalty, and I was made into a full-fledged gang member because I could be trusted not to snitch.

And of course I felt honored, as though the Butcher Cats were the Round Table, the James River was our fiefdom, and Eddie Poe was the Black Knight.

From then on, Eddie took me on as a sort of page or apprentice. My delight in the role reached its summit one hot June afternoon, when he swam from Ludlow's Wharf to Warwick, a distance of six miles, against one of the strongest tides ever known in the river—and walked home afterward! A shaver of twelve! Byron's crossing of the Hellespont amounted to a paddle across a pond by comparison.

As you might expect, my feeling for Eddie at that time was one of abject hero worship. However, this common boyhood attachment was soon to make way for darker sentiments that would contaminate our association forever.

Can you imagine what it is like to have a friend two years older, and to discover that he wants your mother?

FAILING TO FIND enlightenment in the institutional wallpaper, I returned my attention to my old acquaintance—the broad forehead, the classical, oversensitive features—and resolved that as far as I was concerned, this was no longer Eddie Poe. Whatever had passed between us long ago, he was now my patient, and would receive the best treatment I could provide.

I shut the window against the night air's harmful vapors. There being no bed table and only one chair, I placed my satchel upon the edge of the bed. I unbuttoned the patient's shirt—the sallow skin, stretched over visible ribs, rose and fell in short gasps, like a fox at the end of the chase. From my open bag I extracted my bone cup and placed its flattened bell against the patient's left breast. I put my ear to the cup at the other end of the wooden tube, and detected a weak heartbeat, more sluggish than the breathing would suggest. Perhaps it called for a tincture of adrenaline and cocaine as a heart stimulant . . .

"*Are we alone?*"

My expensive French instrument so amplified his voice as to attain an almost biblical resonance.

Startled by this sudden blast I reared back, and in so doing my elbow caught the handle of my bag, whose entire contents clattered onto the black hardwood floor—tins, tubes, bottles of pills, containers of powders, a tourniquet, cotton wool bandages, boric lint, powder papers, my copy of *Mental Hygiene Acts Schedule 15*, my poisons' book . . .

"Startled you, did I, Willie?"

I dropped to one knee and put my alligator bag upright (a graduation gift from Father), and began hastily returning its contents to their proper places. "Somewhat," I replied, not to provide more fodder for his amusement.

"What were you trying to do—kiss me?"

Eddie always had an uncanny way of throwing a fellow off-kilter. In that instant, twenty-five years of adulthood peeled from my skin and I was again on the defensive, feeling foolish and vaguely soiled—literally so in the case of my surgical instruments, strewn upon a floor that had scarcely been scrubbed since the War of 1812.

"I was examining your heart. Your circulation is in poor condition. You have a nervous disorder. Your skin tone is that of a cadaver."

"Willie, can you tell me how long I am going to live? I should love to know, suh. I would make plans."

"Do you experience chest pain? Moments of dizziness?"

"All of it," he replied, and his features turned from superciliousness to despair—apparently even Romantics worry about their health. "It would be appropriate if I were to die here and now. A relief, really," he said as though to himself.

"Are you in pain?" I asked.

"Yes."

"And for how long?"

"As long as I can remember."

Casting his eyes upward (with suspect theatricality it seemed to me), he shuddered and sighed, then his features returned to their normal impression of calm superiority. "I hate to repeat myself, Willie, but are we alone, suh?" he asked, in the soft, Virginia drawl he had practiced to good effect as a boy, though he spent his early childhood in England.

"We are alone, sir. But I can call for assistance in an emergency."

"Good. That is excellent," Poe said, rising to a seated position and cushioning his back with his pillow, seemingly in reasonable health.

For my part, I had already run out of patience, for at Washington College Hospital we take a dim view of malingering. At the same time, I reminded myself that his clinical symptoms were measurable and genuine; though a patient may be feigning illness, it does not necessarily follow that he is not sick.

"Am I to understand that this has all been a performance for my benefit? Cutting shines again, are we, Eddie?"

"What do you mean—*cutting shines?*"

"Oh you know, gumming a person—like pulling the chair from underneath without warning at the Masonic supper."

Poe's gaze became speculative. "That was thirty years ago. A boyhood prank. I am surprised you remember it."

"Fine, then perhaps you'll remember nearly deafening me a moment ago."

His expression became serious. "My presence is no joke, suh, I can assure you of that."

"Then what is your purpose in carrying out this charade? Do you suppose that I lack patients?"

In truth, I had somewhat less than a full caseload, and my patients tended to be the lower sort. My superiors had judged my bedside manner unsuitable for a teaching position, and my cure rate a matter of fool's luck. And the more prosperous patients agreed with him. Perhaps they resented my candor—or rather, the expression it took—my tendency as a war veteran to make quips about death that were offensive to the wealthy.

Or they may have simply disliked my looks: having gone prematurely bald, I determined early on that I would not only flaunt my baldness, I would make a virtue of it. One of my favorite sayings at social gatherings was that I was probably the only human being in the room who did not have head lice. I regarded as my private joke the furtive scratching that followed.

Especially controversial among my colleagues at Washington College Hospital was my eccentric habit of washing my hands between patients and after handling a cadaver. This was regarded as an affectation, a kind of snobbery. Next thing you know, it was said, surgeons will be wearing masks, lest we breathe upon a fellow!

"I apologize for the subterfuge, Willie," Poe said. "The fact is, I'm in a scrape and desperately need your help." And his enormous eyes declared this to be the truth.

"Of course as your physician I shall see to your health and comfort in any way I can," I replied.

He responded with surprising vehemence. "Bugger my health and comfort, Willie! Because of me, a woman was murdered!"

"Murdered?"

"Three days ago in this very city. It was reported in the *Clipper*, did you not see it?"

In truth, I try to avoid newspapers. Reading about the misery of others tends to distract me from my own.

"Very well, Eddie, let us say it was in the *Clipper*. Why have you made this dead woman your business?"

"Because it was done for my benefit."

I think it was here that he snagged my interest—clinical of course—for it is not often that delusions occur in such detail. It occurred to me that his case might provide the basis for an article on artistic hallucination, entitled something like, *Coup d'État: The Rebellion of the Trained Imagination*.

"Do tell me more," I said, weighing a diagnosis of brain fever, for it is a characteristic of this malady that the patient will alternate moments of perfect lucidity with episodes of sheer madness.

"I mean, suh, that a clock has been set into motion. First he destroys my work, then my reputation, and my life and work become irrelevant. Don't you see? He wishes to turn me into the living dead."

"Might this business involve a gentleman named Riley?"

"I beg your pardon?"

"Riley. You were shouting that name as you came in."

"I did?"

"Yes. You were quite specific."

"I know nobody named Riley. You must have been mistaken."

In cases of paranoid delusion, the proper protocol is well established according to the principles of Moral Treatment: after an expression of sympathetic understanding, ease the patient back to sanity by refuting his error, persistently and calmly, with facts from the real world.

"This is distressing news indeed, Eddie. No wonder you were in a state of agitation. But if you believe there has been a murder, don't you think the first place to turn would be to the constabulary?"

"That I did. And spent the night in jail for my trouble."

"On what charge?"

"Drunkenness—what else? These days, anyone who voices an unpalatable opinion is accused of drunkenness."

I refrained from supporting or refuting this self-serving observation.

Continued my old acquaintance: "He is murdering my books, don't you see? And my reputation."

"So you have said, Eddie. But how does one murder a book?"

"First he brands me a madman. Then he establishes my work as the product of a diseased mind. Is it not obvious?"

"But what sort of person would attempt such a thing? Who is this fellow?"

"I am not prepared to say, at present. But be assured that he will stop at nothing, not even the murder of an innocent woman—especially so, for he has a notoriously low opinion of women."

"Drunk or sober, Eddie, did you tell the police what you are telling me?"

"I did. They replied that no innocent woman has ever been murdered in Baltimore. Then they threw me into jail, a filthy place filled with Negroes."

"On a charge of drunkenness?"

"That is what I said."

"I see." Already a credible diagnosis suggested itself—extreme drunkenness, followed by a swelling of the brain, followed by fever, and the pitiable symptoms before me.

By now I suspected that even his time in jail might have been a delusion, and made a mental note to inquire. Would a Baltimore constable incarcerate a white man in a cell full of Negroes? Highly unlikely, it seemed to me.

"How did you come to arrive here in your present condition, dressed as you are?"

"They beat me and took my clothes."

"The constabulary?"

"The Negroes."

"I see." Amazing, I thought, how a man can be barking mad, yet devilishly cunning at the same time. I continued to take mental notes, for the case might enhance my theses concerning the mechanics of dementia—which might, in turn, justify a resubmission to the *Scientific American*. The study would include an exegesis of the character and imagination of Edgar Allan Poe—let that provide sufficient *procedural clarity* for them!

Seen in retrospect, I am embarrassed to acknowledge the secret pleasure it gave me to see Poe in distress. Of course I put my lack of sympathy down to professional detachment; yet for a physician on an emergency case I was having an unusually good time.

"Do *you* think I'm mad, Willie?" He stared at me with the look of a tragic owl.

"You are delusional, Eddie. *Mad* is not a word we use at this institution."

"But the upshot is, you believe nothing I say, suh."

"As a man of science I remain skeptical. For lack of evidence, don't you see?"

Poe nodded, almost briskly, with that peculiar half-smile of his. Immediately I began to suspect that I had fallen into a trap.

"I salute your integrity, suh," he said. "Therefore I demand that you view the evidence. This can easily be done—for the victim of whom I speak is in the morgue of this very hospital."

At that moment I experienced once again the feeling he had produced in me as a boy, of being drawn irresistibly into a realm of Eddie Poe's imagination.

"Is this the murdered woman you mentioned earlier?"

"Indeed it is."

"In the morgue here at Washington College Hospital?"

"Correct."

"I see."

I did not see. Only in hindsight does it become clear that I had been manipulated, that he had predetermined the entire sequence of events from beginning to end. After pompously asserting myself as a man of science, I had no choice but to observe his evidence—otherwise I was not really a scientist.

Rather than applying Moral Treatment to lead the patient to the light of reality, I had become his second, following him into the dark.

"Dear God Jesus, help me to see to see to see to see . . ." babbled the man next door. Alarmingly, his words were beginning to make sense.

For Finn Devlin, Philadelphia was the logical destination. Unlike New York, the second-largest city in America had grown from within, and not by constant immigration. Maneuvering through the myriad gangs of New York would have entailed a whole new set of skills, whereas Philadelphia was familiar turf. When it came to deep-set prejudice, class resentment, blood feuds, and sectarian rivalries, Devlin might have landed in a second Dublin.

The difference between Dublin and Philadelphia lay not so much in kind as in rate of development. It had required centuries for Dublin to reach its current inbred state, whereas in a fraction of that time Philadelphia had become a welter of Quaker Protestantism, nativist intolerance, colonial pretension, and upper-class disdain.

As waves of famished, filthy Irish began to pour into Philadelphia, it took no time at all for the unwelcome arrivals to be dubbed white niggers, with all the fellow-feeling the term implied.

For their part, the Irish were in no mood to conduct diplomacy. Taking their hosts' racial epithet at face value, and having resisted slavery for decades, they responded insult for insult, blow for blow, though outnumbered, outmoneyed, and outgunned.

In a short time this conflict had found its locus in the ancient enmity between Catholics and Protestants. To native Philadelphians, the presence of the Irish signified the first offensive in a papist campaign to dominate America, through a subversion of its ideals. The Gaelic presence was only the vanguard of a vast tide of Catholics, who by their sheer numbers would destroy all that had been sought and accomplished in this outpost of religious freedom in the New World.

Populists of the press urged loyal Americans to defend the country against the "bloody hand of the pope." In the minds of American Protestants, the Irish became an infestation with a common purpose—to establish America as an outpost of Roman Catholicism, like Mexico and Peru.

Rumors abounded. The Irish were said to be arming themselves, undergoing military training in remote locations. Irish students were said to be conducting inquisitions in Catholic colleges, as a rehearsal for the show trials to come, with mock tortures for anatomy lessons.

Protestant Philadelphia responded accordingly. During the Bible Riots of 1844, cathedrals, rectories, and seminaries in Irish neighborhoods were burnt with the tacit approval of the city, along with surrounding dwellings and shops—systematically, block by block, as though it were a campaign of civic hygiene.

(The Irish tried to sue the city for allowing St. Augustine Cathedral to be burnt. The city ruled that they had no right to sue, as they were a foreign group ruled by the pope.)

To be certain, Philadelphia was a disappointment for the immigrant Irishman who sought a new and better life. For Finn Devlin, however, the resulting discord made Philadelphia a city of grand opportunity. Fertile ground for the next revolution. A station on the way to the Promised Land.

CHAPTER THREE

Baltimore, 1849

Mad, *adj.* Affected with a high degree of intellectual
independence; at odds with the majority; in short,
unusual.

—Ambrose Bierce

A turning point in our association occurred when I took Eddie
home to see my pigeons and introduced him to my mother. (Father was seldom in the house during the day or the evening; in truth,
I doubt that Poe ever met him.)

To hear Eddie describe her afterward, you would have thought
Mother was Helen of Troy, and not my mother.

True, she was always known as a beauty. Yet it was impossible for
me to understand the significance of the description. Can one's own
mother ever be anything but beautiful?

(Alas, I possess no physical memory of her. When I close my eyes
I cannot see her face. Yet I remember father perfectly, though I exchanged not more than twenty sentences with him in my life. It is a
harsh fact of life that memories fade when desired, and persist when
least welcome.)

Not long after their first encounter, Eddie began to bring verses to
Mother and to read them aloud. It was beyond my comprehension
that the leader of the Butcher Cats would do such a thing. Of course,
Mother responded with delight, being high-strung herself. It was not
long before she began bringing poems of her own to their meetings,
and they would read back and forth to one another for hours.

Looking back, I see myself as an unattractive child. I would not
warm to myself, were we to meet today. A good-looking boy perhaps,
but far too inward, too skeptical, too tight-lipped when it came to
overt expressions of emotion. Nor, unlike my friend Eddie, was I

disposed to alter my manner in order to secure affection. I made no effort to seduce others by saying what they wanted to hear.

From my perspective, the association between Eddie and my mother seemed to have been invented, made up out of whole cloth. They were like a pair of balloons, blowing each other up to the point of bursting.

Though aware of their rapport, I did not understand its significance at first, nor in what way it might constitute a threat. So I took the position of the interested spectator, eager to share in their enthusiasm. However, as I listened, disturbing feelings occurred within my breast that I did not wish to entertain. Therefore, I took the position that it was all frivolous nonsense and beneath my notice—the poems, the shared laughter, the long silences, the inadvertent touches and ritual kisses, none of which had ever occurred between Mother and myself, not in the same way, not ever.

As the months went by, I came to truly hate Eddie at times. I wished him ill—and as the Negro proverb has it, to wish a man ill is to do him ill. Is that what caused Mother's subsequent decline, and then Eddie's? Had I placed them both under some sort of hex?

As I warned earlier, there are unflattering aspects to this account of myself. They begin to appear, it seems, at age ten.

A more Christian boy would have felt sympathy for Eddie's situation, for here was an unfortunate if ever there was one. A son of stage actors (a drunkard and a consumptive), orphaned at an early age, taken in out of duty by a moneyed uncle in Richmond (codfish aristocracy, a big bug in the export trade, and a notorious tightwad), it is certain that Eddie Poe had had no easy time of it.

It was very sad that he had no mother. Even so, I did not understand why it meant he should have mine.

And when she died—oh! Who could compare with the quality and extent of his grief? The mourning black, the *stricken* aspect he affected, always with an eye to the nearest mirror. (He was, we must always remember, a son of professional actors.)

It has been said that Eddie haunted our family plot in Shockoe Cemetery for years after—indeed, I would not put it past him to have hired some wretch to attend on his behalf.

Who could compete with such an enterprising mourner? Can you imagine how it feels, to have one's *bereavement* upstaged by another?

Following her death, I began to view the ties of sympathy between the two of them in a new way—as the morbid camaraderie of people who have the same disease. This view was later confirmed by none other than the Reverend Thomas Paxton, who termed it "the fruits of oversensitivity and willfulness"—an apt description, and a quality they bred in one another.

After only a minimum of training in the medical field, however, I came to understand that Mother's death was a result of the treatment and not the disease.

When Father sent her to the Hospital For Insane and Disordered Minds, her fate was sealed. Lobotomists and phrenologists probed her skull. She was doused with freezing water and whirled while tied to a wheel. In between these ordeals she was subjected to repeated enemas, in fact I believe she died of dehydration.

This later realization transformed my visceral hurt into something like professional vexation, and a desire to improve the science. Eddie, on the other hand, transformed not a bit. Well into adulthood he continued to visit (or appear at) her grave, visibly overcome with emotion.

Do you see? Even after her death, I held the shells of the relationship, while Eddie ate the omelet. And to pile on the agony, I would carry the stigma of her illness for life—mental illness runs in families, you know. It is in the blood.

True, all of this happened when we were children, and Eddie the child was not to be blamed. In any case, as his physician I would treat Eddie the patient with all the skill at my command.

Still, a small voice within suggested that he deserved it, every bit.

I CANNOT SATISFACTORILY explain how I came to perform the actions I am about to describe. Looking back, it seems as if they were the work of someone else—someone as near to me as my own skin, yet a stranger nonetheless. Having devoted years of study to the mind, I can only speculate as to the motives of the character I call Myself.

In my defense, I did not accede to his demand right away. It was only with the greatest reluctance that I accompanied Eddie Poe down to the morgue.

In truth, I scarcely knew how to get there myself, nor did I want to. For a professional who valued his reputation, the morgue was a hazardous place to visit, in more ways than one.

As I may have mentioned, Washington College Hospital sat immediately next to the medical school by that name, and as a matter of practical necessity the morgue served both institutions. Hence, the mortician on duty acted as death's intermediary, receiving goods from the hospital and delivering them to the school—an essential service, for no medical school will survive long without a supply of cadavers for dissection and analysis.

However, unlike the tumultuous Baltimore of decades earlier, by 1849, fewer cadavers remained nameless, and fewer next of kin were willing to submit the remains of a loved one to the scalpels of supercilious young men.

In response to the chronic shortage, the department developed certain procedural flaws. For example, a mortician might fail to fully and correctly document the description, origin, even the existence of a particular cadaver—especially if it appeared down-at-the-heel. Thus, at any given time, the morgue housed cadavers who might just as well have walked in on their own for all anyone knew about them.

This lack of due diligence, while it troubled the mortician not a bit and aided the college a good deal, placed the attending physician in a delicate position, for nothing will kill a practice as quickly as a connection to a burial scandal.

Ignorance is bliss, when 'tis folly to be wise.

Yet there I was, leading Eddie to the rear stairway to the morgue, feeling our way along the damp wall as we spiraled down into the gloom.

At the time it seemed the only possible thing to do. I had demanded evidence, Eddie had offered to supply it, therefore I could hardly refuse to look at it.

I put the best professional face to the matter—that a visit to another part of the hospital could do the patient no harm; that it was only proper protocol to assist him in separating reality from delusion, by putting his assertion to the test. This is what I intended to write in my report, at any rate.

It was not Eddie's persuasive powers that clinched my cooperation. My reflexive need for objective proof had led me by the nose.

A morgue is never a cheerful place. The unit at Washington College

Hospital was a long, cavernous, windowless basement (the coolest part of the building), smelling of lye soap, chicken gone bad, and rising damp. The walls of blistered plaster had been whitewashed long ago, but had since taken on a green-gray, fuzzy quality. From each wall the cobblestone floor raked down to a drain, so that bodily fluids might be washed away with a single pass of a rubber hose. Directly above the drain stood an elongated wooden table with a surface of polished granite, equipped with two sets of wide buckled straps.

"What are the straps for?" asked Eddie. "In case someone might make a run for it?"

As one who encounters death on a daily basis, I reserve for myself the right to gallows humor. "Not run for it, no," I replied. "But a cadaver can suddenly sit bolt upright. Or it can throw up a stiffened hand or a leg, injuring the mortician. Or, when the body cavity has been opened, a surprising amount of fluid can issue forth, drenching everyone in the room . . ."

"Quite so," he replied, and said no more.

Blinking like nocturnal animals in the intermittent glare and shadow of institutional gaslight, we faced four waist-high tables against the far wall, set between alternate pillars. Each of the tables contained an inert form beneath a graying sheet; in each case the sheet had slipped somewhat, revealing a portion of the occupant's face or leg or torso.

On the far left rested a black-bearded gentleman in his late twenties, with Byron-like curls and a bullet wound in the chest—self-inflicted, to judge by the gray-black discoloration from burning, and the powder tattoos on the fingers of one hand. (He was left-handed, seemingly.)

In the event that his relatives fetched and buried him, his obituary would refer to the death as "sudden," as though somebody had sneaked up to him and said *Boo*.

However, reclamation of the cadaver was most unlikely. The better families of Baltimore did not expect members to end up in the morgue, and if this were to happen they did not really want to know. As for identification, it was all but certain that he had arrived without his pocketbook—indeed, it would not be unusual had the mortician relieved him of it himself.

"Do you think he resembles me?" asked Poe.

"Why on earth would you ask?"

"No particular reason. Do you think he looks the least bit like me?"

"You flatter yourself," I replied. "He is younger, taller, and but for the fact that he is deceased, in better condition."

"I see," he replied, and appeared discouraged.

On the table next to the suicide lay a young shaver who had run into the street near the merchant exchange and was kicked under the front wheels of a freight wagon. The sheet had slipped down to expose his face, which I quickly re-covered while Eddie looked the other way.

Of the two remaining cadavers, one was a stout farrier with liver-colored jowls, whom I remembered having suffered a fit of apoplexy while racing to catch the B&O train.

Lastly, we faced the exhibit Eddie had brought me to see: a girlishly slim female in her twenties, wearing a torn evening dress, with extensive bruising about the torso, and on the neck, indicating strangulation. Her facial features had frozen into an expression of pleading. I began to cover her, but Eddie held me in check.

"Have you seen her before, Willie?"

"It was a police matter, I believe. A prostitute from Fell's Point. We get a lot of that sort."

"Do you suppose there is a record of who brought her?" he asked.

"The police, I imagine. In any case, I do not intend to involve myself by asking. And if it is all the same to you, I would prefer that we left before the mortician returns."

As Eddie observed the corpse it gave me no little satisfaction to see him extract his handkerchief and wrap it over his nose and mouth. For my part, having breathed the stench of a battlefield hospital tent, a morgue is no more unpleasant than a fertilized field.

Removing his handkerchief from his face, Eddie reached into an inside pocket and produced a pewter flask. "I think a sip of brandy is in order."

"Thank you, no." I refrained from telling him that I was a member of the Temperance Brotherhood, for it would only invite ridicule.

After drinking deeply, he peered down at the wretched face and bare, luminous shoulders, with an expression of such sadness that I could hardly credit his next utterance.

"Open her mouth, Willie."

"I beg your pardon?"

"I said, open her mouth."

"What the devil for?"

"So that you can see for yourself. That is my evidence, suh."

"I assure you that rigor mortis has taken place. The jaw will not move in the slightest."

"Open just the lips, then. Do it now, damn it!"

The latter request contained such a note of preemption that I could not but obey. Doubly grateful that the mortician on duty had absented himself for a very long luncheon, I reached down and with my fingers pulled apart the two dry flaps of skin, revealing a set of gums like strips of overboiled beef.

"Do you see that?"

"What are you referring to?"

"She is toothless."

"My dear fellow," I said, "I would hardly expect one of her class to possess a full set."

"She has no teeth at all, Willie."

"Are you sure?" I bent down to peer into the empty hole and, sure enough, there was not a tooth to be found. Even more curious, on closer inspection it appeared that the gums were dotted with dry, bloodless wounds, indicating that the extractions had occurred after death.

Poe reached into his coat pocket, extracted a square envelope, opened it, and turned it upside down. The teeth clattered like tiny bullets on the cobblestone floor.

I do not remember what happened after that.

CHAPTER FOUR

Philadelphia

Text of a speech delivered by Mr. Finn Devlin of the Irish Brotherhood to the Hibernian Society, Moyamensing, Philadelphia County:

American Friends, never let it be said that England did justice to Ireland. The little freedom we have achieved was extorted by force, from men opposed to us on principle.

Before God, I speak only of what I myself have seen. In Ireland, I watched the most absurd, disgusting tyranny. I have seen troops practicing the most cowardly oppression upon civilized men of all ranks and conditions. I have seen twelve men hanged in Dublin for sedition—not against Ireland, but against *England*. In my county, Tyrone, I have seen thirty houses burnt in a single night.

> *Oh, I met with Napier Tandy*
> *An he took me by the hand*
> *He said how's dear old Ireland*
> *How now does she stand?*
> *She's the most distressful country*
> *That ever yet was seen*
> *They're hangin' men and women there*
> *For wearin' o the Green.*

My fellow Irish: we have bought Ireland with our blood. *Ah*, say the holy fathers, *but ye must nae shed blud.*

I tell you, gentlemen, if it were possible to collect all the innocent blood shed by the imperial beast in one great reservoir, the queen and her council might swim in it.

I swear by the blood of the murdered patriots who have

gone before me, had I one thousand pounds, one thousand men, I would be in Erin today. But like you I have been forced to seek a more friendly port.

And so I came to Philadelphia, home of the Liberty Bell. And what have I found?

I found a little Protestant London made of red brick. With public buildings that are bad imitations of their British counterparts. Stately homes that would not look out of place in Regent's Park.

I have seen your fetid, squalid courts, your alley hovels and whorehouses in Port Richmond, Southward, and here in Moyamensing—a faithful imitation of the Seven Dials and the slums of Whitechapel.

And everywhere I have seen the same prejudice: a bigotry every bit as foul. No white men in America are so stigmatized as the Irish—we foreign paupers, we motley multitudes, we white niggers of America.

As every Irishman knows, there are two landlords to oppress you—the landlord who owns your land, and the governor who owns *him*.

I swear that we of the Irish Brotherhood were summoned by Almighty God for one purpose—to carry the battle for freedom to the New World, that we might give voice to the question: *By what right does England rule Ireland? And by what right do the Protestants rule Philadelphia?*

Fellow Irishmen, I will now pass among you with my hat outstretched. I beseech you to think upon your homeland and what she has suffered, and to give as your heart and your heritage dictate.

Baltimore

D o you have any brandy, Willie?"

"I am a Son of Temperance. I thought I told you that."

"No, you did not. Well, you'd better have something. Merciful heaven, do you have these seizures often?"

I opened my eyes. We seemed to be in my rooms. I seemed to be lying on my couch, before my fire, with a pot of tea on the serving table.

Surely one would remember having climbed five sets of stairs . . .

"You are drifting again, Willie. Take some tea."

"How is it that I am here?"

"In the morgue you took some sort of fit. You have been in and out ever since."

I peered at my dusty objects and lumps of furniture. In my customary chair lay Poe's walking stick and valise: therefore, we must have stopped in his room on the way here. Idly, I picked up the walking stick; to my surprise it was of the type that concealed a sword. Despite everything, a part of Eddie Poe was still a West Point man.

"Did you make tea and set the fire?" I asked.

"No, Willie, you did. Do you not remember?"

"Of course. Of course, I remember now." This was emphatically not the truth. "Would you pass me my case, please?"

I opened my alligator bag and extracted a vial of tincture of cocaine. Taken with tea, the medicine soon improved my level of alertness and my nervous tone. As I moved to a seated position, I saw Eddie take several drops for himself.

For a moment it occurred to me that every word he said thus far could have been, and probably was, a lie. Even having suffered a delirium it was not beyond my notice that, for a patient in the throes of a nervous mania, Eddie seemed remarkably lucid and canny. In fact, somehow we seemed to have switched positions, with Eddie the doctor and I the patient.

Again I remembered having experienced a similar sensation at the age of twelve—that Eddie might be leading me into a world I did not wish to enter, just to see what might happen.

"Answer me truthfully, Eddie, if that is possible: What do you want from me? What do you want me to *do*?"

"May I conclude, suh, that you no longer think me insane?"

"To the extent that you are capable of rational planning—or should I say *scheming*—yes. Yet a man can undertake a rational plan for irrational reasons."

"True. At the same time, you must admit I am at an unfair disadvantage, trying to prove a negative. How does one prove he is *not* abnormal? What could I possibly say to reassure you?"

"You might begin by telling me how it is you find yourself here. How you came to be lying in the gutter in front of Gunner's Hall, on election night, in an apparent condition of nervous collapse."

"I am being pursued by Fenian Irishmen. They are trying to kidnap me."

"This happened in Baltimore?"

"No, in Philadelphia. It was in connection with a piece of work I am ashamed to talk about. I came to Baltimore to escape them, and to view the evidence in the morgue with my own eyes."

"Do you suggest that she was murdered by the Irish?"

"Possibly."

"Why?"

"Because someone paid them to. Surely you do not think the Irish capable of planning something as insidious as this."

"Something as insidious as what?"

"The process by which I am to be ruined."

"I'm afraid I don't understand you."

Poe looked at me with pupils like plates: "My dear fellow, do you think that *I* do?"

Philadelphia

Text of a speech delivered by Mr. Finn Devlin of the Irish Brotherhood to the Philopatrian Society, Philadelphia:

My friends, as a newcomer to your country it has come as a shock to discover that there has been no American Revolution.

You may laugh, but it is not a joke. The imperial presence occupies America as completely as in 1775. In 1849, America is a shell of a republic. Put your ear to her, and you will hear "Rule Britannia."

For a sense of America's true position we have only to look to France, America's sister in freedom, whose citizens have proclaimed a New French Republic and rid themselves of the autocrat who stole the throne.

Or let us look to Prague, Rome, Berlin—where the spirit of liberty has set explosions in the streets. Or Vienna, whose emperor fled in terror and whose serfs have been set free.

As Mr. Washington said, *Liberty, when it begins to take root, is a plant of rapid growth.*

But how thrives liberty in the United States of America? What can one divine about a republican government led by a party whose members unashamedly refer to themselves as *Whigs*? And how thrive the serfs on this side of the ocean—America's niggers, black, red, and white?

Tyranny, it seems, when it begins to take root, is also a plant of rapid growth.

Irish-Americans, you were taken to these shores by Almighty God for one purpose—to kindle the New American Revolution. That is the meaning of our suffering. That is our God-given task.

My associate, Lieutenant O'Reilly, will now pass among you. Think upon your homeland and what she has suffered, and give as your heart, your courage, and your patriotism dictate . . .

CHAPTER SEVEN

Baltimore

It has been observed by Gerber, among others, how a sudden injury or shock to the system can strain the mind to the point of delirium—symptoms resulting not so much from the disturbance itself as from the subsequent flight of the imagination into realms of terror that have little to do with the instigating event. This, and the concentrating effect of the cocaine, would account for the behavior of my friend: long stretches of total lucidity, followed by a sudden collapse into delusion and disarray, like a man in a whirlpool.

"Forgive me, Eddie, but you have spent the past hours dropping dreadful hints, with no evidence other than a nameless female cadaver and a bag of someone's teeth."

"I was about to explain when you collapsed. You really must have that seen to."

"I shall see to myself if you don't mind. This is about the cadaver and the teeth."

"I warn you that it is horrible . . ." His face briefly assumed the expression of a man in the throes of great distress, genuine or not.

"If you are going to become fevered and excitable, as your doctor I cannot permit you to continue."

Nodding agreement, he produced from his valise a number of envelopes, in bundles wrapped with twine. He opened one bundle and extracted an envelope. Opening each envelope, he withdrew several squares of newsprint, which he carefully unfolded and laid out on the tea table side by side.

"What is this, Eddie? Are you about to tell my fortune?"

Poe shook his head with a bitter laugh and turned one of the clippings to face me. It was from the *Baltimore Sun*. "Read this, and tell me if you see any mention of missing teeth."

BODY FOUND

FELL'S POINT——The corpse of a woman was discovered Wednesday morning by workmen in an alley near the City Dock. It has been learned by the *Church Times* that the victim was a "fallen woman" and that she had been "interfered with."

"A most disturbing incident," said Constable Dilts, the officer at the scene. "And a reminder of the wages of sin."

On the back of the clipping had been written, "Berenice"—the title of one of Eddie's more tasteless efforts, in which a monomaniac becomes obsessed with the teeth of his once-beautiful, ailing wife, and pulls them out while she is in a cataleptic condition and he in a trance. Reading it caused the hairs on my arms to stand on end, and for a time I developed an unhealthy fascination for women's teeth.

"Answer me this, Willie: Who would know about the poor woman's missing teeth, other than her murderer?"

It hurts a man's dignity to think that a friendship (or a marriage for that matter) can endure simply for lack of an alternative. Yet that is possibly what determined our long-standing association, at least from my point of view.

I had no boyhood companion other than Eddie Poe. Were it not for his company I might never have left the house. Part of my attachment must have stemmed from simple gratitude, for including me in the Butcher Cats; and I can still summon up a lingering aftertaste of the elation I experienced, the day he swam from Ludlow's Wharf to Warwick.

Yet I despised him too, and not only for his theft of Mother's affection. When I was not blaming myself for her death, I blamed him. Nothing in our house—certainly not Father nor I—inflamed her imagination the way Eddie did. Except for Eddie, our house was a model of restraint and responsibility and self-control. He was the rat in the henhouse, the one who created chaos.

Yet our association continued through school, and though he graduated a year before I did, we exchanged letters thereafter and remained, outwardly at least, the best of friends; so that upon my own graduation I joined him at United States Military Academy, West Point, where we arranged to room together.

However, only a few weeks into our first term I began to observe an alteration in my friend's temperament, and from that point my spirit struggled to wriggle free of his grasp.

During our year's separation Eddie had acquired an overbearing sense of his own intellectual superiority. In conversation, his manner was aloof and dismissive. He delighted in gulling anyone he regarded as his inferior (there were many), and was soundly resented for it. For a time a rumor circulated about the college that he was a descendent of Benedict Arnold, such was the popular estimation of his character.

In the short time we roomed together at West Point, I saw that his boyhood habit of exaggeration and falsification had swelled to grotesque proportions—sea voyages he had never taken, famous people he had never met, political and theological insights he did not possess.

Physically, though still decidedly handsome, his deportment took on an inappropriate languor for a young cadet. And he was perpetually short of funds, for which he blamed (with good reason) his niggardly guardian. This funding imbalance he sought to remedy through gambling, with only intermittent success. And he had begun to drink. And, as always, he wrote lugubrious poetry, which he insisted on reciting whether you wanted to hear it or not.

It is to my regret that I never found the grit to rebuke him for these unfortunate traits. Instead, ever the loyal second, I nodded at his arguments, laughed at his jokes, applauded his tales—and planned my escape.

(Lest I appear vindictive in describing Eddie at West Point, note that the Conduct Book of 1830–1831 lists a total of 106 conduct points against him, for lack of attendance in parades, roll calls, classes, and for refusing to attend church.)

For a young man who sought only to do his duty and thereby succeed, Eddie Poe became a dangerous cadet to know. Halfway through the term I gathered my courage and applied for another room, for the stated reason that my roommate and I practiced incompatible study habits—which was, in a sense, true. Eddie accepted that explanation with an equanimity I shall never forget. Nothing he did or said galled me like his indifference to my absence.

In the act of writing that last paragraph, suddenly I begin to realize why Eddie Poe continues to stir up such resentment: *it was because of him that I became a doctor.*

In witnessing Mother's mental deterioration in my friend's company, I came to sense the danger to my own reason. As their mutual transport grew more intense, I spent less time listening to their verses and more time out-of-doors, adding to my collection of rocks and insects. I took refuge in science.

When father brought Dr. Emory to explain to me why Mother would not be living with us in future, my faith in science enabled me to take heart from the logic it represented. When she died, it never occurred to me to put her death to her scientific mistreatment, nor did it seem appropriate, under the circumstances, for me to weep.

In later years, science served me well—up to a point. At Resaca de Palma I removed men's legs and arms by the dozen with hardly a qualm—not because I felt indifferent to their plight, but because I refused to give free reign to my imagination. I did not ask what the procedure might feel like were it to happen to me. Had I indulged in such imagining, I should have succumbed earlier to mental infirmity, or killed more men through medical blunders than I probably did.

My nervous collapse, when it occurred, was the result of simple exhaustion, though some had it otherwise, pointing to my family history of mental instability. According to an alienist assigned to my case, I was not driven mad by what I saw at Monterey, I was driven mad by my mother.

My honorable discharge from the service remains sketchy in memory. I have a bronze medallion on a green and white ribbon, labeled *1846 MEXICAN WAR 1846,* with an eagle clutching a snake on one side and an eagle with wings spread on the other. I once wondered why I earned only the one decoration, but later read that it was the only one issued from that ugly conflict: *you were there. Let us leave it at that.*

For his part, Eddie Poe left West Point in disgrace during my second term, under circumstances having to do with gambling debts.

Opinions differed as to his activities afterward. Some said he had taken a ship to England under the name Henri Le Rennet; others had it that he joined the United States Army as Richard A. Perry.

I made every effort to avoid keeping track of his subsequent life and career—not an easy task in later years with "The Raven" on display on every magazine cover, every bookstore window, every repetition of the word *nevermore*. I wanted no part of the inward stirrings he evoked in his admirers. Despite his artistic gifts, he was not going to do to me what he did to Mother.

Now he sat before me, sipping medicated tea with the delicacy of an aesthete, taking white powder from a salter he carried in his valise (he took it up the nostril like snuff, something I had not seen before), and giving voice to the most outlandish suspicions, in tones resonating with apparent truth.

"Well now, Eddie," I said. "Let us assume for the moment that the victim in the newspaper is indeed the unfortunate woman downstairs. I fail to see where that leads us. And as for the teeth you produced—how are we to know they were her teeth? They could have been anyone's teeth, don't you see?"

"Whether or not they are the same teeth is entirely beside the point. It is part of an ongoing, deliberate attack on the validity of my work."

"Please explain that last bit, for it is gibberish to me."

"Surely you are familiar with my *Collected Tales*."

"I regret to say no." This was a lie, for in fact I read and loathed every page, some more than once.

"Even you, Willie? In America, has the written word become debased to such an extent that old friends cannot be bothered to read one another?"

I found this line of thought more than a little pompous—that a reluctance to read the tales of Edgar Allan Poe sounded the death knell of the language.

"You needn't put it that way," I replied. "It happens that I prefer fact to fiction."

"And what of art, Willie? What of the imagination?"

"I like a good painting. I enjoy a fantasy as much as the next fellow. I dream preposterous events every night for five to eight hours. But when I wake up I am pleased to do so, and I find nothing so tiresome as hearing about the dreams of others."

"Even your oldest friend?"

"Especially so, Eddie."

"I suppose you took no notice of the publication of my tales in *Graham's* and the *Southern Messenger*—Not even 'Murders in the Rue Morgue'?"

"Have you ever been to France, Eddie?"

"No."

"Then why should I wish to read it? Besides, I read a report that was unfavorable."

"Oh really? And who was the butcher on this occasion?" The expression on Poe's face was one I would describe as an unbecoming sneer.

"If you must know, the review was actually the introduction to your *Collected Tales*. Yes, I did purchase it, but was discouraged from reading further by your own editor. The essay painted you as a madman in the vein of de Sade. Not so much an artist as a symptom. I thought he made a valid point."

Poe immediately became so agitated that I feared he would fall into a fit of apoplexy. "Griswold! How hideously appropriate that you should mention him now!"

"I am not aware that I did."

"There is only one *Collected Tales*, and it is edited by Griswold."

"I believe it might have been he. A man of considerable repute, I'm told. A man of character and good sense."

"It is Griswold behind this whole affair. I am certain of it. His entire life is directed against me and my work."

"I see." Indeed, I did—that his mind had again slipped into delusion. "What is your evidence, Eddie? And if you have evidence, why not present it to the police?"

He shook his head wearily, as though dealing with an inferior pupil who had failed to grasp a fundamental point.

"I understand that you think me mad, Willie. Sometimes I think so myself. Yet I beg you, listen to what I have to tell you. At the end, I will abide by your judgment. If you consign me to a madhouse, so be it. If I require medicines and enemas and ice baths, bring them on. But I implore you to hear me out, if only as a tribute to the memory of your mother, and the sentiments we once shared."

Mother. He would bring her into the discussion. How base of him, to use her memory (of which I retain hardly a shred) to influence me!

I refreshed my cup of tea, sat back in my chair and, in spite of everything, listened.

"THE TROUBLE BEGAN shortly after the publication of my *Collected Tales.* Wiley and Putnam had agreed to the venture on two conditions—that I invest in the enterprise myself (I am still in debt over it), and that Rufus Griswold serve as editor.

"I had no objection to Griswold, for we had always been on cordial terms, and he was well known, having edited a well-received—though woefully shallow—anthology of American poetry.

"It wasn't until I received the galley proofs containing Griswold's vile introduction that I realized what had been done to me.

"Griswold treated my tales as you describe—as a literary abomination and an object for clinical study, part of an unsavory niche occupied by the writings of the degenerate de Sade, the criminal Baudelaire, and the whoremaster Rimbaud. His introduction even concluded with a warning that only the most levelheaded reader should partake of its contents; that children, ladies, and people with a history of derangement should be prevented from reading my tales and poems, *by law if necessary.*

"My *Collected Tales* had been murdered—and I had paid for the deed with my own money!

"Soon after publication I received the first newspaper clipping. With it was a piece of paper on which had been written the title of one of my tales, 'The Mystery of Marie Rogêt.' Here it is—do you want to see? Read for yourself."

WOMAN DROWNED
Dreadful Discovery in the Erie Canal
by J. H. Travis *The Republican Compiler*

ROCHESTER——Canalmen received a woeful surprise in the early morning Tuesday upon the discovery of a cadaver floating near Genesis Falls, female, and in a shameful condition . . .

Though I would not have admitted it for anything, I had read *The Mystery of Marie Rogêt*—a mutilated shopgirl floating down the Seine, based on a dreadful crime that took place in New York. As I mentioned, Eddie had never been to France—yet he had spent time in New York. Why would a man abandon what he knew for what he did not know? Figure that one out if you can.

"I take it, Eddie, that you think the combining of the report with the title of your tale was meant to suggest that the one had indirectly caused the other."

"You are not stupid, Willie. Obviously, that is what I am trying to tell you. It insinuates that some weak or twisted mind had read my tale and had been inspired to imitate the deed."

I chose not to reiterate that I quite agreed with Mr. Griswold. There can surely be no doubt that violent or sensual writing, sufficiently vivid, can inspire a diseased imagination to depraved action. However, as a doctor I proceeded to calm the patient through reassurance and flattery.

"On the other hand, Eddie, the clipping might have been sent by an admirer. Someone who read about the crime, and noted a curious coincidence that might interest his favorite author. You must admit that the sender's true motive is a complete mystery."

"Quite right, Willie. A mystery. Remember that the nameless terror is always the worst. Death is not a skeleton but an empty cloak."

"Please continue," I said, noting that his pupils had dilated and his mind had gone off on its own.

"The letter joined with the poor reception for my *Collected Tales*—and, it goes without saying, the loss of my dear little wife . . ." And there it stopped. Slowly his face crumpled as though the bones themselves withdrew. With his broad forehead and delicate mouth he resembled an aged toddler, helpless and inconsolable in the face of overwhelming hurt. As I watched his display of mourning I admit that I was touched—though we must always remember that he came from a family of actors.

Gradually he regained control with the assistance of more medicated tea. "Forgive me. I do not want your pity. I know that you too are a widower. All I meant to say was that I fell into a decline—abetted, I admit, by the use of alcohol. By the time I recovered my senses sufficiently to look after myself, I was nearly penniless. Worse, I had stretched the physical and spiritual resources of my poor little family beyond anything previous—and we had suffered through some difficult times. Purely to fend off starvation, I accepted an assignment from the publishers Topham & Lea—whom I would never have entrusted with the *Tales*, though they could hardly have done worse. Yet this assignment was so far beneath my standard as to be almost criminal."

"Would this be what you would call *hack work*?"

"Not the first time, I regret to say. A few years ago I wrote a textbook on conchology for Topham—under a pseudonym, of course. This new assignment was worse. I was engaged to write the final chapters of a novel by a well-known British author."

"Why?"

"Because the author hadn't written it yet, I suppose. Topham wanted an edge over the competition."

"I regret that I know nothing about the publishing industry."

"You have nothing to regret I assure you. In the meanwhile, other newspaper clippings arrived. You may read this one for yourself:

THE BODY IN THE CHIMNEY
A Thief Meets His Maker
by John R. Basswood *The Brooklyn Eagle*

FLATBUSH——Firemen, upon investigating a report of excessive smoke issuing from a home on Church Avenue, discovered a cadaver wedged in the flue. The owners being out of town for some days, it is thought that a burglar died of thirst . . .

"Eddie, to my mind, this evidence is even more tenuous than the first. Am I to suppose that a body stuck in a chimney is a feature of another of your *Collected Tales*?"

"Correct. Again, with the obvious implication that the two are linked."

"But surely, unlike the female in the canal, your writing can hardly be blamed because a man is stuck in a chimney—especially since, according to the tale, it was the work of an orangutan."

"I believe the sender wished to imply that I am poisoning the general atmosphere. There were many other letters and clippings, as you can see."

"I think that you give your persecutor too much credit," I replied. "It seems more likely that he spent his time scouring newspapers for an appropriate item, and this was the best he could do."

"Well done, Willie. I admire your deductive, scientific mind."

"The same might apply to the unfortunate woman in our morgue."

"But in this case, the package containing the article from the *Christian Times* was accompanied by the pulled teeth."

"And what meaning do you draw from it?"

"I can only suppose that, unlike the others, she was expressly murdered for the purpose."

"What purpose?"

"To drive me to suicide, or insanity, or to stop writing—which amounts to the same thing."

To this I had no rebuttal. Just because a man suffers from persecution mania is no guarantee that he is not being persecuted.

"I think you had better have a little of this," I said, noting his pallor, and produced a bottle from my bag.

"What is it you are giving me?"

"Morphine. Perfectly harmless I assure you."

"Oh, I know about morphine," he said ruefully, and took the entire dose in a single draft.

"Please continue," I said. Though I would not have admitted it, I was thoroughly drawn in.

"I wonder whether you have noticed this, Willie: that upon reaching a certain depth of despair or dismay, one can break through to a state of serene detachment."

"That is what morphine is for, Eddie."

"Finally, I determined to travel to Baltimore and see the evidence for myself. If the woman in the morgue appeared as described in the article, my hope was to enlist the support of my oldest friend."

"Yet rather than making an appointment and stating your case to me man to man, you chose to make a theatrical display of yourself, lying in the gutter and raving like a lunatic."

"It was essential to the course of action we must undertake."

"And what is that?" I noted with alarm his use of the first person plural.

"I need you to sign my death certificate, and to substitute another cadaver for mine. I believe there is an acceptable candidate in your morgue."

I nearly spilled my tea. I scarcely knew how to reply. To say that such a measure was out of the question seemed laughably inadequate. But before I found words to express my dismay, he silenced me with a look of such intensity in those black eyes, that in retrospect I wonder if I was being subjected to mesmerism.

At least it was now clear to me why Eddie had staged his collapse in the street. It would hardly have been the thing for him to meet with me in a healthy condition and somehow die immediately thereafter.

Eddie leaned forward and spoke sotto voce, either because he feared we might be overheard or because it enhanced the mesmeric effect.

"I know that there have been hard feelings between us, Willie, regarding my sentiment for Mrs. Chivers. And I know how bitter memories can turn esteem into disdain. Yet I urge you to take care. Consider that your disdain for me cannot help but extend to yourself. You chose to behave as though a mother's love was finite, as though the affection she felt for another boy could diminish her feeling for her own offspring. I suggest that you, and not I, initiated the heartsickness that brought about her decline."

"Please stop, I beg you . . ." Now it was I who fell into disarray. I was about to take a draft of morphine, then resisted, not to impair my judgment.

"There—do you see, Willie? We are two of a kind. We both know what it is to lose one's mother. We both know what it was to lose *your* mother. You will never have as close a friend as I."

He reached across the table and grasped my hand. "We are brothers. And neither is to blame for what happened. Despite her disposition to melancholy, were it not for your father's inept physician, Dr. Emory, she would be alive today."

"Dr. Emory? *By God!*" I swear that I had not thought of the man in twenty years.

"Ah, so you remember. Dr. Morris Emory was his name. He had extremely thick eyebrows and strangler's thumbs."

"Absolutely right! Astonishing!" I followed only intermittently the discourse to follow, for my mind had traveled elsewhere: I cannot say for certain that Poe knew the circumstance of my wife's death, yet he had unearthed an uncanny parallel between her fate and that of my mother—the two Mrs. Chivers.

In the same way that Father handed Mother over to Dr. Emory, I had subjected my Lucy to the ministrations of Dr. Prebble—no midwife for me, thank you, only the most modern protocols. And as the journals assured me, *there is nothing better than a set of curved forceps* to *assure safer and shorter accouchement and parturition.*

As head surgeon at Washington College Hospital, Prebble had first call on maternity cases, and I never thought to question his ability to carry out this delicate procedure. Only vaguely did it enter my mind that, at the time of Prebble's arrival and subsequent promotion, President Jackson, in a fit of misplaced egalitarianism, had abolished license requirements for physicians and surgeons—*a professional aristocracy*, he called it. Thanks to deregulation, a doctor need never have opened a medical text to set up shop, claiming French training and specialized expertise, with no proof required. In an era of unprecedented quackery, I might have demonstrated a more skeptical spirit when it came to the welfare of my own wife and child—especially given his reputation for stumbling or hesitating over commonplace medical terms and phrases.

Yet I agreed. Why? Because not to do so would betray a lack of confidence in my superior.

Fool!

Prebble was most regretful over the hemorrhage, though by no means critical of his own performance. "An unusual case," he called it. "No one could have predicted a womb of blood with a malignancy of the heart, an unprecedented combination of events to be sure . . ."

Now, years later, I find myself in his debt. Following my term of military service, it was thanks to Prebble that I was permitted to return to residence, since few medical institutions would overlook my history of mental instability and recent breakdown, however well earned.

For the fact that I am able to practice medicine, I have to thank the man who killed my wife.

I became aware of Eddie watching me closely, as though he knew the journey my mind had taken to the rage within. For the first time since we poached pheasant together on the James River, I felt an exhilarating impulse to do wrong, to rebel. To defy the little life I had been compressed into, the tight, dry little man I had become.

With even the most expert mesmerist, the subject must retain an inner desire to do as the practitioner suggests.

What seems remarkable is not only the readiness with which I collaborated with Poe on a project that could ruin me, but the almost mystical collusion of the institution in enabling us to accomplish it.

> **Grave**, *n*. A place in which the dead are laid, to await the coming of the medical student.
>
> —Ambrose Bierce

THE MORGUE AT Washington College Hospital was known to suffer a chronic deficit of cadavers, though the hospital wasted no time or effort in producing them. The school paid well for specimens and showed little curiosity about their place of origin. Therefore, it was hardly surprising that, in the public imagination, the institution had acquired a ghoulish reputation.

Because of our location in proximity to Baltimore's main cemetery, it was generally thought that the deceased slept in their graves there for hardly twenty-four hours before they lay stretched out on a dissecting table at Washington College. Vile speculations grew from there, including the rumor that citizens had been kidnapped live for dissection, and other atrocities as well.

To make things worse, a feature article in the *Baltimore Clipper* by a professional alarmist named Tibbs (accompanying an advertisement for "safety coffins"), advanced the myth that many corpses were buried who were not really dead. One story had it that two grave robbers had unearthed a female cadaver, and as soon as the coffin was open she began to scream. (Some versions of the tale claimed that she had eaten her fingers.)

Of course there was also a perfectly rational basis for the public antipathy regarding Washington College Hospital—namely, the abysmal cure rate; a tendency for patients to arrive with one malady, stay because of another, and die because they contracted a third. Let it suffice to note that, for a variety of reasons, an institution founded as a wellspring of public health had become an object of terror, and seldom would a person willingly go near it once the sun went down.

Given the almost total lack of visitors, the atmosphere in the hospital at night resembled that of a fire station between alarms. Any sense of tasks being done in the normal way disappeared. Staff who worked a second job during the day took naps. Others formed informal clubs, discussing books and playing cribbage and other games in the kitchen and back rooms while awaiting the ambulance bell.

As for the patients on the wards in their fevered slumber, life ground to a standstill at night, with only the ticking of a clock at the foot of the ward to punctuate the empty hours. The halls and stairways took on an atmosphere of still suspension, with only the faint odor of camphor and infection to distinguish it from an enormous crypt, an empty castle, an architectural ghost.

Though it was by no miracle that we carried out our highly incriminating activities, at the time it felt as though we operated under a spell.

CHAPTER EIGHT

Philadelphia

Text of a speech delivered to the Irish-American Literary League, sponsored by the Society for United Irishwomen, Philadelphia:

> To appreciate the depth of the imperial conquest of America, let us visit a bookstand near the Marketplace, and let us peruse the titles on display.
>
> How speaks the voice of freedom in the New World? What new American ethic, what American vision of democracy has found expression on the pages of your novels, poetry, and periodicals?
>
> Ah. I see *Vanity Fair* is popular this year: Mr. Thackery's spiteful vilification of ambition—especially in an ambitious woman.
>
> And in advance of his much-anticipated tour of America, I see that our bookstand is well stocked with the works of the author Charles Dickens, and *his* universe of contented servants and saintly wives. Whose poor bewail their starvation—but not their poverty. Whose servants resent their mistreatment—but not their servitude. Whose villains are bad schoolmasters—not the rulers of the country. And when the well born do go bad, which is seldom, it is because they are corrupted by persons of lesser rank. And of course the worst that can befall a woman is that she might lose her virtue—not that she might be worked to death.
>
> With the spirit of America so infected by submission to imperial authority, do we wonder that Mr. Washington Irving's headless horseman is a Hessian—a European ghost haunting America? Do we wonder that hardly a single tale by Mr. Edgar Allan Poe takes place in the land in which he

lives? What do you expect, in a country whose vice-president, Colonel Aaron Burr, who had fought in the Revolution, attempted to evade a charge of murder by claiming that he was a *British subject*?

With the brains of America hostage to Europe, will not the body follow?

According to the *Tain bo Cuailgne*, the warrior Queen Maeve led her army to victory, drowning the opposing army in a flood of urine and menstrual blood. You, the women of Ireland, were removed to these shores by Almighty God for one purpose—to lead the New American Revolution. That is the meaning of your suffering. That is your task.

My associate, Lieutenant O'Reilly, and his able young assistants, will now pass among you. Think upon your homeland and what she has suffered, and give as your heart, your courage, and your patriotism dictate . . .

Who among us has not felt out of accord with the universe? By the same token, who has not felt as though the Almighty Himself were at one's service?

I say this in another attempt to evoke the feeling of ease that surrounded our perilous project like an aura. From one moment to the next it seemed as though every move had been acceded to by some higher power, that we had only to put one foot in front of the other and doors would open of their own accord.

(Does Satan provide an equivalent sense of ease and delight to *his* children? How is one to know what power is at one's service, and to what end?)

Back in the morgue, the gaslights had been turned down to a mere flicker and the mortician had long gone home for supper, if he ever returned from luncheon. For silence there was nothing to equal it. The cadavers spread along the walls had the presence not of patients but of ruined, discarded overcoats, with no trace of the wearer but bulges and wrinkles in the cloth.

I avoided looking at the sheeted lump containing the toothless young woman. A man can take only so much at one time. Meanwhile, Eddie peered down at the bearded young cadaver with a hole in the chest, assessing its suitability.

Physically, the transfer was clumsy but manageable. By placing an empty table next to the cadaver we were able to roll it onto a stretcher; it was surprisingly light due to dehydration. Grasping the poles at opposite ends, we carried the stretcher up the ramp to the first floor—unconcerned with discovery, for if we encountered anyone it would have been two other men with a cadaver on a pair of sticks.

Nor, thanks to the nature of the institution, did there exist any great danger that someone might take note of our man's absence from the morgue. As an unaudited clearing-ground for the unnamed dead, there was no way to determine whether an empty table meant that the remains had left for the medical school, or had returned to the hospital for forensic diagnosis, or had been claimed by a member of the public.

As we packed the corpse into the wing for the Agitated Insane, I noted that the surrounding babble had if anything increased, though the patients were supposedly asleep. (Often a patient will undergo greater agitation asleep than awake—another instance of the freed imagination doing its worst.)

As we deposited the body of the young suicide on the cot, our neighbor waxed no less eloquent: *"Twin-devil and specter of crazed and doomed mortals of earth and perdition! . . ."*

His monologue seemed to require no pause for rest or breath, and when I hear him in my mind I still experience the discomfiting sense that he was cheering us on, as we rolled the cadaver onto the bed and assessed its potential as a substitute.

The cadaver must have been ten years younger than Eddie—not an insurmountable problem, for death has an aging effect, even on small children. A well-bred young man, to judge by the haircut and the quality of the suit. The coat of fine worsted remained untouched by blood or powder burn, though of course the shirt and vest were ruined.

Every suicide is a poet, sublime in its melancholy. So wrote the Frenchman Balzac in a virtual advertisement for the practice—perhaps an inspiration for the poor devil before us. Or perhaps he fell victim to a poem by Edgar Allan Poe.

Bones of the dead the skull the skull in Connamorrah! . . .

"Willie, please find something to quiet him down."

"He is Dr. Slan's patient."

"How decorous of you."

"I mean that on his morning call Slan would know something had been administered. The patient has been screaming for days."

With the cadaver stretched out before us, Eddie produced an ancient gentleman's traveling case from his valise and, with a surprisingly brisk and businesslike air, took out a throat-cut razor, a strop in a leather case, a pig-bristle shaving brush, a pair of scissors, and even a jar of laurel water: evidently he wished it even to smell like himself.

He then proceeded to cut and shave the beard, and to form a mustache similar to his own.

It is true that a man can groom his own face when blind, but I doubt most men would be able to groom *another* man's face so efficiently. It seemed to me certain that he had given it previous thought.

Still, in part of my mind, we were fifteen-year-old boys again, as I succumbed to that old spirit of high adventure, while I served as proud second to the strongest swimmer in Richmond.

Mere language cannot tell the gushing well that swells and sweeps tempestlike over me signaling the larm of death . . .

He spent a good hour on the job, paying careful attention to the arrangement and disposition of the hair, and I must say I found the result surprisingly convincing—another skill of an actor, by the way.

As he worked, Eddie opined on the process of life and death, describing the former as a proceeding in which human beings gradually become more distinct from one another, and the latter as a proceeding in which we all become alike.

"Is it possible," he mused, "that a life is but a dream issuing from the endless sleep of death? That every personality is an illusion?"

"I have no comment," I replied. "I detest idle speculation about life and death."

Despite my skepticism, I had become fascinated by the transformation of the corpse. To my eye, the likeness went deeper than coloring, shape, and structure; it seemed as if a part of Eddie's essence had been duplicated somehow, as though the cadaver had become a former Poe—a breathless, voiceless, lifeless Poe, while above him stood the new Poe, newly freed from himself.

It is clear to me now that my eyes saw what my mind desired—a common delusion. Match the gender, part the hair at a certain angle, clip the mustache into a certain shape, turn the lip this way or that, and your best friend will see his best friend—if that is what he wants to see.

Eddie Poe was my best friend.

I do not know why a sudden panic came over me at that thought. It seemed as though the full weight of my disappointing life suddenly occupied my stomach—the realization that this was the only friend I had ever had, and for that reason alone I was doing this.

Literally, my bowels melted.

"What is it, Willie? Are you having another one of your spells?"

Though I served in the army, under no circumstance was I prepared to use the bedpan under the gaze of Eddie Poe. For that reason, I left for the outdoor privy, where I had time to reflect.

Thinking in private, I reminded myself that the deeds of this night could not be undone. Whether awake or in a dream, life does not travel in reverse. Looking back, I see that my mind had come to a false conclusion. In truth, the situation was entirely reversible. There was nothing to stop me from returning the cadaver to the morgue where it belonged, bidding Eddie good-bye, and calling an end to this absurd and grotesque enterprise.

Nothing to stop me, but myself.

In truth, by then any decision I might have taken was moot. This I discovered upon returning to the room, to see the cadaver dressed in Eddie's shabby suit and my oldest friend, one foot on the bed, turning up the cadaver's trouser cuff.

"A bit long in the inseam," I said.

"It is a necessary step," he replied, a bit defensively, inspecting the fit of the waist and seat.

All at once I experienced that sense of amused detachment that might well come over a man who has just jumped from a tall building, and can only lie back and enjoy the temporary sense of flying. "I expect the coat could do with an airing. I compliment you for avoiding the vest and shirt."

"There's no need for sarcasm, Willie. To pass for me, he must wear my clothes. Surely that is obvious. It is also obvious that I can't walk through Baltimore in my underwear."

As he brushed the dead man's dandruff from his shoulder it occurred to me that he was about to vacate the premises—escape rather, leaving me to deal with the remains.

He slipped on the coat and turned up the sleeves. "How do I look?"

"I do not feel qualified to render an opinion."

"I'll not forget what you have done for me, Willie. I swear you will be repaid."

"I beg you, Eddie, do not even consider repayment."

"Wish me luck," he said.

"Good luck to you."

"You're a strange, dark fellow, Willie, but you're the best friend I have in the world."

"Do you know, Eddie, I am afraid you may be right."

DICKENS COMING TO AMERICA

by Sanford W. Mitchell, *The Philadelphia Inquirer*

America's reading set is a-twitter over the proposed reading tour of Mr. Charles Dickens. Already appearances by the literary lion have been scheduled in Boston, Worcester, Harvard, New York, Philadelphia, Baltimore, Richmond, and Washington. The Young Men of Boston have announced a public dinner in his honor, and a "Boz Ball" will take place at the Park Theater in New York, where Mr. Francis Alexander has been engaged to undertake his portrait. In Washington, he will attend a levee with the president.

"Here is a son of a haberdasher with no hereditary title, no military laurels, and no princely fortune," remarked Dr. William Ellery Fanning. "His approach will surely be hailed by Americans of every age and condition, and his welcome will be all heart."

ANY FEELING OF satisfaction I might seem to have experienced, any roguish excitement at a boyhood escapade came to an abrupt end with five knocks on my door the next morning.

I had not slept a wink, having spent the night listening to the creaking of my rope bed as I squirmed back and forth, seeking a comfortable position between sandpaper sheets.

I sprang bolt upright. Beads of sweat greased my brow, and more trickled down my rib cage—a fever? I examined the pocket watch on my bedside table: Nine o'clock. I had overslept. Slept? Is it possible that I spent the night in a delirium?

Five more knocks on the door.

More sweat, more blood coursing past the eardrums and a gathering cloud of doom overhead: *What have I done? What am I going to do?*

In my mind, the familiar voice of my old friend whispered: *Remain calm, Willie.*

Five more knocks. Whoever they were, they would not go away. I could feel the brass rails hard and cold against my spine like prison bars.

I stumbled to my dressing table, opened my doctor's bag, and removed Poe's salter of cocaine. "Wait, please. I shall be there in a minute," I called, in a calm, untroubled voice.

What have I done? What am I going to do?

Then came a muffled voice on the other side of the door: *Dr. Chivers! It is nine o'clock and there is an important visitor for Mr. Poe!*

I turned the iron knob and opened the door a reticent six inches. I would not have been surprised to see a robed skeleton on the other side—or worse, a policeman. Instead, I faced the scrubbed, merciless, familiar face of Nurse Slatin, fist upraised, about to knock for the third time, her starched uniform a wall of blue with a white collar, cap and cuffs, and that face, with the broad nose and the permanent stony grimace.

"Yes, nurse, what is it?"

"Mr. Neilson Poe, sir. The cousin has come to inquire after your patient."

For a moment I stood there, tongue-tied. She took this for assent. "Shall I fetch Mr. Poe then, sir?"

"Nurse Slatin, the patient has congestion of the brain and possibly lesions as well. He is in critical condition. He cannot receive visitors under any circumstance."

"Mr. Neilson Poe is paying for the room, Doctor. It would be respectful if you would at least speak to him." Nurse Slatin scarcely moved her lips while talking. Whether in the interest of efficiency or from pure laziness, she uttered words without moving a muscle of her face. Or perhaps it was a result of her calm confidence; for it is a fact of institutional life that minor officials who physically put their hands upon cash, in however small amounts, wield an authority far out of proportion to their station.

"Excuse me, nurse, I should like to get dressed." I said, and gently closed the door.

"Very good, Doctor," came the muffled monotone.

I mopped my face with my handkerchief, crossed the floor to the washbasin, performed my toilet, put on my suit and coat, and checked my pocket watch: ten minutes had passed.

I opened the door. As expected, Nurse Slatin stood rooted to the spot.

"What are your instructions, Doctor?"

"I shall look in on the patient at once. Inform Mr. Neilson Poe that I shall see him shortly in the waiting room. Tell him it must be very quick, for his cousin is a sick man and requires constant supervision."

I headed downstairs, the picture of a harried, concerned physician, while a hollow voice in my mind shrieked: *What have you done? What are you going to do?*

IN EVERY ENCOUNTER, there is a time to sit back, and a time to take the initiative. In dealing with Eddie's cousin Neilson, since there were any number of questions I did not wish to answer, I chose the former approach.

"Sir, am I to understand that you are Mr. Neilson Poe, the patient's cousin?"

"*Second* cousin, as a matter of fact. And you would be Dr. Chivers, sir?"

"*I am, sir*," we said simultaneously, both sides having failed to establish the upper hand.

I shook hands with a gentleman somewhat older than Eddie, about the same height, with a similar expanse of brow and black eyes that must also run in the family.

There, however, the similarity ended.

Neilson Poe was obviously the more respectable of the two cousins, albeit with dirty fingernails and a suit that had not seen a brush in some time. However, he had augmented his appearance in a number of odd ways. Whereas Eddie's chin was clean-shaven, Neilson sported an almost oriental wisp of a goatee. While Eddie grew his dark hair in Byronic curls, the pennant that swept across Neilson's head with the aid of a good deal of pomade had been dyed a sort of purplish auburn.

For several moments, neither of us spoke. The toe of his highly polished walking shoe began tapping the floor, signaling impatience.

I refused to break the pause, for to do so would be to establish subservience. Instead, I pretended to study my notebook, then reached for my pencil and pretended to make a correction, while arranging my features in an expression that suggested deep thinking on an important matter.

"I am sure you understand that the family is extremely concerned about Edgar," he said, at length. "What is your prognosis, Doctor?"

I emitted a troubled sigh. "I am afraid that I cannot be overly encouraging, Mr. Poe. Your cousin is not a well man."

"*Second* cousin, don't you know?" he said, a point he wished to make clear.

"I shall make a note of that," I replied. "In any case, to be frank, the chances are against him."

"I see." Mr. Poe did not seem overly affected by the bad news.

"The patient has a swelling on the brain—a condition we call lobar pneumonia—complicated by transient retardation. I can hardly recommend a visit at this time. Your cousin is not conscious, and there is some risk to yourself, until we know the precise cause of the malady . . ."

"Oh, I wouldn't think of it," he replied quickly, as though I had invited him into a snake pit. "We were never close, my second cousin and I. Quite the opposite, in fact."

"I understand. You are most generous, sir, to accept the burden of his care."

"It is my duty, sir."

"Of course. Then what may I do for you? Why have you come to see me? For I should see to the patient at once."

"I am—I have come—I have come—" The cousin searched for *le mot juste*: either he had no idea why he had come, or else he knew and did not wish to say.

"Out of familial duty, of course," I said, doing his work for him.

"Indeed so. Well put, sir. I thank you for it."

"Your devotion is most admirable, sir. I shall convey to the patient your best wishes when—or I should say if—he recovers his reason. I am sure an encouraging word from a blood relative will lift his spirits enormously."

"Very good, sir. Quite so. Please carry on, then. Be assured that I shall cover all necessary expenses—within reason."

"If there is a change in his condition, I shall see that Nurse Slatin contacts you at once."

We shook hands. His palm had become damp during our brief chat, indicating that I had made him more nervous than the other way around. I watched his back recede down the hall, noting a certain lightness of step, as though at any moment he might begin twirling his stick.

> **Life**, *n*. A spiritual pickle preserving the body
> from decay.
>
> —Ambrose Bierce

It is an unusual thing for a doctor to spend time alone with a cadaver; yet it seemed only prudent to allow a half hour to pass before declaring the patient officially dead.

We doctors have little truck with the dead other than as objects of study. Death, even if it is the normal outcome, is not a state that occupies the medical mind. With a patient's last gasp, the attending physician loses all interest. Following a series of commemorative noises to the relatives he is on to the next patient, the next death, having forgotten the name of the last one.

Not in this case. In my mind the cadaver had *become* Eddie Poe—thanks, I thought at the time, to a remarkably skillful transformation, accomplished by a man with theater in his blood. However, my identification with the corpse may have also been a product of spiritual necessity; to survive this ordeal I was going to have to undertake a number of lies, convincingly—and the most successful lies are the ones we believe ourselves.

Sitting with Eddie's dead body, I felt the urge to weep—certainly not for him, nor for myself, but for all of us. The loneliness of death. That it comes down to this, this, this *silence* . . .

I opened my eyes, looked down at the cadaver—and suddenly the illusion burst. It was as though someone had thrown a stone into a mirror. I saw, really saw, what lay before me, and I nearly cried out aloud.

Dear heaven, I had been in a sort of trance!

Whatever I thought I had seen over the past hours, the young man on the bed before me bore no more resemblance to Eddie Poe than I did. The complexion was darker, the brow narrower, the nose broader; our man was two inches taller, thirty pounds heavier, and a good fifteen years younger than the corpse he was to represent.

I restrained myself from shrieking aloud—unlike the annoying gentleman in the adjoining room.

Too late! too late! I must lift the pall and open to you the secret that sears the heart and daggerlike pierces the soul!

Looking back I sense that I had reached a fork in the road of life, at which one path leads to an uncertain destination and the other leads straight off a cliff. A point where a man must decide whether he intends to proceed with his life, such as it is, or not. I had been considering the question for some time, in the abstract. At the same time, I kept in my alligator bag a sufficient quantity of morphine, should I ever make up my mind.

In that moment, surprisingly, I chose life. Not out of courage, nor hope, nor because life was the path of least resistance. I chose life, that I might live long enough to have a word or two with my dangerous, duplicitous friend Eddie.

NURSE SLATIN, I need you."

"Very good, Doctor." Seated at her station, neither the head nor the lips seemed to move.

"Do you have an address for Mr. Neilson Poe?"

"Who?"

"Mr. Neilson Poe. He is paying for my patient's room. You called my attention to that fact yourself."

"Yes. Mr. Neilson Poe left his address with me this morning. He asked not to be contacted except in a crisis."

"It is not a crisis, but send him a message anyway. Tell him that his cousin—rather, his *second* cousin—has passed away. Request instructions regarding disposal of the remains."

Nurse Slatin paused. A thoughtful expression momentarily swept over her flat features. It was almost as though she were considering the question of life and death.

"Doctor?"

"Yes, nurse?"

"By what time will the room be free? If you can clear the bed by two, there is a brain tumor waiting in the hall."

As I EXPECTED, Neilson Poe replied not in person but by courier. His message contained neither an expression of grief nor an interest in the disposition of his cousin's cadaver. And to my vast relief, nowhere did he indicate the slightest desire to view his second cousin's earthly remains for a last farewell.

Accordingly, in our subsequent communication, he was pleased to accept my offer to assign the collection and care of the remains to Mr. Samuel Ripp, an undertaker with a reputation for producing decent burials of the unloved deceased, at minimal cost to the relatives. For my part, I selected Mr. Ripp as a professional who, for a small additional stipend, could be counted on to overlook the rather large hole in the chest of the deceased, and thereby spare the family the disgrace of a suicide.

Later that afternoon, a pair of nonchalant attendants lifted the corpse onto an ice-filled cooling board. For this I was very glad, for the odor of decomposition might have revealed that our man had been dead longer than claimed. As they removed it from the premises in a wicker transport coffin, I pondered the best route to ensuring that the casket remained closed during the funeral. I did not worry overmuch about the undertaker, for Mr. Ripp would not know Eddie from Adam.

Given his evident concern over expenses, Neilson Poe's invitation to luncheon the next day came as a surprise, and suggested some sort of request might ensue. Less surprising was the venue—the Exchange Hotel, located at the Merchant Exchange. The building, or series of buildings, was an H-shaped monstrosity in the *ramshackle* style, capped by a dome like the pate of a white elephant. Intended as a center for commerce, the venture had to be saved from bankruptcy by renting to an assortment of government offices—including that of the mayor and council. This of course ensured a steady flow of traffic, for every businessman in Baltimore had a reason to bribe a councilman.

In the financial districts of America's three biggest cities (New York, Philadelphia, and Baltimore), building edifices of this sort had become an obsession. Greek, Roman, anything ancient would do, as long as it was grandiloquent and European. I suppose it was meant to impart a feeling of history and permanence—a solidity lacking in the affairs of the tenants.

The occupants of the Merchant Exchange were of course all men, down to the last merchant. Only in the army or the clergy might one have encountered a more homosexual society, in the sense of including only one gender among its ranks.

Fittingly, in its design and function, the dining room was intended to ape a private men's club in the City of London—an expensive and painstaking re-creation, thousands having been lavished on mahogany, brass, velvet, gilt and stained glass, with everything, from chandeliers to spittoons, shipped from overseas.

But in the end, what defined the room, as with any room, were the persons who occupied it.

These were not Mayfair gentlemen. These men—if indeed they were subject to a collective noun at all—were for the most part uprooted, desperate gamblers from any one of a dozen nations, no more than a week away from bankruptcy. They rode on hosses, not in carriages; they did not duel with swords, but in fistfights; their suits had been on their bodies daily for months, as had their underwear, with no bathing required.

Visually, the overwhelming effect on entering the dining room was of an enormous humidor, in which all the cigars had been lit at once. Stepping onto the carpet one took care not to slip on phlegm that had missed the intended spittoons. As for sound, everyone talked as though he wished to be heard from the table at the other end of the room; in the Merchant Exchange, to be overheard was not an embarrassment but a business strategy.

As expected, my table companion was nowhere to be seen. For any Baltimore businessman, to be punctual at luncheon is an admission that business is slack. A waiter in a soiled, vaguely Hessian uniform ushered me to a table and I took my seat in front of a linen tablecloth set with great lumps of silver, each piece stamped with the crest of a nonexistent duke.

To pass the time, I requested a copy of the *Sun* so that I might review the election results. On the front page I noted the resounding victory of an incumbent councilman named *Riley*.

Troubled by the name, I turned to the Books section, that part of a newspaper in which the reader is told which books he should pretend to have read.

DICKENS NOVEL IMMINENT
"A First for American Literature," crows Editor
by Sanford W. Mitchell, *The Philadelphia Inquirer*

PHILADELPHIA——Amid much fanfare, Topham and Lea have announced the forthcoming complete edition of the novel *David Copperfield* by Mr. Charles Dickens.

According to Mr. Topham, "The publication of a major author even before the appearance of a British edition is an unprecedented achievement. It is a triumph for the American publishing industry, a tribute to American know-how, and of great benefit to the American readers."

Readers will remember Charles Dickens as the author of *Dombey and Son*, which makes no secret of its contempt for commerce and for businessmen such as Mr. Topham.

While we readily accede to his first and second pronouncements, we trust that Mr. Topham will leave it to the American reader to discern what "benefits" accrue from Mr. Dickens's acerbic pen.

DR. CHIVERS, SIR, I do apologize."

Neilson Poe loomed above me with his auburn cap of hair, extending his soft right hand. Another reason to ensure tardiness at luncheon: one attains a superior position over one's companion right at the outset.

"We are so terribly busy these days, don't you know?" he continued, as though that were an explanation.

"There aren't enough hours in the day," I replied, grasping his damp little palm.

He frowned slightly, noting the newspaper spread out in front of me. "Surely it hasn't got into the *Sun* as well."

"Only in the *Clipper* at present. But news of his death is bound to spread. Edgar Poe was extremely famous in certain circles."

"Yes, regrettably. Would you care for a whiskey?"

"I am a Son of Temperance, sir," I replied, as the waiter poured the delicious amber liquid into a cut-glass tumbler that might have weighed five pounds.

"I salute your resolution," Mr. Poe said, allowing the light to cast a golden glow through his raised glass, as though he might tell the future by it.

"His passing has put a strain on the hospital," I continued. "There were fifteen women at the front doors this morning, demanding to view the remains. They wanted locks of his hair; some actually carried scissors for the purpose. Morbid, if you ask me."

Neilson Poe shook his head as though weighted down by the folly of mankind. His little goatee waggled back and forth like a finger of reprimand.

"It is the fault of the public school system, of that I am certain," he said. "This is what you get when inferior people are taught how to read. An age of shallow celebrity, when all a man has to do is write something shocking and he will be deluged by brainless young women!"

From his emphasis on the last three words, and from the state of his linen and fingernails, I concluded that Mr. Poe was a bachelor. He was not a handsome man. The hair dye did him no favors. Yet he had an ingratiating quality, an eagerness for agreement.

"My cousin's celebrity," he continued, "was an ill-gotten affair. Poison for the young people."

"I quite agree," I replied. "Yet we must be careful not to confuse celebrity and success, for he had no money."

"Indeed so," replied the cousin, warming to his like-minded companion. "To judge by recent assessments of his work, there can be no doubt that he was on the way down in every conceivable way."

"A sad deterioration in general," I replied. "It might seem cruel to say this, but perhaps he was fortunate to have met his end before he was entirely found out."

"Absolutely! *Dead* lucky, one might say!" and the little goatee went up and down like a bobbin.

I carried on in this sycophantic vein while he drank another whiskey. By degrees, in our mutual view, Eddie was to blame for a general public deterioration, including the rate of public drunkenness and the low voter turnout at municipal elections. Had we continued at this rate for the afternoon, his death might have cured America.

There is no limit to the hatred within families, I thought, as I nodded at regular intervals, echoed random phrases, and retreated into a reverie of boredom. Idly, my gaze cruised about the dining room—and fell upon a lone diner next to a corner window, her face obscured by a book, which may or may not have been a Bible.

It is perhaps unnecessary to mention that she was the only female in the establishment.

For me, the sight of this woman inspired that peculiar sensation of having seen someone or something before—while knowing it to be impossible. (Mr. Emerson wrote about the phenomenon but shone no light on it, leaving the field to quack clairvoyants from Europe and Hindu mystics from Brooklyn.)

Returning my focus to the luncheon, noting that Mr. Poe had ordered a third glass of whiskey, I sped to the subject that was, for me at least, of most urgent importance.

"Mr. Poe, sir, I hope I am not going out of bounds in recommending a closed casket. If truth be told, your second cousin is not a pretty sight. Mr. Ripp can correct the flaws to some degree of course, and at a price, but . . ." I trailed off, wincing gently as though leery of the result.

"Most definitely. The casket must be closed," replied the cousin, instantly. "I had not for one moment supposed it to be anything else."

I feigned a slight cough to mask my expression of profound relief. "That is fine, then. Excellent. It seems to me that all is in order."

"Just as it should be," my companion said, nodding. "The burial will take place tomorrow, in lot twenty-seven. Uncle Henry Herring has kindly purchased the mahogany coffin. The family will take care of the tombstone and engraving. Reverend Clemm will preside—he is a relation of my dear little cousin Virginia, Edgar's late wife."

So many cousins and uncles, I thought.

And did I detect a hesitation, before he pronounced the name of his late cousin? Had cousin Neilson displayed an emotion?

"There is one other thing," said Neilson Poe. "And on this subject I need to trust in your discretion."

"I am a physician, sir," I replied, somewhat miffed.

"No offense intended, Doctor. My second cousin left a will, don't you see? You might wonder that he went to the trouble, since his estate consists mostly of debts. But he did leave his works, for what they might be worth, to my aunt Maria Clemm, who was like a mother to him."

Resentfully, I wondered from whose arms Eddie had stolen Aunt Clemm.

"But he made one specific, and peculiar, request." Neilson Poe paused as though unsure that he would be able to mouth the words. "Edgar asks that his jugular be cut before burial."

"Ah yes," I replied, smoothly. "I am not the least bit surprised."

"Dr. Chivers, sir, I am at a loss as to why not."

"Patients want to make sure they're dead, don't you see, sir. Some request that pepper be pushed up their nose, some want their feet tickled, even cut with razors. Then there is the tobacco smoke enema—dreadful thing—the corpse is played like a bagpipe . . ."

"What the devil are you talking about?" The cousin seemed genuinely discomfited, and I must admit that I found this highly satisfactory.

"Have you read Montaigne, sir?" I asked.

"I'm afraid I haven't had the time."

"There seems to be a creeping suspicion among the general public that the soul is buried with the body. That death might be, simply put, the end. Do you see? Without heaven, the grave becomes a secular hell."

"I understand," nodded Eddie's second cousin, who did not understand in the least.

"Metaphorically speaking, there is more than one way to be buried alive."

"I beg you, Doctor, that is quite enough. How did we get on to this blasphemous subject?"

"Some might regard throat-slitting as desecration of a corpse. However, since it is in Eddie's will, I shall see that Mr. Ripp performs the service you request."

In truth, I would do no such thing. After all, it wasn't Eddie we were burying, and his replacement was demonstrably deceased.

"So that is settled, then," he said, with an air of relief and satisfaction. "Very good. Of course, this will entail a substantial increase in your fee."

"That is kind of you, sir. A closed casket it is, then."

"Without a doubt," said Neilson Poe, evidently pleased at the thought that he would not have to see his second cousin's face, ever again.

MY LUNCHEON WITH Neilson Poe had gone well enough that I might postpone my alternate plan, which was to step off the Thames Street dock and drown on a full stomach. Instead, for no particular reason I wandered the area from Shakespeare Street to Fell Street, amid thick traffic and a pungent mist reeking of manure—nothing like it to clear the sinus.

The docks had enjoyed a seamy reputation from the moment they were built, and were accepted as such by the better neighborhoods. Authorities routinely ignored dance halls, saloons, inns, and broad-minded hotels. As the city prospered around it, the harbor became a favorite-slumming ground for Baltimore's young upper crust, who liked to wander down to Sailortown and gape at the seamen and their trollops as they danced, gambled, and mated in public view.

After a half-hour ramble I found myself at the Light Street dock near Gunner's Hall, the site of my old friend's supposed collapse. For a moment I felt as though I had been drawn there by a magnetic pull.

At the site of a violent or momentous incident, many claim to have experienced a feeling of invisible intensity, like the swirl of air that follows a passing carriage in the street. This is, I believe, the basis for the sighting of ghosts, and what occurred in this case.

Looking at the sodden ribbons wrapped around the lampposts, I remembered that Eddie was found on Election Day. I turned to the buildings on the north side of Lombard Street: not far away was Gunner's Hall, damply festooned—it had been a polling place for the Fourth Ward. Next door to it sat Ryan's Saloon, a thoroughly disreputable inn that leaned against Gunner's Hall like a sot supported by a soldier.

I made my way across the street through enormous piles of steaming manure, narrowly avoiding having my foot crushed under an iron cartwheel, whipped by the braided, manure-encrusted tails of the hosses.

On the walkway outside Gunner's Hall lay a sodden mass of

posters representing various campaigns for mayor and council—including the victorious gentleman named Riley.

Suddenly it occurred to me that Eddie might have manufactured the entire performance out of whole cloth. Had he found a drug that would raise his temperature and produce sweating? Had I been utterly fooled from beginning to end?

I freely admit that I had not ventured near a polling station in a decade. I was not a member of the American Party, nor did I wish to fall victim to its supporters; therefore, I declined to push my way through a gauntlet of Plug-Uglies, to be stabbed with an awl by a member of the Red Necks, or thrust into a bucket of blood. Uncivic of me, I admit.

As I gazed at the ragged bunting, the posters, the empty whiskey bottles, the ends of cigars, the broken clubs suitable for braining, the thought occurred to me: *Eddie must surely have brought luggage.* Immediately I headed in the direction of Ryan's Saloon.

Having to maintain his theatrics for an entire night—insufficiently clad in a cold, rainy season—could have given any man a dangerous chill, let alone a dissipated poet. Therefore he must have rented a place to get warm, and it must have been close by.

By early afternoon, Ryan's Saloon was filled to capacity—perhaps seventy men, most of them drunk since the previous day, having awoken in such distress that they simply carried on in their slept-in clothes. Around me, trickles of desultory conversation took place in a variety of dialects from various parts of Europe, snaking through the air like separate smells. The air itself was, as usual, translucent with smoke. The floor had been spread with insufficient sawdust to absorb the spittle, so that it appeared as though someone had scattered raw oysters about the room.

Across the bar stood a man in his forties, with the build of a blacksmith, thick white side-whiskers with brown tobacco stains, and a perpetual frown.

"Fat fill it be, skipper?" asked the barkeeper, in a Bavarian accent.

"I am looking for Mr. Ryan," I said.

"He is dead. Herr Ryan is dead two years."

"I am sorry to hear that."

"Not the cheneral opinion. He vatered his viskey."

"Might I ask who currently fills the shoes of that mendacious host?"

"I haff that honor."

"Allow me to introduce myself. I am Dr. Chivers, from Washington College Hospital."

"Doctor, I am fery glad you haff come."

The barkeep reached over the bar, as though to shake my hand in welcome. As I began to reciprocate, he extended his right thumb, wrapped in a filthy rag. Having thus seized my attention, he unwound the rag to reveal a knife cut above the joint, festering so that the thumb had attained twice its normal size.

"Is it you haff you a medicine for pain, Doctor? *Ach,* how it keeps me awakened!" He extended the thumb closer to my face. It was a yellowish-black, distended bulb of pus. The thumbnail, the color of blood pudding, had begun to separate from the digit as though deserting a lost battlefield.

Having no alternative, I examined the inflamed digit. As always in such situations, I resented this. I do not understand the Hippocratic Oath. Why must doctors be burdened with a command that applies to nobody else on earth?

First, do no harm. I beg your pardon? Nobody demands such a thing of a lawyer, or a teacher, or a businessman. And as for the command that a doctor must treat anyone who needs it, regardless of their ability to pay: What other citizen of America must eke out a living on his own, and function as a public servant at the same time?

Yet I complied. I always did. It is not only doctors who are held hostage to the neediness of the human race.

"I am glad that brought this to my attention, sir," I said. "Two more days and the thumb would have to come off, without a doubt."

"Two days only?"

"If that."

"What vill you haff to drink, Doctor? Alles ist on the house."

"A large of your best whiskey, if you please," I replied without thinking, while digging into my bag for a vial of iodine tincture.

Immediately I realized what I had done, and was about to cancel my order when it occurred to me how poorly my vow of temperance had served me when it came to resisting Eddie—that sobriety and sanity are not necessarily the same thing.

Service was instant and enthusiastic. The whiskey was delicious.

I would tender my formal resignation to the Temperance Brotherhood at some future date.

I dabbed iodine on the thumb with a bit of cotton. The patient winced—as I would myself, for the stuff stings damnably. Yet he did not complain, for the pain of the swelling was worse. And in any case, the specter of amputation had gained his full attention.

"I wonder if you might know anything about a gentleman who collapsed outside on election night," I asked, as casually as possible.

"Election night? Several chentlemen there vas over the bay. Stabbings and sings of that sort there vas—until the opponent of Riley foted against himself and conceded."

A typical election outcome, it seemed to me. But when Eddie called out Riley's name, was it significant? It would be typical for Eddie to invent a name for death, and to use the name of a politician.

"Did the name Poe come up at any time?"

"Neffer heard it."

"Edgar Allan Poe?"

"Neffer heard of him eiser."

I finished dressing the thumb—in all probability it would require amputation, if not the entire hand—and prepared to take my leave, having wasted my afternoon.

"Take this vial," I said. "Put some on the wound twice a day after bathing it in hot water."

The innkeeper looked at the vial as though unpleasantly surprised. Washing had not been a factor in his calculations.

"If it is not better in three days," I continued, "come up to Washington College Hospital and ask for Dr. Chivers. Here is my card."

"Might it haff to come off?" He asked, as though appealing to my better nature.

"Let's hope for the best," I replied, and raised my glass: "I drink to your thumb. To the health of thumbs everywhere!" I admit that the unaccustomed whiskey may have gone to my head.

The Bavarian frowned at his bandaged thumb as though one might an ill-behaved child. A trickle of tobacco juice took refuge in a whisker while he indulged in gloomy thoughts of amputation and death.

I left my card and turned to leave, when a sudden inspiration occurred—having to do with Poe's reputation for handling his financial affairs.

"I notice that you have rooms to let."

"Ve do, and chip they are at fifty cents."

"Very reasonable indeed. Even so, have you recently had the misfortune of a nonpaying guest?"

The innkeeper's face darkened. "Indeed we haff, *Herr* Doctor, and on election night too."

"Would his name by any chance be Poe?"

"No that vas not the name."

"Henri Le Rennet? Richard Perry?"

"Perry! It was the dodcher's name."

"And he rented the room on election night?"

"*Ja*. Three nights he owes and this morning he vas gone, luggage vas gone . . ." The innkeeper's face brightened slightly: "Is it you are knowing Mr. Perry? Haff you seen him?"

"As a matter of fact, I am after him myself. He owes me some money for treatment received."

"Ah. I vas the luckier for that. He left a suit of clothes—no fest or shirt, but alles vas in good repair. I am getting two dollars for it."

HAVING ASSEMBLED A clear narrative of Eddie's activities on the nights surrounding his arrival and departure, I decided to wander down to the local constabulary. There I made inquiries and, as expected, there had occurred no incident with Negroes of the sort Poe described. Now it became perfectly obvious why he had worn a suit of old clothes: being scrupulous in his dress, and being short of funds, he wished to save his own!

After he left the hospital, leaving his oldest friend holding the bag, I imagined Eddie Poe returning to Ryan's Saloon, changing into his own clothes, retrieving his trunk, and making his escape.

Somewhere near the harbor walked a man in a two-dollar suit, courtesy of a cadaver.

CHAPTER TEN

Philadelphia

The shelves of booksellers are overgrown with Sambo's Woes
done up in covers. A plague of all black Faces! We hate this
niggerism and hope it may be done away with.

—*Graham's Magazine*

J ust above the waterfront, where Dock Street began one of its
sweeping curves, next to a long series of buildings housing newspaper, magazine, printing, and engraving businesses, in a narrow
building of red brick resided the offices of Topham & Lea.

Up and down the street in front of the building, a procession of
drays, Dearborn wagons, coaches, and trotting wagons rumbled down
the cobbles, amid the oaths of drivers and the continual cracking of
long whips.

It being late afternoon, merchants' sulkies and bankers' carriages
had begun to gather in front of the Exchange across the street. Mes-
sengers and clerks rushed in and out of the building to deposit and
trade wild-cat money, state bank notes, and the increasingly common
counterfeit bills.

Located on the third floor behind a heavy oak-paneled door, the
outer office of Topham & Lea featured an impressive display of
paintings by well-known English artists. A glass-fronted bookcase
contained handsome leather-and-gilt editions of the Great Works of
Literature, together with more daring volumes by Byron and the Romantics, and an edition of Baudelaire, in French. Nearby, a large window afforded a view of the forest of masts and sails on the riverfront,
spiking above the blank, flat roofs of warehouses.

A brocade visitors' couch sat against a wall, its cushions worn
shiny by the buttocks of anxious authors. Next to the couch, a narrow Chippendale table contained the latest releases by Topham &

Lea: Thackeray, Scott, Tennyson, and Dickens. Also featured were the collected verses of Professor Longfellow and Dr. Holmes, a twenty-five-cent edition of Charles Brockden Brown and, incongruously, a set of Quaker abolitionist tracts.

Opposite the couch, a door to the inner office featured a brass plaque containing the legend: *Henry H. Topham, Esq.*

Beside the door to Topham's office, behind a small desk piled high with manuscripts and letters, sat a precise, dark-complexioned gentleman with a set of close-trimmed whiskers and unfashionably short hair, wearing a high-buttoned frock coat and an immaculate white neck cloth. Removing a pair of silver pince-nez spectacles, he put aside the latest edition of *Graham's* and rose to his feet, extending a ceremonial smile with the handshake, while his eye took in the visitor with an expression of pleasant evaluation.

"Good afternoon, sah. How may I assist you?"

"Finn Devlin is my name, sor, and I am here to see Mr. Topham. Would you be his secretary?"

"My name is Mr. Bailey. I am the administrator here at Topham & Lea. And I am an editor as well." As Mr. Bailey observed the handsome young Irishman—dark hair, high cheekbones, eyes the color of the sky—his face revealed neither amusement nor insult. "Do you have an appointment, sah?"

"Mr. Topham and I met at Sportsman's Hall, so we did. He expressed keen interest in meself and my work."

Mr. Bailey glanced at the calendar on his desk. "That would have been at the Morrison-Hola match, I expect."

"Aye, that it was. And a grand moment for Morrison too."

"Quite so. You were at a boxing match together, and there you discussed your manuscript?"

"Not at the match, no. It was after the match. Mr. Topham was good enough to invite me to a gathering at his home. And a grand piece of work it is, too."

"And I expect that sometime later in the evening, sah, very late in the evening perhaps, you happened to discuss your manuscript with Mr. Topham?"

"Aye, sor, that is correct."

"And have you actually submitted this manuscript to him?"

"I have done. It has been in his hands one week to the day."

"I am afraid that Mr. Topham is extremely busy. It is unlikely that he has read your work in such a short time."

"That is possible, sor. Yet in any case, I should prefer to speak to him now."

"Mr. Topham is at work in his office. He cannot be disturbed."

"I am not satisfied by your answer, sor."

"I beg your pardon, sah? You are not—"

"Satisfied. Sor."

Something about the visitor's demeanor, his calmness, his certainty of his position—whatever that was—caused the trim gentleman to reevaluate. "Very well, I shall disturb him," he said, and rising from his desk, knocked on the door to Mr. Topham's office, turned the knob, and slipped inside with liquid grace.

A long pause followed. Then the door opened briskly and the little man reappeared, followed by Mr. Topham, a flustered, ostentatiously busy man in a plum coat and a yellow waistcoat who put Devlin in mind of an overfed bird. The cheeks of a man who enjoys a glass of fine wine. A double chin disguised by a precise goatee. Above the smile of welcome, the eyes remained watchful.

At the sight of the visitor, however, Topham's countenance formed a pleased expression. In the saloons and sporting clubs of Dublin and Liverpool and London it was common for flamboyant professional gentlemen—lawyers and businessmen—to seek out the company of athletic young men from the lower classes. Some of these men frequented football and boxing clubs for that purpose. It did not take forever for a well-favored young man of limited means to comprehend the basis for this enthusiasm for the hoi polloi.

"Splendid to see you, Mr. . . . ." Henry Topham paused, embarrassed, waiting for the visitor to supply a name to the void. "Oh dear, forgive me. Of course I remember the face, I never forget a face, but . . ."

"Finn Devlin is my name, sor. And at the Sportsman's Hall it was."

"Ah yes, Irish, of course. The Sportsman's Hall, of course, of course. Smashing match it was, absolutely top drawer." Devlin marveled at the publisher's speech pattern, which suggested that there existed a place in the Atlantic midway between patrician America and patrician England where a man might acquire an accent.

"A grand donnybrook it was and for certain, Mr. Topham," said Devlin. "I am the writer in whom you were kind enough to express some interest."

"Indeed, of course. Of course. A most unusual circumstance, to discover a young writer at a boxing match. And of course you are the writer of . . ."

"*White Niggers of America*. My book dealt with the Irish question, sor. You expressed interest, if I may say so."

"Of course. The Irish question." The contents of the evening had begun to return to Topham's mind. At the match and afterward, the editor had waxed eloquent over the sheer *manliness* of this country called America. In the course of the evening, he had spoken at length about the need for manly writers, writers who carried with them a genuine sense of the grit and the sweat of real American life.

"Whatever the reason for your interest, Mr. Topham, sor, you received the manuscript in your mailbox. Delivered it with my own hands, I did."

"Indeed. Indeed you did just that, sir. Please take a seat." The editor indicated the visitor's couch, and not the inner office. For an aspiring author it was not a hopeful sign, so Devlin chose to remain standing.

"Oh dear," said Topham abruptly, chuckling as though having misplaced his pen. "Ah yes. Allow me to introduce you to my partner, Mr. Bailey. Mr. Bailey, this is Mr. Devlin, a young writer who shows great promise."

"Yes, we have met," said the tidy gentleman, watching carefully. "And I agree that his writing shows promise."

"Mr. Bailey, would you be so good as to retrieve the gentleman's manuscript, entitled— Oh, what was it? Oh dear, there I go again . . ."

"*White Niggers of America* is the title I believe," said Mr. Bailey.

"That is correct," said Devlin.

"Of course. Of course. It all comes back to me now. On the Irish question. Ripping title, grabs the American reader by the throat and simply demands to be read—is that not true, Mr. Bailey?"

"Quite so," replied Mr. Bailey. "It is an arresting argument as well, and quite well put, with some reservations."

I assure you, gentlemen," said Devlin, who was, like any man in his position, ready to snap at any morsel of encouragement, "that the speeches upon which the text is based have been received most enthusiastically by the public."

"I have no doubt of that, Mr. Devlin. No doubt. None at all." Topham flipped through the pages as though to refresh his memory. "An extraordinary piece of work, really. It directs public attention to a most lamentable situation in America, in a style positively throbbing with manly energy. An indictment of racialism in all its myriad forms. Your central thesis reaches to the heart of the rot infecting America today. A remarkable effort, sir, a stunning piece of work and I congratulate you for it."

"That is high praise indeed, sor, coming from a man such as yourself. I am very grateful."

"And you well deserve it. Alas, I fear that *White Niggers of America* is not for us." Topham said this with an air of sad helplessness, as though someone other than himself had made the decision.

"I am confused as to why, sor, given your recent praise."

"Bad timing, I am afraid. The market for racial issues has passed its peak. The American reader is sick of doom and gloom on the subject of race. The reader is looking for something more positive."

"Positive? What could possibly be positive about the situation?"

"You raise a serious question, sir, and it deserves a serious answer. Americans are well aware of the plight of the Irish and the brutal treatment you people have been subjected to. However, that being said, it is time to ask ourselves: What about the *other* Irishman—the Irishman who picks himself up by his bootstraps and makes a go of it, without resorting to beggary and drunkenness and crime? Indeed, I can see a title now: *The Other Irish*. How does that strike you, Mr. Devlin?"

"It matters little how it strikes me, sor, for it is a completely different book from the one you have in your hands. In fact, the book you describe sounds as though it could be written by Mr. Dickens or someone like him."

"Very perceptive, Mr. Devlin. I see that you are a man who keeps in touch with current trends on the ground. From what I have read here, I believe you are capable of telling Americans about the other Irish. I believe that, with proper guidance, you can make the public care about the Irish in the way that Mr. Dickens inspires us to care about the poor."

"Do you not publish Mr. Dickens already, sor?"

"That is true, my friend. Yet at the same time Topham and Lea is searching for an *American* Dickens—don't you see? A Charles Dickens, not of London, but of Philadelphia."

"I do not know if that would suit my style, sor," replied Devlin.

"I understand your hesitation, young man. It is a challenge, that is certain. Perhaps you might wish to discuss the matter with me at another time, over drinks. I think there is much we could accomplish together."

"That would be most welcome, sor," said Devlin. "I have long had a strong feeling for Mr. Dickens."

CHAPTER ELEVEN

Baltimore

I stood at the main gates of the stately old Burial Ground, the city's preferred garden in which to be planted for eternity. Within it slept three generations of Poes, including Eddie's grandfather, Major David Poe, quartermaster general for the city and a hero of the Revolution.

The morning was suitably bleak. A chill mist smelling of coal smoke clung to the cobbles of La Fayette Street as in the distance I beheld the funeral procession—if it could be called a procession, for it consisted of a lone hack containing the Reverend Clemm and Neilson Poe, and a lone hearse containing the deceased. Where were the relatives? Where was the generous uncle who had funded the casket? Where were the grieving cousins who had contributed to the burial, not to mention his literary colleagues—Hawthorne, Melville, Holmes? Where, for that matter, were the young women who thronged the hospital, eager for a lock of his hair?

Given his historic ancestors, not to mention that the deceased was one of the most celebrated—rather, notorious—writers in America, the ensuing ceremony seemed downright secretive.

The Poe family plot lay to the southeast of the Burial Ground, a favored location providing a view of the rising sun on Judgment Day. Even better, it sat as far as possible from the north side, home to stillborn infants, bastards, and suicides, who did not enter through the gates but were passed over the fence.

The site of Eddie's grave pit contained not a single flower, let alone a wreath. Reverend Clemm, wearing what did not appear to be his best frock, took a position at one end of the elongated hole alongside second cousin Neilson, suitably attired in a beaver hat and mourning ribbon.

Two gravediggers lifted the long wooden box from the hearse and set it down, with its lid open to reveal the closed mahogany casket within, courtesy of the absent uncle. Then Mr. Clemm began the service, and I noticed that the funeral party had acquired two additional members.

One was, oddly, the supervisor of the burial ground—a tidy Negro in a shabby suit that was once black, but now appeared almost silver when the light hit it in a certain way. Rather than retire to his quarters in the usual fashion, he remained at the graveside, hat in hand, head bowed, reciting the Lord's Prayer like a fellow mourner.

The second previously unnoticed figure stood by a mausoleum several plots away, the cost of whose construction would easily have paid for a comfortable house and garden.

She was dressed in full mourning: all silk and crepe, with a cameo broach at her throat and a spoon bonnet that concealed the top part of her face, revealing only an oval chin and a delicately formed mouth. The fingers of one gloved hand held a red rose; the other hand grasped a tear bottle, with which she collected the precious liquid, drop by drop. Otherwise, she remained as still as the infant statue by her side.

The burial service was as brief as a Methodist can manage, and the prayers took little time at all. Protestants do not pray for the welfare of the dead but to comfort the living, and on this occasion there were few that needed comforting.

As Reverend Clemm began the benediction and my fellow mourners closed their eyes in communion with their Maker, the woman by the mausoleum chose this moment to approach the grave, slowly and calmly, seemingly for the purpose of placing the rose upon the coffin. Mysterious, to be certain, but readily explicable—no doubt one of his many female admirers had got wind of the ceremony, and had chosen to honor the occasion in suitably, almost laughably, Poe-like fashion.

Meanwhile, at a sign from the burial supervisor, the two grave diggers approached the pit, each with a heavy rope over one shoulder and the lid of the coffin under the other arm.

As they reached the gravesite, Eddie's female mourner moved quickly and smoothly ahead of the gravediggers, extending the rose at arm's length as though about to drop it into the grave.

Then an astonishing thing happened. Rather than drop the flower, she reached down with both hands—and lifted the lid of the casket!

Reverend Clemm stopped in mid-sentence. Neilson Poe appeared understandably alarmed, given Eddie's supposedly severed jugular. As for me, who had the most to lose of anyone, I nearly succumbed to incontinence over the exposure to come: not only was it the wrong corpse, but I had failed to cut the throat as promised—and had collected my fee. I was not only a fraud, I was a common thief!

Nobody stirred or spoke as she stared into the open coffin. For an empty eternity, my heart like a fist against my ribs with each fevered beat, I awaited the screams of horror and denunciation, and my ruin.

The screams did not come.

She turned and looked calmly in my direction—or so it seemed, though I could not see her eyes beneath the veil. Then she spoke, in a Virginia accent with its liquid vowels and Old English character. "He appears as though he were sleeping," she said. "I have never seen him more natural." Then she turned back to the coffin, dropped the flower inside, and gently closed the lid.

Only then did I realize that I had seen this woman before, in the dining room of the Exchange Hotel.

As for my fellow mourners, I do not think the appearance of a dancing skeleton could have produced a deeper chill in the atmosphere. Though it was easy to scoff at Eddie's female following, the appearance of one of them served as a reminder that not one soul in attendance liked Eddie Poe, much less loved him. On the contrary, from the tone of the ceremony it seemed as though every man present had a reason to be glad that he was dead.

Using their ropes as slings, the attendants lowered the box into the grave pit, fetched shovels, and had barely begun to fill the pit when the preacher snapped shut his Bible and the funeral party dispersed.

I alone remained, for I wished to introduce myself to the burial supervisor—whose name was Mr. Spence—to inquire as to his interest in the deceased.

He was eager to comply. "Yes, sah. Mr. Poe used to now and then wander into the Burial Ground," he said. "I recollect plainly his looks and manners, hunting in and out among the plots. He would stand looking at the graves of the Poes, then wander about the others, examining dates and inscriptions with great interest."

Mr. Spence gestured in the general vicinity and we began to trace Poe's steps on his solitary visits: past the Masonic emblems, the death's heads, symbols of the I.O.O.F., the Fraternal Order of Eagles, the Ancient Order of Knights of Mystic Chain; past rows of white marble, followed by older stones of black slate, like a mouthful of bad teeth.

> As you are now so once was I
> As I am now, so you must be
> Prepare for death & follow me.

"He was always very courteous to me, sah, very gentlemanly he was," continued Mr. Spence. "That is why I stayed for the service."

"The mysterious lady—had you seen her before?"

"Only once, sah, and it was not more than one week ago. Fine, fine lady, by her clothes and carriage. He showed her the family plot, and they talked quietlike for a considerable time. When she spoke I thought I heard a accent from somewhere 'round Norfolk."

The lady was Elmira Royster. There could be no doubt about it.

Eddie had taken a fancy to Elmira Royster about a year before he left for college, and in his usual overdone style. As his second in all things, I was apprised of his relations with her in detail, with an emphasis on her physical charms, which he portrayed in typical hyperbole, as he had done with my poor dead mother. While I fully agreed with him, it seemed tasteless to say the least.

By the age of sixteen, unlike his junior crony, Eddie had become a public figure in Richmond who cut an impressive jib at school—Jefferson Debating Club champion, medals in Latin and French, and with a pleasing singing voice; indeed it is impossible to imagine a more favored young man—and what a splendid couple they made!

During their courtship, or whatever it was, I often saw Eddie and Elmira together. He once showed me a pencil portrait of her, languid and apparently asleep. Later he revealed to me that the association had climaxed, if that is the correct word, in some sort of eternal vow.

Perpetually tongue-tied, champion of nothing, who was I to tell Elmira Royster that her Eddie was a duplicitous humbug, with his best qualities spread out on the surface like berries in a market?

Unsurprisingly and sensibly, Miss Royster's father objected to the union, if only on the basis of her age—after all, his daughter was only fifteen. Consequently, Eddie spent his first year at college writing letters proclaiming his love, which were promptly intercepted by Mr. Royster, never received, and never answered.

Two years later, Elmira married into the Shelton family. Her husband subsequently made a fortune in the business of transporting people and things up and down the James, then as the owner of a tobacco plantation a few miles south of the city.

You can imagine what a fuss Eddie made of that early romantic disappointment. I do not know for certain which pained him more—the loss of his true love or the loss of his signed letters. In any case, I soon lost count of the number of times I had sat through that lachrymose tale of woe; it brought my friend many a free dinner and, I suspect, many a paramour as well.

Elmira Royster, his first true love, who wept over his open coffin, yet failed to identify the impostor inside.

Currently at the Exchange Hotel.

ON THE DEATH OF EDGAR
ALLAN POE, 1809—1849
by Ludwig, *The New York Tribune* [Evening Edition]
October 9, 1849

Edgar Allan Poe died in Baltimore the day before yesterday. This announcement will startle many, but few will be grieved by it. Poe was well known personally and by reputation. He had readers in England and in several states of Continental Europe. He had few or no friends. The character of Mr. Poe we cannot attempt to describe in this hastily written article. We can but allude to some of the more striking phases.

His conversation was at times almost supernatural in its eloquence. His voice was modulated with astonishing skill, and his large and variably expressive eyes shot fiery tumult into those who listened.

Outside the public eye he walked the streets in madness or melancholy, with lips moving in indistinct curses. He seemed always to bear the memory of some controlling sorrow.

The social world was for him an imposture. This conviction gave direction to his naturally unamiable character. You could not contradict him, but you raised quick choler. You could not speak of wealth, but his cheek paled with envy. His astonishing natural advantage, his beauty and daring spirit, had raised his self-confidence into an arrogance that turned admiration into prejudice against him. Irascible, envious, these salient angles were varnished over with a cold repellant cynicism while his passions vented themselves in sneers.

He knew nothing of the true point of honor. He had, to a morbid excess, that which is vulgarly called ambition, the hard wish to succeed——not serve, but succeed——that he might have the right to despise a world which galled his self-conceit.

We must omit any particular criticism of Mr. Poe's works. As a writer of tales he was scarcely surpassed in ingenuity of construction or effective painting. As a critic, he was little better than a carping grammarian. His tales will retain a prominent rank. They illustrate a morbid sensitiveness of feeling, a shadowy and gloomy imagination, and a taste for that sort of beauty most agreeable to his temper.

"After life's fitful fever, he sleeps well."

CHAPTER TWELVE

Philadelphia

Wrath, *n*. Anger of a superior quality and degree.
—Ambrose Bierce

The town house near Walnut Street was typical of a certain brand of professional or businessman—wealthy men with no inheritance and no land, who had migrated to the west side as the population of central Philadelphia doubled, retreating from the hordes of immigrants and Negroes who had chosen to disfigure the birthplace of America.

The wealth represented here had been acquired too late for a plantation; too late for one of the great rural estates of the landed gentry; too late for the heightened status, the noblesse oblige, the droit du seigneur of a slave-owner. The latter were now the lords and ladies of the day, whose sons would inherit, as would their sons after them, creating a social class as exclusive and long-lasting as any dukedom.

Questing for nobility in some alternate form, the men who owned these houses had made a virtue—even a fetish—of the urban work ethic, as the embodiment of economic and social virtue. They were part of a new breed of American, destined to uproot the anachronistic plantations and their decadent heirs; whose sheer financial heft would one day open the salons of the landed gentry to industrious fellows like themselves, and their children would inherit the earth.

As an expression of solidarity perhaps, the marble steps to these houses met the broad brick pavement at precisely the same angle; their railings paralleled one another all the way to the end of the street, like the string section of an iron orchestra.

On this morning as on every other, dozens of uniformed Negresses scrubbed the steps and sidewalks with flat stones and sand, whitewashed the trunks of the trees, polished the gleaming brass rails, the door knockers and numerals, also seemingly in unison, like figures in a Swiss clock.

For this rigorous cleansing procedure, water was provided in abundance by the city. Philadelphia prided itself on its water supply, with a tap located in front of every house and stone gutters bisecting each cobbled street—in the respectable areas, at any rate. Wherever the residents owned their properties, each morning the taps produced a veritable river that poured down the street and over the sidewalks, rinsing away the previous day's accumulation of manure and debris and the city was reborn.

However, at Number 207 Chestnut Street on this crisp fall morning, no housemaid whitewashed the steps or shined the brass. That the front curtains remained closed was typical, but not the way they were closed—not with the folds carefully in place and a precise gap in the center, but hastily thrown together with folds aslant. No maid would close the curtains in such a way and expect to retain her post.

As well, the building seemed shrouded in hush, as though the property were holding its breath, transfixed by something gone terribly wrong.

Inspector Shadduck remembered an identical silence having descended upon the barn of a Mexican farmer and his wife who had hanged themselves, or had been hanged by someone else. Either way, as soon as the barn came within sight you knew something bad happened in there.

In front of 207 Chestnut Street the top-heavy bulk of an elderly police van rested on tired springs, like a hippopotamus. In front of the van, two spavined nags with feedbags over their muzzles stared perpendicularly with vacant, startled expressions.

At the entrance to the house, between wooden Greek columns and blocking the front door stood two coppers in pot hats. Previously employed as day-watchers or "Leatherheads," they had had first crack at becoming members of the city's first salaried police force.

Inside the house, past the vestibule, a broad hallway opened onto an enormous, oblong parlor, made larger by two recessed floor-to-ceiling windows at one end. These opened onto an Italian veranda. The windowpanes were of crimson-tinted glass, set in rosewood framing and curtained by a thick silver tissue.

Folds of crimson silk surrounded the recess. Carved gilt-work encircled the room at the juncture of the ceiling and walls. A Saxony carpet quite half an inch thick, the same crimson as the curtains, covered the maple floor.

These decorations served as a sort of frame for a collection of paintings by noted English artists, depicting mythic, sentimental themes—the fairy grottoes of Stanfield, the dismal swamps of Chapman, the forests of Moole—displayed at intervals as though at a gallery and separated by silver-gray paper. Some of the paintings were huge, which lent a distinction to the decor it might not otherwise have claimed.

In further emulation of an art emporium, the room contained virtually no place to sit. In a space the size of a ballroom, guests were apparently compelled to make do with two low sofas of rosewood and crimson silk, and two small conversation chairs, also of rosewood, by the fire; otherwise, they would have to sit on the floor like Arabs in a tent.

So prevalent was the color red in the decor itself that, upon entering, Shadduck's eye at first failed to appreciate the truly spectacular quantity of blood in the room. It spattered the walls, the paintings and pianoforte, rich-arterial blood, soaking the silk and velvet as though bottles of wine had been indiscriminately poured out.

Once the eye succeeded in taking this in, other details became queasily evident.

On the hearth before a dead fire, four large, gorgeous Sèvres vases were now in jagged pieces, while a profusion of sweet and vivid flowers had been spread throughout the area as though in preparation for a spring rite. Against one wall, a bookcase for two or three hundred books stood empty, its magnificently bound contents strewn about. Some volumes appeared to have been cut apart with a sharp instrument, while others remained untouched. There was of course no telling which ones had gone missing, if any.

The corpse in the center of the room should, strictly speaking, have been described as a torso with thighs and arms. The body appeared to have been cut apart with a machete or other large cutting tool, and the severed parts placed in appropriate spots around the room; for example, the feet stood side by side near the fireplace, like a pair of overshoes put out to dry.

As his mother once put it, *Every feller has a dark side, and some have two.* Shadduck had known certain officers like that, smart fellers who enjoyed killing and mutilating. Momentarily he wondered what they did upon leaving the service, what line of work might have suited their taste and temperament.

"Well, I have seen the elephant," commented Watchman Coutts, whose use of the current street jargon served to camouflage a dim mind.

"Sure, and a butchered elephant too," added Watchman Smit, who was a tad brighter.

"Keep low on the levity, fellers," said Inspector Shadduck. "This is a grist of trouble. It will need serious thought."

Not that he knew where to begin.

Shadduck was in his late twenties, tall with a slight stoop and a permanent sunburn, and an older man's eyes with the creases at the outer edges indicating either an acquired sadness or a habitual squint, or both. Almost absentmindedly he slouched about the room, side-stepping pieces of human flesh as one might dodge piles of manure on Market Street.

The leaden smell of blood filled the room like an inert gas. Shadduck had seen this sort of a mess in the army, when cleaning up after a company of mercenaries who had requisitioned golden Jesuses (their own private savior), with or without permission from Command. Land pirates really, no different from British privateers at sea—gangs of common criminals with a license to commit atrocities on specific nationalities.

But that was war. In a war, people are killed and maimed as a matter of course, often for no particular reason. When you found a dead body on a battlefield, you didn't ask what feller killed it, because there could be no meaningful answer.

Now it was Shadduck's job to find out precisely that—who killed somebody else. Killings are disturbing to civilians, and must seem to be put right if the city is to remain governable. That distinction, between the army and policework, had not occurred to him when he applied for the job.

Where to start?

Pausing in the middle of the room, he experienced a slight wave of panic in the crook of his sternum, the feeling he had experienced every time he entered a field hospital . . . Of course. The smell of blood. It still had this effect on him, couldn't look at a plate of blood pudding.

He reached into his chest pocket, extracted a cheroot, and lit it. Thank God for tobacco, he thought, even cheap tobacco was better than nothing.

This new development put the inspector in a considerable pickle. Shadduck had not been given the rank because he was a species of French detective.

To understand Shadduck's position, recollect that the only police force Philadelphia County had ever known descended straight from the medieval police of Europe: a volunteer watch of citizens, plus a daytime constable, who supervised the volunteers and charged fees for his services. The watch was a tedious chore with no thanks to it, and so in practice, when a gentleman's number came up for service he would pay for a substitute, who was usually unemployable for anything else—stupid, illiterate, allergic to any sign of danger. In the usual course of things, watchmen dealt with crimes only when the victim agreed to a fee.

The system changed in 1844, when Philadelphia County undertook to create a police force on the model of New York and London, and directed offers of employment to veterans of the army and the civilian militia. Just out and none too flush, Shadduck wanted the job, and went whole hog in securing it.

Over several weeks he downed consecutive glasses of Old Orchard with former messmates in the militia; having seen action, he was the one to lead the toast to victory and to General Taylor, "Old Rough and Ready." This circle of acquaintance provided him with a popular base, at least for the time being. And his chances were done no harm by the two hundred dollars he sunk into the Swift campaign, not to mention the fact that he was an elbow relation of Commissioner Clark. To be on the safe side, Shadduck even contributed twenty dollars to the campaign of Councilman Wendel Grisse, a canny Pennsylvania Dutchman, who ran on a platform of lawful and orderly streets.

Upon his admission to the force, and being considerably less flush than ever as a result of his political expenditures, Shadduck undertook a campaign of self-advancement that turned out mighty effectual.

In the chaos of war it had been Shadduck's primary duty as an officer to put a solid face to everything, for the morale of the enlisted men—who, when discouraged, tended to desert. As a function of his rank, Captain Shadduck perfected the steady-as-she-goes facade of a master mariner, implying that, though he was not personally in control, he knew the man who was, and had been assured of a satisfactory outcome.

In Philadelphia's current disarray, with a council led by terrified civilians well out of their depth, Shadduck was like an anvil in a windstorm, and promotions accrued.

His streak of good fortune hit an apex with his appointment to the newly created position of inspector—a rank taken from the London Peelers to go with the coppers' designations, and dead certain to infuriate the Irish.

From this high point, as though having reached the summit only to find a cliff on the other side, Shadduck's career began to plummet. First came Swift's announcement that he planned to retire—seemingly to practice law, spend time with his family, and enjoy a fortune mysteriously amassed while in office.

It was as though Shadduck's best hoss had died under him, and after due consideration he chose to back the Independent candidate Joel Jones, the best of a bad lot. If Jones lost the coming November election, Shadduck's goose was cooked; his only hope was that it wasn't Thanksgiving.

Even with a Jones victory, the inspector would occupy a chancy position. Swift had been, after all, a Whig with a minority in council, and Shadduck was, therefore, viewed as a de facto Whig. Democratic knives would be kept sharp, Republican eyes peeled for the slightest lapse or error. Already the inspector could not safely accept even the most innocent private payments from supportive members of the public, and he was feeling the pinch.

In the past, the duties of an officer of the law had been to uphold the morals of one segment of the populace against those of another. In practice, this meant arresting drunks, lewd women, able-bodied beggars, and people found sleeping in a public place. Less public was the policeman's role as the intermediary between politics and business, moving payments from one hand to the other through a network of tailors, carriage makers, and other trades, taking deposit on work that would never be done.

What altered this long-standing arrangement was the increasingly urgent task of riot control. In Philadelphia, with her clean streets in a precise grid pattern, disorder was the enemy, and anarchy was the Antichrist in civic form.

The trouble began in the early forties. Suddenly crowds would accumulate out of nowhere and begin marching down the streets, breaking everything in sight. Gradually the crowds became more violent. (The inflammatory role of gangs could not be underestimated— organized groups of hoodlums for whom disorder and profit followed like seeds and tobacco.)

While clergymen smoothed the ruffled feathers of their terrorized flock, policemen were urgently needed to calm the secular population; to maintain order in the streets and to provide reassuring copy to *The Inquirer*, *The Gazette*, *The Woman's Advocate*, thereby to mollify outside speculators who might put their money elsewhere.

The predicament was mightily complicated by Philadelphia County itself—a series of semi-independent boroughs, each with its own council and bylaws. There existed no officer with a mandate to deal with threats that crossed constituencies. That is why Mayor Swift, at the fag end of his term, and with little support from the county bureaucracy, created the post of inspector.

To date, Shadduck had no physical headquarters, no precise duties, and most galling of all, no uniform. As a militiaman and a soldier for most of his life, he felt out of whack in mufti. This prompted his adaptation of his dragoon kit, with the shoulder patches removed and the chest piece replaced by a six-pointed constable's star, made of copper and containing the state seal. It later came out that his effort at so distinguishing himself had caused shock and scorn among his colleagues, but it was a price worth paying for the sake of his own morale.

To his own surprise, in the first months of service Shadduck discovered within himself an unanticipated interest in policework. His mind cottoned mightily to the task of gathering facts, arranging them into a plausible tale, then testing a prediction, like a scientist and a swami combined.

At a minimum, it gave him something to think about beyond the headaches, a constant companion since the war.

At Monterey, while he crouched behind a line of flying artillery awaiting the order, a bullet from a comrade's .577 Enfield glanced off his skull, putting a hairless stripe in his scalp. The shot knocked him unconscious and later he found that it had affected his thinking in small but disturbing ways. Besides the headaches, he had difficulty putting a name to colors, and would sometimes say one word when he meant another, especially when angry or confused.

Happily, his injury had had no effect on his ability to cogitate. Having no description of his job and no approved procedure to follow, Shadduck's approach to the problem of gangs and rioting was to mimic the innovations of other police forces. He persuaded the commissioner to use paid informants as they had in Boston, so that they might nab ringleaders beforehand on some pretext. As for the riots themselves, he imitated Chicago and Detroit, with their wagons of flying strong-arm squads, who sped to the scene, waded into the crowd with their batons, and proceeded to break heads until the crowd became discouraged. Having no force at his disposal within official circles, he took to employing thugs for this purpose, which raised more hackles in the constabulary.

Nonetheless, these tactics had produced sufficient reassurance among the public that Shadduck now stood in line for the position of commissioner—if he survived the next few months. On the other hand, Philadelphia was now teeming with veterans of the Mexican War eager for his job, not to mention an endless tide of foreigners, with pocketbooks of false credentials and a two-hundred-dollar contribution to the candidate of their choice.

And now this mess. Just the sort of thing to ignite public hysteria, it was only a matter of time before the call went out for a sacrificial goat.

Meanwhile, the press had gone completely out of control. With a new publication surfacing every month or so, there was simply too much appetite for sensation to hold a lid on something like this.

Shadduck was at the crux, the pinch of the game. To survive, he was going to have to puzzle out who did it, or find an acceptable explanation.

In this effort he would require the support of Councilman Grisse, the closest thing he had to an ally now that Commissioner Clark had resigned in disgrace. Shadduck disliked the councilman, but when you are about to fall off a cliff, that is no time to quibble over a helping hand.

It occurred to him that the crime might actually prove useful if it distracted the press from the riots at the ironworks, which were breaking out with the regularity of a steam clock. For once, here was something for reporters to chew on that had no political significance. To get the ball rolling, Shadduck planned to drop a hint to a reporter with *The Inquirer*, that the murder may have been a product of jealousy, revenge, cannibalism—anything to keep the Irish and the Negroes out of it.

But where to begin?

Shadduck turned to face his two coppers, former Leatherheads and as thick as gobs of mud, gazing moon-eyed at the carnage. "Do we have an, an inclusion, rather an inventory, of body parts?" he asked, as though it were a munitions tally.

"Not really, sir," answered Smit, for the thought of counting something had not occurred to him.

"Do so. Coutts, you are to secure a notebook. Take down everything I say."

"I'm naw secretary, sir," said the copper, who was from Herefordshire. "I can naw do shorthand. I can naw write at aw."

"What of you, Smit? Can you put a pencil to paper and make words?"

"Somewhat so," replied the punctilious Smit, who was Norwegian and almost willfully unimaginative.

"In future, everything is to be writ down. In order. For later use."

"Wery good. And who will pay for my notebook and pencil? Already it is out fifteen cents, I am."

Shadduck resisted an urge to stamp on the copper's foot. "Requisition writing supplies from riot patrol, they are always making lists."

Remain logical, that is the ticket, thought the inspector as he shuffled about the room, somewhat more stooped than usual, hands clenched in the small of his back.

"Fellers, take a gander at the mutilation of the victim. The body bears every sign of having been torn apart in a rage. A wolverine might have done it. Yet the murderers made sure we wasted no time in identification."

His two assistants said nothing, because they understood none of it.

With a gesture of his cigar, Shadduck indicated a set of hanging shelves in a corner on which rested the severed head of Henry Topham, of Topham & Lea, the most prominent publisher in the city, like an objet d'art.

"See how the eyes are missing," he said. "But not in the way of a raven. A raven will pluck out the eyes of a cow as preparation for dinner. Here they were taken neatly from their sockets. See also that the teeth have been pulled . . ."

Coutts excused himself. Shadduck paused while the copper went outside for a drink of water.

Uppermost in the inspector's mind was the thought that the victim was in publishing. The book business! If Henry Topham were mixed into any other racket in Philadelphia, Shadduck might have devised a theory by which a colleague or a rival might do for him in such a way— But a *publisher*?

"What do you reckon?" he asked Smit, without in the least expecting an answer. "Who might murder a publisher in such fashion? A failed writer in a pucker over the rejection of his life's work? A dispute over a payment of royalty?" By the expression on Smit's cubic face, even to him it made a weak incentive for such an act.

"Or consider," continued Shadduck, "that the murder might have dirt to do with business. That the answer rests in Mr. Topham's private affairs."

Coutts, looking wan, returned from the street to resume his tally of flesh and bone.

"Observe the decor of the room, Smit," said the inspector. "What do you make of it?"

"It is expensive," offered Smit.

"Note—what would you call it—a *quality* to the furnishings. What word would you put to it?"

"Like a whorehouse," said Smit.

"My word exactly. Mr. Topham was a bachelor. Did he lead a private life that, by, er, some, some . . . well, that is to say, some *sequence of events* . . ." Shadduck worried when he had trouble finding words.

"Sequence of events?" replied Smit, not eager to explore the subject.

Shadduck stood opposite the lantern-jawed Norwegian; the eyes had the comprehension of a cart hoss. "Smit, I want you to find out where the victim has been. What he has been up to. Consult our informants in the free-and-easies along the river, and ask among the Irish. And write it all down. I want a full report."

"Sure, and what am I to ask them for?" asked Smit.

Shadduck sighed deeply. A cart hoss, with blinkers on. No wonder the Norse were known for their toleration—they see so little in the first place.

Interrupted Coutts: "If ye'd care to see, Inspector, I noted something just at this here moment, sir."

"What is it, Mr. Coutts? Something about the color red?"

"No sir, it is the man's shins."

"The shins?"

"There's naw any. They been hacked off and taken."

"How the heck have you come to that conclusion?"

"Me uncle were a butcher, would take me on in busy season. Ye learn to see the animal as the sum o' the parts, so to speak—see? There be the upper leg and knee, there be the feet—but there be naw shin between 'em, don't you know? Yet the arm bones is intact. It beggars understanding what might possess a man to cut a man's legs off and take them away. What might he do with them?"

"He might sell them," replied the inspector.

The Editors
The New York Tribune
Philadelphia

Gentlemen,

Allow me to commend your writer Mr. "Lionel" on his obituary of the late Edgar Allan Poe, for it outdoes in malignancy and injustice all that its author dared to inflict upon Mr. Poe during his lifetime.

By "Lionel," I refer of course to the Reverend Rufus Griswold, who seems to believe that by hiding beneath a pseudonym he can bear false witness against his neighbor without penalty to his immortal soul.

It is common currency among literary circles that Mr. Griswold's hatred for Mr. Poe arises from the latter's refusal of a bribe offered to puff Mr. Griswold's anthology.

Out of charity, this writer prefers to excuse Mr. Griswold on the same grounds that Mr. Griswold explains the work of Mr. Poe: that these are the symptoms of a sick man, for which he cannot be wholly blamed.

I refer to the generally known fact that Mr. Griswold is a consumptive, a disease he contracted years ago in France, resulting in bleeding at the lungs, weakened eyesight, and a weakened mind—symptoms Mr. Poe would well recognize, having lost his beloved wife to the same disease.

For years Mr. Griswold has attempted to foist his bitter future upon the living. Now it seems that his malice and envy extends even beyond the grave.

Truly yours,
R. A. Perry, Esq.

CHAPTER THIRTEEN

Baltimore

I read the rebuttal, which had been reprinted in the *Baltimore Sun*, and another penny dropped. It was now obvious that Eddie's staged death had less to do with newspaper clippings and teeth, and more to do with the desire on the part of an artist to revenge himself upon his critics. It seemed sickeningly clear that Eddie would continue to do so until he was discovered and I was ruined.

In the meantime, how did he expect to earn a living, when he had scarcely been able to do so as one of the most famous authors in America? Then I remembered his mention of a "commitment"—a job of work he found distasteful but remunerative. Clearly he had something in reserve—another, less high-flown means of making a living as a writer.

One thing seemed clear: It was most urgent that I find Eddie and stop him from pursuing his present course. By wringing his neck, if necessary.

> *Mrs. Elmira Shelton (nee Royster)*
> *Exchange Hotel*
> *City of Baltimore*
>
> *Dear Mrs. Shelton,*
> *I trust that I am not out of order in introducing myself, absent of a living intermediary. I am Dr. William Chivers, formerly of Norfolk, where I believe we occupied the same classroom as schoolmates of the late Edgar Allan Poe.*
>
> *I was very surprised to see you at the interment of our mutual friend yesterday afternoon. I would be grateful if you were able to take tea as my guest, tomorrow afternoon.*

Yours in remembrance,
Dr. William Chivers
Washington College Hospital
City of Baltimore

Love, *n.* A temporary insanity curable by marriage.

—Ambrose Bierce

I DO NOT know if Elmira Royster was a woman that other men would find attractive. Though she had skin of a pleasing color and consistency, her nose was far from classically straight. Her lips, though delicate, were not entirely symmetrical, but set in what appeared to be a faint, lopsided half-smile. As for her form, there was no telling what lay beneath all those layers of silk and linen. Nonetheless, from the moment we met across the linen tablecloth at the Exchange Hotel, I viewed Elmira Royster through a haze of imagined copulation.

I had not experienced such an intense sensation in my life—though, as you know, I was a married man. The sad fact was that, in Southern American society, the few circumstances in which a man might meet a woman who was neither servant nor relative—church functions, family gatherings, afternoon teas contrived for the purpose—were purposely arranged to keep ardent feelings to a minimum.

Under such a constriction of opportunity, courtship becomes a process of elimination more than attraction. No wonder that so many men, like Eddie, married their cousins. As for womankind, no doubt this explains the popularity of romance novels, in which a couple's passion for one another is paramount—delicious, because it so rarely happens in life.

I chose a woman who possessed every quality one could possibly wish for in a spouse, with one exception. She was taller than me. A good deal taller. The resulting awkwardness became self-perpetuating; it spread into other areas, and gave our private life a tentative wariness neither of us knew how to acknowledge, let alone cure.

I readily admit to a smallness of spirit throughout my marriage. I am mortified that I was not able to overcome my own squeamishness at this superficial difference. Yet I believe I am not the only man susceptible to arbitrary physical tastes and aversions when it comes to the opposite sex.

In my mind, sexual congress with my wife was like fighting my way through a jungle of arms and legs. This struggle—and it was a struggle—combined with the normally embarrassing aspects of physical intimacy, which resulted in a relatively chaste marriage. (But not quite chaste enough, unfortunately for her.)

Likewise I suspect that there was something about my form or behavior that my late wife could never quite get over, something seemingly trivial that would have embarrassed her beyond measure were it brought into the open. I wonder if it was my smell—for there does exist a doctor's smell, and it cannot be entirely pleasant. Or it could have been something as simple as the sight of my hands, an inability to entirely banish the thought of where they had been. Or perhaps my baldness put her off. Once you begin to make a list, there is really no end to it.

In any event, seated in the Exchange Hotel, I had no precedent for the quickening heartbeat, the roaring in the ears, the rush of blood causing the cheeks to redden, the involuntary and unwelcome tumescence of the loins, the signals of genuine desire—over tea.

What could account for it? I wondered, while liquid sloshed over the rim of my trembling cup. Certainly not her accent—though I found it familiar enough. Nor was I stimulated by her conversation, which seemed strangely elliptical, as though even a comment on the weather contained a second, unspecified meaning.

It might have been her eyes. She possessed floating irises, in which the whites are visible beneath the iris. Common practice has it that such a gaze indicates a spiritually turbulent nature. To the object of her gaze, she somehow gave the impression that she could see my thoughts—a most unsettling idea, in this instance.

My unanticipated passion for Elmira Royster rendered it doubly difficult for me to approach the issue at hand—to wit, that the cadaver in the coffin was not Edgar Allan Poe. It was inconceivable that she did not know this, having wandered the graveyard with him only days before. Yet she had gazed into the coffin with complete equanimity, commenting on Eddie's fine appearance, while looking directly at me.

Perhaps it was not the man in the coffin she meant to describe as looking so well, but the man who had escaped it. Perhaps it was not his appearance, but his disappearance that had pleased her.

All of which assumed that I was in my right mind at the time. Having had little sleep, I was now open to the possibility that it was indeed Eddie Poe we buried—that the substitution had itself been a dream.

"It is unseasonably cold for the time of year," I said, putting a toe into conversational water, however inane.

"It is evah so much colder than in Richmond," she replied, elongating her James River vowels. "I worried that I might not have sufficient clothing."

"Always wise to avoid a chill," I agreed, unnerved by the notion of insufficient clothing.

"Chill rhymes with kill, and a grave to fill," she replied. "That might make a handy rule in instructing children."

"Instructing them about what, ma'am?"

"About life and death, suh."

I nodded thoughtfully and sipped my tea. What the devil was that supposed to mean? Her accent had begun to unnerve me; I had no wish to revisit longings that had tormented me as a young man.

"Rhymes," she continued, "are evah so much more pleasant than spelling things out, don't you think?"

My heart sank. Another poetic sensibility.

"Miz. Royster, I mean Shelton, may I say that I was very surprised to see you at the burial of our mutual friend Eddie Poe."

"Yes, you might say that—in fact, you said the same thing in your note. You are repeating yourself, suh," she said, toying with the silver spoon in her fingers.

"May I ask how you came to be at the ceremony?"

"No, you mayn't, suh."

"Then might I ask why you refuse to tell me?" I asked, cursing her elusiveness, throbbing with desire.

"Dr. Chivahs, do you believe it possible for information to travel between two souls, without the use of the five senses?"

"Certainly, ma'am, if the information has already been agreed upon, as at séances and carnival acts."

"Then there is scarcely a point in my telling you."

"Are you suggesting that you arrived at the cemetery by occult means?"

"Do you mean did I ride astride a broomstick?"

"No, ma'am, that is not at all what I meant." I could feel my teeth grinding together. Despite my passion I was beginning to find Elmira Royster a most irritating woman.

"I went because Eddie asked me to. That is rightly all I can tell you." She sipped her tea, smiling to herself as though a third person had said something amusing.

The conversation continued in this maddeningly oblique fashion until the teapot was empty and my mind had nearly snapped under the strain. It would not be the first time such damage inflicted itself upon me in the presence of Elmira Royster.

"Miz Royster, I mean Shelton, I am going to be utterly frank with you, at the risk of my reputation, my occupation, my freedom—everything I possess. I beg you to answer one question in a straight-forward manner. My life depends upon it."

"Tell me, suh, why do you persist in calling me by my maiden name?"

"I don't know, ma'am. I suppose it is a trick of memory, and feeling."

"Dr. Chivahs, I am right shocked by the, the *passion* in your face. It is well-nigh indecent."

"Forgive me, ma'am, but for heaven's sake tell me—when you opened the casket, *what did you see?*"

She thought about this, or appeared to. "Dr. Chivahs, as a professional man, do you believe in life after death?"

"Certainly, if you mean the life of maggots and worms."

"And what is your opinion of the spirit?"

"I know nothing about the spirit, but believe it is a much-abused word."

"Then you cannot possibly understand when I tell you. Yet I shall. When I opened the casket, I saw Eddie Poe."

"But it was not! You know it was not Edgar Allan Poe in that cof-fin! You know this!"

"Dr. Chivahs, I must ask you to kindly lower your voice."

Indeed, she was correct. Other patrons had turned their heads in our direction, birdlike and in unison.

I leaned forward and repeated my request in an urgent whisper. "Miz Shelton, I am in possession of a pocket pistol, and I swear to you that I will shoot myself here at this table if you do not answer one question with a simple, direct answer."

"You have a pistol, suh? Let me see it."

"I will not," I replied, feebly, for of course I had none. It was the first time since I was a child that a woman had bested me in a discussion.

"Dr. Chivahs, please understand that I do not like threats, especially empty ones. What is your question?"

"What is your relation with Edgar Allan Poe?"

"He is my fiancé. We are engaged."

CHAPTER FOURTEEN

Philadelphia

Never having entered the offices of a publisher before, Shadduck was surprised how friendly and homey it all seemed, like an expensively appointed den, where deep thoughts were shared and everybody understood Greek. It had a pleasant messiness, a what-the-hell quality, papers strewn everywhere, as though an editor had become overstimulated and had run amok.

"Good afternoon, sir," he said to the tanned, tidy gentleman behind the desk. "I am Inspector Shadduck. I reckon you know what it is about. You are Mr. Topham's secretary?"

"No. I am his partner," the gentleman replied, without a hint of displeasure, rising from his desk. "Bailey is my name."

"Bailey—of Topham and Lea?"

"That is correct, sah." Not a hint of irony as the gentleman rose from behind the desk and extended his hand.

"My condolences to you," said the inspector, "over the demotion, the demise of your employer. "Mr. Topham was a mighty fine gentleman, I'm told."

"Indeed, sah. He was like a father to me." Mr. Bailey paused to light a cheroot. His hand shook as he did so.

"You seem jumpy, sir," said Shadduck. "You seem all in a lather."

"I am not in a lather, Inspector. I am tired and bereaved. It has been a vexatious week."

"I understand you, sir. Any feller in your position would feel peevish. Tell me, Mr. Bailey, are you sensible of anyone with the demency to do such a thing? Was an old malice harrowed up in recent times? Mr. Topham in a scrape—any tattle of that sort?"

"Mr. Topham was universally respected. A giant in the publishing field. He was in the forefront of American letters. I weep for the culture of America, sah, with Mr. Topham no longer on this earth." Mr. Bailey exhaled a pensive gust of smoke.

"High praise for certain," said the inspector, glancing about the room. "And I see, both here and in his residence, that he had powerful taste in art as well. Of the sort that might be seen in the National Gallery—*is* in the National Gallery, last time I heard tell."

Shadduck abruptly turned so that he might catch the man's reaction, but Mr. Bailey did not flinch; just a glint of alertness in the eye, enough to suggest that he knew of what Shadduck spoke, that he was not unaware of Mr. Topham's various illicit activities. And so his praise of the man was all humbug.

"Yes, sah," said Mr. Bailey, all too smoothly. "I believe Mr. Topham's collection is—was—second to none in the county."

"And all fraudulent for certain. Like yourself, sir, I am sorry to say."

Though he had never particularly enjoyed it, Shadduck knew how to dress down a man, take his story apart, stick in the knife, and get what he needed. A distasteful but necessary technique, one of many such in wartime, when dealing with civilians.

"I beg your pardon, sah," said Bailey, and Shadduck noticed that his high forehead now shone in the light from the window. "You have lost me there."

"Let us get a thing straight out, Mr. Bailey. You are of the Negro persuasion, are you not?"

A long pause followed, which the inspector filled by examining the titles on the display table. He wondered what it might feel like, if all the information that lurked within these books were imprinted upon his brain. Would he be better off? Would he be any the wiser? "I have heard of Mr. Poe and Mr. Dickens," he continued. "'The Raven,' I read for certain. Just saying the word *Nevermore* is enough to frighten children nowadays."

"True," said Mr. Bailey in a sad whisper that told Shadduck he had him by the ball bag. "They are the most well known among the general public. But they are not necessarily the best."

"How do you know, sir? How do you know what is the best?"

"I cannot tell you, sah. I am only a poor black sambo."

Another pause followed. Mr. Bailey remained perfectly still.

"There can't be many men of color in the publishing business, sir," said Shadduck. "Not even here in Philadelphy."

"That is true, sah." Mr. Bailey leaned back in his chair and smoked his cheroot as though it would be his last, blowing smoke at the ceiling with a half-smile of resignation. It occurred to Shadduck that the faces of Bailey's ancestors formed that same expression when they glimpsed the slave ships gliding into the harbor.

The inspector resisted the temptation to cut the tension. If you wait long enough, everybody talks.

And he did.

"I was born on a farm near Easton, Maryland, sah. My mother was Harriet Bailey. My father I never met, but believe he was my master, Captain Aaron Anthony. When Mr. Anthony died, I was given to Mr. Auld, whose wife Lucretia broke the law by teaching me the letters of the alphabet. I escaped the plantation with a slave map disguised as a quilt. I obtained the identification papers of a free seaman. I came to Quaker City and was taken in by Quakers. I attended the Negro school on Ninth Street. And now I am here." Mr. Bailey shrugged, as though none of it mattered now.

"Well done, sir. I will trouble you no further. Do not hesitate to look me up, if need be."

"It seems I am at your mercy, sah. A Negro makes an excellent suspect when none else can be found."

"We hope to do better in this case, sir."

Outwardly calm but shiny with sweat, Mr. Bailey produced his pocket watch, looked at it, and put it to his ear. "I believe my watch has stopped, sah. Will you give a colored boy the time of day?"

CHAPTER FIFTEEN

Baltimore

I had never been so close to self-murder in my life—and I had been reasonably close, as you know. There I stood upon Kerr's wharf with my father's alligator bag in my hand, staring down at the slimy black water; my immediate plan involved a triple dosage of morphine, followed by a swim in Baltimore Harbor: The morphine would take care of the initial discomfort, and shock would take care of the rest.

First mother, and now Elmira Royster. Eddie had done it again. He had snatched away the only woman I desired, before I had a chance to compete. Would I never be rid of him? Or was he my doppelgänger, preemptively stealing my life?

As the Locust Point Ferry approached, I came up with a better idea: I would pay the fare, take my morphine, and fall off the boat. *Accidental drowning* would be the unchallenged verdict, and I would not end up in the cemetery's north side, and would not be passed over the fence for burial as a disgrace to the dead.

As the boat unloaded its cargo, a procession of riggers, sailors, laborers, and calkers passed by: Irish, German, and West Indians, as well as Negroes who worked the shipyards—lithe and enigmatic, eyes cast downward so that you could not see their expressions, making it impossible to tell the free from the enslaved.

I did not board the ferry to Locust Point, nor did I jump into the sea. What deterred me, in practical terms, was the inadvisability of administering morphine to oneself in public, and the coldness of the ocean at that time of year.

Instead, I found myself walking up Broadway in the general direction of the cemetery, as though I planned to bury myself and save my heirs the trouble.

As with my previous flirtation with suicide, it was not to be. For anyone imbued with the work ethic, the problem with death is that it is too easy to achieve. As any doctor knows, most people achieve it with no effort at all.

And I was hindered by my insistence on thinking of myself as a scientist. In the past few days I had been cast into a whirlpool of doubt and desire which, at the very least, merited attention as a syndrome. It might even enhance my unpublished paper on the forces governing the mind.

Just as a man will do something because it is the last thing he thought he would ever do, is it possible for a man to feel an emotion simply because it is the last emotion he thought he would ever experience?

Around the age of fourteen, I walked into the drawing room and saw my father patting Celia the parlor maid, with whom I had been on friendly terms all my life, on the buttock. Upon seeing me, he withdrew in a state of mild abashment after ordering me to my room.

I wanted to beat my father with my fists, though I did not quite know why. I wanted to tell Celia of my dismay and my disgust. Yet from that day forward, I could not persuade her to look at me when I spoke, and she would leave the room rather than be alone with me. It seemed as though something had broken—as though I had seen or done something that had changed everything.

From that time on, Father too seemed to go out of his way to avoid me. It was as though there existed a parallel home within the home, a basement theater in which events took place that were not to be discussed in the parlor, or seen by the children.

Looking back at relations between the sexes, I see that there were men and there were slaves, and there were also shadow slaves—women willing to minister to a man's desires, in order to live a bit more comfortably. How a marriage fitted into this scheme of things was and is beyond my understanding. Perhaps the existence of slaves created breathing space for the wife, who was likewise the property of the husband, but less owned—if the term can be comparative, or subject to degree.

Was that how it was between my mother and father? Did she dislike him as much as she had reason to?

Nonetheless, over the table at the Exchange Hotel I discovered that the system under which I grew up disintegrates when a man desires a specific woman with unprecedented intensity. Far from domination, such a man will bankrupt himself for her amusement, fall on his knees before her, no matter how many slaves he might own.

CHAPTER SIXTEEN

City Hall, Independence Square, Philadelphia

In our civilization . . . intelligence is so highly honored that
it is rewarded by exemption from the cares of office.
—Ambrose Bierce

S ell them? Sell a man's legs and teeth? Whoever is hearing of
such doings?" Wendel Grisse stared at the report. His tight features formed an expression designed to make the inspector feel personally at fault.

Never speak until spoken to, Shadduck's mother used to say. *Especially
if the news is unpleasant.*

To Shadduck, the Dutchman appeared stretched to the limit.
His skin, once elastic and shiny, had taken on a strained quality, as
though stretched from behind the head. His problem was that, like
many deeply religious men, he did not wish to hear unwelcome information. Since unwelcome information was precisely the inspector's purview, the association was on shaky ground, and already
Shadduck could sense cracks in the councilman's support.

"Heard tell of Waterloo teeth, have you, sir?"

"*Ja.* I am minding that they are the famous British dentures. For
some reason are they named for the battle."

"That is correct. A powerful number of casualties on both sides,
sir. Young fellers, many with very fine teeth. A windfall for battle
scavengers and denturists."

"Pulled the teeth from the mouths of dead soldiers, you are saying?"

"Not always dead, sir."

"*Shendlich!*"

"I reckon I know what you mean, Councilman. The Mexican War
produced a similar kind of truck. Here in Philadelphy there are
mouths full of them soldier's teeth. I hear S. S. White's dentures are

second to none. 'America's Waterloo Teeth,' I hear they are called."

"Greislich!"

"Spoils of war, sir. Shinbones fetch a fine dollar as well, from jewelers. Ivory bracelets are popular with the ladies in France, don't you know."

"And it is from experience you know this?"

"I have with my own eyes seen whole fields scattered with toothless, shinless men. Infantry behind it, mostly. A cavalryman wouldn't stoop to that."

"And here in the city of Philadelphia people will buy such a grisly thing?"

"Trade goods have to come from someplace. With the British impounding every ship with a Negro on board, there's not enough coming in."

"It is unacceptable, this wrongdoing. We cannot have people wearing dead men's teeth and bones. We are not cannibals, sure."

"Not while there are vittles in the market. Food shortages are another piece of calico."

"What is this *calico*, Inspector?"

"A quilting expression of my mother's, sir."

"One thing I do not understand about you military is your sense of humor."

"I apologize. In the field a man grows hardened and rough. Takes time to get a civilized point of view."

"So the murderer may be a veteran like yourself. One who is run amok, *ferricked, ja*?"

"I reckon that is possible. But there is another wrinkle as to the particulars of this case. Mr. Topham kept a splendid home, sir. Fine furniture, with the marks of the best European makers. Walls hung with art work, authenticated by the classy art houses of London."

"There are those who have time and money for artistic work; that is how it should be, sure."

"True, sir. Art is a fine thing. What caught our fancy in this case was that the objects was all humbug."

"Humbug? What is this *humbug*?"

"Counterfeit, sir. Like the soaps and cosmetics and condiments that cannot be had from England at the moment, yet are on sale regardless."

"I have not heard of doings such as this before."

Shadduck surveyed the room. He had often noted its sparseness—nothing but varnished wood and not a fabric to be seen. A highly polished table serving as a desk, empty but for a pen and an ink blotter, and a ledger of the type used by scriveners. A bookcase containing a Bible, surrounded by works on federal law, state law, municipal law, criminal law, trade law, canon law, natural law, and the law of the sea.

On the wall above the bookcase—not framed and hung but painted directly on the wall surface—was the room's only decoration: a starlike thing with a circle around it, that Shadduck knew to be called a *hex*. A strangely sinister term for something his mother might have embroidered on a pillow.

"Mr. Topham was a master of fakery," continued the inspector. "My men traced it all. The furniture was made by a shop in Schuylkill that imitates Chippendales. The paintings were executed by a feller nearby who teaches at the art academy. His students make exact copies as part of their training. After graduation, the paintings sprout certificates of authentication. I reckon every printer in Philadelphy produces a half dozen a year."

"The *deibel*! How is it you have discovered this?"

"We have informants in the field, sir."

Of course. Shadduck's informants. The councilman winced at the sneakiness of law enforcement today. "You must be arresting these wrongdoers at once. Especially the students we must punish, as an example for the young people."

"Arrest them, sir? On what charge?"

"Are you saying that this too is lawful activity, like your book pirates?"

"Something powerful close to it, sir."

"Fraud is not a crime without victims. There must have been complainers, for sure, people who were fooled into buying this humbug."

"No, sir. Complaining would not be in the victims' interests. As an asset, say for borrowing purposes, once they are exposed as fake the pieces ain't worth dirt."

"But the artists who have been copied surely must be complaining."

"That might be, sir. But none of the artists are Americans. Like Mr. Topham's books, the fellers who made them ain't covered by copyrights. There was no actual physical theft, don't you see, sir? The

Reynolds, the Frith, the Herring are still in the galleries where they belong."

"Inspector, you have seemed to become very much the connoisseur of English art."

"I took on a young man at the Academy to inspect the murder scene."

"Another of your *informants*, he was?"

"And well versed in European collections, sir."

"You are being free with the tax dollar. I hope you are exercising diligence."

"I have kept a complete set of records, sir. You may be certain of it."

"I see. Sure, it would be a terrible thing if it were known that the houses of our best citizens are full with swindles. It is *ferfowled* at the highest level."

"What is that, sir?"

"It is rotton! It is *ferfowled*!"

In his mind, Shadduck made a note to tread gingerly on the topic. Grisse's outrage frequently led to baseless crackdowns against new "criminal elements" that were known to everyone but Grisse, in which nothing was accomplished and people suffered for no good reason.

At the same time, Shadduck sensed a possibility that the council-man might see the Topham matter as an election issue, a crime issue, in the way that one invests in a mining venture for a quick return. If that were the case, the inspector had much to gain by entering into a spirit of reform.

"Something else lends the matter urgency, sir. It is the involve-ment of the criminal gangs."

"You mean by this groups of men who do criminal things, yes?"

"Not necessarily, sir, but you are generally correct."

"But if it is publishing of books, what makes them necessarily criminals?"

"I don't understand your question, sir."

"These are smart people sure, and we are in favor of smartness. *Ferfowled* it may be, but if that is lawful practice I might invest in the business myself."

"I reckon you are right that fakery is no great shakes—excepting when blackmail comes into it."

Grisse grew wary. "What is this blackmail you say?" Having been in politics for several years, he was not unfamiliar with the word.

"As my mother used to say, *Man is the only animal that can be skinned twice.*"

"I am not understanding your mother."

"Sir, Mr. Topham had a hand in other tricks of the craft. Birth records, university diplomas, truck of that sort. No way in tarnation can we verify them, sir. Whatever piece of paper a man holds up, he simply cannot be proven wrong—except, sir, by the forger himself. There, I reckon, is your potential for blackmail. A man whose life is a forgery, who then makes his fortune, makes a handsome quarry for blackmail, sir."

"Wery astute. And what are you making of it?"

"I calculate that Mr. Topham kept records, sir. After all, he was a man of the written word."

"*Sheisse.* A book of names Topham had, you are suggesting?"

"I reckon so, Councilman."

"You are saying that prominent Philadelphians are open to blackmail, *ja?*"

"Yeah. It's like a walnut full of maggots, sir."

"What is it that you mean by that expression?"

"A mess of unseen proportions."

The councilman took another gander at his fingernails. "I see. You will be careful, of course."

"What is it I will be careful of, sir?"

"I am reminding you that to lie is not a crime, nor is it a sin."

"True, sir. Jacob was well rewarded for it."

"Well spoken, Inspector. I am liking a man who knows his Bible."

"It is all very well to know the Bible, sir. To believe the whole of it is another piece of calico."

"There it is again, that expression of your mother."

"She was a great influence on me. My father died when I was young. Or disappeared, which I reckon amounts to more or less the same thing."

"Are you an atheist, sir?" The look in the councilman's eye suggested that Shadduck had better craft his answer carefully.

"By no means, sir. On the battlefield, not a day went by when I did not hear men cry out for God and for their mothers. I heard no answer from either, but I knew for a fact that they all had mothers. If you can point me in a surer direction than that, sir, I would welcome it."

"I do not understand your point in any way, Inspector."

"I ask your pardon. I sustained a head injury in the war, as you know."

"Of course. And God bless you for it, you are a credit to the city and a hero of the nation."

"Much appreciated, sir."

"You must tell me what is doing in this murder business. We cannot have murdering in the city."

"Sir, I reckon that Mr. Topham was not just a book publisher. I judge that he drove a whole herd of fraudulent manufacture. Great guns, sir, surely you see the potential of it."

"You are saying that the embargo with the English has made Philadelphia a city of fraudulent wrongdoing?"

"Well put, sir. That is the best face on it. At worst, we have a city of gangsters."

"Inspector Shadduck, you could be in politics, sure."

"Another time, Councilman."

"The city must respond in a *kreftic* manner. We must be stopping this wrongdoing with vigor. As councilman for the Middle Ward I will support your investigation."

"That is good news, sir."

This shin business is most *greislich*. I gave a bone bracelet to my wife last Christmas!"

Situated between Locust Street to the north and Fitzwater Street to the south, the Moyamensing neighborhood paralleled the river around its elbow bend, and therefore did not follow the city's normal street pattern. Instead, an intricate series of narrow lanes twisted their way down to the river, and to Devil's Pocket to the southwest. It was a warren like St. Michael's parish in Dublin, and like it a harbor for illicit and illegal activities.

Easily the tallest and best-repaired structure in the neighborhood, the Black Horse Saloon situated itself on McAfee Court at the mouth of Black Horse Alley; from here, an absurdly narrow passage slithered away downhill, with a sluggish brooklet in the center containing substances of various kinds.

On either side of the ditch stood a row of tiny wooden shanties. Known as "Father, Son, and Holy Ghost houses," they stood three stories high, with one ten by twelve-foot room on each floor. These rooms were rented for twelve and a half cents a day to an entrepreneur who would, in turn, sublet spaces on the floor for two cents each. With such crowding on a daily basis, the few outhouses were always overflowing.

Lacking sun or ventilation, with ceilings six feet high and a family of twelve in each windowless basement, these habitations created as squalid a domestic situation as anything in a London rookery. Yet, were a visitor to venture inside, he might be surprised to see heirlooms on the mantel, pictures on the walls, a teapot and teacups stacked neatly on a shelf, and a crucifix on the wall.

By comparison, McAfee Court in the late gloaming was an oasis of gaiety, offering the visitor both mystic and worldly attractions. At the entrance to Passyuk Lane, a grand bone-fire had been lit for warmth, and now boys and girls jumped back and forth through it— the boyos to test their mettle, the girls that they might marry early and bear many children. In the country it would ensure as well that the crops grew high, but there was no fear of vegetation in McAfee Court.

Other precautions against the evening chill were available in the opposite corner, where a beak-nosed French peddler dispersed spiced gin from a gleaming brass samovar. Among his customers stood four disconsolate nymphs of the pave, banished from the Black Horse Saloon until the meeting's adjournment. With their usual custom beyond their grasp, they ignored the gaunt characters from the soup society, pale as mortuary cloth. Equally, their protectors absent, these judies on the stroll regarded with almost prudish suspicion the young men from the cricket pitch on Chestnut Hill, distinguishable by their camphor-soaked handkerchiefs, held inconspicuously to their noses against the stench, while they rummaged the area for forbidden adventures of various kinds.

Two pigs approached the fire, joined by three colleagues from the next street, with whom they lay down sociably in the gutter.

As BEFITTED ANY meeting on a serious matter the Black Horse contained no women; nor was there a Protestant to be seen—no Slattery, McManus, or Gamaliel. On this evening, the saloon belonged to a grim, intense assembly of about fifty Catholic men in top hats, members of a society known as the Ribbonmen. Leaning intently forward on their walking sticks, their expressions grew steadily hotter while the speaker on the center table performed as fireplace and stoker, raising the cockles of their sectarian ire.

At the bar, orders of hob, nob, and other bevies took place using hand gestures, not to disrupt the speaker's precious litany of ills, injustices, and impending threats. Though the list was as familiar as the stink of their own boots, the congregation would never grow weary of the ritual call for preemptive vengeance, against Protestant and Nativist enemies who would burn Moyamensing to the ground—every cathedral, every house—inspired, as ever, by the beastly English.

The Moyamensing district, dubbed Ramcat by the local citizenry, made wonderfully fertile soil for such a theme, for the slum landlords (with the exception of John McAfee) were predominantly non-Irish, unlike the equally sordid streets of Southwark and Port

Richmond, whose overlords sported names such as Boyle, Cassiday, and Quinn.

Devlin had spoken to many such gatherings since his arrival, and had greatly improved his oratorical skill along the way. With the help of Lieutenant O'Reilly, he had made grand progress in the quest for that which Young Ireland had lacked in the old country—a popular following. Where once he held forth to a scattering of bollixed drinkers, now he regularly hectored packed rooms such as this, crackling with intensity.

With the public alarm over the "Irish problem," and the remedies applied so far—squads of goons, operatives, and informants—the running of the city had become a sneaky, nasty business, a Protestant sort of business, a British sort of business, and that was the making of the Irish Brotherhood. Where once Devlin and O'Reilly had counted themselves lucky with a handful of coppers, now it was a rare meeting they did not exit with pockets heavy with chink.

"Like you, I was born under the ancient scourge of Protestant persecution. Like you, I know the value and the price of civil and religious liberty.

"Like you, I seethe in anger that here in America, the home of liberty, we continue to suffer the almost universally received calumnies on our character and name, lies spread by England, spread as wide as ships can sail or travelers penetrate . . ."

Around the table upon which Devlin held forth, and in a semicircle facing the audience, stood a line of young men, who formed a protective barrier between the speaker and his public. For the charismatic orator, once a crowd had its blood up there could always be danger, whether due to the enmity of an enemy party or the embrace of an impassioned admirer. These young men were able to perform their function as bodyguards without obscuring the view of the speaker because none had reached a height of more than five feet.

These were *Na Coisantoiri*—the Defenders: street shavers who had accepted Lieutenant O'Reilly as their commanding officer, in return for which they received a better life than they had ever known in their born days.

Never in his life had one of these boys worn a proper hat or a set of even secondhand clothes. Now they wore top hats—tipped at a precise angle approved by Lieutenant O'Reilly. Now they sported new duster coats and leaned on stout, pebbly walking sticks made of oak. Where once they had received kicks and curses as street ruffians, now they were given a wide berth—and with reason, for they made an unsettling sight, with clan markings on their faces in pen and ink, accentuating the brow and cheekbones in the fearsome way of ancient Celts and red Indians.

For close fighting, each boy carried blades of various size on his person, which he was prepared to put to use at any moment. Beneath his duster coat, each wore a glass-studded belt about his waist whose buckle had been sharpened to a razor's edge. A few boys concealed barking irons—derringer pocket pistols—filched from an overfriendly fireman or thug. Glimpsed through a soup of pipe smoke, they made a sight as endearing as a pack of wolves. Yet because they were boys and not men, and because they were Catholics every one of them, Ribbonmen looked upon them in the way they might have regarded a squad of budding athletes—with nostalgic longing and a certain envy for their own younger days.

Originally, they were a street gang known as the Daybreak Boys, led by a gaunt twelve-year-old with the seamed face of a worrier, who went by the name of Pistol Ned.

Soon after his return from the war, however, O'Reilly befriended Ned with the gift of a bayonet; from there he proceeded to earn the trust of the Daybreak Boys, by providing instruction in fighting technique. A year later, now rechristened *Na Coisantoiri* and awakened to their Irish root, their short, violent lives had found new meaning in an atmosphere of military solidarity, a higher purpose to trim their daily round of theft, intimidation, and brutality for hire.

Standing on the table, Devlin launched into a kind of history lesson, putting the plight of the Irish on a par with the fall of Athens:

"Here in America, our eyes are open to the filthy web of misrepresentation with which England has surrounded us.

"Here in America, who knows the truth of the Irish? Who remembers that Ireland was already ancient when Christianity exiled the Druids from their sacrificial forests? That Tyre and Sidon bartered with Ireland before Romulus and his brother founded Rome? How Hiberian Celts under General Dathy trampled down the Roman fortifications and were about to scale the Alps, when a handful of needy Normans overran the homeland, fanned the jealousies of rival chiefs, and seized the pleasant plains of Leinster?

"Over seven centuries of slavery, penal laws, and Protestantism completed the work of devastation: what the Vandals had done for Rome, and the Saracens for Spain, Henry and Elizabeth performed for Ireland . . ."

When the heavy front doors abruptly burst open, Devlin instantly saw that they parted at the middle seam—that the kick did not shatter the casing, though it was sufficiently powerful to do so. Therefore, it had been unlatched from the inside, by a traitor within the party. Devlin halted his speech in mid-sentence, and turned to Lieutenant O'Reilly for a signal as to their tactics and route of escape. The Irish Brotherhood had become well used to such abrupt interruptions, whether by Nativists, rival gangs, or firemen.

Nativists were members of a secret society called the Order of the Star-Spangled Banner, whose members had signed a pledge never to vote for a Catholic. By sifting among the ruins of the Whig Party, these anti-immigrant fanatics had managed to cobble together the American Party—also known as the Know-Nothing Party, for its selective memory when it came to criminal acts by its subsidiary groups, who went under names such as the Plug Uglies, the Black Snakes, and the Rip Raps.

If not Nativists, the invaders could be firemen—ruffians who started as many fires as they doused, and allowed many more to burn to the ground rather than see a rival hired for the job; who had taken to attacking Irish of all persuasions ever since the trouble of '48.

Whatever the identity or motive of the enemy, regardless of the issue or controversy or excuse, every mortal in the place immediately began making use of his fists, boots, and sticks in an effort to break the bones of another.

At a shrill whistle from the lieutenant, the boys of *Na Coisantoiri* proceeded to defend the position. Though possessing only the merest grasp of military strategy and discipline, they were eager students of the whiskey dance—a mainstay of faction fighting and the settling of scores, practiced since a century ago, when Irishmen were forbidden weapons by the occupying English. The "dance" was a cover for fight training, in the way of the dances of African slaves in America, whose fight practice gave lethal power to unarmed men.

To be sure, it did the lieutenant good to see the close attention on Pistol Ned's prematurely aged face, as he ducked under a poorly aimed blow from an opponent twice his weight, delivered a two-handed stick punch to the attacker's knee, then used the momentum of the man's fall to break his teeth against the knob of the *bhata*, then on to another without pause. It is always a pleasure for a teacher to see a lesson well learned, and Ned made an outstanding pupil.

As the fighting continued, Devlin made his way to O'Reilly's position at one end of the bar, which afforded a tolerable view of the contest, which the lieutenant followed with the intensity of an athletic coach. Since their partnership, the lieutenant had put no little effort into his little muzzies, so that Devlin and O'Reilly were now powerful men who could put force behind their words. The boys' ability to earn a dollar through robbery and street fighting, when added to what was earned by Devlin's tongue, had secured the financial position of the Irish Brotherhood as well.

Devlin leaned close to the lieutenant's ear, the better to be heard over the din of fists, sticks, and cursing: "D'you mind the style of them? I'll engage they are neither Nativists nor firemen."

"Aye, true for you, Protestants. Orangemen if you go to that of it."

"If that is so we are in for a party fight."

"That is a danger," said the lieutenant, "for the boys are unready for a donnybrook."

There is something infinitely more deadly in the compressed vengeance and hope of slaughter that fuels a conflict between Orangemen and Ribbonmen. To be sure, in a faction fight between Catholics, skulls are broken and lives lost, but they are lost in pleasant fighting—the consequence of the sport, the beauty of breaking as many heads and necks as one can. In a party fight, the very air is loaded with apprehension as to be almost sulphury. The scowls, the grinding teeth, the deadly gleams that shoot from the kindled eye would fry a frog.

"That is the man Kelly at the heart of it," said the lieutenant, indicating the six-foot bruiser with the hooked nose at the other end of the bar, presently downing three fingers of whiskey after braining a man's idea pot. This he had accomplished with his own *bhata*—a fearsome blackthorn implement with multiple notches for men reefed, and a head with lead stuffing to break any bone, and wicked bumps left from branches along the shank, sharpened to tear the skin on contact.

"Kelly it is at the front of it."

"A bad member and it's a fact."

"Put a crack in his head and the wind will come out of him," said O'Reilly, scratching his chin with the nail of his little finger, which he had grown more than an inch long for some purpose.

Continued the lieutenant, turning to whisper into Devlin's ear: *Be dog wide now as I put the heart crossways in them.* He took a step forward and stood in a slight crouch, as though waiting for the moment to spring.

Devlin watched the lieutenant closely from his blind side: a trim, compact man in a duster coat, over the tunic of an infantry officer and deerskin breeches, and shoulder-length hair beneath a top hat set at a precise angle.

The lieutenant had managed the Irish Brotherhood admirably— but at what cost to his immortal soul? To kill a man out of rage and disgust was one thing; to profit from his death was another. True, Devlin was guilty of the deadly sin of anger, and would carry it to his grave and beyond; he did not wish to add the burden of monetary greed to his already compromised soul.

Yet he did not bring up the point. He could not meet O'Reilly's good eye, for it seemed to peer straight through a man. Nor did the other eye bear looking into, for it put him in mind of the eternal pit of hell.

What to make of a man with a missing eye, who did not cover the empty socket with a patch like other men, but left the hole open? Was it intended to intimidate? If so, it succeeded in grand fashion: in normal light the socket put one in mind of a death's head, while in the presence of a flame it would glow bloody red. Meanwhile, the other side of the face might laugh at a good crack like a normal man. As an additional chiller for Devlin came the knowledge that, whatever horrors he had seen for himself, O'Reilly had seen worse, and done them too.

"To cause fear in the enemy," the lieutenant once explained, "you do not simply conquer a town, you burn the cathedral—and with the townspeople in it." Was this what he intended to convey in the Topham matter? Was it a message, a proclamation?

Even if not, most unsettling it was to hear him talk of "harvesting" a man, and Devlin had no stomach at all for the watching of it.

For certain, O'Reilly had a plan on him, and he preferred not to share it with Devlin.

On the saloon floor, the melee continued in waves of sporadic violence, with pauses for drink. True to the lieutenant's observation, the *Na Coisantoiri* were not yet up to a party fight and were getting the worst of it, with two boys badly hurt on the floor and crying for their mothers, though not near croaked. As well, several grown men sprawled about in the bloody sawdust, and a few lay quite still—whether Catholic or Protestant there was no telling, now.

For the most part, however, injuries were superficial. Most of the men swung not true shillelaghs but regular walking sticks of oak and brass, which they waved in the air as though whipping a horse, with none of the skill of the true Whiskey Dance. Nonetheless, it was clear that, were the fighting to go the hour, the boyos would be lost to discouragement if not injury. Therefore, the lieutenant, according to custom, stood ready to claim the lead Orangeman, to call him out and thus spare his own people.

O'Reilly watched the fighting keenly, gauging the rhythm of it, awaiting the proper moment to initiate a match with the "cock of the tin . . ."

"Is that Fergus Kelly?" he cried suddenly, stepping forward and raising his *bhata* against the pillar with a sharp crack. The shout was well timed, for it cut through the room like a siren.

Leaning against the bar, Kelly raised his *bhata* in return, and answered in the traditional way. "Throth and it is that same on the sod here. And is that Dougal O'Reilly?"

"The same, *ma buchal,* and how is your mother's son, Fergus?"

"Can't complain as time goes, and how is yourself, Dougal?"

"In good health at the present time, thank God and gentle Mary."

Kelly's *bhata* gave the bar a thunderous clout for emphasis: "Only take this anyhow to mend your health, ye bloody popist."

"May God help the filthy Protestant who would disturb a civilized meeting of honest men," replied the lieutenant, and delivered a blow to the pillar as if to split it in two.

By now the general fighting had stopped entirely, anticipating a duel between chiefs. All stepped back to clear a space on the floor, that they might witness the sportive crack to come. For their part, the *Na Coisantoiri* took this opportunity to pull their wounded aside in preparation for an exit, for that is the drill—first the diverting action, then the tactical retreat.

"Fergus Kelly, do you have the sand to face me without your bum-boys behind you?"

"There be no bum-boys but yours, Dougal O'Reilly, popist frig that you are, And are those your choirboys I see?"

This exchange signaled the beginning of the stage known as *wheeling*—a ritual joust of wit and insult, accompanied by huzzahs from supporters, so that one built upon the other, until the two came to blows.

"A red nail on yer tongue, Kelly, and a red stone in yer throat, and may the devil roast the jigger off ye."

"I'll see to it that you never comb a gray hair. Your bread is baked, Dougal O'Reilly, and it's a fact."

"It is I who will break your head for you, Fergus Kelly, may you go stone-blind so that you will not know your wife from a haystack."

"Short life and an evil death to you."

"May the devil cut your head off and make a day's work of your neck."

"Cromwell's curse to you. A death without a priest in a town without a clergyman, on a high windy gallows and with Oscar blowing."

"And the curse of sweet Mary on you. May the seven terriers of hell sit on the spool of your breast and chase you over the hills of Damnation."

"Dougal O'Reilly, you popish rascal, I am ready for you. I have what you're going to get in for you a long time!"

"Fergus Kelly, you are claimed!"

"O'Reilly, you'll get it, please God!"

Before the name of the deity had come clear of Kelly's mouth, the lieutenant sprung for him. Making a feint as if he intended to lay the stick on his ribs, O'Reilly swung it past without touching, and bringing it swiftly around his own head, made his move with a powerful backstroke, right on the temple of the taller man. As a reward, in an instant his own face was spattered with the blood that sprung from the wound.

Undeterred, Kelly staggered forward, holding his *bhata* two-handed as an extension of the arm and fist. He was looking to work close, for he was not used to the lieutenant's *pionsa* style, like classical saber fighting, well suited to his military past. Instantly O'Reilly sprung back, and was again advancing with full force when Kelly, turning a little, clutched his opponent's stick in his right hand. Being left-handed himself, the lieutenant struggled to wrench the cudgel back, when Kelly gave him a terrible blow upon the back part of the head, which laid O'Reilly stunned on his face on the floor.

There came then a deafening shout from the Orangemen while Kelly stood waiting for O'Reilly to be in the act of rising, when he planned to deal the popist a blow across the head.

The cool of the lieutenant was remarkable. "Look at your party coming down upon me," he shouted to Kelly, who turned momentarily to order them back—and now the lieutenant was up on his legs.

In fairness, it was impressive to see the cool of both men as they faced one another, eyes kindled with fury yet tamed to the wariness of experienced combatants, calculating upon the contingent advantages of attack or defense.

To the men watching it was a moment of artistic interest as the wiry man and the powerful man stood in opposition. No man's judgment could name the man likely to be victorious. Nor, on viewing these two contrasting frames, made equal by science and elegance of form, could the eye miss the bulges in the trousers of both men—likewise, the gooter of every man in the room, Devlin included, had become similarly dilated with passion for the fight.

Sensing the tension of the moment, the lieutenant raised his cudgel and extended it transversely between himself and his opponent. Kelly instantly placed his against it—both weapons forming a St. Andrew's cross so that the two stood foot to foot, though with the head of the smaller man in line with the chest of the other. Their necks were laid a bit back as was the weight of their bodies, for balance, their fierce but calm features only a foot apart.

Now O'Reilly made an attempt to repeat his former feint, though with variations, taking his measure to land another blow, this time on the left temple. His move was rapid, but equally quick was the eye of the bigger man, whose cudgel was up in ready guard to meet the blow. The two weapons met, with such surprising power that they bent across each other into curves. An involuntary *huzzah* followed from all parties—not so much at the skill of the two men as in admiration of the cudgels themselves, and the judgment with which they must have been selected. And certainly the instruments did their duty. In a moment the two shillelaghs crossed each other in the opposite direction, and again the sticks curved as the two men stared at one another, their eyes burning, while the sight and smell of blood kindled a deeper ferocity.

Now Kelly made a move to practice on O'Reilly the feint that had been practiced on him. Anticipating the blow, the lieutenant stopped the blow with his hand, intent upon holding the staff aloft until he might visit Kelly, now unguarded, with a leveling blow.

As Kelly pulled on the cudgel with his collected vigor, O'Reilly suddenly released his hold; Kelly, having lost his balance, staggered back. A serpent could not have struck more quickly than the action of the lieutenant as his cudgel rang with tremendous force on the unprotected head of his enemy. Kelly fell, or rather was shot, to the floor, as though some superior power had dashed him against it, whereon he lay, quivering spasmodically from the blow.

A peal of triumph rose among the Ribbonmen as O'Reilly stood over the enemy, awaiting his return to the conflict. Yet Kelly did not stir.

Gouge him! Gouge him! shouted the *Na Coisantoiri*.

O'Reilly stooped a little, peered closely into his opponent's face and exclaimed: "Why then, is it acting the dead man you are? I wouldn't put it past you!"

Gouge him! The boys shouted in unison, and began pounding their sticks rhythmically on the floor, in the way that African savages pound spears upon their shields.

Nodding assent, O'Reilly reached out with the little finger of his right hand, the one with the uncut nail, and plucked out Kelly's eye, which rolled onto the floor like a monstrous white tear. Now the lieutenant bent down, took Kelly's eye in his finger and thumb—and put it in his pocket.

No man chose to break the wonderful silence as O'Reilly strode to the bar and accepted a glass of the good whiskey. Meanwhile, able-bodied boys assisted the injured to their feet, while others dropped to their knees and began collecting teeth from the floor.

"I think the sport is over, gentlemen," he said, raising the glass. "Good health to all here."

CHAPTER EIGHTEEN

Germantown, Philadelphia County

A s you approach Fern Rock Station and the country mansions of Meetinghouse Road, well before you reach the open expanse of the Germantown Cricket Club, the fifty-foot wooden tower with its crown of thorns becomes impossible to ignore, being fathoms taller than any neighboring tree or steeple.

The Quakers, Shakers, and Dippers who first settled Germantown regarded the builders of that tower with uncommon hostility—that their first gesture upon arriving in the New World was to proclaim to one and all that the Communists of Economy Manor had reached a point some twenty feet closer to heaven than anyone else.

The occupants of the weaver's cottages at the far side of the pitch would have gladly burned the offending structure down. As though anticipating such an attack, the first thing the Communists built after the tower was a stone wall. Then they constructed dormitories with slit windows on the first floor so that, were an attacker to mount the stone wall, he would be standing in front of a firing squad.

Should the intruder penetrate even further, gun holes were drilled into all outside door frames; as a last resort, it was said that tunnels had been laid to facilitate a quick evacuation to a concealed location.

As far as the Communists were concerned, such precautions came from hard experience comparable to the Jews in Germany. To be at odds with one's neighbors had long ago become an assumption, even a perilous source of pride.

The movement known as communism had been antagonizing traditional guardians of power ever since the fourteenth century, the Dark Ages, when hospital beds and social assistance of all kinds disappeared with the monasteries, and Communist institutions became the hospitals and almshouses of their time.

Naturally, the papacy deplored these incursions, for the stated reason that such sects easily lapsed into heresy—a word with such heavy freight that persecution followed as night follows day, led by militant orders such as the Jesuits.

With the discovery of the New World, it was natural for Communist denominations to look abroad for a more favorable circumstance.

At first, America showed as inhospitable a face as did Europe. Virginia remained strictly Anglican, while Massachusetts was resolutely Puritan—albeit in watered-down form after an excess of witch-burning. The spiritual terrain had been staked out, fenced, and as jealously guarded as in Europe.

In Pennsylvania, however, the first settlers happened to be Dutch Quakers and English utopians, for whom religion was a quest, not a proclamation from above. When William Penn toured Europe with guarantees of religious liberty as part of his "holy experiment," it inspired a rate of immigration to the Commonwealth of Pennsylvania that would not be surpassed until the Irish famine.

Around 1690, forty colonists (the biblical number did not go unnoticed) established a community in an area south of Philadelphia, in what would come to be known as Germantown. Land was purchased with the patronage of Augustin Herrman, a landholder in Bohemia, and named Economy Manor, after the abstemious ethic that prevailed among members at the time.

At first, the physical plant consisted of two forty-foot-square dormitories to house the members and separate the sexes. These rectangular buildings stood on an angle to face a third structure known as the Tabernacle of the Women of the Wilderness—a meeting hall topped by the tower, maintained by anointed priestesses whose purpose was to perpetuate the essence of the colony despite time and change.

Shunned and reviled by Protestants, Catholics, and Anglicans alike, the original sect lasted approximately twelve years; in that time they developed a creed—an eclectic blend of occultism and apocolyptic Christianity—that had nothing to do with the one they arrived with, at which point their Bohemian patron abruptly repudiated the sect and withdrew all support. However, he was unable to reclaim the Pennsylvania property, whose value had appreciated to upward of five hundred dollars an acre. And so the settlers continued to await the coming of the rebirth of the world, watching through telescopes all night long.

In the center of it all remained the Women of the Wilderness, whose knowledge drew increased veneration the more incomprehensible it became, until the sisters were credited with supernatural feats of all kinds.

Economy Manor languished in obscurity until 1720, when Conrad Beisel arrived, a vigorous, practical man, thanks to whom the colony was reborn. By the early part of this century, Economy Manor included a gristmill, a community barn, carpenter and blacksmith shops, a sawmill, a cannery, a woolen mill, a distillery and wine cellar, and five hundred and fifty acres planted in wheat, rye, tobacco, and hemp.

Upon Beisel's demise, the colony again languished until 1847, when it fell under the leadership of a Swede named John Root who had been recently discharged from the army of the Mexican War, and had somehow demonstrated an ability to influence the weather. Root immediately abolished the vow of celibacy, causing particular bitterness among elders who had passed the age of fertility.

By the end of the year Root was accused by a fellow Communist named Jensen, of murdering a Jewish peddler. At the trial, Jensen was standing by a courtroom window when Root appeared in the doorway, called his name, shot him dead, and escaped.

Into the leadership role stepped one Lieutenant Dougal O'Reilly, under whom John Root had served in the Mexican War, and with whom Root had made a private arrangement.

O'Reilly, however, harbored different ambitions. After inspecting Economy Manor and noting its potential as a defensive position for the Irish Brotherhood, he prepared to claim the property for himself, in perpetuity. Immediately he set about getting rid of its remaining cult members—the sisters excluded, for his army of street orphans drew benefit from their cooking, sewing, and nursing skills.

In the months following, male Communists died at an accelerating rate, until within a year the residents consisted of O'Reilly, Devlin, the *Na Coisantiori* and, in their crumbling tabernacle, the Women of the Wilderness.

The Women of the Wilderness seemed to take their new role in stride. Economy Manor had seen so many changes of personnel and doctrine that they had long ago ceased to differentiate between regimes. What they themselves believed was a mystery they were not prepared to answer, if indeed they knew themselves.

Surprisingly, they continued to accept single women from outside the commonwealth as new members. By what process and to what creed these conversions took place was, like everything else about them, a mystery.

By 1849, Economy Manor was a ruin. The only buildings standing (and only just) were the dormitories and the tabernacle. Of the rest, all that remained were foundations—massive, medieval-looking edifices made of stone, out of all proportion to the makeshift wooden buildings they had supported. When the remaining structures collapsed as well, it would appear as though a race of supermen once occupied the land.

In the men's dormitory candles had been extinguished early, as was the usual practice after hard fighting. Bunked in their Spartan quarters like schoolboys at Eton, those members of the *Na Coisantiori* who remained awake tended to their injuries with the assistance of three sisters, keen for a taste of motherhood after a lifetime of pointless celibacy.

From the kitchen below could be heard a low rumble of conversation, a meeting of high command.

Blur-'an agers!

Devlin pushed the torn shred of newsprint across the table after reading the article for the fourth time; this he swapped for the half-empty bottle of Old Pepper.

"You wonder at the cheek of the man," replied Lieutenant O'Reilly. To Devlin, in the meager light of a single candle, O'Reilly's empty socket was like a bottomless hole.

DICKENS COMING TO AMERICA
by Sanford W. Mitchell, *The Philadelphia Inquirer*

America's reading set is all a-twitter over the planned reading tour of Mr. Charles Dickens. Already appearances by the literary lion have been scheduled in Boston, Worcester, Harvard, New York, Philadelphia, Baltimore, Richmond, and Washington. The Young Men of

Boston have announced a public dinner in his honor, and a "Boz Ball" will take place at the Park Theatre in New York, where Mr. Francis Alexander has been engaged to undertake his portrait. In Washington, he will attend a levee with the president.

THE LIEUTENANT HELD the scrap of newsprint to his good eye and pretended to read, though in truth he could barely discern his own name. But by the way Devlin had harped upon this man Dickens during speech after speech, O'Reilly suspected that Devlin had something in mind, should he appear close at hand.

As an American for whom personal advancement was the whole purpose of life, the lieutenant could never see the point behind his partner's eruptions. Nor did O'Reilly comprehend the depth of Devlin's anger. Why would a man waste his wrath on a man he had never met—and a writer of books? No doubt it was the same inner rage that inspired him to stab a publisher in the mouth with a marlin spike.

There are two ways to disguise a conspicuous crime—by cleaning it up, or by making it worse. As always, O'Reilly made the best of a delicate situation, and proceeded to turn Topham's demise to his own material purpose.

Though Irish by race, there existed a gulf between the two men that would only grow wider—between an American citizen looking to his future in the New World, and a new immigrant, still seething over injustices that had driven him there in the first place.

Despite his allegiance to the spirit of America, O'Reilly continued to pay lip service to the auld sod: in America as in Europe, to be an accepted member of a race and religion could mean the difference between prosperity and death. Only a fool discarded bonds of blood and history out of hand.

In recent weeks, however, the first cracks had begun to appear in what had been a solid partnership, along the fault line between pragmatism and idealism. Whereas on the surface the ambitions of the two men meshed nicely, their inner reasons for attaining their objectives were as different as Ribbonmen and Orangemen.

For Finn Devlin, the imminent American tour of the eminent British author rekindled deep, ancient grievances that could not possibly be satisfied other than by the violent and painful death of its object.

Lieutenant O'Reilly on the other hand, as in the case of the late Henry Topham, had begun to see in the Dickens matter a material advantage to himself—although in this case the victim must remain live and kicking.

After all, O'Reilly had lost an eye for America, and the debt would be paid in full.

A man's ambition is binary in nature. One part seeks immediate satisfaction, the other part focuses on more lofty goals. The two objects are not simultaneous, however. For the fulfillment of the highest ideals, much depends on a good horse and a full stomach.

The immediate goal the lieutenant had in mind was simple. He wanted fifty thousand dollars. With that amount in his possession, a man could afford to keep a carriage, to display sufficient turnout to be invited to the better homes. Political influence would follow, higher purposes and greater advancement—witness McMullin, leader of the True Blue Americans, who took over the Moyamensing Hose Company and was about to run for office in the Fourth Ward.

O'Reilly regarded Devlin's idealism as a dangerous asset, to be watched carefully. Having squandered his young life in a doomed battle for an imaginary Ireland, the younger man could not be trusted to act in his own interest. At the same time, it was Devlin's grand foolishness that lent him his silver tongue—the grand crack that it takes to move men, that would one day talk O'Reilly into a position of political power.

As every businessman in Philadelphia knew, the easy money, gained through ownership of land and slaves, had been swallowed up by the great families; such was the level of competition today that no man could achieve advancement and remain entirely within the law. Ownership of a public servant had become essential to long-term success.

In Philadelphia County the American dream was still possible. Any man, no matter how low his birth, could attain success and honor and a house in the country—as long as he had an assemblyman in his pocket.

In the long term, Devlin would be the making of O'Reilly by attaining political office. Even in the short term, the man's mouth earned a good dollar, though the purse remained well short of O'Reilly's fifty thousand.

For the present, therefore, it was essential that their philosophical difference remain out of sight. This was not an impossible task, for Devlin remained so absorbed in his political preoccupation that he barely noticed the opinions of others. The mere fact that O'Reilly was of Irish ancestry, in Devlin's mind, meant that the work of the Irish Brotherhood proceeded purely out of their shared aspirations for Ireland, their hatred for the imperial beast.

For O'Reilly, the challenge lay in restraining Devlin from undertaking suicidal, symbolic acts, destroying symbolic buildings and symbolic people. (Mayor Swift, having caught Devlin's early notice as a Whig on an antiriot platform, escaped assassination only by the black of his nail.)

"You say Dickens was invited to a party with the president?" said O'Reilly with feigned outrage. "Scarce is the American author who has received such an honor."

"Oh, you can be sure that there is more to it than that," said Devlin.

"In what way are you thinking?"

"D'ye not see? Negotiations have taken place in secret rooms. Negotiation between nations always begins in the realm of 'universal' ideas. Once established as sentimental allies, reciprocity will follow, then reunification, and Britain will have it all, box and dice. And what then of the Irish in America? Will there be more coffin ships? And to what New World will we sail?"

"Be serious, man," replied the lieutenant. "Britain and America are on the cusp of war as we speak."

"A distraction," said Devlin promptly. "You may be certain of maneuvers behind the scenes, in the map room."

"If that is true, it is a bad picture you paint for certain," said O'Reilly.

"It cannot go unheeded or unanswered," said Devlin.

"Indeed, you can turn it into a fine speech."

"A speech? Do you not see what is at stake?"

"The British beast again, is it? The theme has gone over well in the past, yet I fear it is wearing thin."

"The coming of Dickens is a deeper provocation and must receive a resounding reply." Devlin's hand shook as he handed over the bottle.

"Well, *me auld segotia*, aren't you the quare hawk? Revenge must be taken calmly, you must surely know that as an educated man."

"I would be the calm man to see Mr. Dickens come away from his levee with the president stretched out on a board. And he would be calm as well."

Inwardly appalled by the thought, O'Reilly strove to keep his objections on a practical level. "Such a feat would take more than the work of a shillelagh. It would take guns at the least and I do not think we have the marksmen for it."

"A levee is a public occurrence, is it not? The smooth, confident bugger, out with the president on the lawn, mingling with the toadies. It would take no great skill to sidle up with a pocket iron and put one into him. Or better yet, there could be an explosion . . ."

By the far wall, forgotten in the intensity of the discussion, sat Sister Genoux, sandwiched between the stove and a small wooden table pulled up to one side. From this position she could stir a pot of stew while engaging in her primary occupation as a cigarette roller. With methodical smoothness she cut papers and Virginia plug, rolled shredded tobacco into the papers to form a tube, then glued them together with paste. With tobacco and papers prepared beforehand, she could complete the entire process with one hand, by the dozen, and smoke a cigarette herself while doing so—and stir a pot of stew besides. Later she would trim the ends and put them in a box and sell them to the shops on Chestnut Street.

It was said that she came from a family of Jacobins and that her grandfather had accompanied Paine on his return from France. Though there was no way to tell whether or not this was true, with such a revolutionary pedigree she had impressed Devlin mightily.

"There will be no explosion," said the lieutenant, firmly. "The president led the Buena Vista charge. We will do no harm to Old Rough and Ready."

"The president is a Whig. I'll hold that he is overdue for it."

"Be sensible, man. Such an action would come down very hard on the Irish, something so bold and bald. Churches would burn in the Catholic wards everywhere, and there would be lynching for certain. Such a thing is hard to countenance just for one's own satisfaction.

It might even serve the opposite purpose by making a martyr of the very man you despise."

This produced a thoughtful silence, which relieved the lieutenant somewhat.

"You could kidnap him," said Sister Genoux.

Supper being an afterthought after an afternoon of fighting, O'Reilly had overlooked the presence of Sister Genoux. Had he kept her in mind, he would not have allowed the conversation to proceed so far in this direction, since the woman could stir up Devlin's radical passion like her pot of mutton stew.

"Kidnap him?" asked Devlin, and met her gaze with his beautiful blue eyes.

Petite, dark, solemn, with a doll-like regularity of features, Sister Genoux was the youngest of the Women of the Wilderness. Though she had to be at least a decade older than the Irishmen, she retained the form and complexion of a marriageable woman. O'Reilly knew from Devlin that she had learned cigarette-rolling from her father, against the objections of her mother, who smoked a pipe.

The lieutenant was about to quiet the sister with a retort, then thought better of it. Though he distrusted her influence on Devlin, O'Reilly was a practical man, prepared to accept wisdom from any source, and he knew instantly that her notion had merit.

To kidnap Dickens under the flag of the Irish Brotherhood. Surely there would be a goodly amount of ned to be made by such a gesture, perhaps a profit not unadjacent to fifty thousand dollars.

A pretty thing indeed.

"What do you think?" asked Devlin, sensing interest in the lieutenant's hesitation. The sister too observed carefully, in the way that one might evaluate two horses up for auction.

"I think the notion bears thinking over. D'you wonder how much he might be worth? With the threat of war what it is, one side might pay as well as the other, to avoid a bad business."

"That is possible," replied Devlin, "but it cannot be simply a matter of making ned. There is a message we must carry to the people."

"Quite so," replied the lieutenant, keeping his thoughts to himself. Lighting his cheroot, he gazed at the puff of smoke like an idea made visible.

Continued Devlin, "Once he is in captivity we might persuade him to put his name to any manifesto at all. And the papers will print it for certain."

Out of O'Reilly's line of sight, the sister nodded agreement. "It is a wonderful thing," she said quietly, "the eloquence of a terrified man."

Having struck an accord over the thrust of the matter, the two partners lapsed into their separate brooding silences, and ate their stew like men who had not taken food since breakfast. Soon after that, the lieutenant made for his bed, leaving Devlin and the sister alone together.

"Take him for ransom is *très bon*," she said, as she fired a twig in the stove and lit a cigarette. "But I am thinking that you have something else in mind. Cut off his head, yes, that would cause a fuss, in America and Britain *aussi*. Is that what you are thinking?"

"Aye, Sister Genoux. That is what I am thinking. Whatever the ransom, Mr. Dickens will never comb a gray hair."

"You are just like my father," she said, with a bitter laugh and an outpouring of smoke.

A MASSACRE OUT OF SHAKESPEARE
Astor Place Riot Claims up to 40 Lives
by Harlen C. Penny, *The New York Tribune*

NEW YORK——As Britain and the United States edge ever closer to war over the Oregon border dispute, anti-British sentiment erupted in a frightful riot at the Astor Place Opera House yesterday, where as many as forty lives have been lost following a performance of Shakespeare's *Macbeth* by the British actor Charles Macready.

As the angry crowd roiled, one window after another cracked, pieces of bricks and paving stones rained onto the terraces and lobbies, so that the Opera House resembled a fortress besieged by an invading army rather than a place meant for the peaceful amusement of a civilized community.

The death toll to date stands at 31 civilians dead, some 30 or 40 wounded from gunfire, and more than 100 soldiers, police, and civilians injured by paving stones, clubs, and other weapons.

Responsibility for the disaster points to a group of Nativist agitators led by the writer Edward Z. C. Judson, who goes under the pen name Ned Buntline. In print and in speech, Judson portrayed the rivalry between British MacReady and the American actor Edwin Forrest as a test of American vigor against a lingering imperial presence.

Officials are not questioning the wisdom of proceeding with the much-publicized Charles Dickens tour, under such incendiary conditions . . .

Baltimore

Sir:

 Our mutual acquaintance is in terrible distress. I shall have accommodations reserved for you at the Swan in Norfolk. My coachman will collect you there. It is imperative that I see you.

Sincerely,
Mrs. Elmira Shelton (née Royster)

A s you might imagine, it was not out of concern for Poe's welfare that I so eagerly booked the 4 A.M. steamer to Richmond, having secured a temporary replacement at Washington College Hospital.

This latter arrangement proved an easy matter. I was no more popular with my peers than ever, nor would my few patients object, being for the most part semiconscious. Even Nurse Slatin made no protest over my abrupt departure, for in my sleepless condition I had become downright dangerous.

The side-wheeler, part of the Old Bay Line, shuddered its way out of Baltimore Harbor and down Chesapeake Bay in the first light of morning. Soon we were chugging past the oyster boats and skipjacks (like plumed herons with their sharp, elongated prows), and gradually the odor of dead fish and sewage surrendered to an air that would cure the lungs of any ailment. As I leaned over the railing, suddenly a bluefish surfaced just below me; for a second my customary urge to jump overboard left me and I rejoiced at the sight, a sensation that settled into a mild exhilaration over the simple act of breathing.

There could be no doubt Elmira Royster had been the cause of my sleeplessness, and my unfamiliar enthusiasm for life. Poe's distress be damned: for the first time in years I looked to the future without becoming tired.

Soon thereafter, seasickness came over me and I found myself leaning over the railing for another reason entirely. I was miserable for the next eight hours, and it came as a relief when the stink of dead fish and sewage returned, indicating that we were nearing the James River and Richmond. It seemed almost worth the misery of the voyage, that first step on dry land, the sheer luxury of treading a surface that did not move underfoot.

The Swan Tavern, despite its prestigious location near the capital building, was nothing more than a glorified boardinghouse. A once-elaborate hotel in the latter stages of decay, it looked like a cake left out in the rain, or a setting in one of Eddie's tales. It seemed obvious that Elmira Royster had chosen the Swan because it was Eddie's customary lodging—being perpetually short of funds, and no doubt looking to her for a temporary infusion of cash.

The carriage that collected me had likewise seen better days, as had the two horses with swollen hock joints and visible ribs, and the white-haired Negro at the reins, whose livery consisted of a long, ash-colored duster coat and a tattered straw hat.

Inside, the carriage exuded the stale sweetness of mildew. The seat sagged, and had been worn right through in places so that the coarse hosshair cushioning poked through like stubble. Yet it was comfortable enough, and as the carriage clattered up Broad Street toward Church Hill I was treated to a short window tour of the city in which I grew up. How it had changed! The cholera outbreak of the previous summer having abated, the hustle and commotion of city life had returned to the hills overlooking the bright islands of the James River where I had wandered as a boy. As well, the city had acquired a new dignity—or pretentiousness, depending on your point of view—thanks to the new courthouse, built on what was once Town Back Creek, where once we would fish brookies. Predictably, the edifice was vaguely Greek, with a dome so white in the sunlight as to strain the eyes.

Like most American cities, in Richmond the transition between urban and rural was a matter of blocks, not miles. Soon the road narrowed to a gutterway, as we overtook a gang of manacled slaves, recently purchased, on the march across the mountains to the Ohio River. A short time later we were trotting amid plantations of tobacco, flax, and corn, tended by brown, bent figures with sacks tied around the waist.

Just as the faulty springs of my vehicle had become all but

unbearable for the coccyx, the carriage abruptly turned down a gauntlet of enormous chestnut trees, whose branches all but met overhead. It is a characteristic of chestnuts that in autumn their leaves do not fall immediately, but remain on the branch for some time; the leaves above and beside me resembled little brown hands, rubbing in the wind, making a dry rattling sound, a sort of ghostly applause.

The chestnuts soon gave way to enormous magnolia trees surrounding a family graveyard, to the right of the driveway and in front of the house—a single table-monument and four granite obelisks, surrounded by iron-lace fencing. In between these monuments stood a quantity of small children's gravestones, scattered in the overgrown grass.

There was nothing grand or Gothic about the mansion itself, which resembled an institutional brick building—a small courthouse or library perhaps—with six deep-set windows and four plaster pillars in front, like sticks of dough, framing a set of front steps and a mounting block. Clearly the residence had not been created with the Virginia landscape in mind, but occupied the middle of the lawn as though dropped out of the sky. Behind the house and to the left stood a number of empty slave quarters made of brick, once whitewashed but now stained by water and fungus into a patchy green-gray.

From this evidence I concluded that another plantation-owner had leased or bought the fields, leaving the original family to crumble along with the buildings.

The elderly Negro who answered the door was easily as ancient as my driver. Along with the general condition of the house, this suggested an establishment on its uppers, in which the servants remained out of age and loyalty.

"Yessa, Dr. Chivahs," he said in an extraordinarily resonant baritone, extending the welcome one affords a bill collector. "You is expected, sah."

I followed the old gentleman's surprisingly lithe frame down a wide hallway whose walls had been stenciled with abstract shapes. At the end of the hall we reached an almost empty drawing room, with two chairs and a tea table situated in the center of an oval Turkey carpet. There were no pictures on the walls, and the fireplace had evidently been cold for months. I began to wonder if anyone lived here at all—or was it a stage setting, created especially for our meeting?

"Miz Royster will be with you in a moment. Would you care for a whiskey, Dr. Chivahs, sah?"

"No thank you, sir, I am a Son of Temperance."

"As you wish, sah." Nonetheless, he continued to hover about, as though expecting something further to develop, and rightly so.

"On second thought," I said, for I could endure his stare no longer, "it has been a long day."

"As you wish, sah."

The butler indicated a chair by the table, there to await Elmira Royster (whom I still could not acknowledge as Mrs. Shelton for some reason). Nonetheless I chose to remain standing, for as with Neilson Poe at the Exchange Hotel, there is something about being discovered sitting down that reduces one to a subordinate level.

The butler returned with a glass of whiskey on a small silver tray and set it on the table. "Purely medicinal, I assure you," I said to his retreating back, and wondered why I had felt the need to explain.

"It is the brand your friend was drinking when first we met," said Elmira Royster from the doorway. "You were watching it evah so longingly, and I felt sorry for you."

If erotic longing is a cause for pity, I must have made a pathetic sight as I gaped at the figure in the doorway—her skeptical eye, her lithe, supple form, her slightly aquiline nose, her quality of psychical distance contradicted by the rapid motion of her bosom.

"When last we met I was a Son of Temperance," I replied, weakly. "Presumptuous of me to say it, I know."

"In what way was it presumptuous, suh?" She wore a plain, thin cotton dress of the sort worn by Negro servants. The simplicity of it struck me as angelic and provocative at the same time.

"Presumptuous," I replied, "to assume such dominion over oneself."

"That is rightly true. We are all creatures of the flesh, and the flesh is weak."

Beneath the dress, she did not appear to be wearing a corset. A silver mourning locket hung by a chain to a point between the swell of her breasts, each of which would have fitted into my hand.

"Do you know why I invited you, Dr. Chivahs? Do you know why you are here?"

With my mind in a fog of desire, I had no idea what to reply. This was perhaps not the time to mention that I did not care a fig about Eddie Poe, that he had given me nothing but trouble since he entered my life as a boy, that the thought of him in trouble filled my heart with inexpressible joy.

Nor was it the time to say that I had come because I needed to see her, to be in her presence, in the way that a dipsomaniac needs a drink. That I would leap like a trout at the opportunity to look at her face, let alone hear her voice, smell her violet scent. Had I expressed my thoughts outright, she would have been well advised to have me shot, if only as a precaution.

While my mind scrambled for words with which to explain myself in an acceptable manner, my body acted of its own accord. Aghast at what I was doing, I arose from my chair, stepped forward, and placed my lips directly upon hers. She did not resist, nor did she call for help; on the contrary, for a moment she grasped the nape of my neck with one tentative hand in order to press her mouth more firmly upon mine.

Our lips parted. My mouth felt swollen as though bee-stung, as Elmira Royster sank into a chair beside the tea table.

"Dr. Chivahs, I declare that I have nevah experienced such behavior from a gentleman in my life."

Nor had I, though I once witnessed similar activity between seamen and their women; and I had heard of such behavior among Negroes, and the Irish as well.

"I assure you, ma'am, that I am appalled by myself. I scarcely know what to say in my defense."

"The less said about it the better," she said. "Of course it is understood between us that this may not go one step further."

"Why?" I croaked without thinking. The whiskey glass shook in my hand as I raised it to my lips.

She seemed mildly affronted by the question. "*Why*, you ask? The fact that I am in this room alone with you is in itself a disgrace, suh."

"I agree that my action was reprehensible, ma'am. But allow me to point out that you did not resist."

"I did not slap your face, if that is what you mean."

"That is not what I mean, ma'am."

"Very well, suh. I agree that the flesh is weak, mine included. Can a heart so full of corruption also contain the Holy Spirit? Can good and evil exist at the same time, in the same body?" She asked me these questions as though I might venture an answer.

"I do not have the faintest idea," I replied. "I am a freethinker."

The corners of her mouth moved upward, though her eyes continued to evaluate. "Freethinkers never know anything for certain. I wonder how you manage to leave the house."

"I mean to say that I am open to suggestion and argument."

"Dr. Chivahs, are you familiar with the marriage vow?"

"Certainly, ma'am. I swore to it myself, once. In fact I am a widower."

"And I am a widow." Elmira Royster frowned slightly, as though the word evoked a distant memory. "I never liked the word *widow*. It makes me think of spiders. And *widower* is very much like *murderer*, don't you think—as though a man *creates* a widow? Such sinister words for such a melancholy condition!"

I ventured no reply. The room was warm and she exuded violet. My mother's clothes had smelled of violet, from the sprigs of orrisroot that lined her linen drawer.

"How much better is the word *engaged*, don't you think? Yes, Dr. Chivahs, I am engaged, even if I am not to be married."

Once again her mouth formed an expression of ambivalent amusement. "Ephesians Five: '*Wives, submit yourselves unto your own husband, as unto the Lord.*'"

I could not tell if she was declaiming the verse or mocking it. "You must have loved Mr. Shelton a great deal," I said, feeling inane for not the first time.

"I did not, suh. I hated him. He was a brute. I might as well have been one of the staff—he beat me when he felt like it, and he violated me when he felt like it. If I refused, he would simply visit one of the slave girls. At any sign of an independent spirit I was mocked, in public if possible."

"Was this beastly behavior not noticed by others?"

"I imagine that it was. But among the couples we socialized with the situation appeared no different from ours. Through experience I became attuned to the weapons men and women use on one another. I could hear the subtle barbs, uttered in a private code and therefore guaranteed to wound; and the response—the ways in which a woman makes light of her husband's behavior in a social setting.

"But now my husband is dead, suh, and all that he did is gone with him. And I am engaged to a man who would rather plunge a quill into his own eye than cause me pain."

My mind struggled to concentrate, for I was literally quivering with hatred for her late husband, and for his oversensitive replacement. "Ma'am, how is it possible to be engaged to be married, without contemplating marriage itself?"

"I am a practical woman, suh. Engagement without marriage places our association in exactly the place I want to be."

"I am glad of it, ma'am. I recall that the last time Eddie married, his bride was all of thirteen."

"My fiancé's relations with women have nothing to do with using her, carnally or in any other way. Eddie loved little Virginia, suh. He worshipped her. Cherished her. And when poor Virginia became consumptive, he loved her all the more. He went without food in order to purchase medicine for her. In her weeks of dying he never left her side, not once, and when she passed away he was like a walking corpse himself."

"And yet he seems to have made an impressive recovery."

"On the contrary, my fiancé is in desperate distress."

"Yes, you said so in your letter."

"Those were his own words, in a letter to me."

"May I see the letter?"

"Certainly not, suh. It is my personal correspondence."

What an infuriating woman, I thought.

"However, I can tell you that it concerns some Irish gentlemen," she continued. "Briefly, it seems clear that Eddie is in peril, suh. As you are his best friend—"

"Ma'am, as your fiancé, he is at this moment my worst enemy."

A silence fell between us in which, in my imagination, my mouth found hers, my arms wrapped themselves around her waist, and I pulled her close so that I might feel her breasts, swollen beneath the soft cotton of her dress. Her mouth was surprisingly cool . . .

"Doctor, you astonish me."

"Please forgive me, ma'am," I said, momentarily convinced that she could read my thoughts.

"Dr. Chivahs, I think it would be best if we prayed together."

I honestly did not know how to respond to such an outlandish suggestion, other than to accede.

We joined hands—which in itself made the moment worthwhile—and softly she said a prayer. I felt her breath on my face; it smelled of leaves.

> *As we endure this mortal coil*
> *Allow us not our souls to soil*
> *Let our desires dormant lie*
> *To be released when we die*
> *At Thy feet our passions poured*
> *In praise for Thou, our Loving Lord*

"Amen," we said together.

She opened her eyes and looked into mine. "Dr. Chivahs, I wonder if you are capable of sustaining an association of the soul?"

"Ma'am, I am afraid I have not given my soul much thought."

She nodded, as though the answer would suffice for the present. "You must go now. I surely do hope your hotel is comfortable."

"I do not think I shall be comfortable for some time to come."

"A woman must be firm if she is to stem the tide of a man's sensual nature. She must set limits and abide by them. I may need your help, for Eddie's sake. In which case I must trust in your honor, suh. Otherwise I do fear we mayn't meet again."

"I shall do my best, ma'am. As I mentioned, I am a freethinker."

Soon after that I left the house. Two ancient Negroes waited for me at the door of the ancient carriage.

"Have a safe trip, sah," said the butler in his improbably resonant voice, and the driver bowed his head. Altogether, I experienced the distinct feeling that I was being mocked.

CHAPTER TWENTY

Baltimore

Repentance, *n.* The faithful attendant and
follower of Punishment.

—Ambrose Bierce

Dr. Chivers, there is a gentleman to see you. I believe he is a constable." Nurse Slatin articulated this information as though she
had acquired police powers herself.

I cannot adequately describe my distress at this news. For days I
had been going about my rounds with a display of cool professional-
ism, while bearing an inward turmoil that permitted me neither to
eat nor sleep. At the mention of *constable* it required an effort not to
throw myself out the window.

In the days since our meeting, I had not for one moment recovered
from Elmira Royster. Night after night I lay awake, listening to the
creak of my rope bed, tormented by imaginings I had not experienced since my youth, when the sight of a girl's bare arm would return in the night to brush against my lips, producing a temporary
fever and an inflammation of the loins.

The only plausible reason for a constable to visit was that Eddie
had been exposed. Whether dead or alive it scarcely mattered; what
mattered was that Poe was not where he should be—underground.

I did not throw myself out the window. Nonetheless, I kept my
morphine ready.

Under the policing system of the day, Baltimore constables were
appointed by a warden under the direction of an elected official, as a
reward for the applicant's support during the last election. This was
universally understood and accepted.

The constable in this instance had surely given good service to some clan or sect or ethnic society, for he radiated confidence in the security of his position, despite a lack of anything resembling knowledge or training, or even a command of the English language.

"You being Dr. Chivers please, sir?"

"I am he."

A mass of folds resembled a smile. "It is good profession, Doctor. It is hoped my son to be doctor. Any man can be doctor in America."

"Democracy is a powerful stimulant to advancement," I replied.

"I apologize, Doctor, to be interruption between your works."

"That is all right, Constable, I am sure it is an important matter."

"A disturbing communical from the Philadelphia Municipal Police we have had." The constable glanced down at his notes, which were taken in a foreign language. "It concerns a . . . a hunting, sir."

"I'm sorry but I never go near the forest."

"No, sir, hunting it is. *Hunting.*"

"*Haunting*, you mean."

"Yes."

A pause ensued, during which I formed a civil reply to such an absurdity. "Poltergeists are outside my area of scientific expertise, Constable," I said, with an air of restrained amusement. "Here at Washington College Hospital, we deal with the living—if only just."

"Ha, ha. That is funny one. But I must to ask you the question: Am I understanding you were present at the death of Edgar Allan Poe the writer?"

"Indeed I was. I am sure Nurse Slatin can produce the full report for you."

"That is not what I am seeking, sir. I am to understand you were friendship of Mr. Poe?"

"We were chums, yes. However, we hadn't seen each other in years."

"But you would to recognize him, is so?"

"Oh I recognized him, all right. Though he was very near death."

"So. I shall my report giving that Mr. Poe was positively identified by . . ." Here the constable produced a piece of paper from one coat pocket and a monocle from another, and read aloud: "*the attendant surgeon at the time and place of his death.*" He removed the monocle: "No?"

"Indeed I was. Might I ask what this has to do with your haunting in Philadelphia?"

"I am not free with that informative."

"If I cannot know what the problem is, how in heaven's name do you expect me to answer your questions?"

"I see no reason not. Man name Rufus Griswold claim he is feisted by Mr. Poe in the night, horrible threats given. It is in the business of the police to follow such when the victim has the good stansion."

"If this was the Griswold who penned Mr. Poe's obituary, then he might be suffering from a malady known as remorse. Rufus Griswold did Mr. Poe a good deal of harm, and for no good reason."

"I will write down," replied the constable, and did so in another language. "But there is complication."

"There are always complications."

"Is a bed murder in Philadelphia. I am bringing the newspaper for you, I do not read the English greatly."

POE IMPLICATED IN TOPHAM MURDER

by Sanford W. Mitchell, *The Philadelphia Inquirer*

PHILADELPHIA——Not a few have noted aspects of the grisly murder of Mr. Henry Topham which correspond with uncanny accuracy to incidents in the work of Edgar Allan Poe, whose *Collected Tales* were published not long ago, in which murder, mutilation, and torture serve as recurrent motifs. Given the stormy relations between the late author and Mr. Topham, it is to be wondered whether the similarity was not a product of deliberate design.

Inspector Shadduck, the officer responsible for the investigation, demurs. "There is no need to alarm the public," he said. "Murderers seldom read novels, much less imitate them."

"Your hands is shaking, Doctor. Is the palsy?"

"A slight case, yes. Am I to believe that Mr. Poe is a suspect in this murder?"

"Is public sensation over hunting of Mr. Griswold. There is

demanding to updig Mr. Poe for easing of the public mind. Let us hoping it is not necessitation."

I nodded sagely while my stomach roiled. "I agree, sir, that it would be a great shame to wake the dead."

M̲Y̲ ̲S̲E̲C̲O̲N̲D̲ ̲V̲O̲Y̲A̲G̲E̲ from the land of Lord Baltimore was no more comfortable than the first. Between episodes of seasickness my thoughts went to the subject of death—the gravitational pull of escape, from everything, to be enveloped in black velvet, back to the infinite womb . . .

Having disembarked in Norfolk Harbor, there being no hack available at the dock, and therefore obliged to find my own way, I walked to the Kaiser Brothers livery stable, where I was permitted to rent a rancorous saddle hoss for an outrageous sum. As well, I was provided with a map to the Shelton estate drawn by the manager, a Negro freedman by the name of Brooks.

The distance to the Shelton estate was farther than I remembered. By the time we trotted onto the property, between the eerily rustling rows of chestnut trees and past the cemetery, my inner thighs were aflame with saddle welts, which would make my trousers a torture and leave me waddling like a sailor for days.

By the time I stood stiffly onto the mounting block by the front stoop, the elderly Negro coachman had already materialized to take the reins, while Elmira Royster stood behind the screen door, holding the visiting card I had hastily sent ahead the day before.

Shifting from foot to foot in order to restore feeling and movement to my legs, I noted her dress, which was the same as at our previous meeting, or one just like it. Already I could smell violet.

"Dr. Chivahs. I am evah so surprised."

"Forgive me, ma'am, for arriving without due notice. I left Baltimore in some haste."

"You look peaked, suh, you appear right consumptive. I declare, when is the last time you have eaten?"

"Eating is out of the question. On this occasion it is I who am in terrible distress."

"Then you are most welcome to come in, suh. Will you take another glass of whiskey on this occasion?"

"I certainly shall."

I followed her down the hall—mesmerized by the swing of her body beneath her dress—and into the drawing room, while wondering why the devil I had come, what did I expect? After the constable's visit I had acted with the instinct of a trapped animal and fled—but by what logic did I expect Elmira Royster to be of assistance to me, a woman who seemed seldom in her right mind herself?

Or did I seize on this new emergency as an opportunity to act upon my aching desire for her, an ever-present pressure like a fist beneath the sternum, pressing on the *Rectis Abdominus* so that the taking of food became an absurdity?

In my wretched state, one thing remained self-evident: *Somehow Eddie Poe must be stopped.* The sentence roared in the mind, and to this end Elmira Royster was my only lead, being in written contact with the scoundrel.

The drawing room was furnished—or unfurnished—as it had been when last I was here. Elmira Royster sat at the tea table, crossed her legs beneath her dress, and gestured that I was to be seated as well.

"My sakes but the house is chilly for this time of year, is it not?"

"Yes, ma'am, and almost vacant. When I was last here, I confess that I wondered where you really live."

"I declare, that is a question I sometimes ask myself. Where do I live? Where do you live, Dr. Chivahs?"

"In my mind for the most part," I replied, surprised to hear myself say it. "Certainly not in Washington College Hospital, I hope."

"If one lives in one's mind, perhaps life is all a dream," she said, and her eyes shifted as though something were written on the center of my forehead.

Of course as a scientist I detested empty mystification and all that promoted it, if only because it reminded me of Eddie Poe and his fetish of death and dreams and grotesques.

"I do not agree that life is a dream," I said, raising my voice. "In fact, I *know* that it is not. A war teaches you that, if nothing else. An amputation is not a dream, ma'am, I assure you, and my patients would all agree with me."

Elmira Royster did not seem discomfited in the least. Yet my outburst must have had some effect, for when she spoke she seemed almost reasonable. "After Mr. Shelton passed away, I began to simplify things. I sold the property except for the house itself, and freed the slaves who wished to go. When the remaining staff leave or die, I shall sell the house too."

"An admirable plan, ma'am, and I applaud your treatment of slaves. It is more than Jefferson ever did."

"I believe I once said that a wife is a sort of slave. It gives us something in common."

"Many have noted a similarity."

"It goes away when the spouse is departed."

"Indeed. With nobody to give the orders, there is no one to obey."

"Not so, suh. We take orders from a higher power, through Christ our Lord."

"Believe me, ma'am, I would not dream of contradicting you."

"Sarcasm ill becomes you, Dr. Chivahs."

"I was not being sarcastic in the least."

We sat in silence while the elderly and all-observing butler placed two glasses on the tea table between us: three fingers of whiskey for me, and a glass of what appeared to be lemonade, but which could have contained anything.

"I will be in earshot, Miz Shelton," murmured the butler, with a significant glance in my direction.

Despite the fact that every word we uttered would be overheard by the staff, I decided to speak plainly. "Ma'am, I am here because I am utterly smitten by you, and because I am in desperate trouble. I don't know which comes first."

"That rightly makes two problems," she replied. "Which do you *think* comes first?"

"The Philadelphia police have requested that Eddie be dug up—and you know as well as I that it is not Eddie in that grave."

She frowned slightly. "*Dug up?* My soul, why would anyone do such a thing?"

"There is a public outcry in Philadelphia. It seems that Eddie staged spurious hauntings in a spirit of revenge."

"He haunted Mr. Griswold?" Her eyes glinted with interest. "After that obituary I am not surprised."

"The name of the writer was, I believe, a Mr. Ludwig."

"Yet it was Mr. Griswold, suh. It was a most vile eulogy. Eddie was livid."

"Do you mean that Griswold wrote under a pseudonym"

"Of course. They all dice each other up under pseudonyms. Eddie was fond of the practice himself. I called it a form of cowardice, but he differed. *Truth must always wear a mask*, was his opinion."

"You have put your finger on the problem, ma'am. Having left his mortal body, at least as far as the public is concerned, at present Eddie is nothing *but* a mask. He can destroy anyone he likes, being forever anonymous."

"But surely, suh, to do so he would need an associate—someone with an interest in supporting him, and in covering his tracks. Someone in the publishing business, perhaps."

"That was nicely put, ma'am. I expect that might well be the case."

"Thank you, suh." Elmira Royster appeared amused, which I found infuriating. "Eddie once remarked that he would like to become a ghost, stalking the halls and frightening folks out of their skin."

"Then you knew that he was planning this insanity?"

She shrugged, as though it were a trivial matter. "He mentioned it in one or another of his letters. I neither approved nor disapproved."

"You are in touch with him, then?"

"Of course. Eddie and I are, after all, engaged."

"Pardon me, ma'am, but I swear that he is the most selfish beast I have ever encountered. I have risked everything for him, and he is cutting shines again!"

Once again my mouth had surprised my mind with its unintended frankness.

"I don't rightly know what you mean by *cutting shines*," she said.

"Eddie does awful things just to see what will happen. He always did. Now that he is 'dead' he is free to act upon his morbid fantasies, and take responsibility for none of it, and with no critics to complain. We—you and I—have become his creative materials. He is experimenting with our lives—just to see what will happen! Oh, it is monstrous! . . ."

I do not remember what happened after that.

*　*　*

I awoke to the fragrance of violet and a woman's mouth against my forehead. I did not move. When I finally opened my eyes, Elmira Royster was kneeling close to me, in her plain cotton dress, with no sign of a corset beneath.

"I was testing you for fever, suh," she explained. "You are abnormally warm."

"Test me again. One can never be too sure."

She put her hand on my chest and her lips on my forehead. "You are still very warm," she said, and straightened up again.

"I am afraid I must have fallen into a delirium. It happens occasionally. A war injury. Nothing very serious. Please excuse my behavior, whatever happened."

"For a man in a delirium, you were remarkably polite. You were able to climb stairs without assistance. You were raving about experiments, and about something called flying artillery, and about butchery—but it all made perfect sense to me."

"Ah yes, I remember saying that," I said, which was an utter lie. "It is a feeling I experienced in the war, of being an experiment in some monstrous laboratory. Run by some godlike creature, nothing friendly, driven by morbid curiosity, like a boy dissecting a frog."

"I declare, that is a strange notion of the Savior."

"I don't know that I mentioned Him."

"You described the Son of God, dissecting a frog. God, manifest not in the flesh but in the laboratory."

I decided to change the subject. It would not be the first time I had observed religion to turn an intelligent individual into some kind of imbecile.

"I wish they wouldn't use the word *flesh*," I said. "It makes me think of raw meat."

"Dr. Chivahs, I do fear that you are becoming delirious again."

Indeed, I did feel the need to close my eyes for a moment, and by the time I opened them again an uncertain amount of time had passed. I was alone in a room which appeared to be a library—and on the second floor, to judge by the trees outside. I was lying on a velvet couch. The floor was bare, with no carpet; in fact, other than a fireplace, a desk, and a chair, the room stood entirely empty of furniture. Only a wall, containing bookcases, interspersed by open windows, which emitted much air but little light.

Having little to look at, I closed my eyes. When I opened them again, there she was.

"It is late in the day," I said. "You must shut the windows at once, for reasons of health."

"I disagree, suh. It is a curious assumption, that the harmful vapors are *outside* the house."

"I am a doctor, ma'am, and it is my professional judgment. Should you choose to ignore it, I hold you responsible for what happens as a result."

The omniscient butler, of whom I had by now formed a thorough dislike, entered with a tray. "The brandy, Miz Shelton, ma'am," he murmured in a tone of resentful resignation, primarily directed at me.

"Thank you, Mr. Washington," she said, as though she were speaking to a business colleague. "Kindly set it on the bedside table, if you please."

With a not quite undetectable sigh, Mr. Washington poured three fingers of brandy into a plain glass tumbler and put it before me. "Your health, sah," he murmured, nodded to Elmira Royster, and was gone.

"I was a Son of Temperance before Eddie arrived," I said. "You will probably think ill of me, for transgressing my oath."

"'Sufficient unto the day are the sins thereof,' " she replied, and in my imagination we kissed.

She sat on the couch beside me, which made a tight fit, so that I could feel the warmth of her body.

"Forgive me, Elmira, but . . ."

"Dr. Chivahs, my name is Mrs. Shelton."

"If you insist, ma'am."

"You were meaning to ask a question, suh. What is it?"

"What is your understanding—no, what I mean to say is, what are the *terms* of your engagement to Eddie Poe?"

"I don't rightly know what you are suggesting, but there are no plans for a marriage, as I have said before. We wished to stop the rumors. People can remain engaged for decades, and nobody says a word."

"Then I am to understand that there is no . . . no passion between you?"

"Kindly watch your language, suh. But yes, that is why I am engaged to Eddie. I could never be engaged to you. I would find it evah so stressful."

Infuriating as usual, yet the warmth of her hip against my side encouraged me to continue the conversation.

When I describe my feelings for Elmira Royster, please understand that the word is not *love*. To say that I liked Elmira would be stretching it. To say that I needed her in order to remain alive, would be more to the point.

"I am trying to imagine you as a freethinker," she said. "A freethinking doctor! How do you know where to cut?" And for the first time I saw her laugh out loud.

I myself did not laugh. At her mention of my profession, the entire catastrophe of my present situation struck me in the stomach with terrible vigor.

"Miz Royster—"

"I am Mrs. Shelton."

"Mrs. Shelton, I beg your pardon but let me restate the facts of the case. They want to dig Eddie up. There has been a sensational murder in Philadelphia, and Eddie is a suspect, or rather, his ghost, at least for the present. The upshot of it is, if they dig him up I shall be utterly ruined—and, incidentally, Eddie will be suspected of murder. If you care anything for your fiancé—and I would rather you did not—you must help me to reach him."

She hesitated, which I took as a hopeful sign, though it tormented me beyond endurance that his welfare was uppermost in her mind.

"Eddie is in Philadelphia," she said. "He has found work there under a pseudonym. I have his address."

"That would be most helpful. Thank you."

She stood, crossed to the writing table, took pen and ink—and stopped. "No. I do not think so."

"You do not think what, ma'am?"

"I do not think I shall give it to you, suh."

"Why not in heaven's name?"

"Because I must protect Eddie. From you."

Damnation.

"Why on earth would you say such a thing?"

"I declare that any man with your wayward sentiments is not to be trusted alone with my fiancé."

"Ma'am, I am a doctor. I do not take lives, I save them." Hearing myself say this, I did not know whether to laugh or cry.

"I will assist you on one condition, suh," she said. "I shall go to Philadelphia with you."

"Surely that is out of the question, ma'am. How could such an arrangement be possible?"

"We will travel as man and wife. As Mr. and Mrs. Henri Le Rennet. And that is my last word on the subject."

OTHER THAN ON the open sea and in the Sahara desert, only in America is a man truly sovereign and self-determining—if only because here it is uniquely possible for him to disappear without a trace, and to transform into somebody else, without leaving the country.

Without alerting a soul—partner, enemy, creditor, police, mistress, wife—a man may leave his house on Monday, catch an omnibus to his bank, withdraw all his money, travel five hundred miles, and literally be somebody else by the beginning of next week, with a new partner, a new mistress, a new set of creditors, and no one to call him to task.

Liberty takes many forms, some more savory than others.

Every man has a dream, and mine was simple, if somewhat far-fetched: as Mr. and Mrs. Henri Le Rennet, Elmira Royster and I would travel to Philadelphia via Baltimore, locate Eddie, and one way or another end the threat to my life and reputation.

But what then? Return to Washington College Hospital, and a life I found so devoid of interest that I contemplated ending it, on a daily basis? Would Elmira Royster return to her shell of a house and her tactical engagement to await the demise of her staff, and her fiancé, and herself? How much better if she and I were to simply continue together to San Francisco, as Henri Le Rennet and his wife Elmira, and begin anew, leaving Eddie Poe behind, and ourselves as well!

I imagined inventing a suitable French ancestry for Mr. Le Rennet, and purchasing certificates to prove it. I might join the church of my wife's choice. I might set up a private practice, patching people up, treating their aches and pains, delivering their babies. For the first time since my birth I might be, dare I even pronounce the word, *content*.

CHAPTER TWENTY-ONE

City Hall, Independence Square, Philadelphia

Councilman Wendel Grisse, not for the first time, was deeply troubled over the presence of Shadduck in his office and his city. Was it possible that he had brought a snake into the house to control the vermin, only to see it turn on the family?

Many times he reviewed his actions of the past year, and was unable to find his mistake. For what did he deserve this troublemaking?

The need for professional policemen had become urgent after the disturbances of forty-four, when the only officer on duty was the sheriff, with no budget to pay or arm a *posse comitatus*. Then the militia refused to step in over a dispute with the city over reimbursements. By the time a force of firemen had been cobbled together (led by Mayor Swift, in a frightful display of grandstanding), the rioting had gone to anarchy and madness—churches and businesses were burnt and many were killed and injured.

What a terrible humiliation for the county, to think that Philadelphia, the city of brotherly love, could not impose the most rudimentary law and order!

More humiliation for the county followed, when the state assembly passed an act requiring the city and surrounding townships to hire a force of one policeman for every hundred and fifty taxpayers. The law went so far as to specify that the force be "able-bodied," indicating that the senior government regarded local officeholders as idle buffoons who could not be trusted.

Seeing the spree of patronage hiring to come, and the resulting opportunity for political advancement, Wendel Grisse, a German immigrant and a pillar of the Pennsylvania *Deutsch,* ran for office on a platform of law and order and a clampdown on criminal wrongdoing. In this he secured support from the militia, who then delivered sufficient votes to secure victory—literally so in some polls, where voters for Grisse arrived in covered wagons.

Grisse's first action as a spokesman for law and order was to convince Mayor Swift that, since riots seldom confine themselves to one township, an officer must be brought on staff to oversee and coordinate the effort. As well, on the principle that a politician's duty is to dance with the suitor who brought him to the ball, Grisse proposed that a militiaman be appointed to the position and that he should report, *naturlich,* to himself.

As a militiaman and a war veteran, as well as having contributed to Grisse's campaign, Shadduck suited the position as though it had been tailored to his measurements. And for the first few months the appointment seemed inspired, as Shadduck buckled into his new task with an energy and competence seldom seen in municipal politics.

Early on, however, Councilman Grisse sensed trouble. With the ink hardly dry on his covenant with Philadelphia County, already the inspector had begun to burrow his way into the structure of government, on his own. Then came the announcement that Shadduck was to advise Commissioner Clark, whose respect for military men was out of all proportion. Grisse was not consulted on this, and was not made party to whatever passed between them. Then came another unpleasant surprise, when Mayor Swift announced the forming of new riot control measures under Inspector Shadduck—again, with no consulting of himself, Wendel Grisse, the councilman who fought and won the last election on the issue of law and order!

The commissioner later paid for his snub when a scandal erupted in the press involving brothels, and that fixed his flint for sure. Yet Shadduck could not so easily be brought to heel, having no scandals outstanding and, to Grisse's discomfiture, having contributed to the mayor's campaign as well as his own.

It was by now clear that Grisse's patronage appointee meant to ignore the normal duties of fealty and obedience, and had set off on his own. To the councilman it was a vicious stabbing in the back; worst of all, to retain any credit as the law-and-order representative, Grisse was in the excruciating position of having to appear supportive!

Still, the two remained on outwardly friendly terms. Grisse prided himself on his ability to keep things always friendly, even with treachery afoot.

But the danger the inspector presented was not over. This past August, Shadduck took another step on the road to—what? What was he after? This is what haunted Grisse while lying awake at night in the absence of sleeping . . .

In quelling a riot in Moyamensing, Shadduck saw fit to deputize the Bleeders, a gang from Schuylkill, to pacify the mob—which they did in short order. In fact, it was said that several members so took to the work that they became coppers themselves. Imagine—wrongdoers in the police force! And for this Shadduck received commendation in the *Public Ledger*!

But most unsettling was his collection of informants from the lower classes. The inspector had cited their use in the city of Boston, cleverly omitting to mention that informants were paid money for their information. (Grisse and the rest of council had assumed that they had it beaten out of them.)

Unknown to council (willfully so in most cases), law enforcers had previously been paying informants out of their own pockets; however, by bringing the use of informants into the open, as part of the business of riot control, such payments now came under the city budget. Imagine, were it known that the city paid spies to tattle on its citizens! For sure there would be no incumbent Grisse this time next year, were such a thing made public.

Nor did council anticipate the alarming powers it gave the inspector himself, to have informants at his beck and call. How many informants did he keep? Nobody knew. What information did he possess, and about whom? Nobody knew.

It was known for sure that Shadduck kept files in military fashion. Where did he keep them? Did a file exist on Wendel Grisse? Could something be brought forward to ruin him, should he make trouble for Shadduck?

In his own self-defense, Grisse had had no choice but to secure informants of his own—paid from his own purse—and worse shame, they found nothing. Shadduck had no gambling habits, consorted with no loose women, kept the schedule of a train, and drank nothing stronger than beer.

When the position of inspector was first created, his purpose was to restore law and order. This was taken to mean bringing the Irish and the Negroes under control. However, though the Topham murder involved neither Irish nor Negroes, the inspector had taken charge by default—there being no other officer whose job it was to inspect anything. Now his inquiries had taken him into areas of Philadelphia life that were never intended to be any of his business.

Having brought the Negroes and Irish under a semblance of control, in Grisse's view, Shadduck's proper course was to stand steadfast and to ensure order, so that Philadelphia might return to its former glory as the model of American civilization, the most orderly city in the republic, with the finest water system in the world.

The councilman could foresee a day when the inspector's prying eye would turn on respectable white people. For the first time it occurred to him that riots might not be the beginning and end of criminal activity, that other wrongdoing might be afoot; and that he might not want to know.

COUNCILMAN GRISSE LOOKED down at the report on the table in front of him, written in the most atrocious hand imaginable, illegible to any civilized man—let alone one like himself, for whom English was his second language. Besides, in normal society, gentlemen communicated by speaking, and then they shook hands; they did not submit a "report."

What did Shadduck intend to do with this report? Did he plan to table it before the council? Was it a trap of some kind—was Shadduck making a paper noose for Wendel Grisse's neck?

The inspector sat across the desk from Grisse in an expectant position, head forward, rangy arms draped over his knees, raw wrists protruding from the sleeves of his absurd uniform, the picture of earnest sincerity, and it occurred to Grisse that he was expected to make a comment on what he had read.

Accordingly, the councilman formed a benign, thoughtful expression, stroking Shadduck's "report" as though it were a cat. "It is interesting thing, this, sure." Grisse said. "A shocking thing, no doubt. But, Inspector, I do not understand the writing."

Shadduck tried not to show his displeasure, for Constable Smit's writing was perfectly clear to him. Unlike the politician, who lives by word of mouth, the better part of an army officer's life was spent reading orders and requisitions, put on paper by semi-illiterate aides. And the councilman had had the report in his hands for more than a week!

"Would it be the truth that you have not read the document, sir?"

"I have the jist of it," replied Grisse, unnerved by the inspector's tone. "*Also*, before taking this further I would wish to hear your thinking on the case."

An officer who doesn't read his reports. Swallowing his exasperation, Shadduck cleared his throat, fidgeted with his hat, and undertook an explanation: "It comprehends—I mean that it *concerns* the Henry Topham murder, sir."

"I can comprehend this, Inspector. I am not a dolt."

"I mean to say, sir, that it concerns Mr. Topham's business interests."

"He was a dealer in forged artwork and documents; you have made this accusation before."

"I suspicion that Mr. Topham was the biggest toad in the puddle, sir. With the publishing business as cover, he was, when you get to the quick of it, a forger."

This was most alarming to Grisse. Like everyone in the commonwealth he retained memories of the last such crisis, when the Bank of the United States went down in an ocean of bad paper. "What things were forged? Bank drafts? Stock certificates?"

"Could be all of that and more, sir. But in connection with the murder I have uncovered an unsavory side to the publishing business itself."

"Indecency, do you think?" Grisse's lips pursed together; with his elbows on the table before him, he reminded Shadduck of a praying mantis. "If that is so, the indecency must be stopped at once."

"I mean piracy, sir."

"Stealing books, do you mean to say?"

"Stealing writers, more like."

"Somebody is kidnapping a writer? That is absurd."

"Our nation has no treaty with England, sir, as you know. It seems British authors published here needn't be paid. As far as I reckon, the race to pirate British books is the mainstay of the American book trade. Agents are planted in London publishing houses. Manuscripts and galley proofs are stolen and shipped to Philadelphia. Topham was not a publisher, sir. He was a thief."

"With no laws broken, I think that is not a thief but a good businessman."

"The American writers are not happy about it, sir. In order to compete, they must write their books for nothing."

"It is the free market, sure, and we do not decide what Philadelphia reads."

"I am suggesting a possible push to murder him, sir. And with powerful savagery."

The councilman did not like this feeling of being led, one methodical step at a time, to a location not of his choosing. "Very well, you must be arresting all authors to be questioned on this matter."

"That is an expensive proposition, sir, but I thank you kindly for your support."

"Begging your pardons, Inspector, what is it that I am supporting?"

"The investigation into Mr. Topham's murder, sir."

"I see. *Ja, naturlich,*" replied Grisse, confused, thinking, *If only it was the Irish to blame.* "I am hoping you are giving no credit to the speculations of the newspapers. All this haunting talk and the horror tales coming to life and the ghosts and some such."

"No, sir. We will look into natural explanations first off."

"It is unwholesome, this talk. It is morbid and not Christian, and must be stopped."

"Best we disprove it then, sir. I have made a request to the Baltimore constabulary. We'll produce Mr. Poe in his coffin if we have to."

"Wery good, Inspector. I am most impressed. Continue please with your . . . reports."

Shadduck nodded, stood, saluted smartly, and exited the room, leaving the councilman in a state of profound agitation. It appears that when a city creates a police force, wheels are set in motion. One thing can lead to another, with unpredictable results.

The threat was not Shadduck the man but the change he represented. A voice within told Grisse that Philadelphia would never again become the city he once thought it was, or wanted it to be.

CHAPTER TWENTY-TWO

Philadelphia

Let us dine Boz, let us feed Boz,
But do not let us lick his dish
after he has eaten out of it.
          —*The Philadelphia Inquirer*

For a moment, Dickens forgot that he was on a train.

Certainly he knew it was a train when he boarded. Since then, however, it had become not a train but a cocoon, stuffed with indeterminate shapes cloaked in damp serge and worsted. It was the same cocoon that had prevented him from seeing the magnificent vestibule of his hotel in New York, or the spectacle of Broadway itself, or the architecture of the railway station. Once again this same moving, sweating, muttering human wall surrounded his seat, spitting tobacco juice on the floor, scribbling in shorthand, and eyeing his every move.

The journey from New York to Philadelphia required a train and two ferries, and would take between five and six hours. Already he was feeling fidgety and trapped. He looked down at his hands as though they belonged to someone else. Dispassionately he watched them pluck at one another, as though bent on parting skin and bone. *Whoever owns those hands should see a doctor . . .*

Dickens would have given anything for a good English cigarette. Yet there were none to be obtained in the colonies other than by rolling it oneself. Dickens had made several attempts to do so, but his nervous fingers were not up to the task, and the twisted result resembled a woman's curling papers. Lacking his preferred smoke, he had resorted to cigars. They made his tongue sore, but at least he knew which end to put in his mouth.

Now he felt a sore throat coming on, which worried him. Was it the cigars, or the onset of a cold? Tobacco was the lesser evil by far. Smoking would not cause death, but with colds you never knew. It would be ironic if his trip to America killed him. A high price to pay for a few weeks' respite from one's life and one's wife.

"Oh, Mr. Putnam, would you be good enough to find me a glass of water?"

After replying in an incoherent drawl, his American assistant muscled his way through the crowd to comply. Dickens watched his retreating back, with a sigh: thus far, only the man's style of ties and waistcoats appealed to him. He was not even certain where the man came from, or how he came to be his assistant. "An official appointment," was the only explanation.

As Dickens drank his water, through the heel of his glass he thought he could see the eye of a reporter, peering down his throat.

It had been a miserable Atlantic crossing, in a shuddering, smoking hulk of a steamer. For the first five days Dickens lay seasick in his tiny, suffocating cabin, on a bed like a flattened muffin, with pillows like slices of bread. No sooner did he find his sea legs than a terrific storm pulverized the vessel. For three days the *Britannia* lurched and throbbed and shivered its way through waves the size of warehouses while her passengers lay in their cabins, huddled in the fetal position with sickness, distracted by terror—not of drowning but of burning to death.

The *Britannia* had barely reached Boston Harbor when the first reporters clamored aboard to shake his hand, pester him with questions, and scrutinize his appearance—though not to assist with his luggage. His new friends accompanied him on the packet ship to the dock, where more gentlemen awaited him, reaching out to shake his hand, fingers grasping for him like the antennae of sea creatures. A circular wall of overcoats then surrounded him, hustled him forward, and stuffed him into a waiting brougham.

On the way to his hotel, having summoned the courage to peer out the carriage window, he could see nothing but other hacks, their windows open, with heads sticking out and fingers pointing at him all the way.

Inside the hotel another swarm awaited, filling the vestibule and the lobby to capacity and wound to such a pitch of excitement that the manager had found it necessary to station two stout porters to block the grand staircase, hands joined. Otherwise, the crowd would have chased Dickens all the way to his bedroom to watch him change his clothes.

As he escaped up the stair, someone called out: *Mr. Dickens, would you be kind enough to walk entirely around the room so that we can all have a real good look at you?*

"If you don't mind, I shall have a good look at myself first," he replied. "I could be an impostor, you know."

Through every waking hour since his arrival (other than in the bath or water closet, thank heaven), Dickens had not had five minutes to himself. Every move he made, every breath he took occurred in the company of vigilant gentlemen with notebooks, who spelled each other off like firemen. Over time he noticed that a sort of daisy chain took place, with one gentleman introducing the author to another—who, at the end of his shift, handed him off to another, and so on throughout the day. Even his nights were not necessarily his own. At one point, hours after he had retired, a group of singers, inspired by one or another of his books, stood in the hall outside his door and serenaded the boots he had left out for cleaning.

On the other hand, he might have dreamed this last episode: seeing and dreaming tended to merge when the two worlds were equally fantastic.

From what he had managed to see of Boston and New York by peering between a pair of shoulders, or from a carriage, or the window of his room, urban America possessed a disconcerting brightness, a brittle unreality, a shimmer—in the way that things look when one has taken too much of a stimulant. As well, everything seemed to be in motion; even the buildings had an agitated quality, as though worried that they could at any moment be torn down and replaced by something bigger and better.

Not that Dickens had had a moment for reflection during the public dinners, receptions, balls, assemblies, and dignitaries without end, with always at least three reporters scratching his elbow. It was a level of scrutiny he had not experienced since his birth. At first, the fuss over him pleasurably inflated his self-regard; but it was not long before he realized, to his puzzlement and hurt, that to be famous is not the same as to be admired, or even liked.

Each morning, after a night of rapturous embraces, songs in his honor, and eloquent tributes to his genius, Dickens would pick up the morning newspaper, and would scarcely recognize the brute who went under his name. *Rather thick set and surprisingly short; wears entirely too much jewelry; very English in appearance, and not the best English . . .*

As an Englishman, this sort of comment struck him as distressingly physical and personal, this almost medical interest in his "jug-like ears," his "dissipated mouth," his "surprisingly dark complexion," his "stubby, simian fingers." Nor, despite their own tendency to slovenliness, did his critics lack an eye for fashion. *His whole appearance is foppish and partakes of the flash order,* went one scribe, which sounded scarcely simian to Dickens. Indeed, these reports so lacked consistency that he wondered if he might have a doppelgänger in the city, a thoroughly unpleasant double, set on ruining his reputation.

When he absentmindedly combed his hair at a dinner table because it was in his eyes, the discussion required eight column inches in the *Daily Advertiser.* During an informal debate on female beauty, when he referred in jest to a lady's "kissability," he was upbraided for coarseness in every lady's publication in Hartford, and was the object of cautionary sermons next Sunday on the deadly sin of lust.

Although American journalists viewed him with skepticism (though not yet with that unfriendly feeling that would later become so violent and even malignant), their sense of critical distance did not inhibit them from presenting their manuscripts—to be read, assessed, and returned, together with any alterations he thought proper, preferably by next morning, at which time they would discuss its publication in England.

And the letters. Bales of them, wrapped in twine, awaiting his attention at every stop. One gentleman from Cincinnati requested that he write an original epitaph for the tombstone of an infant. A Southern gentleman thought Dickens might provide him with an autographed copy of a poem by someone named Leo Hunter, to an expiring frog. A woman from New Jersey wrote that many funny things had happened to her family, and many tragic events also, and that she had all the records for a hundred years past, which Mr. Dickens was to arrange and rewrite and send her half the profits. An elderly lady from Pittsburgh urged him to write an exposé of Mormonism (about which he knew nothing), and to lecture on its evils worldwide.

At other times it seemed as though he had been admitted to a national orgy of self-flagellation over the inferiority of American culture, as though they expected a literary messiah to rescue them from their miserable state and lift them to the heavens. How disappointed they must have felt that he did not float above the ground!

And always the same question nagged: If the Americans found his appearance and manners such a disappointment, why were they so eager to take a look at him? Was he unusually ugly, like a sideshow exhibit? Or was he to be seen for no other reason than that others had seen him? Did celebrity in America engender itself, build upon its own substance like a fungus?

In New York, he was met at the station and given a golden key by a stout gentleman claiming to be the mayor, whose assistant immediately took it back again. He was then surrounded, hustled out of the building, and deposited in an open carriage. Seated in this vehicle he was paraded down Broadway in a procession that resembled the funeral of a royal, excepting that the corpse was expected to wave. Citizens roared on either side, many of whom could not have read *any* book, let alone his book.

Following a pause barely long enough for him to change his clothes and empty his bladder, Dickens was fetched from his hotel on Broadway and frog-marched to the first of several "Boz Balls." This was a genial gathering of three thousand celebrants, for whom the Park Theater had been turned into a ballroom, its walls covered with white muslin and adorned with huge medallions, each representing one of his novels. The stage itself was made to represent a Gothic setting, on which a singer performed appropriate English songs, while a seemingly unending series of *tableaux vivants* represented scenes from his works. Most imposing of all was the portrait of Dickens himself over the proscenium arch, jug ears and all, with a laurel crown hovering above in the grip of an eagle. It was not clear to him whether the eagle was in the act of presenting the laurel, making off with it, or dropping it on his head.

This morning he was awakened, stuffed with breakfast, and put on the train for Philadelphia. The train consisted of three cars: the ladies' car, the gentlemen's car, and a car for Negroes—the last painted black. Every second window was open, and from each a spray of spit emanated like down from a burst feather pillow.

Once seated, he had turned away from the watch chains of the men in the aisle only to face another wall—of faces in the window, noses flattened against the glass like children at the sweet shop.

At last the train seemed to be pulling out of the station. Wheels clanked and rattled beneath him and the car lurched forward, while the engine in front screamed like a dying horse, lashed and tortured in its last agony.

"Mr. Putnam, do you have a lucifer?" he called to his American assistant in the opposite seat.

"A what, sir?" Putnam noted the unlit cigar, leaned forward, and obliged. "Round here we call it a match."

"A match for what?"

"I dunno. For a cigar, maybe."

"Have you ever been in England?' asked Dickens.

"In print I have sir, like most Americans," said Putnam. "But not otherwise. We are a reading people here, sir."

Dickens had never encountered anyone quite like Putnam: a strapping, square-jawed young man with a Frenchman's taste in neckties— soft bow, soft collar—that gave him the look of a foppish boxer.

Though impressed by the egalitarian spirit behind the open train carriage, it caused Dickens not for the first time to wonder at the American love of chewing tobacco, and their disregard for the spittoon. Even now the gentleman in the seat behind Putnam was busily employed in cutting a plug from his cake of tobacco, whistling softly to himself—another favorite pastime of this cheerful, resourceful people. When he had shaped it to his liking, he took his old plug out of his mouth and deposited it on the back of the seat in front of him, while he thrust the new wad into the hollow of his cheek, where it rested like a large walnut or a small pippin. Finding everything satisfactory, he stuck the point of his knife into the old plug and held it up for Dickens's inspection, remarking with the air of a man who had not struggled in vain that it was *used up considerable*. Then he tossed it out the window, put his knife into one pocket and his tobacco into another, placed his elbow on the sill and his chin in his hand, and appeared to fall instantly asleep, still chewing regularly and spitting out the window, though unconscious.

Such vignettes of American life took place between encounters with gentlemen he did not know from Adam. For not the first time, he wondered: Does the spirit of liberty grant any man the freedom to bother any other? Are all men free to finger his coat, jab his ribs, ask him personal questions, and grow shirty if he fails to deliver a satisfactory reply?

For the writer of books, a normal day is spent for the most part in his own company, staring out the window, and engaging in a controlled sort of dream. To find oneself perpetually on display and on duty morning, noon, and night was neither natural nor wholesome, nor did it bring out the best part of his character. Well before the Hartford appearance, Dickens had already begun to feel chronically ill-used, cheated, outraged. It became his secret pleasure to identify the hypocrisy and cant of Americans—though he knew perfectly well that, were a score to be taken on cant, the English would beat them raw.

In public, Dickens began to speak openly of his views on poverty, slavery, and especially on copyrights—the three subjects his colleagues in London had specifically warned him against. Especially, he was to avoid the last, which would only cause bad feelings and make him appear pushy and mercenary.

As a matter of fact, whether or not they found Charles Dickens up to their standards, a significant number of Americans had read his books. The windows and stalls of bookshops groaned under the weight of his titles; tobacconists featured boxes of Little Nell Cigars and Pickwick Snuff; he had even seen pillows with his portrait embroidered on the surface, so that the owner had the honor of sitting on Charles Dickens's face.

And for all this he had not been paid one bloody red cent!

The injustice of it made his blood boil. He felt like a musician required to play concerts in return for a percentage of receipts—concerts for which the audience, however affluent, would never be required to pay. For a man who had worked in a blacking factory as a child to buy his father out of debtor's prison, it was a bitter pill to swallow, day after day.

After a long evening and several glasses of champagne at a public dinner in Hartford, he gave an impromptu speech on the forbidden topic. He reminded his audience how Walter Scott had died in penury at sixty-one, despite there being thousands of devoted readers across the ocean who would, given the opportunity, gladly have paid him a small fee. He reminded Americans that just because two nations had historic differences, it did not mean that their citizens must abandon a sense of fair play.

The applause he received was decidedly tepid, and the press the next day decidedly hostile.

You must drop that, Boz, cautioned the Morning Post, *or you will be dished. It smells of the shop rank.*

The shop rank! A common retailer! Splendid, how they managed to hone in on the circumstance of one's upbringing!

The theme of his humble origin was taken further in later editions—no longer presented as a badge of honor but as a bad smell. Suddenly it seemed as though he had come to America with no purpose but to wring an unearned profit out of hardworking Americans.

At a minimum, went the current line, Dickens had shown singular ingratitude for his warm acceptance in the Land of the Free. *Biting the Hand That Applauds Him* went the lead in one report. Over the following days, the words *dollar-hungry* magically welded itself to his name. Some writers went so far as to refer to him not as the author but as *the son of a haberdasher.* (Had they done proper research they could have taken it one step further, for in truth he was the son of a *failed* haberdasher.)

A résumé that had once endeared Dickens to democrats as a "self-made man" had entirely changed its significance, and had become a source of his discredit.

Most galling of all to a proud writer, in every account, every description, every reference to his person or work, the writing itself was ill-researched, ill-observed, ill-put, and unoriginal. Even in the weeklies, which gave a chap a few days to think about what he should write, the articles scanned like letters of blackmail, in which an anonymous criminal pastes strips of received text on the page, not to subject his own handwriting to scrutiny.

In England, it was scarcely unusual for one writer to insult another. At bottom, every writer is in competition with every other, living and dead, for a place in the memory of Man. Nonetheless, in London it was understood that if one writer were to disparage another, he owed it to his victim and the profession itself that the assassination be well put.

Most frustrating was the inability to mount a creditable response.

In England, Dickens would have cut his critics to shreds in a single letter to the *Times*. In America, where myriad publications littered the newsstands like leaves in fall, he would have had to devote his life to writing rebuttals.

Disapproval of his views on copyrights spread even to respected American authors—who had everything to gain themselves, for they would no longer be required to publish books for nothing in order to compete with the British. Nevertheless, despite having chanted his praises in speech and print, even Washington Irving and Oliver Holmes joined the malignant chorus. Suddenly his books, once thought guided by the hand of God, had been exposed as cheap swami tricks, done for a fast dollar.

How disillusioning, to feel the undertow of class hatred in this bright, noisy, extravagant democracy. How mortifying, to feel the dead hand of pedigree pulling one down, even here.

With this understanding, one sleepless night in New York, Dickens's fevered attention turned to slavery in America. The existence of the institution as a part of daily life became for Dickens like the hunchback in the room, whose deformity must never be mentioned; having no outlet for discussion, the deformity grew in the mind to a staggering size.

Only an idiot would suggest that England possessed an iota of moral superiority. Hypocrisy was Dickens's specialty; he had made a career exposing and mocking it. In the case of slavery, he was well aware how England's much vaunted crusade had destroyed colonial economies and served the interests of the East India Company.

His response to American slavery was not so much political as sensory—a revulsion at the physical atmosphere it produced. That one person could *own* another affected the subtext of human intercourse; it changed the air one breathed.

In America, the principle of ownership of human beings had become integral to trade, and as trade goes, so does the mind and heart. The institution became part of the human vernacular, as America became a society consisting of the owners, the owned, and citizens in-between—the majority, or what one might call the *somewhat* owned. A man's tailor was not quite as owned as his slave and his wife, but he was more owned than the man who ran his cattle.

In this atmosphere, Dickens had begun to suspect why Americans so resented him: having taken on the assumption that as they owned his books, they owned the author. Hence, what was for Dickens a visit to a foreign land was, to his American readers, a homecoming.

Having come home, Dickens's duty was to appear as his readers had pictured him in their minds, and to behave in the way that they thought an eminent author should behave. In introducing the copyrights issue, he had spurned their sense of ownership by denying that he had already been bought and paid for.

In his mind, Dickens was far from home; indeed, it had been the entire point of the journey from the beginning. Worry had always made him ill, and his latest bout of ill-health in London he attributed to worry over Catherine, who had become more despondent after each pregnancy. As a result, the house on Doughty Street had become more a hospital ward than a home. Life with his poor wife was no longer an occasion of happy excitement but a well of dismal foreboding, which aggravated his own morbid tendencies, his shortness of temper, and every other quality he disliked in himself.

Always prone to nervous exhaustion, shortly before embarking for America he had suffered a bilious attack and nervous prostration that put him in bed in that hospital of a house for three weeks.

Now he felt something else coming on—an illness of some kind. *Not a fever, surely.*

"Mr. Putnam," he shouted to his secretary in the opposite seat, for it was impossible to be heard otherwise. "I need to remain in seclusion for at least three days. I think I am getting a cold." Already he looked forward to recovering his thoughts, writing letters, finding himself again—no public dinners, no assemblies, no extended discussions about his taste in waistcoats.

His assistant shook his head slowly and certainly, as though Dickens had suggested that they jump off the moving train. "Sir, I reckon that will be a hard row to hoe," he said.

"I'm baffled by these ruralisms of yours. Do you mean that a man may not become sick in America?"

"No, sir," answered Putnam, with the accent on *sir*. "You are free to get as sick as you can get."

"Then why is it, as you term it, a difficult row to sow?"

"The actual saying goes . . ." Putnam started, then thought better of it. "Well, to start with, you have your artists waiting for you, sir."

"Artists? In the plural?"

"Two of them, seemingly. A Mr. Alexander, who plans to paint your portrait, and a Mr. Dexter, who will sculpt your bust."

"When in heaven did I agree to this madness?"

"It seems they wrote you in London, sir. And received a reply to the effect that you greatly looked forward to it."

"Damnation. I wanted the voyage so badly that I agreed to anything. What a fool I was, to commit to what I could not envisage."

"Everyone who comes to America does that, sir."

"I suppose. Or who joins a war."

"Or who heads out West. Did you know, sir, that *out W*est is a term sometimes used in place of *dead?*"

"You don't say! Extraordinary!" Dickens was surprised to discover that at some point in the previous exchange he had extracted his notebook and had written two hundred words.

The train lurched to a stop with such suddenness that he feared for his teeth. He was immediately lifted to his feet and propelled down the aisle and onto the platform, to behold many more pairs of boots and shoes, and the glow of a great many cigars, and the sound of spit slapping the ground. Eventually by slow degrees the steam from the engine cleared, and heads and shoulders emerged, and reacquainted themselves with the boots.

SEEN THROUGH THE window of the moving carriage, Philadelphia was a clean and handsome city, alarmingly regular, with not a crooked street in sight. Observing the posture and the manner of pedestrians who passed up and down the walkways on either side, Dickens thought he could feel the collar of his coat begin to stiffen, and wondered if he should buy a new hat, for lack of a wide, Quakery brim.

Dickens cleared his throat and noted that his cold, or fever, or whatever it was, had begun to ease. This came as a relief, for you never know with a cold—it might take you *out West*. He laughed to himself at the picture this put in his mind, and wrote it down in his notebook.

The Georgian entrance to the United States Hotel, as seemed to be the rule, positively teemed with expectant citizens. They poured from the front doors into the street on his arrival, obstructing traffic and slowing the carriage to a standstill. Dickens pulled down the window and put his head outside for a better view of the building opposite the hotel, a white marble replica of the Parthenon, magnificent and ghastly at the same time, for it seemed utterly bereft of life.

"Good heavens, Mr. Putnam, is that a tomb?"

"In a sense I guess that is so, sir. It was once the Bank of the United States—do you see the letters over the columns? I expect you know the sad tale."

"Ah yes, the Bank of the United States. I suppose one might call it the Tomb of Investment."

"That is a fair way to put it, sir. The Catacomb of Worldly Hopes, you might say . . ."

The two continued in this light vein, the author's pencil scratching away on his lap, until the carriage came to a halt, the door of their carriage swung open, and Dickens was plopped like a raisin into a pudding of humanity, and paddled along by outstretched palms.

Inside the hotel, Putnam appeared at the grand staircase to meet him. He had somehow found the time to go to his room and change into a purple vest and an even brighter cravat. As before, his athletic frame contradicted the effect, as did his serious, watchful expression.

"Mr. Dickens, sir, I am afeared that the garden I mentioned is rockier than previously guessed. Do you recollect your correspondence with a councilman by the name of Wendel Grisse?"

"Not a word of it."

"Claims he asked if it would be all right to invite a few friends. 'To shake hands with the great man' was the way he put it."

"Thanks to your description, Putnam, I remember it even less than I did before."

"Well, anyway, you agreed to it, sir. And Mr. Grisse seems to have a passel of friends. His entire district, as a matter of plain fact. He put a notice to that effect in the *Gazette*."

"He expects me to hold a levee? That is out of the question, and that is my last word on the subject."

"I will pass that on, sir," said Putnam, and disappeared behind a moving curtain of serge and tweed.

*   *   *

NEXT MORNING, NESTLED in blissful solitude, Dickens opened his eyes to the music of the doorbell. It pinged gently as though tapped with a spoon. Pleasant enough for the first five pings, but by the fifteenth it lost its charm.

His rooms in the United States Hotel were comfortable, even luxurious: a parlor, a bedroom, a bathroom, and a room for the serving maid, which would remain unoccupied by reason of decency. However, the position would be filled on a live-out basis, in fact he had asked to see a selection of applicants later that day.

Dickens put on his morning coat and leather slippers, stopped in the parlor to fetch a cigar, and swung open the front door, expecting Putnam, or tea, or possibly a rasher of bacon, looking forward to the new day, and some time to himself.

On the other side of the door he found neither Putnam nor tea nor bacon, but a harried-looking gentleman with a high, shiny yellow forehead that might have been polished with a dry cloth.

"Mr. Dickens, sir," announced the gentleman. "On behalf of the United States Hotel I bid you good morning and welcome."

"That is all very fine," Dickens replied, "but who are *you*?"

"I am the manager of the hotel. And I declare that it's been a spell since we received such a public man as your own self."

"So it would seem," said Dickens, who grew instantly tired despite his night's rest.

"Your public awaits, sir. Philadelphy is ready to pay their respects to you."

"Good heavens, man, did not my assistant make it clear that I did not wish to hold a levee?"

"Notwithstanding, I reckon you must," said the manager.

"*Must* is not a pleasant word, sir. I remind you that I am your guest, not your doorman."

"I am sorry that I can't fix the language, sir, but you must receive, there is no choice in it."

By now Putnam had appeared behind the manager, in his usual coat and a cravat of bottle-green silk. Dickens thought it better to admit them, lest a third figure appear with heaven knows what demand.

"I am sorry Mr. Dickens, sir," said Putnam, with the look of a man who had run up against a stone wall. "It was too late to publish a retraction in any form, and now the public has arrived. If you don't bite the bullet, you will be darned unpopular in Philadelphy."

"Not unpopular exactly," corrected the manager, studying his fingernails. "Our citizens aren't long of riling up, and the *Gazette* could flay you like a wild cat."

Dickens was about to become wroth, but thought better of it, for he was scheduled to appear before the public for several days and did not wish to be treated like a wild animal. "In heaven's name, let them come, then."

"Oh, they'll come all right," agreed the manager, as though it were a foregone conclusion, and opened the door.

Up the stairs and through the hall they poured like water until the room was clogged with humanity. Peering through the open door Dickens glimpsed a dismal perspective of more to come.

"You'd better take a seat," said Putnam, "while there is room for you."

One after another, dozen after dozen, score after score, up they came, all to shake hands with Dickens. And such varieties of hands: thick, bony, limp, rigid, damp, papery, coarse, and smooth. Such differences of temperature, such diversities of grasp. Still up, up, up they came, ever and anon, while the manager's voice could be heard above the crowd: "There's more below! there's more below!" Followed by the voice of Putnam: "Gentlemen, you that have been introduced to Mr. Dickens, will you now clear? Will you clear and make a little room for more?"

Indifferent to Putnam's cries, they did not clear at all, but stood where they were, bolt upright, staring. Just in front of him crouched two gentlemen from the *Gazette* who had come to write an article. They regarded their subject with heads tilted in opposite directions: if Dickens cleared his throat, it was noted by one; if he rubbed his nose, it was recorded by the other.

Behind him wandered other guests, whose interest lay in phrenology and physiology, observing him with watchful eyes and itching fingers. When he turned suddenly he saw that one of them had been examining the nape of his neck, and he thought he glimpsed a pair of calipers. At intervals another of them, more daring than the rest, would make a quick grasp at the back of his head, touch it, then vanish in the crowd.

And still he could hear Putnam's voice—now so muffled by the crush of humanity that he seemed to be calling from underneath a feather bed: "Gentlemen, you have been introduced to Mr. Dickens, *will* you clear? *Will you clear? . . .*"

Eventually they began to trickle away; but as soon as the way was clear, in glided a new parade of expensively dressed gentlemen, every one with an expensively dressed lady on each arm. At the end of the procession, in walked a triumphant individual, a Dutchman with a German accent who introduced himself as Councilman Grisse, the author of this travesty. The Dutchman offered Dickens neither a thank-you nor an apology, and addressed him with no more consideration than if he had been purchased, paid for, and set up purely for the delight of his friends.

Finally they glided away, still in pairs, for dinner—to which Dickens had not been invited. Seemingly, the Boz Balls have a way of evaporating when one is out of favor with the press.

There now remained only the stragglers: threadbare gentlemen with a ghostly aspect who, having attained admittance, didn't know how to get out again, and appreciated the warmth. Another one had wedged himself behind the door and stood there like a clock, long after everyone else had gone.

It was by now late afternoon, and beneath his morning coat Dickens was still in his sweat-soaked nightshirt and dressing gown—had it been a dream? If not, he now knew how a corpse must feel after the visitation.

Foolishly, he supposed that his day was over.

"Now you must see the maids," Putnam said—and, wouldn't you know, in came the maids.

HAVING HAD SLAVERY on his mind of late, the procession of maids depressed Dickens even more thoroughly than their predecessors had. In England, though he had spoken and written on the servant problem, in private he had not been overly disturbed by the topic. When not working, he preferred to worry about his health and prospects, and the state of his marriage, and the perpetual pang of anxious unhappiness that had dogged him since his youth.

It is a paradox of foreign travel that it provides occasion for examining oneself, in the emptiness between places and events, while one is doing nothing but simply going from one place to the other. A time for self-refreshment—that is, assuming that one is not surrounded by people remarking on one's every twitch . . .

In the applicants came, four of them—two Negresses, one Irish, and a Frenchwoman. The Irishwoman was chewing tobacco, whereas the Frenchwoman smoked a cigarette. When he had recovered from the shock of seeing a woman do such a thing in his parlor, it occurred to Dickens that the Frenchwoman was smoking quite a good-looking cigarette.

He returned to the task of evaluation. All four women came well recommended and equally presentable. Having been selected by the hotel manager, there was not the slightest possibility that he would receive less than excellent service, no matter whom he chose.

But it could not possibly be the Irishwoman, for that would do him no good, brooding about the Corn Laws and the famine and its aftermath, all over again. He had done the subject to death in print, had exhausted every ounce of moral rhetoric he possessed. Now he could muster up nothing but a banal, monotonous hatred for Lord Russell, beacon of laissez-faire, who saw a half-million starve rather than risk "a distortion of trade."

Now he observed the two Negresses, fine-looking girls with ebony skin and a heartbreaking shyness of manner, and it dawned on him that he could not look at them without the most hideous thoughts coming to mind. What would it be like to *buy* such a woman? Were he to do so, would he ever again approach Catherine, in one of her moods? Why would any man put up with a free woman, when he could *own* one? And in that moment of demeaning speculation, Dickens understood how the mere existence of slavery made an ogre of a man . . .

"*Excusez, monsieur.* You are staring at me for a long time."

"*Pardonez-moi, madame, mais il y a une bonne cigarette, là.*"

"*Merci,*" she replied. "*Voulez-vous une cigarette, monsieur?* I sell one to you for two cents."

"That would be most excellent," he replied, and she extracted a cigarette from the folds of her dress, and the transaction was made.

Dickens lit his cigarette, savored the rich, mild smoke in his mouth, and blew it out in the shape of an *O*. An excellent cigarette indeed! Tightly rolled, it was made of fresh, pure Virginia leaf. After going without for days, it surely made one of the most satisfying cigarettes he had ever tasted.

"*Où avez-vous obtenu ce cigarette, madame?*"

The Frenchwoman laughed at the question. He liked how she threw her head back when she laughed. "*Mais, monsieur,* I make them myself."

"Remarkable! You don't say! I am impressed!"

"It is for me a business, what they say, *on the side*. I learn it from *mon père*."

Miss Genoux, who went under the name Sister Genoux, was a mature but comely woman in her mid-thirties and a member of some sect or other. This latter circumstance did not alarm Dickens as it might have done at home. From what he had seen and read, half the Commonwealth of Pennsylvania belonged to some Communist experiment, whose members sought either a return to Eden or the Second Coming and a quick end to it all.

Astonishing, how this Utopian stream threaded its way through the country, from their Constitution to their institutions and so on, flowing downward like lava, even to their farming methods. Despite her Georgian architecture and her English books, America began as a rash Continental experiment, in many ways more so than the English, and the undercurrent remained.

Through Sister Genoux, perhaps Dickens might gain an insight into France, a country that was currently unavailable to him as a public person. And he had often thought of writing a book about the revolutions taking place in Europe, seemingly in every country but England. These thoughts proved useful in supporting his decision to hire Miss Genoux as his housekeeper; yet the truth was that he desired her cigarettes.

CHAPTER TWENTY-THREE

Philadelphia

It is not easy for a man to travel incognito after the age of thirty-five. The problem has nothing to do with the risk of discovery from the outside, but with the physical challenge of identifying oneself as someone else, of saying and writing a name other than one's own on a consistent basis. The instinct to do otherwise is almost animal: when asked his name, only by a supreme effort can a man avoid pronouncing the one he was given, however skillfully he might prevaricate in other ways. Though everyone speaks unfamiliar names on a daily basis, applying one to oneself requires an extraordinary amount of practice, not to sound like a complete fraud.

As the 4 A.M. steamer *Richmond* rattled and lurched its way up Chesapeake Bay to Baltimore, at Elmira Royster's urging I rehearsed my new cognomen—Henri Le Rennet—by introducing myself to strangers at every opportunity.

It being a French name, pronunciation added to my implausibility in the role. And to be sure I did not like the name, although I could well understand the need for it. It had been one of Eddie's several aliases when evading gambling debts, and might prove useful in contacting him through an advertisement in a Philadelphia newspaper.

To me, the fact that I now had Eddie's name seemed bitterly ironic. Elmira Royster and I could not step out of his shadow even for a moment. This knowledge enhanced my resentment over their "engagement," and my doubt as to whether the association between them had been quite as spotless as claimed.

Still, I did my best to pose as a gentleman whose history did not in the least resemble mine; on several occasions I caught myself imitating the little I knew about Frenchmen and how they behaved, and feeling like a complete fool.

Elmira Royster suffered no such qualms as Mrs. Le Rennet. To be someone other than herself, and French to boot, gave her an almost sensuous delight as she elongated her vowels and pursed her lips, swanning about the vessel with Monsieur. Le Rennet in tow—the latter mostly silent, in the hope of appearing unable to speak English.

The *Richmond* docked in Baltimore Harbor. We proceeded directly on foot to the Anchor Inn, I with a muffler covering the bottom part of my face, turning my head away from the steady traffic of carriages, gigs, drays, and an omnibus, any one of which might have contained a colleague or a former patient.

We chose the Anchor Inn because it sat closest to the docks, where recognition would be unlikely, for the clientele would be seamen and other transients from away.

The innkeeper greeted Mr. and Mrs. Le Rennet without misgiving—for if we were not the establishment's normal clientele, our age and style of dress in no way implied an immoral association. From the saloon we were led up three floors to a tiny room beneath a gable, furnished with a bed, a chair, a wardrobe, a table, and nothing more. The bathroom and lavatory were situated at the end of the hall one floor down. I later learned that the amenity served forty-six rooms. Standing with our two suitcases, Mr. and Mrs. Le Rennet completely filled the room so that the innkeeper was obliged to stand in the doorway, enjoying our upper-class discomfort with tiny, impish eyes.

"Do you have anything larger?" I asked.

"And with a couch?" added Mrs. Le Rennet.

"For that I recommends the Willard, ma'am," he replied and retreated downstairs, laughing at his little joke.

"I am sorry that it is not the Willard," I said.

"Oh, I don't mind a particle," she replied. "I am sorry you will have to sleep on the floor."

I SPENT A miserable night. Though Elmira Royster was most generous with the blankets, the floor was damnably hard, for I had little fat for cushioning, less so perhaps than ever before.

The next day I had become so lame that she relented. The result of this was that we slept the next night in the bed with two suitcases separating us, like a knife and fork in a drawer both in position and rigidity.

At the same time, she had no objection to occasional kissing, and there was never a doubt about our physical regard for one another. For this reason, and for the hand-holding, I put up with the Bible readings and the prayers on the train from Baltimore to Philadelphia. There is no limit to what a man will put up with, given desire and a shred of hope.

For any newcomer from the South on a walk down Chestnut Street, Philadelphia seemed almost impossibly flush and well fed, in fact even the hard up seemed comparatively healthy: the peddlers on the sidewalk (*Sleeve buttons, three for five cents!*), the cane men, toy men, toothpick men, the old woman squatted on the cold stone flags with her matches, pins, and tape, the young Negro mother, begging with coffee-colored twins on her lap; the omnibuses clanging down the street, the one-horse postal wagons crammed full of letter carriers in gray uniforms, not to mention the precise regularity of the streets—all combined to create the impression of a place where nature had truly been conquered and harnessed, and put to better use through the ingenuity of Man.

Elmira Royster had a different view. "There is something terrible going on beneath the surface of this place," she said, for no apparent reason at all.

"What on earth gives you that idea?"

"Experience, suh, and instinct. Anything this perfect has something to hide."

> MR. AND MRS. HENRI LE RENNET *wish to speak to* MR. RICHARD A. PERRY *on a matter of utmost urgency. Currently residing at the United States Hotel, Philadelphia.*

Located in a warehouse near the river, the offices of the *Philadelphia Morning News* consisted of a huge room with frosted windows along one side. One window had apparently been broken, then temporarily covered over with newsprint. A cloud of smoke shrouded all within so that one could see the occupants' legs with perfect clarity but little else. At the center of this cluttered, confusing space stood a huge worktable, at one end of which two women appeared to be drawing illustrations; behind them, at an upright table like an artist's easel, a compositor, in a smock that might once have been white, arranged small bits of metal in what looked to be a huge, segmented cigar box. At intervals, two husky young men came to fetch the full boxes and replace them with empty ones. Everyone worked or walked with a slight slouch, as though oppressed by the rhythmic clatter of the iron printing press in another part of the building, like an assembly of metal skeletons performing a jig, all the day long.

The remainder of the room—that which was not littered with stray paper, dropped pencils, and empty bottles—consisted of small wooden tables piled with paper, behind each of which burrowed a man, like a rodent taking shelter. Other men occupied chairs at varying distances from a battered potbellied stove, reading newspapers in a forward position, as though about to spring to action at any moment, with hats and coats on despite the stifling heat. Each consumed a form of tobacco, whether gnawed between the teeth or swelling one cheek like a squirrel. Beside each chair sat a spittoon.

At the reception counter, Mr. and Mrs. Le Rennet awaited service for an absurd amount of time, and no amount of bell ringing seemed to make a difference.

Eventually a lantern-jawed woman lumbered up to the counter, with an inky apron and a scowl that would wither a plant. "What?" she asked succinctly, her meaty hands splayed out on the counter's scarred surface, arms braced as though prepared for a stiff wind.

"My wife and I wish to place an advertisement in your newspaper," I said. "Perhaps we have come to the wrong place. Perhaps we should speak to the *Inquirer*."

"No you ain't," she replied, immune to any insult short of a blow to the head. "Give it here."

I produced the text, which I had labored over all night. Our lady of the flowers calculated the price for one week's notices, and the transaction was complete.

"There was just one other thing if you please, ma'am," said Elmira Royster, exaggerating her accent slightly. "We have always been so admiring of one of your correspondents."

"Which one?" asked the woman, startled by the thought that someone here might be worthy of admiration.

"I believe his name is Mr. Rufus Griswold."

"Land sakes, woman. Haven't you heard?" Her eyes widened, her voice lowered to a scandalized whisper, and she became almost girlish in her dismay. "Mr. Griswold is possessed by the devil. Mine own eyes have seen it."

"How terrible for you," replied Elmira Royster, with an encouraging frown.

"It turned out a blessing. For I have found the Lord since."

"God love you for it," replied Elmira Royster, taking her hand, "and may He welcome you into His arms on Judgment Day."

"Amen, Sister," and the two appeared about to embrace.

"Forgive my interruption," I said, fearing that the conversation had gone off-track. "Where did Mr. Griswold suffer his breakdown?"

"Here in this very office. Mr. Griswold were troubled, uncommon troubled, days before, mumbled to himself, stared at nothing much. Then he come in first thing one morning, hollering that the fiend chased him clear up Dock Street, then starts to bawl about something laying for him, wouldn't let him sleep, come at him from the mirror or the window, or just out of thin air. Then he took a fit, threw a chair right through the window over there, land sakes, it nearly fell on a gentleman walking by outside—well, if that ain't possessed, you tell me what is."

"I don't doubt you for a second," I asked. "But possessed by what?"

"Fellers here says it was Mr. Edgar Poe as died lately. They say he had a good reason. But I say it was the work of the devil."

"And where is Mr. Griswold now?"

"In the madhouse, has been ever since. Fellers here taking bets on when he gets out, but he never will. The man is possessed, I do believe it."

> **Ghost**, *n.* The outward and visible sign of an
> inward fear.
>
> —Ambrose Bierce

SITUATED ON EXPANSIVE grounds to the west of the city, the new Pennsylvania Hospital for the Insane had the well-groomed look of a university or government building. There were no bars in evidence; upon entering we encountered none of the racket I had come to expect in such a place—no calling for forgiveness, no wailing for one's mother.

"I am Dr. Chivers from Baltimore, and this is my assistant, Nurse Slatin. I believe we are expected."

The receiving nurse, a pleasant woman of middle age, the sort who won baking contests and participated in sewing bees, assured me that I was expected and welcome. "The superintendent regrets that he cannot conduct you personally, owing to his heavy schedule. He commends you to Dr. Rush, who is a resident. Shall I fetch him for you, Doctor?"

"Please do, nurse. We are most grateful to you."

I scarcely expected to meet Dr. Kirkbride on a few hours' notice. Nor did I wish to do so on this occasion, for the eminent Scotsman was a sharp Quaker and not easily fooled. In truth, I hoped for an intern, and as green as possible. It is the very devil to maintain a fiction with an experienced alienist, one accustomed to sensing the lie in the air.

As we awaited the arrival of our guide, Elmira Royster and I engaged in our accustomed gay banter.

"Why on earth did you call me Nurse Slatin? I declare, the name sounds obscene."

"Might I remind you, ma'am, that I am *somewhat* familiar with hospital procedure. Both names must correspond to the faculty roster in Baltimore."

"Were there no other nurses at your hospital? I should very much like to meet this Nurse Slatin. I think you are making a private joke at my expense."

To which I had nothing to reply, for indeed I was, and now felt ashamed of myself. Private jokes are a coward's revenge.

We wandered about the waiting area, glancing at the various figures coming and going, and to look at them I would not have known the attendants from the patients. Of course I speak visually; the conversation of the mad people was plenty mad enough.

Dr. Rush turned out to be a young, pie-faced gentleman from Maine, of Nordic extraction with a halo of fine blond hair, a premature bald spot, and an almost comically earnest dedication to Dr. Kirkbride's Moral Treatment.

"We house rich and poor folks together, to keep things fair. Purging, blood letting, and twirling are not practiced. We have no strait-waistcoats, fetters, or handcuffs—though we do require the tranquilizing chair from time to time when someone gets all het up."

I feigned interest, while my mind returned to the Hospital for Insane and Disordered Minds, where my mother had been subjected to all of the above, as well as generous doses of jalap, syrup of buckthorn, tartarised antimony, and ipecacuanha—all of which made the patient violently ill in various ways, according to the hypothesis of the week.

"What on earth is *twirling*?" asked Nurse Slatin, which should instantly have given us away were Dr. Rush capable of suspicion.

"Try to recall, nurse," I said, as though gently admonishing a colleague, "that in Maryland it is known as *whirling*. The patient is strapped to a platform and whirled at high speed to send blood to the brain."

"Of course," replied Elmira Royster. "I declare, you Northerners have some outlandish ideas."

"It was thought to stimulate the mind," added Dr. Rush, shaking his cottony little head to indicate his disapproval. "It was darned painful, and to no good effect."

"If the effect is the point of it, why do they continue to administer it?" asked my companion.

"Nurse Slatin, you just hit the nail on the head," replied Rush, instantly smitten.

A whitewashed hallway branched out at the end into a series of long galleries with wards in each one. Patients flocked about us, unrestrained. In a corner, a group seemed absorbed in a bilbo catcher, in which they took turns attempting to cup and balance the ball. Not entirely to my surprise, Elmira Royster joined them and took her turn, and was able to cup the ball on the second try, to general applause.

In between wards, a common area had been established, which resembled the reading room of a gentleman's club, with a fireplace, chairs, and tables, where inmates read, knitted, and played skittles and other games. Quite as a matter of course, we were introduced to Dr. Rush's wife and another lady, chatting with a throng of madwomen, both black and white. The two women were graceful and handsome, and it was not difficult to believe that their presence had a highly beneficial influence.

On one wall had been written an inscription: LOVE ONE ANOTHER, which seemed like very good advice to me.

Leaning her head against the chimney piece, and with a great assumption of dignity and refinement of manner, sat an elderly female, decked out in scraps of finery as though having looted a pawnshop. Her head was strewn with scraps of gauze and cotton so that it resembled a bird's nest. She was radiant with imaginary jewels, and wore a pair of gold-trimmed spectacles. As we approached, she gracefully dropped upon her lap a very old greasy newspaper, in which I dare say she had been reading an account of her presentation in court.

"This," said Dr. Rush, advancing to the fantastic figure with great politeness, "is the hostess of the mansion, sir. It is a large establishment as you see, and requires a great number of attendants. She lives, you observe, in the very first style. She is kind enough to receive my visits, and to permit my wife and family to reside here."

The madwoman bowed condescendingly, and my guide continued. "This gentleman is newly arrived from Baltimore, ma'am. Dr. Chivers, this here is the lady of the house."

"Does Lord Baltimore still flourish, sir?" She asked.

"He does indeed, ma'am," I replied.

"When you last saw him was he well?"

"Extremely well," I said. "I never saw him looking better."

The lady seemed delighted by this. After glancing at me for a moment as if to be sure that I was serious in my respectful air, she stood, stepped back a few paces, sidled forward again, made a sudden skip (at which I jumped back a step or two), and said: "I am an antediluvian, sir."

I said that I had suspected as much from the start.

As Dr. Rush gently eased me away, the lady and I exchanged the most dignified salutations, and our party continued on. The rest of the madwomen seemed to understand that it had all been a play-act, and were highly amused. One by one, Dr. Rush similarly made known to me the nature of their several kinds of insanity (each seemed aware of everyone's mistaken assumption but her own), and we left them in the same good humor.

"Dr. Kirkbride's method puts their own delusion plumb in front of them, in its most incongruous and ridiculous light. Gradually they see the humor in it, and when that happens I'll allow they are half cured."

"I have read of the method, and applied it myself only recently," I replied, reminded of Eddie Poe. In that case, however, had I refrained from Moral Treatment and taken a traditional approach, Eddie would be in the bughouse yet and I should not find myself in this desperate situation.

As for the wards themselves, instead of the usual long, cavernous space where patients mope, pine, shiver, and rattle about all day long, the wing was divided into tiny but separate rooms, each with its own window. Glancing in, one saw a plant or two upon the windowsill, or a small display of colored prints upon the walls, which were washed so white they made one blink.

Another wing housed the orphans of suicides and the children of the insane. The stairs were of Lilliputian measurement, fitted to their tiny strides, and furnished as though for a pauper's doll house.

However, though all of it inspired me greatly as a scientist, as a desperate felon my area of interest lay elsewhere.

"Has the institution kept an inventory as to the various disorders and their causes?" I asked.

"Indeed yes, and they are many and various. There are the injuries to the head, of course, and ill-health of most any kind (especially fever), and intemperance, and use of opium and quack medicine. Many folks go insane from loss of property, loss of friends, loss of employment, grief. In this state, religious excitement is a frequent contributor to mental disease, as are metaphysical shocks of various kinds."

"Ah yes," I put in, quickly. "In that latter category I suppose you would place Mr. Rufus Griswold, the writer."

"One of our more well-known patients, yes. A difficult case, as they frequently are in a forced admission, which tends to reinforce feelings of persecution."

"Because they are in fact being persecuted," Elmira Royster piped up.

"Precisely, ma'am. We doctors are his persecutors—as is anyone who would seek to change the habits of another."

"Is he charged with a crime?" I interrupted, for the conversation had the smell of philosophy.

"Causing a public disturbance is the charge. The report allows he made quite a spectacle of himself. Caused a passel of damage at the newspaper in which he is, or was, employed."

I turned to Elmira Royster: "An interesting case, would you not say so, Nurse Slatin?"

"Indeed, Doctor. I declare, Dr. Rush, that I should be ever so grateful for an opportunity to observe the patient."

I did not catch what passed between them, but instant agreement followed. "However," said Dr. Rush, "I must caution you folks that the patient is still delusional, though he appears perfectly normal in all respects."

"I believe that is the case with many men," replied Elmira Royster, and I wondered what she meant by that.

DR. RUSH KNOCKED politely, and after a considerable pause we were favored with a "come in, please" from within—uttered, or rather sung, in a reedy, preoccupied voice. Through the open door we were favored with a view of the occupant, dressed in black, stooped over a table, and writing with a quill—a virtual emblem of the poet at work; in fact I suspected it to be a pose for our benefit.

"Good afternoon, Dr. Rush," he said without looking up from his work. "It is good of you to come."

"Please forgive the distraction, Mr. Griswold. And how goes the writing, sir?"

"Painful and laborious as always, but we carry on." The patient had not yet looked up from his work.

"Dr. Chivers and Nurse Slatin, permit me to introduce you to the Reverend Rufus Griswold. Mr. Griswold, these folks have come from Baltimore to observe our work here. I trust that is agreeable to you."

After a pause, the patient set pen, ink, and foolscap at precise angles on the table's leather surface and rose to greet us. As Dr. Rush continued to explain our business to him, Elmira Royster silently drew my attention to the foolscap, on which a poem, or part of one, had been written and rewritten, its words and phrases scratched out and replaced until there scarcely remained a word visible. With difficulty I made out the following:

> *And peering through a lattice*
> *Of a humble cottage near,*
> *I see a face of beauty,*
> *Adown which glides a tear,*
> *A rose amid her tresses*
> *Tells that she would be gay,*
> *But a thought of some deep sorrow*
> *Drives every smile away.*

"It reads like Eddie on a bad day," whispered Elmira. "It does not scan—and what in heaven does *adown* mean?"

I did not attempt to reply, having no appetite for poetry, well written or not.

With remarkable care, Griswold had transformed his tiny room into a miniature library-study consisting of a couch, a writing desk, a chair, and a small Turkey carpet. Every vertical surface was filled with books, neatly stacked in improvised bookcases made of raw lumber from the asylum workshop.

The patient appeared to be perhaps thirty, slender, sharp-nosed, and pale, with hair of Romantic length and a parson's beard—the latter no doubt a relic of his years as a Baptist clergyman, suggesting that the transition from preacher to man of letters remained incomplete.

As we were led to expect, Griswold did not seem the least bit mad. He greeted us like a perfect gentleman, apologized for the size of the accommodations, and bade Elmira Royster to seat herself on the couch. Of course, hardly had she settled her skirt when Dr. Rush took up the space beside her with unseemly eagerness. I preferred to stand.

Seating himself at the desk, Griswold spoke of his days here at the institution as though it were a trip to a spa. Seemingly, the peace and quiet had done him no end of good. In fact, after years devoted to the selfless tasks of an editor, critic, and mentor to poets, he at last felt the creative sap coursing through his own veins, praise God, and had been writing almost nonstop ever since.

"I expect you would find me impertinent," said Elmira Royster, "if I were to ask for a short reading. I am evuh so fond of poetry, suh, and I hear so little, and if you were to favor us with a verse I should be so pleased." If her James River accent had become anymore pronounced, we could have hummed to it.

"It would be an honor I assure you, ma'am," replied Griswold. (It was clear that, deranged or no, the editor retained an eye for a well-turned ankle.) After a moment of reflection and throat clearing, he began to read aloud, in a high-pitched, ministerial drone.

> *She whom I see there weeping,*
> *Few save myself do know,-*
> *A flower in blooming blighted*
> *By blasts of keenest woe.*
> *She has a soul so gentle,*
> *That as a harp it seems,*
> *Which the light airs wake to music*
> *Like that we hear in dreams . . .*

As he read, Elmira Royster raised her handkerchief to her mouth as though moved, and I distinctly heard a suppressed snicker. At my silent urging she regained her poise, and after a pause at the end, made admirable use of her handkerchief, dabbing at one eye as though touched to the marrow.

"Such skillful alliteration, suh! 'Blooming, blighted, and blasts'— do you not think it remarkable, Dr. Chivahs?"

"Indeed so, Nurse Slatin. I have never heard anything quite like it." In truth, I found it disconcerting to witness Elmira Royster dissemble with the skill of accustomed practice, indicating a thespian bent she held in common with her fiancé.

However, as a practitioner of Moral Treatment, Dr. Rush was having none of it, and proceeded to enunciate his objections: "To me the verse did not read properly aloud, sir. In order for the speaker to make sense, the phrasing became most unnatural. And I do not see how anything can be 'blasted by woe'."

In an instant, Griswold fired at Rush a look of such undiluted venom that I should not have been surprised had he tried to plunge his pen into the doctor's eye.

"Remember, Mr. Griswold," Rush continued, not in the least discomfited by this outlay of malice. "You are under treatment for delusional behavior. As your doctor it is my duty to dispute you on errors of fact. If you have a rebuttal, please let us hear it."

The patient did not reply, but fell into a sulk and refused to look at anyone. "A typical manifestation of delusion, when confronted with reality," observed Dr. Rush. "First the rage, then the whimper."

"I do hope you will forgive me, suh, if I ask you a question," said Elmira Royster, coy as usual.

"By all means," replied Dr. Rush; with his fat face and cottony halo of hair, he could have been the sun itself.

"I wonder, was not the patient exhibiting the normal reaction of an artist to criticism—first rage, then a disappointment and sadness?"

"You intrigue me, ma'am. Please continue."

"You will think me a terrible fool, but is it suitable to apply Moral Treatment to a poet? If we did, I do rightly fear there would be no poetry at all."

Dr. Rush became thoughtful—though I doubt that there was much in it other than the desire to ingratiate himself further. "You make an excellent point, Nurse Slatin," he replied. "We must always take into account the divine madness behind music and art."

I resisted the urge to lash out at the both of them, for disseminating Eddie's pernicious cant.

"I thank you, nurse," said Griswold, who had emerged from his sulk and now affected a dignified air. "Your defense of the poet was most gracious, and profound."

"Indeed so," I said, eager to redirect the discussion, which Elmira had an unnerving way of diverting from its charted course. "And if such a distinction may be made in the case of the poet, perhaps it might also apply to the possessed."

This inspired the puzzled silence I had hoped for, and I forged on. "Perhaps we scientists have no business meddling with people who see goblins and ghosts. No matter how consistently one might expose a thing to be fraudulent or mistaken, one can never prove absolutely that it is not ever true."

"In the same way that science will never prove that our Lord did not rise from the dead," said Elmira Royster, entirely distorting the meaning of what I had just said.

"Amen," replied Griswold, and a bond was forged between them, and it occurred to me that, in steering this discussion, she possessed a better compass than I did.

The young doctor was by no means put out by any of this—on the contrary, he seemed to take extraordinary delight in each argument, however inane. "I declare that this is the most fascinating discussion I have undergone in months," he said. "I promise you that I shall take your points under advisement, and bring it up with Dr. Kirkbride at the earliest opportunity."

He produced a notebook, reseated himself on the couch, and began scribbling with great intensity, ceding the floor to me, which I had already ceded to Elmira Royster.

Rising from the couch, she leaned upon Griswold's desk so that her wrist and a part of her forearm stood approximately six inches from his nose. Certainly he could smell violet.

It is almost indecent, the ease with which a woman can induce a man to explain himself fully. Were I to attempt the same feat I might have cajoled the patient for hours, bullied him with my education, frightened him with his grim prognosis and their terrible cures; as a physician I might have emptied my entire arsenal, and accomplished less than the baring of a woman's wrist.

"Are you acquainted with Philadelphia, ma'am?" Griswold asked in muted tones, as though about to provide directions to his club.

"I am surely a stranger here," she replied. "A Southern lady new to the city."

"When you are settled in you will note that every street is laid out at right angles. As a native Vermonter and a man of artistic bent, I seek respite from the stultifying regularity that has been imposed upon the city by the founders. Being sensitive to ugliness in all its forms, I am frequently drawn to Dock Street as it winds its irregular course, like a country road, to a land of the imagination."

It is impossible to adequately portray the self-congratulatory unctuousness of the man. He reminded me of a clergyman who has taken up the selling of miracle cures.

"Every evening at eight o'clock," Griswold continued, "I have made it my practice to leave the office and take a stroll. Dock Street at night, free of the commercial bustle, with its wet cobblestones aglimmer in the intermittent gaslight, becomes a tonic for what I like to call the poetic sensibility."

"*Aglimmer?*" I asked, being unable to restrain myself.

"Aglow," he tersely replied, and returned his attention to Elmira Royster, who appeared, of course, utterly rapt.

"I confess that in such moments, alone in the city, I feel closest to what I like to call the poetic muse. It is a level of sensitivity very much to be striven for. But of course, once found, it must be expressed morally and responsibly, and true to our covenant with our Lord. In this I am sure you agree, ma'am."

To my horror, it seemed almost as though they were about to kiss.

"I could not possibly agree more," she whispered, her vowels like honey on a stick. "*And thou shalt love the Lord thy God with all thy heart, and with all thy soul, and with all thy mind, and with all thy strength.*'"

At this, Griswold's excitement reached such a pitch that he nearly sprang from his chair. "The first commandment! How could I have missed it?"

"*They on the rock are they, which, when they hear, receive the word with joy . . .*'"

"Don't tell me . . . I have it—Luke! Luke . . ." Unable to name chapter and verse, Griswold literally blushed.

"Chapter eight, verse thirteen," she replied, and smiled down at him as though it was their shared secret.

I confess I could barely listen to this pompous, sanctimonious banter. "Is that why you so disapproved of Edgar Poe?" I asked, with no good objective in mind.

"Of course," snapped Griswold. "He did not glorify the Lord. He directed the reader's attention to ungodly thoughts, and a morbid cast of mind."

"Because of your dislike for him, did you hound him with a newspaper clipping and a bag of teeth?"

Griswold turned to Dr. Rush: "Is this gentleman a fellow patient?"

Before Dr. Rush could summon a response, Elmira Royster intervened. "I do agree completely, Mr. Griswold," she said, while her eyes sent me an unmistakable message: *Shut up.*

A period of sulking on Griswold's part followed; she smoothed his hackled fur until he deigned to continue.

"It was in that poetic state of mind, attuned with the poetic muse, that I became immersed in the gathering night, the stars above in their ancient transcendence. By some instinct I turned—and there was a gentleman on the walkway some distance behind. I could discern neither his face nor form; I could not even tell whether he was moving or standing still. He was an outline against the sky, framed by the warehouse at the curve of the street.

"Even at that distance, I knew that he was looking at me. And against all reason, I knew exactly who he was.

"I turned away with a shudder and quickened my pace forward. When I felt I had covered sufficient distance I turned around again—

"The figure had decreased the distance between us by half!

"My unease surrendered to panic as I broke into a dead run, glancing behind me at intervals, at the trim figure in the frock coat, whose face I could discern more clearly each time he passed under a lamp, and who was gaining on me with every step.

"I stopped, exhausted. I cried out, bent forward, hearing no sound but my lungs crying out for air.

"With the fatalism of a man caught in a guillotine, I turned my head—and he was gone. May the Lord be praised!"

"Amen," echoed Elmira Royster.

"Or so I thought at the time. I continued on my stroll, though no longer attuned to the poetic sensibility, until I reached the corner of Spruce Street, where a passing omnibus caught my eye—and I swear to Almighty Christ that in one window was the face of Edgar Poe! Oh, Ludwig! What have you done?"

"*Ludwig?*" I asked involuntarily, completely thrown, while Elmira Royster nodded slowly to herself, as though a suspicion had been confirmed.

"I will never be rid of him, thanks to you!" cried Griswold, and abruptly fell into a fit.

Already Dr. Rush was calling for assistance as the patient writhed on the floor, his mouth literally foaming, while his limbs twitched in the way of an insect on its back. A leather restraint was placed between his teeth, but before it could be tightened, Griswold managed to croak out the name *Ludwig* once more.

"Has this happened with him before?" I asked Dr. Rush.

"More than once," replied the resident, with a sigh of gentle perseverance. "Ludwig appears to him as sort of demon."

"I do believe I know why," said Elmira Royster.

"Do tell, ma'am," replied Dr. Rush. "I am darned eager to hear what you have to say."

"Ludwig was the author of Eddie's beastly obituary. It made him nearly go mad to read it . . ."

Desperately I signaled Elmira Royster to proceed no further, and thank heaven she complied.

"Do you mean to say," asked Dr. Rush, retrieving his notebook and pencil, "that *Ludwig* is a pen name Mr. Griswold has used in the past?"

"It is indeed, suh," she replied. "If the patient is possessed, it is by a part of himself."

"I believe you have a study there," I said to Rush. *The Pseudonym as Doppelgänger.* It could justify a piece in the *Scientific American.*"

"By heaven, that is an excellent title," said the resident, writing it down, while Rufus Griswold twitched at his feet, leather straps pinning his arms to his ribs and a restraint in his mouth. In a moment, two orderlies placed him in a stretcher and carried him away for a rendezvous with the tranquilizing chair.

ELMIRA ROYSTER HAD insisted that we stay at the United States Hotel for two reasons, neither of which could I disagree with.

In the first place, accommodations at the United States included a small parlor and a couch. This was for the best, for I was beginning to become groggy from lack of sleep. It is not an easy thing to sleep beside a woman with no contact permitted. It is not only the avoidance that rankles, but the fact that, when on occasion inadvertent touches do occur, one lies for hours in a rigid, inflamed state, with sleep a laughable impossibility.

Her second reason for choosing our accommodation was that it would discourage Eddie from cutting shines. At the United States Hotel, the lobby and halls would be packed with bookworms and newspapermen, eyes peeled for the author Charles Dickens. With recognition a virtual certainty, Eddie would not attempt something clever or dramatic. He enjoyed a risk, but was not about to jump off a cliff.

The letter arrived with surprising promptness by the evening post, addressed to M. Henry Le Rennet, United States Hotel, Philadelphia, in Eddie's punctilious yet elegant hand. (At school he would practice his handwriting for hours at a stretch on the *F*'s and *S*'s alone.)

> Mr. Le Rennet,
>
> Must urgently meet with you alone at the Black Horse Saloon on McAfee Court, Moyamensing, at two in the afternoon. Commend me to Mrs. Le Rennet, with whom I shall speak at an early opportunity.
>
> Most truly yours,
> Mr. R. A. Perry

"I declare, that I am at a loss as to why he would wish me absent. We are, after all, engaged." This, in a tone not of outrage but curiosity.

Elmira Royster reclined fetchingly on the Empire recamier, where I had slept, or rather squirmed, the previous night—a mahogany piece by Quervelle, outrageously carved with rosettes and paw feet, on which a hunchback dwarf might get a good night's sleep.

"Doubtless he is concerned for your safety," I replied, though I doubted his concern for anyone but himself. "Moyamensing is a district not unlike the docks in Richmond. Women who venture onto its streets carry knives, if they go out at all."

"Perhaps I shall do missionary work there," she replied, a bit petulantly. "Surely there are souls to be saved in such places."

"As a Protestant, ma'am, missionary work would be an excellent way to have your throat slit in Moyamensing."

"Such gallantry," she said, exaggerating her vowels. "I hope the sight of my blood won't be too much for you."

"What I mean to say is that I shall be hard-pressed to look out for my own neck, let alone yours."

"I see that your priorities are clear, suh."

"Forgive me, please . . ." I said as I stepped up to that dreadful recamier, grasped her shoulders, and planted my mouth upon hers. For a moment it almost seemed as though her lips moved gently with mine, but the mind can play tricks.

"You need to be put in a cage," she said, swanning from my grasp. She entered the bedroom and closed the door, leaving me sitting on my ugly couch, staring out the window at the grand, hollow husk that was once the Bank of the United States.

CHESTNUT STREET TEEMED with traffic, every sort of truck, wagon, cart, and coach, grinding along. The cobbles had worn away at the edges, so that the hard wheels of the carriages bounced and lurched, creating an incessant rattle and din that would drive you mad.

Between the larger vehicles, two-wheeled delivery carts threaded their way along at reckless speed, obeying no rules, causing more broken legs than all other carriages combined. To me it seemed as though the sheer acceleration of life in Philadelphia necessitated myriad violent outcomes that would have been avoided at a slower pace.

Everywhere I looked, I saw evidence of an underlying inhumanity. On the corner of Sixth Street, I observed a policeman looking on benignly while a cart ran clear up onto the walkway, and nearly took a child beneath its wheels before the horrified eyes of its mother. This was none of the policeman's business; his main function being to settle disputes between drivers with the aid of his club. Meanwhile, in the intersection at Market Street a small company of wretched sweepers risked life and limb so that the combined excrement would not form an insurmountable barrier and stop traffic altogether.

No wonder Eddie resorted to the bizarre; what excitement can mere fiction add to such an environment?

Despite my unfamiliarity with the city, I had no difficulty in locating the omnibus to Moyamensing. Once underway, the wheels rumbling beneath our feet, I was surprised by the prevailing silence among the passengers, who scrupulously avoided each other's gaze, each one seeming to fear the other, though there were no Negroes in evidence.

Looking back, I see that I had stumbled upon one of the many differences between the North and the South: in the South, the assumed menace was a member of the black race; in the North, it was any stranger at all.

Moyamensing had once been a separate township with its own central square. Then, Philadelphia began expanding like floodwater, blurring boundaries between constituencies, then absorbing them entirely; meanwhile the exponential growth in population entailed constant destruction, construction, and renovation. As a result, signs of Moyamensing's once independent character had all but disappeared. Homes had been long ago divided into apartments, then subdivided into rooms, while gardens gave way to shanties, enlarged as the need arose into tenements, constrained by no law other than brute necessity.

If Philadelphia seemed cold-blooded, to my eye this was a hellhole, and I felt the impulse to return to the United States Hotel—which I would have done well to follow.

Under a cloud of menace I circumnavigated the square: around the periphery, children picked through accumulations of garbage piled a foot or two high; while a Gothic procession of exhausted women, old and injured workers, and gaunt, dangerous young men shuffled along between piles of manure. A cart rumbled past, pulled by dray animals in appalling condition, splashing my trousers with filth. A mule with what looked like scabies, sipping from a crude trough in front of the saloon, looked up at me and made a sound like a steam whistle.

A pessimist by habit, I entertained little hope of persuading Eddie to behave like a friend. On the contrary, in our thirty-year acquaintance he had done so precisely once, the day he admitted me into the Butcher Cats—and for that he had extracted more than a pound of my soul.

And yet, a quarter of a century later, I still felt in his debt—because he treated me as a human being.

Fool!

I suppose I hoped to persuade him into breaking off his engagement with Elmira Royster. I suppose I based this hope on the tenuous assumption that, as a Virginian, he understood the position in to which he had forced her, and retained a shred of honor toward the weaker sex. Surely it was unacceptable that a woman should be held to an engagement with a dead man!

Unless Eddie did not intend to remain dead.

This terrible worm of a suspicion had been gnawing at the back of my mind for several days, and now it presented itself in all its degraded glory. What a fool I had been to take Eddie's stated intention at face value! To find out the truth? To prevent the taking of innocent lives? To, in effect, sacrifice his life for the good of another? Had I not (though I would forever deny it) read the same sentiments in his *Collected Tales?* Was the pattern not obvious—the hysteria, the sentimentality, the gore? Was it not clear that this was just another of Eddie's phantasms, brought to life?

Fool! In my misguided loyalty to a cad, I had made myself a criminal, while Eddie, who had initiated the whole ghastly mess, risked no penalty at all. In America, there is no law against disappearing. On the contrary, given the size of the country and the freedoms it claims, one is positively encouraged to do so.

It is often the way that two thoughts follow one upon the other with such rapidity that they constitute a pair. Thus, with the bitter realization of having been duped came the wickedly satisfying notion that Eddie might be induced to disappear—from the face of the earth. In short, I wished to murder him. This might seem excessive to some, yet it made a terrible sense, for in one decisive stroke I might thereby obtain Elmira Royster and my own happiness, and put an end to the tyranny of Eddie Poe.

Predictably, there remained the *how.* I was not so dedicated to causing Eddie's death that I would willingly pay for it with my own. On the contrary, for the first time in my memory, life did not present itself as a chore—if I could gaze at the face and form of Elmira Royster.

Immediately, a third realization took its place like a perfectly aimed dart—*you are a doctor.*

One could be killed by medical treatment, it happened more often than not. I had enough ammunition in my father's medical bag to dispatch half the population of Moyamensing. *Death due to natural causes*—Oh, happy phrase!

Yet the prospect was a dream, a phantasm. Eddie had not driven me to murder—not yet.

The Black Horse Saloon stood as the centerpiece of the square by comparison to its neighbors, which were poor constructions, their windows bandaged with mattress ticking, leaning precariously against one another like wounded men. Improbably narrow lanes spread like fingers off the square; down each passageway, lines of ragged wash dangled a few feet overhead for as far as the eye could see—a testament to the resourcefulness of womanhood, there being no running water.

On the saloon's covered veranda stood two boys not yet in their teens, with the pale, pinched faces of street urchins. Sporting top hats and duster coats, they leaned on rough walking sticks like miniature men about town, saying nothing, gazing in every direction but mine. I did not make anything of this, other than that the youth gangs of Philadelphia seemed unusually well turned out.

The far end of the saloon's interior consisted of a long bar backed by an enormous mirror, which had the effect of doubling the size of the establishment, and its supply of liquor as well. In front of the bar, an open area provided space for dancing and fighting. Around the open area, tables had been crammed back to the walls so close together that the shoulders of adjacent cardplayers actually touched; an excellent arrangement for fleecing the sailors who formed the bulk of the clientele—rootless and untraceable, with nothing to do until departure but make marks of themselves. (It occurred to me that the presence of sailors might explain the young men outside as well. However, I was wrong in this.)

Tobacco smoke poured from each table as though a series of small campfires had been lit. In the nonexistent space in between, four barmaids, aged between twelve and sixteen, wearing short dresses and boots with bells attached, threaded their way through the room with customers in constant, crude contact, a shabby imitation of the girls at the Atlantic Garden in New York.

By pressing my back against the wall I squirmed my way around the room to where Eddie sat, at a small corner table next to a rear exit, alone. I recognized him instantly, for he had scarcely bothered to disguise himself other than to lose weight and shave his mustache. Surprisingly, the latter adjustment altered his appearance substantially. Shaped like a black arrow, Poe's mustache had forced one's gaze upward to those enormous, ineffably sad eyes and the brooding forehead looming above—the picture of author gravitas. Sans mustache, however, the face assumed the perfectly normal proportions of a blandly handsome gentleman of military bearing, with a longish nose, a prominent chin, and a tight, almost prim mouth. He looked like the sort of man you occasionally meet at horse races and gentleman's clubs—the risk-taker who loses every wager and lives for a change of luck. Likewise, his clothing—the ancient beaver hat, carefully brushed and oiled, the threadbare yet blindingly white collar, the tattered neck cloth and mended gloves—suggested a gambler in extremis.

"Willie. I am so sorry. O God, it is horrible!" And he promptly began to weep. Not an unusual greeting from Eddie, in my experience.

"I should think you would be sorry. Do you know the danger you have put me in? Dear God in heaven, they are talking about digging you up!"

The tears subsided. Head in hand, theatrically disconsolate, he sighed and shook his head. "That is not what I meant."

"Of course not. Harming a friend never entered your mind, did it?"

"You do not understand my situation. I stand accused of an appalling crime. Now that I am dead they are painting me as a monster—don't you see? It is worse than ever. He has won!"

"Do you mean poor, haunted Griswold, whom you have driven barking mad?"

"Yes. Or rather, no. I did no such thing."

"You did not haunt Mr. Griswold?"

"Far from it. I went nowhere near him."

"Then what is your explanation for his present condition, the story that he tells?"

"He is haunted by himself. That is what happens to Baptists who do evil." Smiling at his private joke, Poe took a small sip from a water glass, three-quarters full of an amber liquid that may or may not have been tea. It seemed clear that the man was in an inebriated state.

"Willie, did you not see what he wrote about me? And under the name *Ludwig*—he couldn't have been more obvious, he has been using it for years. Especially when he wants to carve up a competitor, and duck the rebuttal. Talk about kicking a man when he is down. To commit such an atrocity against a dead man—and to hide beneath the name of *Ludwig*!" Overcome by the enormity of it, he paused to take a generous sip from his glass, then smiled to himself in self-congratulation, for it was a fine speech.

"Of course he assumed that no rebuttal was possible. However, being alive, I sent a letter to the editor, objecting to this libel of the dead, the sheer cowardice of it, and presented a few counterthrusts into the bargain. Under a pen name of my own, of course. I had to avenge my good name. Surely you can see that, as a West Point man."

"And that is what drove him mad?"

"Griswold has the wit of an ox. One thrust and he keels over."

"And that is just what you wanted, Eddie—was it not?"

The eyes, with their usual expression of melancholy intoxication, grew suspicious as well. "I do not know what you mean."

"You had no interest in preventing such horrors as that poor toothless woman. She was but a prop, in a sideshow, for my benefit. You used your death for no other purpose than to take revenge against the man who ruined your *Collected Tales*."

"I admit that your analysis contains a grain of truth. I was utterly ruined by him, you know. And yet the affair has gone beyond Griswold. It has taken on a life of its own, and with it a new ghastliness. Willie, there has been a savage murder. The murdered man was my publisher here in Philadelphia. Now I stand implicated in the press, though supposedly dead, and Griswold had nothing to do with any of it!"

"And how did you reach that magnanimous conclusion?"

"He was in the madhouse when the murder occurred."

"I see."

"No. You do not see. The story came to life, to the effect that my ghost committed the murder—a silly public legend, but the press caught hold of it in suitably sensational tones, and now it is regarded as proven fact. Do you see the horrible irony? If I were known to be alive I would immediately be charged with murder—and what could I say in my defense? Don't you see? I am condemned to death-in-life, buried alive, and even that is not the worst—for I am now a slave as well!" Again, Eddie indulged himself in a round of blubbering.

For my part, I could barely keep from executing a horizontal lunge for his throat. "Therefore, am I to understand that it was never your intention to remain dead? That you planned to emerge from hiding after taking your revenge, take a bow—and leave your old friend Dr. Chivers to suffer disgrace and imprisonment?"

"Far from it. I would claim to have been under a powerful drug. It is well known that people are buried alive regularly, due to medical error."

"Excellent. A medical error committed by me. And with my reputation already in tatters, how would I explain the cadaver that happened to be under your name?"

"I would say that it happened subsequent to my revival. An error on the part of the grave diggers."

"You, sir, are a liar. Now tell me how you came under suspicion for murder as well. I am interested, from a clinical viewpoint."

"Did you happen to read my tale entitled 'the Man Who Was Used Up'? It appeared in *Burton's* . . . Pardon me. I had forgotten that you do not read my work."

"I suppose you expect me to apologize." I ordered a glass of whiskey from one of the serving girls, in order to calm my nerves.

"The tale concerned a man who had in effect been dissected in battle. A satirical piece, but someone took it literally. And when Henry Topham, the publisher, was discovered in a dissected condition, the connection took on a life of its own."

"There is no underestimating the stupidity of some readers, I suppose."

"Especially when they are critics," he replied, and burst into tears once again.

I took another sip of my whiskey. "Eddie, I am concerned about your peace of mind," I lied, for nothing concerned me less at this point. "You are clearly in a state of nervous exhaustion. Not to mention the misery you are causing your fiancée, Mrs. Shelton. Would it not be better all around if you were to move elsewhere as Richard Perry, wipe the slate clean, and start afresh?"

"No doubt," he replied. "But, Willie, when I say that I am a slave I mean it in the most literal sense. I am the literary equivalent of a plantation Negro. Except that the work is more degrading, I swear to you, Willie . . ."

Suddenly Poe stopped speaking, as though someone had given the order.

"Ye'd best drink up, me old trout," said a voice behind me. The accent combined an Irish lilt with the flat tones of a northeaster—and there remained something military as well, the clipped consonants of command.

Eddie glanced longingly at his glass. "This was to be a private meeting, Lieutenant," he said. "We agreed to this."

"True for you, you're right there, but privacy is a relative thing is it not?"

I turned to look up at the man behind my chair, and beheld a military carriage for certain, and what looked to be an infantry tunic beneath his coat. As well, the man was not without troop support, for behind him stood the shavers I had encountered outside the saloon.

Like the shavers, he wore a duster coat over his tunic, and a top hat set at a precise angle, but of better quality and fit.

The face was handsome if low bred, but for one of the eyes—or the lack of it, for the socket gaped as empty as the skull on a bottle marked *Poison*.

"How do you do?" I said, unable to look away from the empty eye.

"And top of the morning to yerself, sor," replied the lieutenant, and his smile was anything but warm. The upper front teeth were missing, which made the canines appear more prominent than usual.

"Might I ask your business with us, sir?" I asked.

"Yes, you might," he replied, and ventured nothing further. I took my gaze from the empty socket to the other eye, and realized that it had been watching me closely, that the blind eye had been a kind of decoy.

When I turned to my companion for enlightenment, Eddie's expression suggested that I had been taunting a poisonous snake.

"Willie, please forgive me."

I began to experience nausea. "What have you done to me now, Eddie?"

"I told them I would convince you to go back to Baltimore, that you would say nothing, that it was unnecessary to take drastic action. Now I see that I have led you into a trap."

"Leading me into traps has become a lifetime hobby, hasn't it, Eddie?"

His eyes grew enormous in their appeal for sympathy, as another group of top-hatted shavers appeared behind his chair, led by a fellow with a prematurely aged face. "Yer want carryin' or will yer come with us on your own hook?"

"'Fore we tap yer yockers fer ya," offered one of the others, meaningfully raising a stick with a knob the size of a man's fist.

Poe rose to his feet with an expression of utter defeat. "I am truly sorry, Willie," he said.

"Sorry for what?" I asked, though not overanxious to hear the answer, as he disappeared out the nearby back entrance, followed by a column of former street Arabs who did not reach his shoulder.

"And now ye'll come with me, sor."

Obedient as a waiter, I accompanied the one-eyed gentleman to the front door, for there seemed no point in doing otherwise. As the crowd respectfully parted to allow us to pass through, it seemed obvious that I would scarcely find an ally in the building. Once outside, I might have had a slight chance of making my escape on foot. Or probably not.

"What do you want from me?" I asked as we stepped outside.

"The truth of it is, sor, I want you to disappear," he replied, and turned to face me. I did not argue. I was slightly taller, but he had the stick, and with notches down one side—for drawing blood? Breaking a head? For men killed?

"Ah, me old sweat, yer a military man if I am not mistaken?"

"Yes. I was a doctor at Veracruz."

"There it is. For that service I will leave yer with yer life and a warning."

"Believe me, sir, I consider myself amply warned already," I replied—humbly, obsequiously, like a condemned man to a magistrate about to reduce my punishment. *Coward!*

Below the veranda on which we stood, a group of the youngsters watched with interest. It seemed as though we were actors on a stage, playing a scene for their benefit. Then, as though at a signal, they began to tap their sticks on the cobbles—randomly, so as to make a sound like hailstones on a roof. Then, led by the scrawny shaver with a prematurely old face, they began to chant a word I did not recognize, that sounded like *huge him*, which made no sense to me whatsoever.

"If ye ever sees me again, ye'll not see me again," he said, and the empty eye tilted in my direction, and something darted toward me.

"Sir, I do not understand . . ." I began to say, when suddenly I was looking at the empty socket and the floor at once, and I realized that he had plucked out my left eye.

I heard a scream, which I think must have come from me,

drowned out by laughter below and the clatter of hail on a roof, and then another scream, which seemed to tear out of my throat as my hand clutched the wet round thing hanging from my left cheek like a peeled plum . . .

The fact that there was still vision meant that the muscles and optic nerve remained intact . . . *Think*, a voice hissed in my brain, *Use your brain, think.*

I had undergone a *traumatic globe luxation*, of that there could be no doubt.

Someone began shouting a vain plea for help while my mind scrambled for footing, like a cat about to fall off a roof. *A test. A test of the mind.* Experimentally, I closed my eyes; the eye continued to stare at the palm of my hand, which meant full *luxation*—the eye had been plucked far enough out of the socket for the eyelid to close behind it.

The pain. Do not faint. Think.

Someone continued shouting words I did not recognize as I rose to my feet (I was not aware of having fallen), one hand cupping that precious, fragile thing, held by threads of muscle and nerve, which would fall apart like a boiled onion should a sudden move of my hand break apart the *sclera* . . . *Think.*

No blood. Good. Momentarily I felt overcome by dizziness—shock, which is often attended by fainting . . . *This must not happen.*

As I burst into the saloon, no doubt making a most unusual noise, patrons looked up mildly, watched me for a brief moment, then returned to their cards. The barkeep, on the other hand, seemed to understand that something serious had occurred—to me, at least.

Whiskey! Whiskey and a looking glass! These improbable words issued from my mouth as I made my way to the bar. Before me the crowd parted as though I were mounted on a horse—the momentum of a screaming man with his eyeball in one hand.

The eye which remained where it belonged now beheld a young barmaid with improbably red lips, running up to the bar, boots jingling in a way that made me think of Christmas. In her hand she extended a small round looking glass, arm at full extension, not to venture too close to the grotesque thing that was me. Now the barkeep appeared before me with a bottle of whiskey. "That will be one dollar," he said most sympathetically, and would not release the bottle until I produced that amount with my free hand.

In my mind I pushed away the pain, the pain of no pain, of a knife that has sunk too deep . . . *Do not faint!*

For an uncertain amount of time I remained in a dark bubble, as though nothing in the world existed but me and my eye, as though I was *in* my eye. With the whiskey as an internal and external lubricant (even in my desperation I did not trust the local water), I handled the organ with the delicacy of a watchmaker, remembering the technique employed by eye surgeons I had assisted in the field—albeit removing eyes, not putting them back. Carefully I fed the tendrils of muscle and nerve back into the socket with one hand, while my other hand, with agonizing slowness, gently rolled back the precious globe of tissue like a snowball, pausing to allow the sclera to stretch to its fullest . . . Done. I completed the operation—or must have. Looking back, I do not remember it having been done by me.

Using my handkerchief as a pad and my cravat as a pressure bandage, I covered my eye, not knowing if it would ever see again. Worse, a perverse part of my mind feared that I had inadvertently replaced my eye backward, and that I must spend the rest of my life with one eye staring within.

Having only one eye, my ability to perceive distances had gone, yet I had no difficulty retracing my route back to the United States Hotel. In the crowded omnibus, none paid the slightest attention to the swath of fabric covering one side of my head. I expect it came as a relief to these Northerners—one less gaze to avoid.

Given the continued presence of its famous English guest, I had come to expect a throng of the curious in the lobby of my hotel, but what greeted me upon my arrival went far beyond precedent. Not only members of the press and public milled about, but the police as well. The gathering had a different quality than when I had left. A tense politeness predominated, and when they looked at me at all in my disheveled state, it was with the expression of people who had more important things to think about.

Everyone appeared to focus on the hotel staff, from the manager down, with questions I could not hear but whose answer entailed a shaking of the head. Near the reception desk a particularly tight group had convened around a tall, athletic, bespectacled gentleman in a French cravat, who seemed greatly exercised by something or other. No doubt the outspoken English author had committed yet another error of protocol; according to the press he had by now quite outworn his welcome with the American public for his presumptuous remarks on slavery, not to mention his mercenary, self-serving demand for royalty payments from American publishers of his books.

None of this was of interest to me, for my eye throbbed abominably from the abuse and its aftermath, and I was eager for a dram of morphine. As well, I looked forward to my reunion with Elmira Royster, to whom I planned to lie outrageously to the effect that Poe, as a man of honor, had released her from their absurd engagement.

Freed of him at last, at the cost of an eye, it was my hope that my misfortune would awaken her instinct to nurture and nurse. Given some affection for me and a broad interpretation of Scripture, we might spend our time as I had longed to do since we first met across a white linen tablecloth in the Exchange Hotel.

Fool!

There is a quality to an empty room, even if it is pitch black, that tells you upon opening the door that nobody is home. As a doctor, I had come to recognize the sensation from entering a room shortly after the patient has expired; so much so that the taking of the pulse became a formality. Now the familiar feeling of absence came over me, and as I turned up the lamp my hands trembled with dread of what I might see. For I had no doubt that Lieutenant O'Reilly would slit a woman's throat as easily as he would take out a man's eye. He was, after all, an infantryman.

Not until I had turned up every lamp and searched the premises was I satisfied that the sensation I had experienced was not of a corpse in the room, but of an empty room, period.

But if Elmira was not dead—where was she? For it was now dark outside, and unthinkable that even she would be so rash as to venture onto the streets alone at night. Therefore, she must have left *with* someone.

Of course.

The note, placed on an arm of that dreadful couch, written on hotel stationery in a meticulous, steady hand, would have been utterly predictable to anyone but a fool such as I.

Dear Dr. Chivers,

Forgive me for my sudden departure. I hope that you will not think me rude. Nor, as a gentleman, should you be altogether surprised. We are, after all, engaged. What God hath joined together, let no man put asunder.

Sincerely yours,
Mrs. Elmira Shelton

From my pocket I retrieved the letter from R. A. Perry and the significance of its last line became clear: *Commend me to Mrs. Le Rennet, with whom I shall speak at an early opportunity.*

Clearly it was a private signal. And what was her response? *I am at a loss as to why he would wish me absent. We are, after all, engaged.*

I think I read the letter again, marveling at its clarity and concision, though the handwriting seemed somewhat blurred. I do not remember what happened after that.

CHAPTER TWENTY-FOUR

Oh, Dickens! the Atlantic was thy Rubicon; on its broad waste thou didst shipwreck much fame and honor. Wonderful indeed that thou shouldst, in a day, turn two million admirers, friends, into despisers! Whilst the arms of millions were stretched to receive thee, and thou betrayest them, and sold them to a publisher!

—*An American Reader*

It seemed a high price to pay for a cigarette.

Dickens lay under a coarse blanket on the floor of what he knew to be a Conestoga wagon—popularly known as a "prairie schooner," for it was shaped somewhat like a boat, with angled ends and a floor that sloped to the middle so that barrels wouldn't roll out when climbing or descending a hill.

He had seen pictures of these wagons, but they appeared more comfortable and commodious than was the case here, for it had no springs at all. However, when his captors permitted him to poke his head out to breathe, it became clear that the vehicle had a certain charm, for the canvas bonnet glowed from the lights outside, making it seem as though he was inside a cloud. Less cloudlike was the continuous jolting, wrenching the spine this way and that. Detracting further from the feeling of airy lightness was the top-hatted young gentleman seated on his chest.

"Young man, I'm afraid I cannot breathe. Would you mind?"

"Cock yez up with it," said the young man with the voice of a boy soprano. "Or I fib yer idea pot fer yer."

Though his understanding of the response was incomplete, Dickens said no more. Nonetheless, the young man removed himself from Dickens's chest to take a seat on the floor beside his head, with his stick at the ready, its dreadful knob hovering directly over the author's *idea pot*.

"Where are you taking me?" Dickens asked. As he expected, no answer was forthcoming.

In any case, he had a good suspicion that he was about to take residence at an establishment known as Economy Manor, home of the Women of the Wilderness, of whom Miss Genoux was one.

It was a high price to pay for a cigarette—if cigarettes had comprised the limit of his association with Miss Genoux. In truth, this was not the case. With the Frenchwomen's free and open encouragement (he had heard such talk of the French but disbelieved it), they had engaged in certain intimacies.

Dear heaven, Catherine must never know.

Beginning with her fine cigarettes, within a very few days his affinity with Miss Genoux had grown well beyond that of a housekeeper and her employer, orders given and received. At first he enjoyed watching her as she expertly rolled, trimmed, and stacked her smokes like little pyramids from Egypt, or logs from Canada. Only in the company of musicians and jugglers had he so enjoyed an exhibition of physical dexterity, and all for his benefit! Her pianist's fingers, her serene, uniquely French features, her white skin, aquiline nose, small, girlish breasts—oh, she was a pleasure to look at; but that was nothing compared to her conversation.

Her grandfather knew Robespierre. Her father knew Fourier, the feminist. She had had the benefit of hearing both. Such a radical shift in such a short time, from the Reign of Terror to Fourierism; from monarchism to terrorism to communism. So many *isms* to navigate in three generations!

Her explication for the failure of the revolution was admirably succinct: "In a revolution you never kill the ones you want to kill. Only their symbols."

"Oh, I don't know," he had replied, puffing happily on his cigarette, for he enjoyed an argument with a woman. "I can think of a number of Britons who would serve the country better with their heads gone."

"Yet they are the ones who always get away." Now it was Miss Genoux who became gloomy.

"Perhaps so." Again, Dickens felt the sensation of insignificance any author of fiction undergoes in the company of actual experience.

She shrugged, in a way that struck him as essentially French. "*Vraiment*, you English have no stomach for revolution, you are too squeamish. You, how should I say, shrink away from the body fluids."

That gave him a mighty laugh. Not often in his life had a woman caused him to laugh like that, though Catherine had, once or twice, years ago.

"We English did have one revolution," he said. "It produced Oliver Cromwell. A dreary prig with warts."

Miss Genoux threw her head back when she laughed and displayed a set of perfect teeth. Smiling to herself, she took a cigarette delicately in her fingers, held it to her lips, lit it with a Lucifer, and allowed the smoke to waft over her face, like a veil.

"When we were with Fourier we lived in a phalanx in New Jersey."

"What is a phalanx?"

"It is what you would call a dormitory, but nicer. Where there is no private space necessary." She laughed inwardly. "My mother was a *fairy*."

"And what is a fairy?"

"Their duty was to cure lovesick young men. There was what some call "free love" in the phalanx, but with restrictions. The personality types must match. With the personality types of *ma mere et mon père*, there was too much difference."

"And that ended their marriage—because they couldn't stand each other? My goodness, what a thought!"

"But of course. When the types are wrong that is all there is to say. Mother took a good deal of pleasure in her life after, and so did *mon père*."

Never had Dickens spoken of such matters with another man, much less a woman—and an attractive woman at that. He hoped that she would attribute the redness of his complexion to the consumption of claret, thoughtfully provided by the management. "Is it possible that one's personality type might change over time, and cause things to fall apart?"

"Of course. That is what happens, isn't it?"

A pause followed, while they smoked, their private thoughts swirling around the room. Dickens gazed at his cigarette and it occurred to him that his hands were no longer shaking, that he felt relatively calm.

"Your system strikes me as infinitely superior to what we live with today," he said, and became gloomy again.

"Yes, but not in all ways. The phalanx was too much work for everybody—so much digging, so many rocks and trees. They said that digging clods of earth would make better thoughts, but it seemed to me that our thoughts became cloddish instead."

Dickens stubbed out his cigarette and in doing so realized that his other hand had been busily writing for heaven knows how long.

HE HAD RECENTLY traveled to Paris, and the city had made an immense impression on him—whenever he was alone for long enough to take things in. Being a family man, with him traveled their five children, with Louis the courier for his correspondence, and also Catherine's sister Georgina, who would fall into a heap and die were she not invited. And of course Catherine's maid Anne accompanied her as nurse and confidante; and two of the servants were needed to perform the usual duties; and, of course there was Catherine herself. With such a suite of followers, it was not easy to see Paris.

Perhaps that is why he suffered insomnia. A part of him longed for a bit of solitude, in which the only thoughts he must take into account were his own.

Late at night, proclaiming sleeplessness, he would vacate the marriage bed and step onto the streets of Paris, often with his overcoat over his nightshirt. Paris: glittering, shimmering, yet with an unambiguous clarity to everything, providing a glimpse of life other than in dark, ugly, relentlessly domestic London. There was no doubt in his mind that his fascination with Miss Genoux had to do with his visit to Paris, and his subsequent fascination for all things French.

While enjoying Miss Genoux's company, it was the furthest thing from his mind that she might be part of a plot to kidnap him for ransom. What could be sinister about a Communist settlement—especially in an establishment called *Economy Manor*?

When the young blue-eyed Irishman appeared at his door, at first he thought it a mistake, that he had rung the wrong bell. Only when Miss Genoux greeted him by name and stood aside for him to enter did he suspect something might be amiss. Handsome in a boiled-down sort of a way, the Irishman dressed like one of the gangsters who frequent the pubs along the embankment, and carried a walking stick that was all too familiar to anyone who had frequented the gin palaces of Whitechapel.

Surely the hotel staff would never have admitted such an individual unless a guest specifically requested that they do so—either personally, or through his housekeeper.

"*Excusez-moi, Monsieur Dickens,*" she said when the young man came for him. "*Je suis désole.* Forgive me."

Miss Genoux seemed genuinely sorry, and such was his fondness for her that Dickens experienced a perverse urge to comfort her, to say *not to worry*.

Already he supposed he was about to be kidnapped—though the term did not sit well with him, for it implied a child or a small goat. In any case, resistance seemed pointless and self-defeating. His captors were a gang of criminals possibly, but in all probability it was for a good cause. Perhaps Miss Genoux had been coerced into becoming an accomplice—though he somehow doubted that. She did not strike him as a woman who could be coerced into doing anything she did not wish to do.

Idly, Dickens wondered what sort of price he might fetch on the ransom market. Certainly, his views on copyrights and slavery had not enhanced his value with the Americans. On the other hand, it would be bloody embarrassing were a Briton to be butchered in America, with the two countries verging on war.

It was an alarming situation to be certain, but interesting at the same time. And with his recent spouting over slavery, he could scarcely feel sorry for himself; any trepidation he might feel was surely nothing compared to the bleak hopelessness experienced by an African tribesman, no less innocent than himself, kidnapped for a lifetime of slavery or death at sea.

Lacking proper springs, when the prairie schooner swerved off the main road (which was plenty rough in itself), Dickens was afraid that if this sudden spate of violent, unpredictable lurching continued for any length of time it would do his back an injury. As the ponderous carriage tumbled from ditch to pothole, the jolts seemed enough to dislocate all the bones in the human body; at one point Dickens and his captors were flung together in a pile, like rugby players.

Eventually, at the command of the driver, the wagon rumbled to a halt with a great amount of snorting from the horses and the creak of leather harnesses. Immediately his young companion hoisted Dickens to a semi-upright position and, together with his fellows, slid him like a pole off the back of the wagon, where he promptly fell in a heap on the ground.

Above and around him a number of young men had gathered, dressed in the rakish way of his abductors, as well as a number of crones wearing wide bonnets and dresses the color of rats. Prominent among the former was the spare, handsome young Irishman, and another fellow of about the same age who appeared to be missing an eye. Beside the one-eyed man stood a young rowdy with the face of a codger. Dickens knew that face; he had seen many like it in the blacking factory, where he worked as a child.

Miss Genoux was nowhere to be seen.

"Charles Dickens, sor," said the man with one eye. "There is a fellow writer in the house. You might fancy meeting him."

CHAPTER TWENTY-FIVE

Inspector, I am expecting that you know what our meeting concerns."

"Yes, sir. The Henry Topham inquiry. I have prepared a full report."

A deep weariness came over Councilman Grisse as Shadduck reached into an inside pocket of his ridiculous uniform and produced a sheaf of paper about as thick as the end of his thumb. Grisse noted that it was written in the same indecipherable hand as the last.

"*Mein Gott*, Inspector, I cannot read that."

"Sir, I would not have taken you for a commander who don't read his reports."

"Inspector, I am not to be questioned from you as my inferior."

"Pardon, sir. Right you are, sir. Still and all, you did ask for an explaining."

"What I wish is that you please to give me the, what you call the *jist* of it."

"Yes, sir. Well the jist is that we've got a deal of trouble, sir. When it comes to trouble we've got the whole elephant."

Grisse's eyes became glassy with incomprehension. "*Gott in Himmel*, what is that you are saying?"

"It is the Irish behind it after all, sir. Behind the murder of Mr. Topham. I calculate it to be one of their gangs."

Grisse nodded gravely, though he felt a slight sense of relief, that at last they were on familiar ground. "How are you knowing this?"

"An informant, sir. I cannot speak of his identity for he is in a tight spot himself."

"But of course. We would not wish to be troubling one of your informants."

"He is with a gang, sir, with an Irish name I cannot pronounce."

"A gang of Irish criminals? They must be arrested for this wrongdoing."

"Indeed so, sir. But it is a bigger pickle on account of the fact we have no reason to arrest them."

"A gang of criminals and you have not a reason to arrest them? Then how is it you know they are criminals?"

"That is a fair question, sir. You have tackled the jist of it again."

"I do not see how have I done this."

"I reckon it is a political crowd—leastways for the time being. Most of your criminal gangs have political origins of some breed or other, sir."

"What is this you mean by politics?" asked the councilman, feeling apprehensive. "Surely you are not suspecting a political party."

"*Irish* politics, sir. What they have over in Ireland. We have seen this happen before, as you know."

"Sure, when it is between Irish the fighting *es ist sehr greisslich*."

"This crowd is led by a Fenian-type feller who heads up an effort called the Irish Brotherhood. Gives a darn good speech too. An informant heard him address the Hiberian Society, so I went myself. *Darn* good speech. But what stood out in my reckoning was the times he mentioned publishing. Still, a real firebrand, that feller. It is all in the report, sir."

"Yes, of course, of course it is in the report." Grisse slipped the document into a drawer and closed it firmly. "Please continue, Inspector, I wish to be hearing it wery much."

"Turns out the Fenian has a partner. One-eyed feller, gouged out probably, saw action, officer class, claims to be. Rounded up a herd of street Arabs then staked claim to some doings in Moyamensing."

"Were you knowing this officer? In the war maybe?"

"Sir, a good many men were in the war. But I reckon that explains the mess at the Topham place. He weren't mad at Mr. Topham, sir. He darn well *harvested* him."

"*Greislich!*"

"The rest was to impress the competition, is my judgment."

"That is *nicht* possible!"

"Oh, it is an open secret, sir. Ask any dentist."

"This is not politicals it is *cannibals!*"

"In a way of speaking, yes, sir. Then I got to cogitating. A couple of days ago we had parley with Mr. Topham's second. Name of . . ." Here Shadduck checked his notebook, which was so thumbed it resembled a small brush. "A Mr. Bailey was his name. Feller had nothing to say, but he was plumb scared shitless. More a-feared than you'd expect in a feller with nothing to say."

"How were you knowing that he was so frightened?"

"As a veteran I have seen fear before, sir. Just as I seen them other things."

"Of course. *Das ist gannonk.*"

"What?"

"I ask pardon."

"That is all right. Well, the fear in him told the tale. Told me for certain a political type gang was involved, don't you see? As I said, the manner of Mr. Topham's disposal was a sign of that."

"How could you ever be concluding that?"

"A criminal-type gang would either shoot Mr. Bailey dead or pay him a sum of money. A happy silence either way, don't you see? That is how criminals do their business. But the political breed makes a different piece of calico. Your political type puts a powerful terror in people, takes pleasure in it. If it is political, we are in a tight pinch, with no telling how it will come out."

"What is it about the publishing business," asked Grisse, "that is making for such wrongdoing?"

"That is the question in my mind, sir, you have penetrated the heart of it."

Grisse sat back in his chair with a mournful sinking of his own heart. Philadelphia, the birthplace of the nation, was reverting to a savage state. There was no doubt about it. One day this deterioration will be noted by the press and the public, and officials who presided over the mess will be out on a rail. All the more reason, thought the councilman, to continue his reluctant support of Shadduck. Surely one day there will be a need for someone to blame.

"I think you are having the situation well in the hands, Inspector."

"It is all in the line of work, Mr. Grisse, sir."

"Then as part of your work I am asking what you are thinking of doing about *this.*"

Extracting a small, thick envelope from an upper drawer, the councilman upended it on the table.

Out of the envelope rolled a human eye.

CHAPTER TWENTY-SIX

Philadelphia

Of late, it had not been an uncommon condition for me to awaken in a bad state, yet this one beat all. As I surfaced into consciousness, despair and hatred poured over me like a pail of vitriol—brought on by my oldest friend, who had ravaged my life and career, and had stolen from me the only two women I had ever adored. Even putting aside the former complaint, my mother and Elmira Royster were plenty enough to provoke a man to homicide.

But there was another logic, however twisted, at work in my mind. By dedicating myself to killing Eddie as my archenemy, I shielded myself from the overwhelming alternative—that I had somehow brought these disasters upon myself. In other words, the enemy was either Poe or Chivers. It was him or me.

As though to confirm my position, from the moment when I decided that I must kill Eddie I experienced no more thoughts of suicide. With Poe dead I could rest easy, if not happy, and die content, if not at peace. And if I died by dangling from a gallows, when the trap beneath me collapsed and I plummeted through space with a rope around my neck and my head in a sack, my last thought here on earth would be a happy one: *Eddie Poe is gone.*

However, if I wanted to murder Eddie, first I was going to have to find him.

Lying on the carpet in my room in the United States Hotel, I became aware of the letter beside my hand. I rose carefully to my feet, reread the letter (reading was easier with two eyes), then tore it into strips and ate it, washed down with a tumbler of whiskey. Then I entered the bathroom, took the bandage off my eye, and examined myself in mirror. My head looked like something that had been dredged from the bottom of the sea.

The eye throbbed menacingly, but it could perceive light and shadow and discern vague patterns. On the other hand, it bulged like the eye of a fish, bloodred, with splotches of orange for contrast.

As well, and not surprisingly, my face appeared deranged. Seen in my present condition I would drive women and children shrieking from my presence. This would not do. If I were to find and kill Eddie Poe, I would have to somehow impersonate a normal man.

I pulled the bell for service. I fetched my bag, opened it, and applied a dressing to the eye, which I covered with a clean bandage just as the valet appeared, a fleshy, young fellow in his late teens, with an armful of towels and an array of tiny boils on his forehead.

"I should like my bath drawn at once," I said.

"Certainly sir. What did you do to your eye, sir?"

"Don't you know better than to pry into a man's affairs?"

"Yes, sir. Beg pardon, sir." The valet eyed me warily, he knew I was a bit off. I was going to have to come up with a better response to inquiries about the eye, for it was bound to come up again.

From this point forward, I set about impersonating a rational man, by doing what a rational man would do. I bathed. I put on clean linen. I shaved my face and filed my fingernails (ragged fingernails will give you away every time); I trimmed my sideburns and removed the pathetic sprigs of hair from my bald scalp. I applied cologne. I put on my suit, freshly brushed by my valet, and tied my cravat with no assistance and no mirror.

Grooming: the sign of a sociable, reasonable man, the disguise of a savage. Beware the man who has something against you, and has recently been to his barber.

I paid my valet a generous gratuity, which relaxed him somewhat, but he remained leery of me. To glimpse madness in a man is a bit like watching him vomit: you can never look at him in quite the same way again.

Having disguised myself as a civilized gentleman with a bandage on one eye, I made my way down to the reception area—the bandage gave me a rakish air, I thought—and surveyed the company. And took in much, for there is nothing like being out of one's mind to stimulate the perceptions.

The lobby buzzed with newspapermen as usual, but there was a strained feeling to everything, the drawn agitation you sense in crowded hospital waiting rooms, and on the faces of rail passengers following the announcement of an indefinite delay.

"I am Mr. Le Rennet in Room 207, and I wish to make certain inquiries." I said this to the watchful, uniformed Negro behind the counter.

"I see you did an injury to you eye, sah?"

"I have a stye."

"A stye, sah. Had un meself. Dandelion poultice go good fo it. Draw out the poison like a worm."

"Thank you for the medical advice, sir. I appreciate it."

"No mention, sah. And what else do you want knowing?" The smile remained reassuring while the black eyes drilled into me. *Does he know?* I thought. *Does he know I am mad?*

Nothing for it but to go the whole hog.

"Sir, I wish to ask you a private question concerning my wife, Mrs. Le Rennet. It is of a confidential nature and you may expect a substantial gratuity. Do you recall seeing my wife leave the hotel?"

"Yessa. She had a small bag—an overnight bag—and she was in the company of an Irishman, sah."

"Did she leave with this Irishman willingly?"

"That is a hard one to judge, sah. Fo' sure, if I thought otherwise he'd of been shot." The desk clerk glanced meaningfully downward, which I took to mean a weapon under the counter.

The Irish. How many times had the Irish come into the discussion for no apparent reason, and with sinister implication? Or did the Irish figure into any sort of unrest in America—just as the Mexicans did a few years earlier, and the Apaches, and the Negroes of course?

Perhaps every era has its Problem People—underdogs who cause trouble for everyone else. To be sure, the complaint is invariably legitimate, their grievance just; in some other place and time someone has done them inestimable harm. Yet human time passes in a blur, sufficiently fast to elude the fastest draw, the speediest revenge, so that the victim's wrath falls upon the head of someone who has done him no harm, someone who remains unaware of his own symbolic nature, why he should have been singled out for attack.

"Pardon, sir," said the young man at the end of the reception counter. "I wonder if I could take a moment of your time."

The police? If so, he was one of a special sort, to judge by his dress and grooming, and by the bulge beneath his coat. "By all means, sir," I said, calmly and reasonably. "I am at your service."

"Did I hear you happen to mention the Irish there, sir? Mind telling me what made you do that?"

"A personal matter," I said.

"Please come with me, sir," he said, and I obeyed, convinced that he was either a private detective or a gangster—yet new to the field, for the face had an earnest, naive quality I had seen on the faces of recent recruits, convinced that they served their country by losing their limbs.

I ASSURE YOU, sir, that I am not a constable," Putnam said, with a small beer in front of him. (For my part, nothing less than four fingers of whiskey would do and the fingers of butchers at that.) "I have the honor of serving as the American assistant to Mr. Charles Dickens."

"That is an honor indeed," I replied, nodding, not believing a word of it, performing a fine impersonation of a reasonable man.

We occupied a small table in the hotel saloon—a situation reminding me all too keenly of my meeting with Eddie, the one-eyed man, and all that followed. Like the Black Horse, the room was packed with men—but only men, no absurdly dressed servant girls nor ladies of easy virtue, nothing to counter the stablelike atmosphere that attends any all-male public gathering. As in the Black Horse, and the Exchange Restaurant for that matter, the air shimmered with the combined odors of smoke, tobacco spit, stale armpits, and crusted, crumbling feet—not precisely what the architect had in mind when he fashioned the elegant decor. Had he first obtained an insight into the nature of the clientele, a more appropriate choice might have been a tublike, porcelain expanse, with a drain in the center of the floor so that it could be hosed out like a stable, and a removable roof that could be doffed like a cap, ventilating the room.

"I overheard your mention of the Irish, sir. It interested me considerable for reasons that must remain private."

Cleverly, I saw the flaw in his position. "Privacy is the right of every white man. If you make such a claim, surely you do not expect me to do otherwise."

Putnam looked startled, as though winged from an unexpected direction. "You have scored a fair hit on that one, sir. I congratulate you."

I did not trust this young man, if only because he dressed like someone in the theater. I did not approve of the pattern on his waistcoat, and was bothered by an urge to feel the texture.

Putnam took a tactical sip of his small beer and continued. "I will make a clean breast of it, sir. My information is not known by the Philadelphia police, nor by the press. I count on your discretion."

"I have an interest in avoiding both professions," I replied. "If we are to undertake an exchange of facts, I count on your silence as well."

The young man leaned forward. "Sir, the fact is that Mr. Dickens has disappeared and I am afeared that he might come to some harm."

"Do you mean from an Irishman? Of course, everyone suspects the Irish of everything."

"And with good reason, sir."

"Perhaps so."

"On the other hand, the situation may be perfectly innocent. Mr. Dickens has been darned twitchy of late. I would not be surprised were he to head out on his own, if only to get away from his admirers. On the other hand, and this is most worrying, he did leave with an Irishman, who was admitted to Mr. Dickens's rooms in advance."

"A highly unusual circumstance."

"Exactly my thought, sir. Mr. Dickens knows no Irish in Philadelphia, and it is hardly the normal thing for Irishmen and Negroes to walk in off the street and gain access to private rooms in a respectable hotel. So I made inquiries. The Negro at the desk—the one you spoke to—said that it was Mr. Dickens's housekeeper who admitted the Irishman. Fact is, I met her myself—a woman from New Germany, and French."

"One can never trust the French," I said. "They are a self-indulgent, bloodthirsty race, like the Irish, the Spanish—and Catholics in general."

"I am not of that view, sir, being Catholic myself. But it adds up to a passel of foreigners."

"It was an Irishman who conducted my wife from the hotel," I said.

"There you are, sir. These two events cannot be entirely separate."

"Indeed so," I replied. However, in my mind it was not the conjunction of two Irishmen but of two authors that suggested something other than coincidence at work.

Despite our common interest, I was unprepared to reveal all to Mr. Putnam. In particular I chose to omit the part of my tale that featured Eddie Poe and myself. If I was going to kill Eddie I would have to be clever, as I would, for madness does not exclude cleverness. Anyone who has been in a war will tell you that.

I made a show of cogitating while I concocted a reasonable lie. "I suspicion that my wife has been abducted for money, and I can only sit and wait until a demand is made."

"Perhaps so. However, not to be indelicate, sir, but am I to believe the Negro at the desk when he said that your wife left *willingly?*"

Having been caught out, Mr. Le Rennet made a show of containing his feelings. "You have an extraordinarily acute sense of hearing, sir. You must be some sort of detective." And I swear to you that I burst into tears.

"It would not take a detective to see that you are having a pretty tall time of it, sir."

"Are you a detective?" I asked, wiping my eye with my handkerchief.

"No sir, I am but a public servant. My function is the protection of persons my superiors deem politically sensitive. Mr. Dickens is one of those persons, sir. On the slavery issue, many Americans wish him ill, especially in the South."

"To be frank, sir, I have never read Mr. Dickens and don't give a damn what happens to him. It is my wife I am concerned about," said Mr. Le Rennet, voice breaking with anguish. "Please excuse me, sir, I wish to retire for I am not well." Seemingly overcome, I arose to take my leave.

"It is my understanding that you are a widower, Dr. Chivers. Or have you recently remarried?"

I stopped in mid-stride while my mind scrambled for purchase. Composing my face into a reasonable expression, I turned. Putnam gazed up at me like an amazed divinity student, shaking his head in wonder at the complexity of the universe.

"I beg your pardon, sir," I said, as though he had told me a mildly amusing joke. "My name is Henri Le Rennet."

"Sir, I do not believe any man named Le Rennet would make such a general statement about the French. Not to mention that the name itself is a known pseudonym of the author I mentioned earlier, Mr. Edgar Allan Poe. The *late* Edgar Allan Poe. Mrs. Le Rennet—or Mrs. Shelton, depending—would surely know this, having been engaged to him herself."

I returned to the table and signaled the barman for another four fingers of whiskey. "What of it?" I said, feigning defiance, for I had been well and truly found out and there was no point in pretending otherwise.

"I hear they are about to exhume the body," said Putnam, with an expression of innocence and wonder. "That ought to be real interesting."

CHAPTER TWENTY-SEVEN

Philadelphia

Having been raised with no father and therefore no countervailing influence over him, Shadduck had spent his youth either following or running from his mother's advice. *Always dress properly*, she had said, and continued to do so in his mind. *The bad gardener quarrels with his rake. Bad the crow, bad the egg. Those that lie down with dogs, get up with fleas* . . .

Shadduck's mother had been dead three years by the time of the Mexican War. Since then, when it came to proper dressing, Shadduck had always felt more comfortable in uniform, and remained careful of the men he associated with. Another product of his mother's rearing was a tendency to sit back and consider, when the temptation was to plunge into immediate action. *Act in haste, repent at leisure.*

A detached human eye sat before him on Grisse's table, staring at something over Shadduck's shoulder. There is something unnerving about an unblinking eye—even when it is attached to its owner; surely the man who sent it intended to cause a chill of horror in the recipient, and thus provoke him to rash action.

Thanks to his mother, Shadduck did not do this. He did not reel back in horror at the sight. He pondered it calmly, as though it were an interesting specimen at a medical school.

To Wendel Grisse, the inspector's detachment was horrifying. The councilman had unveiled his grisly secret late in the meeting to achieve a telling effect—that he might glimpse the man beneath Shadduck's seemingly guileless exterior.

Disappointingly, Shadduck's response was not at all telling. In fact, the inspector stared down at the object with an almost bovine lack of intensity. This alarmed Councilman Grisse more than ever: Could one ever trust a man so filled with *kreft*?

Both men stared at the eye, which lay there like a shelled raw egg whose membrane had somehow remained intact, primordial and terrifying, like the eye of a Cyclops.

"Who's eye is that, do you s'pose?"

"I am not free to be saying that information."

"Suit yourself, sir. But I can't be no help without the facts."

Shadduck's indifference was genuine. As far as he was concerned he had a full plate before him with the Topham business, and the councilman was welcome to deal with the eye himself.

For some time the two sat in silence. Shadduck waited for the mind of Councilman Grisse to boil in his own predicament.

The envelope had arrived by messenger. By the time Grisse became aware of its contents, the deliverer was nowhere to be found. As the named recipient of the horrible thing, Grisse feared that he might be seen as somehow involved—even responsible. This was a treacherous position in itself.

The worst of it was that the councilman might be expected to oversee the investigation. He was, after all, the law-and-order incumbent; and for political reasons he had rashly proclaimed himself Dickens's bosom friend, his host in Philadelphia. What a fool he was to lend his name to the Englishman's visit—for that is surely why Grisse was selected to receive the *greislich* gift. He had welcomed Mr. Dickens publicly in the newspaper, put his moniker to the visit as though he himself were behind it.

Now his detractors could claim that, having invited a dignitary to Philadelphia, Grisse had failed to secure his safety. And an election only a month away!

While Councilman Grisse squirmed in his private dilemma, Shadduck put his mind to the Irish gang that had done for Mr. Topham, and the force he might be able to summon for combat. To rely on an outside constabulary was out of the question, for he had no authority with which to command them. And outside the function of riot control he had only Coutts and Smitt to call on. Yet it was certain that the arrest had to be conducted as a military maneuver, if it was to succeed without a passel of bloodshed.

"Inspector, I repeat that I am showing this eye to you as a matter of the most confidence."

"Yessir. But if I am to make something of it, I must put a name to it."

"Very well. Inspector, I believe the eye is belonging to Mr. Charles Dickens."

"Charles who?"

"Dickens. He is an English author."

"The author staying in the United States Hotel?"

"*Ja*, that is so."

"Great guns. Is this true for certain?"

"Sure. There was inside a letter saying so."

"What did it say, sir?"

"For yourself you can read this." Councilman Grisse extended a folded sheet of paper stained by some sort of fluid, now dry; it made a crinkling sound as Shadduck spread it on the table before him.

> *Councilman Grisse, Sir,*
>
> *You are looking at Charles Dickens's left eye. You have one week before you receive the right one too. A week after that we will send you his head.*
>
> *To see that the right eye remains where it is you are to set about the raising of fifty thousand dollars and await further notice. Any contact with the police will have disastrous consequences.*
>
> *Sincerely,*
> *A company of desperate men*

Shadduck read the letter twice. The wording felt Irish to him. "Fifty thousand dollars is a passel of money, sir."

"It is a terrible number. But I am noticing the handwriting. It is good handwriting, no? Not the handwriting of your reports."

"I judge the hand to be clear is all I can say."

"I am telling you it is university man who wrote this." From the moment he entered civic politics, Grisse had made a study of mimicking the handwriting of educated men. Hence, on this rare occasion, Grisse knew something that was beyond the inspector's ken.

Shadduck appreciated this, and observed the councilman closely. "Do you reckon that the writer might be a Dublin Irishman with a gift for oratory, sir?"

"Irish? I am not knowing what is Irish."

"Yet it has an amount of flair, don't it? A style to it?"

"I do not know what you mean by this *flair*."

"Never mind, sir. I will cogitate the matter on my own."

It was now clear to Shadduck that the men who had murdered Topham were the men who held Dickens—which made for a knotty situation. *Take your time with knots, or you will only tighten them*, his mother would say. It would be a poor piece of policework if he were to resolve the murder of Henry Topham, only to kill Charles Dickens.

And great guns, if it ever became known to the press! Wars have been declared with less provocation than the murder of an eminent man on foreign soil.

Accepting that the same parties had committed both crimes, Shadduck judged that the two must have been joined up somewhere. Was it over a crime? Was one crime committed to evade discovery of the other? Possibly, but Shadduck thought not. When it came to the actions of desperate men, it was unwise to put to ingenuity what you could put to chance, or fate, or stupidity. In his experience, events had a natural way of coming together in patterns—curious patterns to be certain, but patterns nonetheless.

As for Councilman Grisse, recent events did not bode well for a second term. Above all, the kidnapping must not be made public, no matter what happened to the victim. In a sense, terrible to say, it might be the better outcome if Dickens were to be buried in an unmarked grave.

However unlikely it might seem, part of Grisse's mind could not resist thinking that in some way Shadduck was responsible for all of it. That his overreaching had stirred up a hornet's nest whose inhabitants were giving no end of trouble. Grisse had never been in favor of a professional police force. It was a recipe for abuse and wrongdoing in itself, to create a class of people whose business it is to ferret out crimes, bring every skeleton into the open—whatever the consequences to the city's stability and repute.

Who, in the pursuing of happiness, has not committed a crime? And is it not possible that a great man may even have committed a great crime? For certain that is not a good thing, but it is the way of the world.

In Inspector Shadduck, the councilman had begun to glimpse the consequences of bringing a man into a police position who did not recognize that more harm could be done by destroying a prominent person, than by the crime he might have committed; that the enemy to be fought is not crime but chaos.

"I think we agree, Councilman, sir, that the matter of Mr. Dickens must be kept entirely private—for the safety of the victim."

"*Gott in Himmel* I am hoping so!"

"The snarl is in the newspapermen, sir. If they get their snouts into it there will be no stopping them."

"They are like wild animals for sure, they are sinking their teeth into anything and damning the consequence."

"Sir, it has come to my attention that the doctor who signed Mr. Poe's death certificate is currently here in the city. Thinking on Mr. Griswold's experience, the hauntings and such, it is a possibility that Dr. Chivers and Mr. Poe entered into a blackmail scheme of some sort. As a precaution, I have asked the Baltimore force to proceed with digging up Mr. Poe's grave."

"Yet more blackmail, you are talking about. Inspector, I am thinking now that every man in Philadelphia is blackmailing someone else."

"That is too big a thought for my mind, sir, though I reckon that to profit off a climate of fear is not unknown in the world. But that is not my point, sir. Once the press gets wind that they are exhuming Poe's body, speculation will spread. I reckon we might feed them the notions we have discussed in this room—our suspicions of the doctor, that there is more than meets the eye—and will be handed a couple of days' grace while they chaw over it."

Councilman Grisse eyed the inspector with admiration and abhorrence. Learning so fast, settling on solutions so readily, Shadduck liked his work too much for the good of anyone.

POE TO BE EXHUMED
by Harrison Diggs, *The Philadelphia Eagle*

After due consideration the City of Baltimore has authorized Baltimore law enforcers to exhume the body of the author Edgar Allan Poe at once, at the request of the Philadelphia police. Sources close to the case suggest a possible connection with the Henry Topham murder. "The situation is at a delicate stage, and there is no intended disrespect for the dead" said a senior official who asked not to be identified. "We will have more to say when the investigation is concluded."

CHAPTER TWENTY-EIGHT

I was awakened by six knocks on the door—too insistent for a servant, too heavy for a woman. This left two possibilities—the Irish or the Police.

Six o'clock in the morning. I rolled out of bed in my nightshirt, opened the drawer of my bedside table, and withdrew my loaded flatlock percussion pistol, a militia revolver I had purchased from the valet. (Anything, it seemed, can be purchased from the staff of a Philadelphia hotel, there is really no need to leave one's room.)

"Who is there, please?"

I stood at the door with the barrel of my pistol extended before me. If the voice was Irish, I would open the door and shoot him. If it was the police, I would leave the door closed, and shoot myself.

"Putnam here, with important news."

Putnam. Large, young, bespectacled Putnam. In a sense, his presence came as a relief, for I had begun to sag under the accrued weight of my various fabrications. Putnam was the one man who knew my real identity, to whom I could tell, up to a point, the truth. I had no need to conceal my name, my position, nor to hide my association with Eddie—only my intention to kill him. As for Elmira Royster, he seemed to regard her as having no tactical significance.

I opened the door to admit the muscular fellow in a conspicuous vest and a tie that resembled the flag of a Balkan nation. "Please enter," I said. "I shall ring for coffee."

"Cripes, man, what are you doing with that thing?"

I looked at the weapon in my hand. "I bought it for my own protection, sir."

"It appears to be loaded and ready to fire."

"That it is. I did not know who was on the other side of the door."

"I admire your optimism."

"Optimism? How so?"

"In allowing yourself only one shot."

With remarkable dexterity, Putnam produced from beneath his coat a four-shot pepperbox pistol with fluted barrels—an impressive firearm but one that required experience and training. "This is what I prefer," he said. "Made in Belgium—you can't beat the Belgians when it comes to rifling."

"Was it provided as part of your line of work?" I asked, for I continued to suspect that he was a detective.

"It was my own purchase, not official issue. Why do you ask?"

"The fact that you can afford to purchase such a firearm on your own hook leads me to suspect that you are a Pinkerton man."

Putnam appeared startled, which pleased me a good deal. "How so, sir?"

"So well dressed. So well equipped. And your use of the term *official* issue suggests that you work for a large firm."

Putnam sagged visibly. As we would have said in Richmond, he had been snarled proper. "It is a new type of service, sir. I do not entirely comprehend the structure of it myself. I trained for the cavalry, but as a college man it was decided that I should assume other duties in the capital."

Putnam returned the gun to its holster beneath his coat. "While I am not convinced of a relation between the disappearance of Mr. Dickens and that of your, er, wife, I am not ready to ignore it."

"By which I take you to mean that your superiors are not ready to ignore it."

Again, Putnam appeared slightly abashed.

The man was new on the job, that much was certain. He had the perpetually startled look I had seen on the faces of nineteen-year-old sons of landowners, recently promoted to captain, upon assuming dominion over the actions of a hundred and twenty men.

"Were you in the war, Mr. Putnam?"

Putnam appeared embarrassed. "No, sir, I missed it. My own fault really. College men were moved to a different sort of training. More political, you might say."

"We live in a democracy, sir," I said. "Everything is political."

"I'm not sure I want to parse your meaning, sir. It might be construed as seditious."

"You federal people alarm me, sir. You create more and more laws, more and more ways a man can go wrong. You're like quicksand—a man finds himself sinking deeper and deeper."

"I take it you are a Southerner, sir."

"I am."

"Well, of course it is natural for you people to defend your way of life. But abolition is an inevitability—as an intelligent man surely you see that."

"You weary me, sir, with your Yankee patronization, but never mind."

Putnam produced a tattered notebook with a scuffed leather cover. "This is what I have come to show you. I discovered it among Mr. Dickens's effects. It appears that the French housekeeper who admitted his Irish abductor is a member of a sect in Germantown. That is where I believe we will find Mr. Dickens—and, God willing, your, er, wife."

And, I suspected, Eddie Poe as well. "Germantown, you say? That is south of here, is it not?"

"That is not your concern, sir. But you have my assurance that I shall keep you informed of developments."

"Nonsense, sir. I am coming with you."

"You are not, sir."

"I am if you retain any hope of secrecy. Besides, I am a doctor. Knowing the Irish temperament, you will need one."

CHAPTER TWENTY-NINE

Germantown, Philadelphia

The accommodations were not *so* bad as they might have been, but they were less than ideal. The room reminded Dickens of the ward of a shabby hospital, the rows of rope beds unoccupied but for two on either end. The rest were empty, with their blankets in a rumpled condition. Next to each bed, a grim, broad-brimmed hat hung on a peg. To Dickens, it looked as though the occupants of the room had simultaneously got up and gone to the privy, and would be back at any moment.

Seated on a bed with his back against the wall (there being no pillow), with nothing to read and nothing to smoke, Dickens pondered the preoccupied gentleman at the far end of the ward, who had ignored his arrival and had not spoken to him since. The inhospitable fellow had turned his end of the ward into a small office, with a bed and a table and a large quantity of paper, on which he wrote, as far as Dickens could tell, twenty-four hours a day.

When the one-eyed man and his young ruffians brought him up here, the only light in the room was the writing lamp. When Dickens awoke next morning (having slept surprisingly well in his clothes, on a strange bed), the first sound he heard was the scratching of his cellmate's quill pen.

To his immediate left, above the door, was a grim clock, which uttered every tick with a kind of struggle. At a table beneath the clock sat something alive with skin of rust, possibly one of the women present at his arrival, in a rat-colored dress and a black bonnet.

"I bid you good morning, madam," Dickens had said, but received no reply.

Should he be afraid for his own welfare? He supposed that he should; yet there had existed a certain unreality about the entire escapade, a strangeness that made it difficult to take things seriously—though he supposed that he would take them seriously enough if a gun were placed at his temple.

One thing was certain: between the locked door, the slits for windows, and their rusted chaperone by the door, it was entirely pointless to think of escape.

"I beg your pardon, madam, but might I visit the privy?"

The thing nodded at the pitcher on the floor next to his bed. Beside it was a commode.

"Ah yes. Quite so. Excellent."

Squatting beside the bed, shielded by an upraised blanket, he remembered the children's quarters in the workhouse where such indignities were a constant condition.

For Dickens, the silence was hardest to bear. As a man who made sense of things by saying them aloud, he required discourse in the way that a lamp requires kerosene. Without another mind to share his impressions of the past hours, he was at a loss to make any sense of them at all.

And how curious it was! Who were these people—the young ruffians in long coats, the Irish, the odd-looking women? Not to mention Miss Genoux, whose company he had so much enjoyed and who had betrayed him so casually. He could envisage her rolling cigarettes by the guillotine, the tumbrel rolling in—with Dickens a passenger.

And what to make of his fellow prisoner, the writer—if that is in fact what he was? For all Dickens knew, his companion might have been a scrivener, copying documents at halfpenny a page.

Mortifyingly, it occurred to him that upon his arrival in this hospital or whatever it was, he had responded to his silent companion like a cartoon Englishman by not speaking unless spoken to—after all, they had not been formally introduced. At last it occurred to him that, when one is held hostage, or whatever it was, surely one might hurdle the usual formalities and exchange a greeting.

"I beg your pardon, sir," he said after clearing his throat rather more loudly than he had intended. "This is terribly forward of me but I wonder if I might ask you for the time."

"Eight twenty five," replied the writer, without looking up from his desk. "It says so on the clock."

"Of course. That large, clanking thing over the door. Forgive my ignorance, but would that be morning or evening?"

The gentleman stood, crossed to one of the slit windows, peered out, and returned to his table. "Evening, suh, I believe."

"Quite. Thank you very much, indeed. Well and good then. Actually, to be perfectly frank, I wonder if I might be so bold as to introduce myself: Charles Dickens is my name."

The scratching of the pen stopped, and the gentleman at the table turned in his direction. "I am aware of that, suh. I am Edgar Allan Poe." He turned back to his work and the scratching resumed.

"Well, God bless my soul! By heaven, now I recognize you, sir. You had me confused, without your mustache. Come to think of it, Mr. Poe, weren't you supposed to have died?"

"That is true, suh. And in a sense, I did."

"Ah. As a metaphor, perhaps."

"Perhaps. I am, after all, breathing, at present." The scratching continued, like a small rodent trying to escape from a paper box.

"Quite. Excellent, then. Top drawer."

It was clear to Dickens that Poe was in low spirits, for he had often fallen into a similar condition himself. "I dare say I am familiar with your work, sir. 'The Raven' is a stunning piece, words beyond meaning, pure music, really. And of course your tales as well—an impressive body of work, though I am surprised that you haven't tried your hand at a novel."

"There is no money to be had in it, suh," replied Poe. "A tale might be bought by a magazine, but a novel will not be bought at all— unless the author has the means to publish it himself."

"Ah yes, of course. Well, I am with you there, in fact I have stated it publicly—indeed, I seem to have fallen into some disfavor in America as a result . . ." Dickens stopped abruptly as a thought occurred to him. "If I may ask, Mr. Poe, does my position on copyrights have something to do with my present circumstance?"

"Nothing whatsoever. In America, everything comes down to money, suh. It is the national language."

"Sadly, I tend to agree. I salute you, Mr. Poe. for having made the most of a fallow field."

"Did I? Well, yes, I suppose I did. It would have been different had I been able to secure an English readership."

"Do you mean that your countrymen might then have sat up and taken notice?"

"Precisely, suh. For an artist in America, to have been born here is in itself evidence of inferiority. However, by writing something mildly shocking, one can easily become infamous as well. Invisibility to infamy, with no pause for renown."

Momentarily it occurred to Dickens that they were talking about Poe the author as though he were in fact deceased—as though the man seated before him was not Poe but a ghost, looking back upon his life on earth . . .

Dickens glanced at the clock, then at the thing seated by the door who could with little alteration pass as an Egyptian mummy; now his glance fell on the rows of hats—whatever had happened to their owners? he wondered. Then with a shudder it occurred to him. *This is not unlike a tale by* . . .

"God bless my soul," he said aloud.

"Perhaps now you remember," continued Poe with a sigh of weariness. "I wrote you a letter in forty-six, and we corresponded briefly. You did me the favor of accepting a short tale I had written for possible publication in England. Not to chastise you, Mr. Dickens, but I have not heard from you since."

Poe's accent surprised Dickens, for he had never thought of the man as a Southerner. However, there was no Southern cordiality in his voice at present. "Ah. Ah yes. I believe it was entitled 'The Cask of Amontillado.'"

"And what was your opinion of it, suh?"

"Forgive me, Mr. Poe, but is that why I have been brought here? It seems like a deal of trouble, to kidnap a man in order to discuss a manuscript."

"That is not the case, suh. I am a prisoner as much as you are, though for a completely different purpose."

"I assume that I am being held for ransom—but that cannot be the case with yourself, given that you are supposed to have passed away."

"I am not a hostage, suh. My situation is worse. I am a slave."

"You are writing under duress, sir?"

"Very much so."

"What if you were to refuse?"

"There is someone dear to me also held hostage for that express purpose, suh. Whether for politics or personal gain—and I am not certain which—these are desperate men, suh, hardened men. Violence is not a horror for them but an expedient."

Frightened by the specter of violence, yet relieved at having any sort of empirical explanation for his situation, Dickens rose from his bed, wandered to the other end of the room (conscious of a pair of ancient eyes boring into his back), and offered his hand.

"Whatever the situation, sir, it is better to have company. I am very glad to meet you, Mr. Poe, even on this occasion."

"Would you care for a cigarette?" asked Poe. "It is the one thing we receive in quantity."

"I accept with pleasure," replied Dickens, and Poe handed him a small packet of ten.

Dickens savored the thick Virginia smoke. "Am I correct in assuming that you are acquainted with a Miss Genoux?"

"You are indeed, suh. Though *acquainted* is hardly the correct word. I have never been to France."

"Yet you wrote the excellent 'Murders in the Rue Morgue.'"

"It was not the French who interested me. It was the orangutan."

"So am I correct in thinking that you know nothing of Paris?"

"Not a bit of it, suh. It is my view that, if you bother to read sufficiently about a place, you will know more than did the inhabitants of the day."

"And what of the Irish, Mr. Poe? What do you know of them?"

Halten sie! It was the voice of the thing by the door. Dickens had not expected it to speak German, but he did not expect it to speak English either.

"I do beg your pardon, madam," he replied. "No need to call out the troops."

Dickens turned back to his proper place, but was restrained by Poe, who had a grip on his coattail.

"I dislike repeating myself, suh, but what did you think of it?"

"I beg your pardon, sir. Think of what?"

"My tale, suh. 'The Cask of Amontillado.'"

"Dear heaven, man, under the circumstances it seems odd that your submission of three years ago should remain uppermost in your mind."

"I am a writer, Mr. Dickens. My work is always uppermost in my mind—how it is being received. Is that not how it is with you?"

"Of course, that is so," Dickens replied, knowing that it was not *always* true. As a journalist, he had some time ago ceased to care about his style of writing and speaking. If his style pleased the reader that was all to the good, but it was not as though it would change if not.

"A writer is grateful for any response, even if it is discourteously late."

"You seem adroit in collecting injuries, sir."

"Injuries do accumulate, that is true."

"Very well," said Dickens. "In return I should ask for the favor of knowing where I am and what is presently happening to me. Will you agree?"

"Certainly, suh, though you may be overestimating my grasp of it. Please be frank, and so shall I."

"'The Cask of Amontillado.' I shall have to think back. It was, after all, three years ago that I read it."

"Three years is not the longest time I have had to await a response from an editor. But it is a long time just the same."

"I do apologize for my rudeness. Between the fuss made over *Dombey and Son*, *Pictures from Italy*, and a bit of European travel, I had a good deal on my plate."

"How fortunate for you."

Dickens lit another cigarette. Tobacco smoke served as a wonderful stimulant for the memory.

"'The Cask of Amontillado.' What a fine piece—what a model of economy and distilled irony. Think of it—a Mason murders a Mason by shrouding him in masonry! Quite stunning, really—and told in less than twenty-five hundred words! Dear God in heaven, were I to undertake such a tale I should have required that number simply to describe the vaults!"

"That is high praise, sir, and I thank you for it. And yet you saw fit not to publish."

"That is true. Unfortunately, it was not for us. I did not make the decision easily. But my colleagues at the *Daily News* came to the same conclusion."

"Might I ask why? *Godey's* saw fit to publish, and it was well received here. But then, I suppose you are about to say that the British are more discerning in their taste."

"I am about to say nothing of the sort. You art-for-arts-sake people think taste is everything—don't you see? Your tale was rejected because it contained factual irregularities that might confuse the European reader."

"Facts? The tale is a work of fiction, suh. What have facts to do with it?"

"Mr. Poe, have you ever been to Venice?"

"Of course not."

"Yet your tale takes place at the Portale di Venezia—the Carnival of Venice."

"Not so. I indicate nothing of the kind. The tale takes place during carnival season in an unnamed Italian city."

"Yes, Mr. Poe, but anyone who has spent a week in Venice will recognize Mr. Fortunato's costume as originating at the Portale di Venezia. Not to mention the fact that Fortunato is a common Venetian name."

"Nonsense. Fortunato is a play on the word Fortune. Surely to God that is obvious, suh. Yet for the sake of argument, I shall give it to you that the tale takes place in Venice. What then?"

"In the end he bricks Fortunato up in the cellar. I shall never forget the exchange: *The amontillado! Yes, yes, the amontillado.* What could be more horrifying than having one's murderer agree with everything one says?"

"Indeed that is the point, suh, and you explicated it well."

"But there is one problem, Mr. Poe: there are no basements in Venice. Venice is below sea level. Do you see? Had your avenger lured Fortunato into his vault, they would both have drowned."

Poe lapsed into silence. It was plain to Dickens that he had touched a nerve.

"It seems to me," Poe said eventually, "that is the difference between us. A matter of approach. You write about the world, about other people. I write about myself—and I include my dreams. There are drawbacks on both sides, as I have discovered while reading your work."

"I don't quite know what you mean by that," replied Dickens, and a long silence ensued. Seeing that the conversation had dried for now, the Englishman returned to his rope bed and lit another cigarette.

Writers are notoriously touchy when you bother them with facts, but they tend to recover quickly.

"By the by, Mr. Poe, what is it that you are working on at the moment?"

"David Copperfield," came the reply.

The Texas Paterson he wore beneath his coat had stood by him throughout the war, so that Shadduck now regarded the gun the way another man might his dog or his horse.

It was not official issue. As far as top brass was concerned, a cavalryman was a dragoon, his conveyance was a hoss, and his primary weapon was a saber, and that was the end of it. Shadduck had bought the percussion revolver from a Texas Ranger, who had seen it to good use in Indian fighting. Unlike every other revolver on the market, the Texas Paterson shot every time.

A heavy pistol, and with the long barrel to boot, yet it was not at all awkward on the field, worn outside the coat. However, as a concealed weapon for an urban policeman it left much to be desired. Stuffed down the belt of his trousers in its Colt holster, the weapon shifted constantly. More than once he had had to make furtive shifts in his clothing, in public. At the moment, the Texas Paterson sat across the inside of his thigh, so that its greasy metal surface assumed the heat of his body. He shifted so that it rolled over to the outside leg, and that was more comfortable.

He was in unfriendly territory. How unfriendly remained to be seen.

"What is that fecking thing in your trousers, Inspector?" Of course, McMullen had noticed the weapon the moment the inspector entered the room, and could easily have ordered him disarmed, which Shadduck would have taken as a signal to flee the building.

"An old service weapon, sir. For sentiment more than protection. No offense meant."

"None taken. I carries a pocket iron, for the line of the suit. Yours does not show your uniform worth spit. Though I doubt anything would."

"I will cogitate on that advice, sir."

To Shadduck's eye even a single-shot pistol seemed redundant in McMullen's case, for the man seemed more than adequately protected by two muscular young toughs in pot hats and loose-fitting fireman's jackets, beneath which any number of weapons might be stored, in case their enormous cudgels proved inadequate to the task.

The meeting took place in Sportsman's Hall, one of three saloons owned by McMullen, the other two being the Black and Tan and the Fourth Ward.

Sportsman's Hall was a three-story affair: The top floor housed a dance floor featuring an orchestra of piano, violin, and cornet and a repertoire of "Green Grow the Lilacs," "Skip to My Lou," and "Jimmy Crack Corn"; it was a popular spot for trimmers—thieving whores—to meet their marks. The second story featured an arena in which dog and raccoon fights would occur, as well as bare-knuckle boxing matches for a purse of five dollars. Should there occur a lull in the action, the duty of the waiters was to fight each other.

The serious drinking occurred on the bottom floor, where customers were regularly drugged and robbed. To ensure a smooth operation McMullen had forged an agreement with the police whereby knocked-out patrons would be brought to a prearranged location, where constables could remove their inert bodies to the precinct house, there to be charged with public intoxication.

McMullen's estimable rapport with the city's law enforcement apparatus was one reason Shadduck had settled on him as a potential associate. Another was that he also served the community as the leader of a gang known as the True Blue Americans—who, as a secondary enterprise, manned the Moyamensing Hose Company. This made McMullen de facto head of the biggest gang in Philadelphia County, and the busiest fire department as well. It was a natural fit, given the Hose Company's disposition to setting their own fires.

Shadduck needed troops—and of a higher caliber than he was going to get from the various Philadelphia County police forces. As well, if he was to have a future beyond the coming election, he had best round up a stouter ally than Councilman Grisse.

In addition to his other services to the community, William McMullen was about to run for election himself for president of the fourth ward, under the banner of the Native American Party.

Like many men in private business, McMullen had come to see public service as a necessary part of the business climate—thanks to President Jackson.

In the more than ten years since his presidency, the memory of Old Hickory may have faded, but the effects of his reforms had not. In axing state and federal laws, as well as regulations and standards among the professional classes, in thereby ceding power of judgment to the common man, the president had set in motion a process that would be felt for generations, and would prove once and for all how much easier it is to remove laws than to pass them.

Thanks to Jackson's reforms, nearly every public office in America was now an elected one. The pathways to power were myriad and open to an extent unprecedented since the Middle Ages; a determined man had but to secure the delivery of a few hundred votes to be on his way to the top.

According to Jackson, a white man could do anything he set his heart to, if sufficiently inspired. In this he had himself as an example. If Andrew Jackson could become president of the United States, it followed that, if the people elected a man to build a bridge, or play Hamlet, or set a broken bone, and if he set himself seriously about the task, success would be the inevitable result.

The radical implications were alarming to men who had gone to the trouble of acquiring an education. Yet the sayings of Old Hickory made perfect sense to the common man—and in America, what the people believe is always true.

William McMullen was one of the first businessmen in Philadelphia to listen beyond the apocalyptic shrieks of the Whigs and to recognize the value of radical democracy to his own interests. With a platform in public office, an enterprising man could whip up for himself one enormous sphere of influence.

Like so many men with their eye on politics, McMullen had groomed himself to approximate the look of a general in the Mexican War—the drooping mustache, the shoulder-length hair, the goatee trimmed to an inch beneath the lip. A ginger-nut redhead and a former lightweight boxer, he sported an expensive suit and a broken nose. His skin seemed to have been rubbed raw with sand, and his features depicted a jagged, anxious, careworn character. Yet the moment he became interested or incensed, his features took on a youthful, concentrated intensity, and it was said that he could deck a man twice his size with lightning speed.

McMullen faced Shadduck across the table as though for a game of invisible poker, nursing a glass of what appeared to be whiskey and milk.

"Cock yez up with it, Inspector," he said. "And why I should give over good men to some fecky in the ninth in a fecked-up uniform over a fecking blackmail game? Pay the feckers and feck off is what I say."

Shadduck paused before responding, though he had anticipated the question and his answer. "I reckon there be mutual interests here, Mr. McMullen, sir. Stability is vital. Public unrest is bad for businesses of all kinds."

"You're the fecking razzer, why come to me about it?"

"The rascals are Irish, sir. And they're politicals. I thought this might interest you—in light of your future plans."

"Mind yerself, Inspector. I rankle at Irish insults."

"As do I, sir. I deplore intolerance of all kinds. But I reckon for a native-born American there is a distinction to be made. There is a difference between native Americans like yourself and the present inflow of Irish republicans. A powerful difference, sir. One you might wish the public to understand—should you proceed with your candidacy."

The eyes flashed and Shadduck knew he had scored a point. "My candidacy? Did you get this fack from yer peaches?"

"A feller needs facts if he is to act in a proper manner. Being a Nativist and not a Whig, you need a firm position on the issue, sir."

McMullen had not considered this. He was new to politics. "I'll go to bail that they are not like us, and they fecking don't want to be."

"Worse, sir—they seek to bring their battles to the New World. They seek unrest and upheaval. They give the Irish a bad name. Or if I may say it man to man, it gives yourself a bad name, Mr. McMullin, sir."

"It is true if you go to that of it." McMullen took a thoughtful sip of his milk. "Give it to me again why you are not using your fancy razzers."

"Because they have no jurisdiction in Germantown, sir. And as it is a gang we face, I am hoping the presence of a superior force will encourage desertion among the enemy. I am a peace officer, sir, and seek a peaceful resolution wherever possible."

Another sip of milk, while McMullen waited for more.

"And there is the kidnapping victim," continued the inspector. "It is a prominent gentleman is all I can tell you. If it were known he was taken prisoner by Irish, let alone put off his feet, it would cause . . . unrest. All in all, best keep it out of the public sector, sir."

"Twelve firemen you want?"

"That would be just adequate, sir. I could do better with sixteen. The site might be well defended."

"And what is the advantage to meself? I know you mentioned it but I have forgotten."

"The gratitude of the city, sir. A high position in the sight of respectable men. And a bright future for your own men as well. Should firefighting lose its appeal there is a fine career to be had in the police department."

McMullen regarded Shadduck with speculation in his eye. "Inspector, where in the bowels of Christ did you get the nose on you?"

"Pardon, sir, I don't get your drift."

"Where are you after learning your fecking tacticals?"

"It was the war, sir. Alliances is everything in a war. With outside powers, and within the army itself."

"Particular that last, I imagine."

"You are correct, sir. A bad assignment in the field can be a death sentence. A man's worst enemy can be the first lieutenant of his own regiment. Private excitements blaze even in the heat of battle. Men are shot in the back while not necessarily in retreat."

"A frequent occurrence in Philadelphy these days," said McMullen. "I'll go to bail that soon there will not be an honorable man in the county who does not have a fecking knife in his back."

"We in the police force are in a similar scrape, sir. It is a feller's duty to make the most of himself. Yet he who seeks his fortune takes on the cares of the world."

"Who said that last?"

"It was my mother, sir."

McMullen's expression softened—as would the face of any American man at the mention of *mother*—and he extended his hand.

"Shadduck, you are some can of piss. Should I make the decision to enter public service, I hope I can count on your support."

"You will have it, sir. That is for certain."

Shadduck felt the barrel of the Texas Paterson against his thigh and it felt a mite silly now. In civilian life, not all power comes from the barrel of a gun.

CHAPTER THIRTY-ONE

Economy Manor

"Mr. Dickens, suh, am I to understand that *David Copperfield* is now complete?" Poe said this with a concealed weariness indicating a loss of patience with something.

"Of course it is. I should never have come to America without having submitted the final number. I worked day and night on it. We meet our deadlines, sir."

Poe seemed not to care about deadlines. "Then I take it, suh, that you know how the story ends?"

"Certainly, sir. That is what outlines are for."

"I do not do outlines myself. For me they inhibit the poetic spirit."

"That is all well and good with the writing of poems. Try it with a novel and you will find yourself in an unholy mess."

"Point taken, suh. Then perhaps you can be of assistance to me on a number of themes."

"Am I to believe that you wish me to assist you in fabricating my work? In palming it off to the public as my own? What an obscene suggestion."

"I suggest to you, suh, that your work will be stolen from you in any case."

"Yes, well, in a sense that is true. But I give up on that one, Mr. Poe. I am sick to death of the copyrights issue. it will never be solved in my lifetime; I simply wish to go home."

"Since you have nothing to gain or lose from its publication in America, is it not to your advantage, as an artist, that your tale be told in the way that you mean it to be told? I am a different sort of writer, suh, with a different outlook on life. Do you really want me to tell your tale for you? For that is what I am obliged to do, or someone dear to me will suffer grievous harm."

"Isn't that curious?" said Dickens. "It never occurred to me that anyone might be held hostage other than myself. A self-centered occupation—hostage."

At this Poe laughed, perhaps for the first time since he won a swimming contest as a lad some twenty-five years ago.

It was by now clear to Dickens that he was in a grim situation and might need Poe's assistance to come out of it in one piece. In life, as in politics it seems, one must learn to rise above principle.

"Very well, Mr. Poe, I shall help you to complete your damn forgery. But under protest."

Poe nodded gravely, then preceded to finger through the manuscript before him the way a bank teller counts a pile of dollar bills. He had marked specific pages by turning over the corners; every few pages he stopped at a notation, gave it long consideration, muttered something, and carried on. Having worked his way through the entire document, he stopped, sighed, and turned to Dickens with the look of a lawyer on a bafflingly complicated case.

"Mr. Dickens, as you can imagine, I have many technical queries about your protagonist. I take him to be in some measure yourself; therefore, it is probable that Mr. Copperfield's inconsistencies are also your own. Well and good. Yet one development baffles me completely: The incest, suh. *Where in hell's kitchen are you going with the incest?*"

Dickens opened his mouth but no sound came forth. Had he been asked about the last time he fornicated with sheep, it could not possibly have produced a deeper glaze of incomprehension and alarm.

Poe handed Dickens a cigarette, which he accepted readily, and was grateful for the proffered lucifer, that his companion would not observe his hands trembling.

"Mr. Dickens," continued Poe, "you may write for the pulp trade, but you are not an author who treats his reader as a fool. And yet again and again you hint at deeper, darker currents just beneath the surface, without revealing precisely what they are. Setting aside the amative, may I say erotic, affinity between David and Steerforth, I would be most grateful if you would explain the incestuous love between Agnes Wickfield and her father. To be certain, you have seeded it masterfully throughout the text; yet how does it end, suh? How does it resolve itself?"

"Mr. Wickfield? Ah yes—Mr. Wickfield," replied Dickens,

thinking back. For the surname had changed several times before publication.

Poe shuffled through the manuscript, produced a number, and continued. "You wrote this chapter, sir, I have it in its entirety. It is entitled, *Agnes*."

"Agnes was the name of our cook," said Dickens. "She was a good cook, and I thought she would be chuffed by it."

"Accepted, Mr. Dickens. Yet listen to what Mr. Wickfield, her father, says about the relations between them. All I ask is that you tell me what it means."

Turning up the lamp, Poe read from the manuscript:

> My love for my dear child was a diseased love, but my mind was all unhealthy then. I say no more of that. I am not speaking of myself, Trotwood, but of her mother, and of her. If I give you any clue to what I am, or to what I have been, you will unravel it, I know.

A long silence followed, and Poe grew impatient. "Come, suh, surely you cannot deny the self-loathing in the speech. Its manner of expression suggests a man who cannot bring himself to say where his 'diseased love' for his daughter led him. At the very least, suh, what does he do next?"

"Whose speech is that, did you say?" asked Dickens.

Poe's enormous eyes rolled with impatience. "Mr. Wickfield, suh. The father of Agnes—"

"Ah yes. Agnes. Gentle Agnes."

"Gentle Agnes, exactly so—who, unless I am very much mistaken, is to marry David, and they will grow old together in a state of connubial bliss."

"That is a rough approximation of what happens, yes." Dickens never liked plot summaries of his work, thinking that they revealed his innate shallowness. He always felt he showed better in the details.

"Which brings me again to the question, suh—what is to be the outcome of incest? What natural justice will put it to rights and settle the score? Will Agnes murder her father by giving him a sleeping draft that is a bit stronger than usual? Will he hang himself? Or does Agnes's mother return in some way—in a dream perhaps, or as a ghost, or as an awakened corpse, to confront Mr. Wickfield with his sin, whereupon he is found in his bed the next morning, dead, and on his face an expression of ineffable horror?"

Dickens struggled to recall writing the passage. What, indeed, had he been thinking of? "Sir, were I to take your approach and question every line I wrote, I should have found myself confined to the writing of short tales—*extremely* short tales, if I may say so."

"Are you telling me that Mr. Wickfield's speech means nothing, suh? That he might as well have been singing ring around the rosy"?

"Mr. Wickfield feels remorse over his employment of his daughter during her most marriageable years to take the place of his dead wife. Otherwise he would not so willingly give her up in marriage to Copperfield and lose her companionship. Sir, my deadline was drawing very near and I needed a resolution."

Or perhaps, Dickens thought, it was something he scribbled down during a sleepless night. He had known many such nights at the time. If he wrote it in that state of mind, there was no telling what he was getting at.

"Yet incest explains everything, suh, does it not? Did not Mr. Wickfield drink himself to sleep each night? Did he not gaze upon Agnes repeatedly with an expression of anguish? There is only one satisfactory narrative, suh: a man in the throes of grief looks upon his daughter, who suddenly becomes his wife incarnate. He succumbs to passion, and only when the deed is done does he realize that he has violated his own flesh and blood . . ."

"Stop!" cried Dickens. "Good God, man, what the devil are you talking about? That is not the world of David Copperfield! That is not benevolent, sad Mr. Wickfield. Many men take to drink in their later years, and not because they have committed incest."

"Then what *is* the reason for his drinking, suh?"

"Surely you can't expect me to answer for a character's every twitch . . ."

"If you will pardon me, suh, for a man to violate his daughter is a bit more than a twitch."

"Please, Mr. Poe. From the bowels of Christ, I beg you to put that line of inquiry out of your mind. There is no incest in *David Copperfield*. I pledge to you that no thought of any such nature crossed my mind in the writing of the tale."

"*My love for my dear child was a diseased love . . .* " I ask you only to tell me, What does it mean?"

"I admit that I cannot tell you off the tip of my tongue. Perhaps it slipped in of its own accord."

"And you rejected 'The Cask of Amontillado' because Venice has no cellars!" replied Poe, with a certain bitterness in his tone.

CHAPTER THIRTY-TWO

Germantown

Putnam and I rode to Germantown on rented saddle hosses, resentfully obedient animals at best, like hired thugs. The federal agent had for once eschewed his normal flamboyant style of dress for a more appropriate set of hunting tweeds. He wore his belt and holster around his hip in the way of a penny-dreadful gunfighter, which I confess I found a bit overdone.

More irritating was his riding ability, which was well beyond my own—he had trained as a cavalryman, after all, before his present calling. My thighs cried for mercy at the speed he kept up, and I knew I would be crippled next morning. My riding ability was further impaired by the fact that I remained blind in one eye and could not perceive distances with any accuracy, so that every pothole became an unanticipated jolt that nearly knocked the molars out of my head.

We thundered past a field containing bristling stalks of Indian corn; they looked like a crop of walking sticks, all hard edges, like the bristling firs set against the sky. To a Southerner like myself, the Pennsylvania landscape seemed overrated, a two-dimensional spectacle even for a man with two eyes—suitable, perhaps, to the two-dimensional morals of its inhabitants.

In rural America, life made a person simple, in ways both good and bad. No man bred in the city can fully appreciate the isolation that attends country life, and its effects on the human soul. How each settlement becomes a small, stagnant pond, where life forms develop without interference from the "outside"; whose laws are determined by the will of a patriarch, where justice is what seems legitimate to fewer than a dozen men.

It occurred to me that this was Eddie's America—whose inbred inhabitants became inured to the grotesques they had made of themselves.

Economy Manor was a remnant of an even older form of settlement, one that preceded the remaining farms in the area—and even more isolated as well; a remnant of the German penchant for forming cults around activities and ideas, from the hunting of boars to breast-feeding children at the age of twelve. A time when every dispute over philosophy or doctrine had the capacity to become the basis for a way of life.

Compared to the rest of Germantown, the woods surrounding Economy Manor created a small island of primordial swamp in the midst of a garden. Conifers that dated to wilderness times. Fruit trees that had gone to seed for so many generations as to resemble the limbs of giant hags, contorted this way and that by the pressure of surrounding birches and alders. The result was an impassable wall of vegetation, pierced by a narrow driveway that might have been the entrance to a medieval fort.

Above us, like a celestial scarecrow, the crumbling tower added a sinister touch to the disheveled property, as though proclaiming a purpose behind this vegetative pandemonium.

The driveway was so pitted with holes and trenches as to be scarcely a drive anymore; we dismounted and walked rather than risk splitting a hoof or breaking a leg. Eventually we reached a stone wall surrounding a clearing about the size of a football pitch, containing what seemed to have once been a tiny village. After tethering the hosses beyond sight and sound, we crouched beneath the wall, peered over, and took stock.

Had we ventured upon a field of dinosaur skeletons I should not have experienced a stronger sense of having wandered into something that belonged to another age. The wall itself was of a type of masonry that had not been practiced for at least a century. Within its boundaries, the foundations of collapsed buildings and the construction of the few remaining ones belonged to a time when men worked not for money or ambition, but as repayment to God for something done or not done by some distant relative in biblical times.

Putnam spoke in a rather officious whisper, as though we were on a training exercise. "There are three inhabited buildings, if you count the church in the middle. He must be in one of them."

"Well and good," I said. "However, these sects often segregate the sexes; therefore Mr. Dickens and my wife may not be in the same building."

"I was not aware of that."

"Try to remember, Mr. Putnam, that we are not on the same mission. I don't give a hoot about your hostage. I am here to rescue mine."

This was all bombast of course, and a lie besides, since my warped objective was to murder my old friend Eddie. I felt my pistol under my coat; with only one shot, and only one eye, not for the first time did I feel out of my depth. Not for the first time was I seized by the panicked impulse to simply get up and run away, flee, disappear, and do . . . something else.

"I plumb knackered myself bringing you along," said Putnam. "It will be a black mark on my record for certain."

"Nonsense, Mr. Putnam. Had you left me behind in Philadelphia, I should have gone straight to the press, thereby triggering an international incident. Precisely what your superiors engaged you to avoid."

"Point taken," replied Putnam, but he appeared to take no comfort in it.

"What procedure are we going to follow?" I asked. "I am only a simple doctor; you are the professional with all the expertise."

"Dunno," he replied, at length. "I need more information. A better vantage point."

Suddenly, in the way that a dog moves when he sees a squirrel, my companion leaped the wall and traversed the clearing, in a crouched scurry used by infantrymen on an advance through open country, as far as the stone foundation of a ruined barn.

He disappeared inside the foundation. Seconds later his head reappeared as he waved impatiently for me to follow. I did so, but with less grace and slower speed.

Now we found ourselves behind a wall of rough stonework in what was once a shallow cellar. Before us and perhaps twenty paces away stood two plain, tall buildings shaped like oblong boxes, separated by a sort of pagoda with the absurd steeple sprouting out of its cap.

"We must wait until we know where the hostages are being kept," said Putnam.

"How long do you suppose that will take?"

"Dunno. I am a federal agent, not a fortune-teller." It was the first time I had seen Putnam become testy, and I began to suspect that he too was out of his depth.

We waited, crouched on our haunches against the masonry, staring at the darkening sky awaiting the moon, each utterly uninterested in what the other was thinking. Then I sensed a vague rumble, a slight earth tremor, which became a furious clatter from the direction of the front gate, and in rolled a prairie schooner, hosses in a lather as though doused with whipped cream. The driver, whom I recognized at once, hauled furiously on the reins, the wagon lurched to a halt, and out tumbled a number of shavers in duster coats, in a great hurry.

"The driver is O'Reilly," I said. "We are in the right place."

"You recognize him from a considerable distance," said Putnam. You must have seen him at close quarters."

"Close enough for him to pluck out my eye."

CHAPTER THIRTY-THREE

Economy Manor

After several hours attempting to collaborate, having filled the room with cigarette smoke as an opaque defense against Poe's absurd interpretations, Dickens had begun to experience a sensation of having died already, in his sleep perhaps. Now he faced eternal punishment for his sins as a writer—for what could be worse than to have one's work perversely misinterpreted in an eternal, Satanic seminar?

As a literary interrogator Poe was relentless, being eager to have the thing over and done, and with no wish to invent a word more than absolutely necessary. At the same time, like all writers of tales, Poe had acquired firm opinions about what constituted acceptable fiction, and Dickens's explications fell well short of the mark.

"Suh, as I see it, being a demon in human form, Uriah Heep might disappear into thin air before he can be charged with any crime, as the beast incarnate. Or better yet, at some moment during his trial, before a stunned magistrate, Heep's flesh might fall away to the bare skeleton, which would clatter to the floor in a pile of bones."

"Confound it, Mr. Poe, you weary me with your ghastly ideas! Where did you unearth that one? Not from anything in *Copperfield,* surely."

"On the contrary, suh. From your text, how is any conclusion possible other than that Heep is a supernatural being? Look at your descriptions of him, suh. At every opportunity you evoke his 'cadaverous' appearance. In other movements he resembles a serpent. In his speech he resembles a vampire—that produces no reflection in a glass. Why plant these seeds of meaning, if not to reveal Heep as beyond human?"

"This might seem mundane to you, Mr. Poe, but I described him thus so that the reader could identify him next time he appears. Surely you don't expect the casual reader of a serialized novel to recognize more than one primary quality per character."

"And all you mean to point out about Mr. Heep is that he is *thin*?"

"Well, it could never be, simply, *thin*. C*adaverous* sticks more firmly in the mind, don't you see. But, Mr. Poe, just because a man is thin, even cadaverous, it does not follow that he is a supernatural being."

Then what, suh, am I to make of the following?" Poe rose to his feet, cleared his throat, and read aloud, in the resonant voice that had held audiences spellbound over "The Raven":

> . . . the poker got into my dozing thoughts besides, and wouldn't come out. I thought, between sleeping and waking, that it was still red-hot, and I had snatched it out of the fire, and run him through the body. I was so haunted by this idea that I stole into the next room to look at him. There I saw him, lying on his back, with his legs extending to I don't know where, gurglings taking place in his throat, stoppages in his nose, and his mouth open like a post office.

"I like the post office comparison," remarked its author. "Really, I don't think I've seen that before."

"Odd that you should say that, suh, having written it yourself."

"Perhaps, but it might just as well have been written by someone else, for I have no memory of it whatsoever."

"With so little thought given to it, no wonder you are so prolific."

CHAPTER THIRTY-FOUR

Economy Manor

W ord reached O'Reilly of the impending raid as he was conducting business in Moyamensing. Shadduck was well known in the township and his activities closely monitored. When Shadduck somehow cobbled together a *posse comitatus* out of a gang from the Fourth Ward known as the True Blue Americans, the lieutenant was informed of this within minutes. Then further word arrived that the gang was preparing to head south to Germantown, and O'Reilly concluded, correctly, that his enterprise had been blown. One of his party had peached. Economy Manor was subject to attack.

Shadduck had been a worry from the moment he first appeared. To begin, he was not confined to any particular township, and could cross boundaries at will. And his police methods, with his paid informants and hired toughs, set members of the criminal class against one another, corrupted the gangs from within.

To the Irishman such tactics seemed to belong more to the realm of civil war than to the activities of a constable or watchman. Seen in hindsight, it would have been better had Shadduck been put off his feet straightaway. But there was no point in crying over spilled milk . . .

An hour after, having snatched the *Na Coisantoiri* from their various occupations, the prairie schooner thundered out of Moyamensing to Germantown Avenue—past the orchards and the linen works, past solemn bearded gentlemen in broad-brimmed hats and enormous women in white bonnets, past the Mennonite church and the Quaker church and the Baptist church and the Pietist church, until at last the spire of Economy Manor beckoned in the distance. Whipping the horses to further exertion, in his imagination O'Reilly speculated on the snake in their bosom—for certainly there was one.

Seen in hindsight, it was inevitable that Shadduck would seek out a member of the Irish Brotherhood. But who was the bad member? Who was the snitch?

In his mind, like the rising moon, O'Reilly saw before him the face of Finn Devlin. The partner had always been capricious, always righteous, always ready to perform some suicidal deed for a symbol. Money mattered nothing to him, nor even his life. Here was a man perfectly willing to assassinate Old Rough and Ready, the president of the United States—simply to avenge himself on an author . . .

Now it was clear. Devlin planned to kill Dickens, whether or not the ransom was paid. Then he would provoke a donnybrook with the police. A grand battle, an irresistible opportunity for martyrdom. The Irish Brotherhood would be consumed in a grand blaze, along with O'Reilly's fifty thousand dollars, and he would never be mayor of Philadelphia.

Putnam and I peered over the stone foundation while a curious scene took place before us by the light of the rising moon.

Moving at a run, O'Reilly disappeared inside the building to the right of the church, while the shavers milled about the wagon with grave expressions on their thin, pale faces. Now the sound of shouting from inside the building, while another group of young men poured out of the building to mingle with the others in a state of great agitation. Now out of the building came a good-looking young man, followed closely by the lieutenant, waving his cudgel and speaking furiously to the younger man in a foreign language. Then O'Reilly turned and struck him in the face with a sweeping gesture and the younger man went down with what appeared to be a cut above one eye. Moving quickly, O'Reilly crouched beside the man and lifted his hand, and from personal experience I knew exactly what he was about to do.

He was stopped by a series of sudden, urgent cries from the direction of the front gate; now a shaver with the face of an old man appeared at a full run, elbowed his way past the other boys, and spoke to Lieutenant O'Reilly—something about coppers, and a word that sounded like *saddle*. O'Reilly immediately rose to his feet and, without another glance at the young man lying on the ground, gathered his young men in what looked to be a football huddle. At a shout they dispersed in orderly groups of a half dozen, each apparently with a sense of purpose, while the young man on the ground slowly rose to his knees, then to his feet, then disappeared inside the building in the middle that must have been a church.

"The church," my companion hissed into my ear. "They are keeping him in the church."

From inside the church, if that is what it was, came more shouting, but with one voice distinctly female. With the look of a decision taken, Putnam drew out his four-barreled pistol and prepared to vault the stone foundation, just as the church door opened and the young man reappeared with blood streaming into one eye, in the company of a dark-haired woman with a pale, round face, pulling at his arm and pleading in French and English and a third language as well.

Non mon ami, it is *pas necessaire,* you do not have to do this!

Leave me, woman! *Coimhéad fearg fhear na foighde!*

As the two engaged in their furious jabber, out of the church came a half-dozen elderly crones, each with a small sack made from a bed-sheet. At first they seemed to be about to follow the man and woman into the building to the left. Short of the entrance, however, they turned abruptly and made their way together through the tall grass toward the woods to the rear—then suddenly vanished, all at once, as though by witchcraft.

The man and woman disappeared into the building.

"Dickens is there, for certain," said Putnam, and over the wall we went.

THE LITERARY DISCUSSION was silenced by sounds of anger and urgency, then the sound of feet on the stairway. As they entered, the ancient sentry beneath the clock abruptly rose to her feet and shuffled out the door and down the stairs without a word.

"A good night to you, Sister," said Dickens, then recognized the figure in the doorway as the young Irishman who had accompanied him from the hotel.

"Good evening to you as well, sir," he said to the young man, then turned to his female companion with an expression of deep sadness. "And to you as well, Miss Genoux. I see now that any affection you expressed for me was simply to gain my trust. How stoic of you to indulge me in such a fashion. I hope that my presence did not disgust you overmuch."

"I beg you do not make a laugh of it, sir," she said. "Monsieur Dickens, *jesuis desolé*. I am so sorry. So unhappy for what he is going to do."

"I do not understand you," said Dickens, and turned his attention to the young man with blood coming from a wound over his eye. The eyes were remarkably blue, and never in his life had Dickens seen eyes staring at him with such clear, pure hatred. "You should know, sir," he said feebly, "that I have written extensively in favor of Irish rights."

When the young man laughed, it contained so little merriment that Dickens hardly recognized the sound.

"Your countrymen, sir, your people, slit the throats of Irish children in my village as if they were pigs, sor. I watched it all, sir, from the crawl space under the house, saw it with my own eyes, sor, ten years old I was. It is too late for the sympathy of an Englishman, sir, I don't want it."

"You are such a fool with your symbols," said Miss Genoux, bitterly. "While you fight your symbols the murderers are gone, gone away, *mon ami*, the beast, he always get away!"

From the expression on the young man's face, she might as well have been shouting at the moon.

"I thought you were different but you are *la même chose, tu comprends*, you and Marat, you are just the same!"

"Revenge is never perfect," replied Devlin softly, taking out of his coat pocket what appeared to be a knife but which on closer inspection turned out to be a spike, of the kind used by sailors to splice heavy rope.

"Are ye Catholic, Mr. Dickens, sir?" he asked.

"Church of England, actually, but my attendance is poor, said the pale man with the tired eyes, lighting a cigarette. "Why do you ask, sir?"

"Because ye might want to say a prayer."

THE PINCH OF it was that Shadduck had had neither time nor resources to survey the field beforehand, or even send an advance party.

Through informants, Smit was able to provide a general picture of Germantown, which suggested that the enemy zone would be more or less typical of the area—cultivated fields, orchards, and settlements, with intermittent small forests serving as windbreaks and woodlots.

The company having assembled two hours after schedule, the ride to Germantown had been hindered by dissenstion among the men—they were, after all, thugs and goons in private life, with general devilment their principal incentive.

By the time the company reached Germantown the sun had dipped below the surrounding fringe of trees, and the sheer impassability of the wood surrounding Economy Manor became evident. Seeing this, Shadduck ordered a halt and called Smit to account.

"Sure and the thickness of it is shocking to me also," said Smit.

"We're policemen," added Coutts, standing beside Smit as support, "we are naw red Indians."

"Leave me alone while I cogitate on it," said Shadduck, lighting a cheroot.

"What am I saying to the men?" asked Smit.

"Tell them to play some cards."

The original plan had been for his men to take two positions, from which they would advance in a pincer movement, rolling up the left and right flanks of the enemy, forcing a retreat to the open rear. Being young men, there was every possibility the enemy would desert, leaving Shadduck with a simpler mission and lower attrition on both sides.

A reasonable plan in theory, and standard procedure for a limited action. And completely out of the question.

Two tactics suggested themselves: either fall back or continue. Given the uncertain loyalty of his troops, there was every chance the former would degenerate into mass desertion, abandoning Mr. Dickens to his fate. *Don't throw out the dirty water till you get in fresh* went the saying. And so they would advance. However it must be done at once, for the property's one road would be impassable after dark, even with torches.

When Smit had assembled the men at the edge of the wood, Shadduck ordered horses to be tethered, torches cut and wound with kerosene-soaked cotton, and issued a command of silence as they advanced on foot down the overgrown driveway to within sight of the enemy camp.

As anyone might have predicted, silence—or indeed any sort of discipline among this company of goons—proved impossible. Most had brought alcohol to guard against the chill, and even the sober fellers were unprepared to obey any command other than to go out and beat somebody up.

By now the task for Shadduck was to maintain order in his own mind, for he was in danger of making a balls of the entire operation. Using a combination of experience, logical elimination, and inherited wisdom, he had blundered into a hole. *Every man has a fool up his sleeve . . .*

Notwithstanding the pacifist convictions of its Communist founders, the enemy position turned out to be admirably defensible, and all but immune to surprise. Whatever the hour or season, an invader must funnel out of a hole in the woods, at most two or three abreast, to face a clearing and, beyond a stone wall, a fully assembled defense at a shooting distance of no more than twenty paces.

This is precisely what had happened to Shadduck and his *posse comitatus*. Indeed, it was only because the shavers lacked artillery (or any medium-range weapon) that Shadduck's company avoided immediate annihilation. Looking across the low bushes at the assembled enemy beyond the wall, the inspector felt a kinship with Indian fighters who underestimate Apache warriors and are reduced to hairless corpses, one by one.

For sure he was in a scrape.

It was no comfort that the enemy troops were between ten and twelve years of age. Shadduck had seen plenty of units that age on the Mexican side, well drilled and effective. And Shadduck had made inquiries about the *Na Coisantoiri*, enough to know that there were a good many of them, and all of them had taken weapons training of some sort. A few carried pistols for certain, but most relied on identical heavy-knobbed fighting sticks, each one three feet in length. Shadduck had seen these sticks in action and it was a sobering display.

His own company of men was, as his mother would say, another piece of calico.

It is not unreasonable for the respectable citizen to envisage a gang as a sort of militia, with a command structure and a sense of camaraderie. In the case of the True Blue Americans, however, that analogy went off-course.

The True Blue Americans were an amalgam of two trade gangs, one a band of butcher's assistants called the Butcher Boys, and the other a party of printers' devils and apprentice bookbinders known as the Roach Parade. The former group, predictably, liked to employ butcher's cleavers and other implements of the trade, while the latter preferred to work with their hobnailed boots, brine-hardened fists, and their teeth, often filed to points.

Though as likely to fly at one another as at the enemy, the True Blue Americans did possess a sort of uniform—a blue stripe sewed onto the outside seam of their trousers, and an oversized plug hat, dyed blue and stuffed with leather and cotton. This alteration made it possible to withstand a blow to the head from a rock or a brickbat. However, it made their heads appear huge.

It was a matter of debate which gang possessed the superior arsenal, but Shadduck would have bet on the cudgels of the *Na Coisantoiri* for their effectiveness at both close and medium quarters. Held at arm's length, the knob would break a man's skull from a distance of five feet. Move inside and the shaft with its sharpened branch ends could tear off his face with a quick swipe.

Observing the overall situation, Shadduck saw that he would be a fortunate officer to get out with his own skin.

As the two companies traded insults from a distance, working up their temper and nerve, it became clear that close contact fighting must be avoided at any cost.

In the war, any commander on the field who did not wish to be shot in the back obeyed certain cardinal rules—one of which was never to lead his unit into close quarters fighting without a clear and obvious advantage. In this case, he saw none.

Of greatest worry was that the enemy had been trained under a single command, the gentleman on horseback thirty paces away. Shadduck noted the way he would speak in a low voice to an assistant, who would relay the order forward according to protocol. Shadduck recognized the leader as O'Reilly, a familiar figure in Moyamensing. His eloquent partner, however, was nowhere to be seen. Shadduck wondered why.

One thing was certain: to avoid bloodshed on both sides, that officer must be shot. *A stitch in time saves nine.*

"Request parley!" Shadduck shouted out, and took several paces forward so that he now stood halfway between his men and the wall. In a moment O'Reilly's head and shoulders appeared above the wall, his single eye focused as though to bore a hole straight through him. Shadduck stood there in silence. *If you have nothing to say, say nothing . . .*

Shadduck watched the feller with one eye as he stepped forward to within ten paces, carrying his cudgel casually like it was a furled umbrella. Shadduck saw the notches in the stick and wondered what they meant.

"Inspector Shadduck is your name I believe, sor."

"And I suspect you are Mr. O'Reilly, sir."

"*Lieutenant* O'Reilly if you please, sor."

"Maybe so. I am told your are a veteran of the war, sir. And I have heard other things besides."

"A veteran of the war like your own self." O'Reilly opened his duster coat to reveal an infantry tunic.

To Shadduck's eye, neither the man nor his tunic looked like officer material. However, he said nothing about this. *Never call out a man until you know what is behind him.*

"And what else did Mr. Devlin have to say?" asked the Irishman. "He is an acquaintance of yours, I think."

"I have never spoken to the man, sir."

"Yet he has spoken to you is what I'm thinking."

Even while speaking, Shadduck's mind was elsewhere, forming a new plan.

Unknown to the inspector, Lieutenant O'Reilly was no more interested in a donnybrook than his enemy. Unlike men who fight for causes, he knew what he wanted. He wanted fifty thousand dollars. If a donnybrook took place and officers of the law were killed, he would be a hunted man, and would have to uproot himself again, begin again. This O'Reilly was willing to do, but not without his fifty thousand dollars.

"What is it to be, Inspector Shadduck?" Riley called. "Is it a pitched battle you have in yer mind?"

"You know me then, do you, sir?"

"True for you, Inspector, you are the talk of Moyamensing. And you with your squealers, sure, you must know me as well."

"I reckon that is a fact, sor. As an officer charged with violent disturbances, I am obliged to make certain inquiries."

"There is no violent disturbance here, sor. You have come in error."

"Maybe so. Still, it is my duty to act on my suspicions, sir, and to satisfy them for myself."

"I am an honest man for certain. You may feel free to ask what you like and I will answer all of it."

"Have you ever taken out a man's eye?"

"I have, sir," replied O'Reilly, and held up his little finger with the long nail. *"If thy eye offend thee, tear it out."*

"Did Mr. Dickens's eye offend you, sir?"

"I do not understand what you mean," said O'Reilly, now certain that he had been betrayed by Devlin.

"According to his wife, Mr. Dickens's eye was hazel in color. The eye you sent the councilman was blue. Therefore, I have hope that he still has his two eyes."

"I have never read Dickens," replied O'Reilly.

"Yet you have him here on the property, do you not?"

"I have not kept track of the books in my library," replied O'Reilly, baring amber teeth, the front ones missing.

"To hold a man against his will is a criminal offense, sir. As an officer of Philadelphia County I must arrest you on a charge of kidnapping."

"Kidnapping is a hanging offense, sor."

"That is so."

"I am not certain of your investigation, Inspector, and I put little faith in your deputies." O'Reilly scratched his chin delicately with the long nail of his little finger.

"Nor I yours," replied Shadduck. "Respectable fellers do not hire children in their defense."

"My lads are well paid and well fed and fully under my command. Can you say the same, sor?"

"I don't have to, sir. My aim is not to capture enemy territory but to enforce the law of the land."

"An interesting distinction."

"To be sure."

"You were a cavalry officer yourself, Inspector Shadduck. You have experience in the field. Surely you are not counting on this pack of wolves for support. As their commanding officer, do you even know their names?"

O'Reilly had pegged Shadduck on that one, for the inspector did not know a single one of their names. *An officer who doesn't know his men.* Is that what he had become?

"We are civilians now, sir," said the inspector. "I suspicion you have noticed there is a difference between war and peace."

"No, sor. Or if there is a difference, it is a subtle one."

With the grace of an athlete, O'Reilly vaulted the stone wall on the balance of one hand; in doing so his duster coat opened and Shadduck could see the markings of an infantryman.

"We are officers and gentlemen, sor," continued O'Reilly, stepping forward. "And it will always be so. Might it be a more pleasant affair for all concerned if we were to keep it between ourselves?"

"I am not here to fight a skirmish with your men, sir. I am here to place you under arrest."

"Surely we two have seen enough young blood for one lifetime," said O'Reilly, then held aloft his cudgel with the notches in the stem. "Do you know what this is?" he asked.

"I do, sir. It is what you people call a *shillelagh*."

"You pronounce it well. It is made for the Whiskey Dance. A grand thing is the Whiskey Dance."

"What are you leading to, sir? I do not understand what you are suggesting."

"A fight between champions, sor. It is a grand tradition among my people. And yours too, with your gunfighters in the West."

"Only a fool takes up an unfamiliar weapon, sir. It is a poor gardener who does not know his rake."

"Come, sor. You have taken saber training for certain."

"I was an officer in the cavalry, it is true."

"There we are then. For certain the two are nearly the same, if you go to that of it. Indeed, the saber-trained fighter has an advantage. Being infantry I have only bayonet and marksman training, and that will offer no help with the *bhata*."

"You are barking at the moon, Mr. O'Reilly. I will not be goaded into fighting you on your own terms."

O'Reilly turned to the worn-looking little fellow now seated on the wall nearby. "What do you think, Ned? Do you think our man is to be *goaded?*"

In place of a reply, Ned took out a pistol and aimed it directly at Shadduck's chest. By the way he held the weapon it was clear that he was comfortable with it. At the present distance he had an excellent chance.

"This young gentleman is known as Pistol Ned," said O'Reilly, as though he were introducing his son. "A young man of rare accomplishment. It is said that he shot a man in the throat from, oh, about your distance—at the age of six."

Shadduck said nothing. *Let the other person talk. You never know what he might tell you.*

"Come now, Inspector Shadduck," said O'Reilly, as though disappointed. "Your silence disappoints me. To enjoy the Whiskey Dance, you must enter fully into the form and the ritual of it. Let me begin, sor. Now is the moment when I address the cock of the tin: *Is that Captain Shadduck? Is that the cock of the tin?*"

So saying, O'Reilly nodded behind him and one of the *Na Coisantoiri* threw a cudgel over the wall that landed at Shadduck's feet.

Shadduck quickly picked up the weapon, at which signal the *Na Coisantoiri* began to rap their cudgels rhythmically against the stone wall like savages (which they resembled with the marks on their faces), making a sound like a herd of tiny horses galloping down a cobblestone road. For his part, O'Reilly began a strange little dance, a sort of jig, while he shouted traditional insults at the inspector, to huzzas from his boys.

"May the devil cut the head off you and make a day's work of your neck!"

Huzzah!

"May the seven terriers of hell sit on the spool of your breast, and chase you over the hills of Damnation!"

Huzzah!

"And the curse of Crumble to you!"

Huzzah!

"The treatment of the boiled broken little fish to you!"

Huzzah!

O'Reilly cut the distance between them in half, while the troops on both sides watched carefully. He cut a graceful figure, holding his *bhata* as though it were an extension of his arm and fist, feet moving rhythmically forward and back, ready for the strike.

Shadduck abruptly dropped his cudgel, pulled out the Texas Paterson from his trouser belt, and shot O'Reilly in the face.

O'Reilly hit the ground on his back, dead already, as though he had been struck down by the hand of God.

Putnam and I eased our way up the narrow, ill-lit, evil-smelling stairway to a door behind which we could hear muffled shouts and the sound of feet. Already my heart was racing over the deed I was about to undertake. I thought, if there is anything more stressful than to murder, it is waiting to murder. It would be ironic at the least were I to take a fit and die over the prospect of killing Eddie.

At the top of the stairway, Putnam stopped and turned in my direction; looming over me in the darkness. For the first time he appeared not as the gauche dandy but as something quite different—thanks, probably, to the enormous weapon he carried in his fist.

"I suggest you stay behind me at all times, sir," he said, and immediately burst through the door.

I took out my pistol and stepped into a room with many beds, like a hospital ward. Putnam stood with his back to me, seemingly frozen to the spot, watching two men fight a duel, sword against spike. I recognized Eddie's sword as having come from the walking stick he took into the hospital, seemingly ages ago. His opponent was the young man with blue eyes, and with blood covering one side of his face.

With one foot forward and his sword at full extension, Poe was able to keep his wiry young opponent on the defensive and off-balance; evidently his saber training had held, somewhat. Meanwhile, by a table covered with writing materials stood a pale, worried-looking man in a soiled bottle-green coat and a mustard waistcoat, nervously smoking a cigarette.

"Willie!" cried Eddie when I came into view. "Dear God, what a friend you are!"

"Yes, Eddie," I replied. "We are friends for life." Then I lifted my pistol, aimed it at his chest, and fired—and in that moment our eyes met, and I was certain that he knew all that he had done to me, and how much I hated him for it.

But I missed.

The bullet sailed through the air and shattered a window at the other end of the room. I did not have access to another round.

"Jesus Christ!" cried Putnam, nearly deafened by the blast, as the young man with what appeared to be a spike in his hand momentarily turned in my direction—and Eddie took advantage of the opening to execute a lunge.

With a sigh, the young man looked down at the spreading stain on his shirt beneath the rib cage, then sat on the floor, legs spread out like a toddler, while the dark-haired woman crouched in the corner let out a howl like an animal.

PISTOL NED AIMED his weapon straight at Shadduck's chest. The inspector's Paterson did likewise, but the contest was not equal, for the boy made a smaller target, just a head and shoulders behind the wall.

"Don't do it, Ned," he said. "If you hit the mark, you will be hanged for it. If you miss, you will be shot. These fellers need you. The lieutenant is finished. You are their leader now." Shadduck's voice took on an almost singsong tone, as though to appeal to whatever was left of the child in him.

Ned's careworn expression did not change. Shadduck heard the snick of a hammer pulled back. In his peripheral vision he saw top hats appear over the wall, like young aristocrats observing a boxing match or a hanging.

"The Daybreak Boys you were once called, is it so?" continued Shadduck. "And I reckon that is what you are now. You are not an Irishman, Pistol Ned. Nor are your men. You are an American, and you are a leader of Americans, and you have no business hanging for a foreign country."

A long, deliberate pause followed. Even the True Blue Americans behind him had fallen silent. Then Shadduck heard the snick of Ned's hammer, and the shaver pulled back his pistol. Momentarily catching Shadduck's eye, he nodded briskly, then disappeared behind the wall. Shadduck returned the Paterson to his belt, took a deep breath, and lit a cheroot. He was thinking, Pistol Ned is a sharp young feller, with a future. A useful informant, as well.

Assured that any danger to himself was past, Smit appeared beside Shadduck in the clearing to offer congratulations. "Sure, and that was a very close scrape, sir."

"Not especially," replied Shadduck.

IN A SITUATION of chaos, a man reverts to habit. In this case, I attended to the wounded Irishman.

"Will he die?" asked the pale woman with the French accent as she knelt beside me.

"The puncture did not appear to have pierced an organ. With pressure maintained on the wound he will take a while to bleed to death. As for the head wound, it will not heal unless it is sewn."

"We must take him away from here. You will help me."

"Madam, why on earth would I do such a thing?"

"Because that is how you will ever again see your wife. You wish her alive, *n'est pas?*"

In my peripheral vision the tip of Poe's sword appeared. "You tried to shoot me, Willie," he said, with more than a note of hurt.

"You were already dead, Eddie. I thought it best for everyone that you remain so."

"It concerns Elmira, does it not? It has to do with our engagement. Oh, my dear fellow—"

"It could be any number of issues, Eddie. Such as the fact that they are about to dig up your grave. And we know what they will find, do we not? Remember, it is not your signature on the death certificate, Eddie, it is mine. I am the criminal, not you."

"Oh dear. I had not thought of that."

"My life is over, Eddie, thanks to you. All I ask is that you do not turn this into one of your little vignettes of jealousy and revenge and horror. If there is one thing I beg of you, Eddie, please do not write about me and put me in a damn magazine."

Poe seemed momentarily at a loss for words. As far as he was concerned, I was supposedly his best friend in the world, and, therefore, the best friend of his genius. If anyone would want to save his literary reputation, at whatever cost, surely it would be his friend Willie.

That is how self-centered a poet can become; like an open nerve when dealing in his own sensibilities, while utterly incapable of imagining what it might be like to be somebody else.

Another pair of legs appeared beside me, in a pair of soiled green trousers. "If you will excuse me, sir, my name is Charles Dickens, and I believe Mr. Poe saved my life a moment ago. As an Englishman I will defend him to the death if need be."

"Am I dying?" asked the young man on the floor, who was only partially awake.

"You are coming with me," Sister Genoux hissed into my ear. "You are going to help. Or I swear to you that you will never see your wife alive."

THE TWO POLICEMAN remained standing by Lieutenant O'Reilly's corpse while the covered wagon containing Pistol Ned and the Daybreak Boys rumbled out of the compound and down the drive on their way back to Moyamensing.

"Sure, they are bad members and will be trouble," said Smit, pursing his lips and shaking his head in a way that reminded Shadduck of a rooster on alert.

"I reckon we'll have some of them fellers on the force one day," he said.

"Inspector, it is shameful the way you joke about things sometimes."

O'Reilly's corpse lay flat on its back, arms spread like Jesus, eyes wide open, an expression of surprise in one, and with a hole in the center of his face mouthing a silent *o*. Looking at the empty socket, in his imagination Inspector Shadduck saw a faint glow, like the last coal in the hearth to die.

Fire!

For a veteran there is no more alarming word in the language, even from a distance. Shadduck wheeled around and dropped to one knee, half-expecting a bullet in the back. Instead, he saw pot-hatted men beneath their half-dead torches, sharing bottles of whiskey and smoking.

"Who gave that order?" he shouted. "Who gave an order to fire?"

Smit took Shadduck's arm and helped him to his feet. "Sir, it was not an order," he said. "It is a fire."

FOR THE SECOND time in our lives, Eddie and I found ourselves on either end of a stretcher containing the inert body of a stranger. Devlin was much heavier than his predecessor, being alive.

On this occasion, Eddie held the rear position, which I preferred because it spared me having to look at him. "I didn't mean to ruin your life, Willie," he said. "Why would I want to do such a thing?"

"I have no idea, Eddie. It seemed to come naturally to you."

"Whatever has happened between us, even the latest incident, as far as I am concerned you are still my best friend. If I have done you a disservice, I swear that I will make it up to you."

"I doubt that very much, Eddie."

"You will see."

We maneuvered the stretcher clumsily down the staircase and through the door, then followed Miss Genoux through the long grass behind Economy Manor. Over her shoulder she carried a sack of belongings, presumably retrieved from the church.

By the flattened grass in front of us it occurred to me that we were in the path of the old women I had seen leaving the church earlier, before they seemed to disappear by magic. Halfway across the clearing, however, I began to make out what can only be described as a hole in the forest, a tubular passage that might as well have been a tunnel. It appeared to be another way out of the property, a century-old way of escape, carved through the forest in case of attack by enemies who never materialized, if they existed. There was no telling where the tunnel led, if indeed it led anywhere at all.

We stopped for breath. "Sister," I said, "can you not see the futility of all this? We will surely be overtaken by the police."

"I am not worried about that," said Miss Genoux, lighting a cigarette.

In the distance behind us, I thought I heard a voice shout *Fire*.

THE BLAZE OCCURRED in the central building. It had been ignited from inside, so that the high steeple served a flue, drawing the heat upward. By the time Shadduck had mounted the stone wall for a better look, already the garland on top was in flames, so that the burning tower illuminated the property like an enormous torch.

Fire!

After receiving an offer of double pay for the additional work, the True Blue Americans were persuaded to perform their professional function as firemen. However, there being no hose nor an apparent water source to draw from, all that could be done was to give the building a wide berth until it could be determined which way the flaming tower would topple.

As the area brightened to near-daylight visibility, it occurred to Shadduck that, in addition to Smit, Coutts, the True Blue Americans, and himself, there was an additional presence—two gentlemen, one of whom appeared vaguely familiar.

"Good evening, sir," said the shorter man. "I am Charles Dickens, and this is my assistant, Mr. Putnam."

"Mr. Dickens," replied Shadduck. "You are just the feller I was looking for."

We stumbled down the long-forgotten pathway (being in front I took the branches in the face), over roots that had turned what was once a path into a series of low hurdles. I was too preoccupied with my footing to glance behind me in order to ascertain the source of the light. I assumed it to be coming from the torches of our pursuers. Out of sheer physical and spiritual exhaustion, I welcomed them in my mind, whoever they were.

Trudging along behind me, sagging under the weight of our mutual burden, Eddie kept an uncharacteristic silence, and on the few occasions that he spoke it was with a preoccupied air. As for me, my anger against him was now a spent force that had transformed into a sort of bewildered awe. As well, succeeding waves of mental nausea came over me, much like the panic I had experienced during the ordeal in Washington College Hospital. The enormity, the sheer inconceivability of my situation began to overwhelm me, along with a series of mental pictures—memories of the war, the hospital tent, my mother, like a whirlpool spinning me down, black, unfathomable . . .

*   *   *

I WISH TO commend everyone present," said Dickens, "for doing such an excellent job of it."

Shadduck turned to Putnam. "Who are you really, sir?" he asked. "Whom do you represent? What is your interest in the case?"

"I am a federal agent, sir," said Putnam. "And the case may have resolved itself."

LOOKING BACK, I imagine that procession of fools through the absurd overgrowth of vegetation as eyeless creatures snouting their way out of the depths of the earth toward an assumed opening in the prehistoric quest for air and light and life. So it was with Miss Genoux, Eddie, myself, and our mutual burden, shuffling and stumbling our way along with no object but forward—and it does not matter where forward leads, if it is the only possible direction. As for the patient, he spoke only to complain of the pain, and to speculate on his proximity to death. I replied with something to the effect that, if it was death he worried about, pain was infinitely preferable to no pain. This medical commonplace only seemed to confuse him.

Whatever awaited us at the other end, from that point on I knew that I would be leading an existence that bore no resemblance to the one I had lived before. This thought bothered me not a bit. I had given up on any hope or expectation from the moment I had fired my pistol at Eddie, and missed. How typical. Since my old friend's reappearance in my admittedly unhappy life, it was safe to say that nothing had gone according to even the most short-term planning. At every turn there awaited a profound, unexpected shock to my past experience and future prospects. Like a man caught in a maelstrom, I could only submit to its power, go where it took me, wait and see.

We emerged from the forest into the light of a near-harvest moon, to find ourselves in a tiny overgrown graveyard whose markers were made of a soft white stone that actually seemed to glow in the dark. Six thin, plain obelisks leaned at oblique angles, each one surrounded by smaller stones, all dated, I was certain, within a month of each other, thanks to one or another epidemic—diphtheria, smallpox, scarlet fever, measles. A new disease arrived with each new wave of immigration, an influx of misery as varied and endless as the waves of the sea. Thrashing our way through the long grass I noticed other stones topped by skulls and crossbones, which had been painstakingly carved, accompanied by a cautionary message indicating a drowning, a hunting accident, someone kicked by his horse, and a warning that the reader be also ready. I failed to understand the point of this, whether it meant to imply that a sudden death was somehow more unpleasant than a lingering one, or that, with a bit of luck, one might give it the slip altogether.

The tiny building had been a Pietist church belonging to a congregation that had died out during the last century—there were not many followers to begin with, to judge by the size of the church.

The graves told a tale that might be summed up as: following successive epidemics, and seeing no end other than their own eventual demise, surviving members of the community simply became tired of burying people and went their separate ways.

The rough-hewn oak door at the rear of the church grunted its obdurate refusal as Miss Genoux pulled repeatedly on the rusted iron handle, and it was not until we set the patient down on the overgrown grass and added our combined weight to her effort that the door finally swung open with a shriek like a metal bird, causing Eddie and I to fall back upon the ground, while Miss Genoux disappeared inside.

After finding our feet again, my old friend and I took up our burden together for the last time, carried the Irish patient into the dark, musty room, and installed him in what appeared to be a rough pew. I examined his wounds. The forehead was still open, but had ceased to bleed. The opening in his side had begun to seep clear liquid, but the area was cool to the touch, and the swelling had not increased. By the light of a lamp held by a seamed ancient in a rust-colored dress, I changed the dressings.

"Am I dead yet?" asked the patient.

"Not as dead as you deserve to be," I said.

"Please do not joke about it," said Miss Genoux, kneeling beside the pew, wiping his forehead with the hem of her dress.

I turned my attention away from the patient into the gloom of the house of worship, and could make out the figures of elderly women. A half-dozen rough pews had been set in a square around a stove made of bricks, built at the same time as the building itself, in order to keep the congregation within a few degrees of freezing to death during a Sunday sermon in January. For certain, little warmth would have emanated from the pulpit, which stood so close to the ceiling at the end wall that the minister, if he was not a dwarf, must have had to preach on his knees.

"Dr. Chivahs. I am surprised and glad to see you."

Elmira Royster stood up from her position close to the stove, which she had taken in order to keep warm in her simple cotton dress. As had happened ever since I first saw her from my position beside the grave of Edgar Allan Poe, she put me at a loss for words.

"Good evening to you, ma'am," was my inadequate greeting. "I am very glad to see you as well."

"What have you done to your eye?" she asked.

"I am told that an ancient cure for a cynic was to pluck his eye out. That is what happened to me, madam."

For an instant our eyes met, and I felt a peculiar ache in my sternum. Then, as might be expected, someone else caught her eye. "Hello, Eddie," she said. "I am very glad to see that you are alive."

"Elmira," said Eddie, and his eyes became huge, with a most soulful expression on his handsome face, and I could barely resist stopping up my ears with my fingers not to listen to the saccharine sentiments that were sure to follow. However, as it had done so often in the recent past, fate decreed otherwise.

"Alas, madam, I am no happier than before," said Eddie. "My dear little Virginia haunts me still. The only time I can ever be at peace is when I am alone, holding her in my heart—or when I am in my grave."

"It was never my expectation that you would be a husband to me. I do not want another husband. I had one and that was enough."

"Then we are agreed, madam. Hence, with the greatest of respect, I must ask you to also agree that we put an end to our engagement."

With that statement, Eddie caught my eye with an almost imperceptible nod as though to say, *There.*

As far as Shadduck and the company were concerned, nothing further could be done until it was established which way the steeple would go down. The True Blue Americans, even in their role as true blue firemen, were understandably uneager to commit themselves either way. Nobody wants to find himself standing underneath a flaming beam, least of all a Philadelphia fireman.

As it happened, the tower collapsed upon itself like an upended telescope and then, like a felled tree, toppled to the left—and at once it was clear that the dormitory was finished, for the roof caught fire as though it had been coated with turpentine. Immediately the firemen set about the task of protecting the remaining building from wayward sparks.

"Is anyone inside?" asked Shadduck, without knowing what he would do if there was.

"An Irishman," replied Putnam. "Heavy with drink, I am afraid. No hope for him now."

"And a quantity of writing materials as well," said Dickens, with a measure of satisfaction.

SHOCKING DISCOVERY IN BALTIMORE
Author's Remains Stolen
by James Preston Wilcox, *The Philadelphia Inquirer*

The undertaking, initiated by Baltimore police, to exhume the body of Edgar Allan Poe was thrown into confusion Tuesday when investigators at the family plot in Baltimore Burial Ground discovered the grave to be empty. Police believe the felon to be either a party of grave robbers, or an admirer of the late Mr. Poe, whose work often dealt in bizarre and morbid themes. "Such undignified treatment of human remains is a serious crime," said Policeman Rennick, "and will be dealt with severely."

CHAPTER THIRTY-FIVE

S hadduck stood in the offices of Topham and Lea, noting the lack of clutter.

"Mr. Bailey, I reckon it is pretty well clear that your Mr. Topham was murdered by the Irish. With Mr. O'Reilly a veteran of the war, the shinbones said it all."

"The shinbones, sah?" asked Mr. Bailey, with the look of a man who was being subtly tortured.

"And the teeth of course," replied Shadduck.

"I do not follow you, sah. Am I intended to?"

"A barbaric practice, for certain. Yet here is where you might help me out, sir. I reckon it is an uncommon thing for such men as would do such a thing to have such a deep acquaintance with the ins and outs of the publishing business. Do you not agree, sir?"

"Though the Irish are avid readers, I am told."

"But other than pirated titles, Topham & Lee is not in the book business, financially speaking."

"You are wrong, sah. We continue to publish the most important books in America."

Shadduck crossed to the table by the door and examined the abolitionist tracts—cheaply bound and written, every one written or edited by a Nathaniel Washington Bailey.

"That is so, Mr. Bailey. This occurred to me, sir. The importance of it—to yourself, no less than anyone."

"It is important," said Mr. Bailey, whose hand shook as he lit his cheroot.

"It was not your race that caught my attention but the books you made. The difference between your interests and those of Mr. Topham. That you might have done better with another . . . partner came to my mind, if you get my meaning, sir."

Mr. Bailey opened a desk drawer and extracted a bottle of whiskey and two glasses. "May I offer you a drink, sah?"

"You may, sir. I am not presently on duty."

"Do you wish to wipe the glass? Many do."

"That will not be necessary."

Mr. Bailey got up from his desk and began to wander the room, touching various books as though for the last time. Only after touching each of his titles, and having taken four fingers of the amber liquid, did he find his voice.

"As you may know, Topham & Lea was founded by Quakers. Abolitionists—though we colored folks sat in separate pews."

"Does that latter fact rile you up, sir?"

"No, sah. Only that there are various ways of being helped."

"I don't follow your drift."

"No matter. My writing in the *Alton Observer*, up until my editor was lynched, had made a sufficient impression on them that my benefactors established the firm—as a platform for my essays and poems. Of course such an enterprise required an experienced publisher, and Mr. Topham's name was well known, even then."

"And who is Mr. Lea?" asked Shadduck. "I reckon I should speak to him as well."

"There is no Mr. Lea," replied Bailey. "Mr. Topham felt that a second name lent weight to the imprint. I need not tell you that the name *Bailey* was out of the question."

"A sensible business decision. But I reckon it might make a feller a mite peevish."

"Quite so. As did Mr. Topham's next move—which was to devote the firm to other products, more remunerative than discussions about slavery and lynching and the coming Fugitive Slave Act. But of course as a policeman you know this side of it. Mr. Topham certainly paid you enough to look the other way—and of course he was a principal supporter of Councilman Grisse."

Shadduck winced. "All this is well known to me," he lied.

"Of course when it came to this . . . shift in priorities, I could say nothing to my benefactors. Can you imagine, sah? With Henry Topham's word against mine, Sambo best hang himself on a limb, save hisself the indignities that goes wit' a lynchin'."

"There is no need to be sarcastic," replied Shadduck. I get your drift."

"And yet for all of my experience with white men, I was still susceptible . . ." With a small laugh Mr. Bailey poured himself another glass. Shadduck had not yet touched his.

"I confess to having been moved by a manuscript written by Mr. Finn Devlin. *White Niggers of America* was the title. Though I knew the term *white nigger* well (it is part of the no-nothing vocabulary), for the first time it occurred to me that the term might apply to something other than a man's color. And so I arranged a private meeting with Mr. Devlin, at which I spoke more frankly than I ever had—he had created a metaphor you see, which created a rapport between us, albeit a false one.

"I spoke admiringly of the work, but made it clear that it required a good deal of revision. I mentioned also that Mr. Topham remained an impediment to its publication—I admit this to you—and I spoke frankly of Mr. Topham's endeavors in the realm of fraudulent manufacture, and was specific about the profits that accrued. After all, it was my function to maintain two sets of books.

"When next we met to discuss the manuscript, Mr. Devlin introduced me to his partner, Lieutenant O'Reilly. Being of a more practical nature, Mr. O'Reilly presented me with a business plan that included a change of administration here at Topham & Lea. Upon acceptance, they murdered Mr. Topham."

"Surely you could not see into the future, sir."

"I did in this case."

"He was a bad member, Mr. Topham."

"Yes, sah. A corrupter of everything he touched."

"He must have riled you fearful."

"No, sir. One learns early on where anger gets you. I wished to continue my work for the betterment of my people. To do this I needed the protection of a white man. The Irishman had made a better offer, and Mr. Topham could go to the devil. And the queer thing of it is—he did."

"He did what, sir?"

For the first time in their short acquaintance, Mr. Bailey allowed himself a small laugh. "He went to the devil. A black man does not deal in money a great deal, sah, we trade on the barter system mostly among ourselves. Before knowing Mr. Topham, I did not imagine the lengths a white man will go to for money."

Mr. Bailey drained his whiskey, set it in the precise center of his desk, crossed the room, and opened the door. "Shall we proceed to the jail, sah?"

Now it was Shadduck who took a generous sip of Mr. Bailey's whiskey.

"According to my mother, sir, there are four kinds of homicide: felonious, excusable, justifiable, and praiseworthy. I have enough on my plate dealing with the first kind to be making distinctions over the other three.

"*Let the big dog eat*, is another thing my mother used to say. By which token I think she would tell me to let the small dog eat too."

Mr. Bailey shrugged. "As you like, sah. I believe I mentioned before that I am at your mercy."

"I do not accept that, sir. For I would not want to be at yours."

CHAPTER THIRTY-SIX

Philadelphia

DICKENS DEPARTS
Farewell and Good Riddance to Outspoken Scribe
by Sanford W. Mitchell, *The Philadelphia Inquirer*

Charles Dickens's unlucky visit to America is finally at an end. Having been treated like a spoiled child throughout, and having thoroughly worn out his welcome, he leaves our shores in the humor that often follows too lavish a bestowal of sugarplums on spoiled children. Unlike his arrival, his departure for Boston will be a quiet one, with no special events planned. Mr. Dickens will depart by sailing ship from Boston Harbor on Friday next, in the company of his American secretary, Mr. Richard Perry.

The phaeton carriage containing the literary gentleman, his assistant, and their combined luggage clattered smartly over the cobbles of Chestnut Street, elbowed its way through the hansom cabs and the moving vans and the two-wheeled delivery carts, past the grandiloquent husk of the Bank of the United States, on its way to the railway terminal. There were no cheers in its wake among the small gathering of curious Philadelphians outside the hotel, only scattered criticism:

"Thinks a deal of hisself, don't he?"

"Dresses like a tout, looks like to me."

"He was of the lower sort, you know."

"Swarthy too. It makes you wonder."

"Bit of a skirt chaser I fear."

"And tight as a chicken's arsehole."

Only when it turned out of sight did the small gatherings of curious Philadelphians (none of them in any way official) began to disperse.

"I believe Eddie will be happier in Europe," said Elmira Royster.

"He certainly preferred it as a setting for his tales," I said.

"Mr. Dickens will be happier over there as well," said Putnam. "I reckon Europe is a better place for writers all round."

On this occasion, Putnam wore a plain brown tweed suit of the type favored by railroad inspectors and Pinkerton men. When I remarked on the transformation, he explained that Dickens's file had made mention of the author's flamboyant style of dress. On advice from his superiors and with a modest allowance, Putnam had affected a similar fashion in order to establish a rapport. "It was not something I enjoyed. It felt effeminate."

"We are grateful for your assistance, sir," said Elmira Royster to Putnam, taking my arm. "And we rely on your discretion on certain matters."

"The requirement is even more imperative in your case, ma'am," said Putnam. "In fact, it is of national importance. I am instructed that if either of you reveals a word about the events of the past few days, serious official consequences will ensue."

"I will take it to my grave," I said, feeling the warmth of her hand in the crook of my arm.

CHAPTER THIRTY-SEVEN

Baltimore

Responsibility, *n.* A detachable burden easily
shifted to one's neighbor.
                    —Ambrose Bierce

We sat in the dining room of the Exchange Hotel, looking into
our glasses of whiskey.

"It is a dreadful business, Mr. Poe."

"Dreadful indeed, Dr. Chivers."

"It makes one wonder."

"One does indeed wonder, that is true."

"How far Americans have traveled down the road to hell."

Neilson Poe ordered another brace of the amber liquid. He had
already had four. "Exactly the point, sir. Down the road to hell." And
his finger hit the tablecloth with a thud.

"How are the relatives bearing up?" I asked. I had drunk less, in
fact there were two full glasses on the floor by my ankle.

"Not well, Doctor," he replied, and his beard wagged back and
forth. "Not at all well."

Seated at our linen-covered table in the dining room of the Exchange Hotel, I was once again struck by the family resemblance between Neilson Poe and my old friend Eddie—the sweep of the
forehead, the large moist eyes. Then all at once it became clear to me,
the intention behind his odd choice in hair color, which was to disguise the resemblance between them as much as humanly possible. If
it were not for his dyed hair and his wispy little beard, the similarity
between the two relatives would have been remarkable; they might
have been twins.

"If what you say is true, Doctor—that Edgar has been sold to the medical school for dissection . . ." At a loss for words to describe this enormity, Neilson Poe could only sigh, and shake his beard.

"It is a grisly business," I replied. "And yet, when one considers the content of his work, somewhat ironic as well."

"You have said it, sir!" Neilson Poe nodded vigorously; again I had managed to establish a rapport, with precious little effort.

Like Eddie, this was a man who longed for approval. But there were dissimilarities between them as well, not of blood but experience. Whereas Eddie's mouth suggested sensitivity, Neilson's mouth appeared sharp and defensive. Lines had burrowed into the skin at the corners until they threatened to cut his chin off from the rest of his face. And whereas Eddie had been pristine in his toilet and wardrobe even in impoverished circumstances, his second cousin, the prosperous lawyer, permitted himself dirty fingernails and linen that was less than fresh.

For several moments we contemplated the fate of Eddie's cadaver, sold to an anatomy class as a subject for dissection. (In actual fact, the indignity was double—the corpse having been bought and sold twice.)

As a man who seeks agreement from those around him, for Neilson Poe any pause without an obvious explanation was cause for concern. Therefore, I maintained silence, while my companion wound himself up like the spring of a watch, until the toe of his highly polished walking shoe began tapping, and he could stand it no longer.

"Dr. Chivers, may I be frank with you about my second cousin Edgar?"

"By all means," I replied. "It has not escaped my notice that there was some bad feeling between you."

"The truth is, sir, my second cousin was a monster. As you say, for him to be dealt with in such a monstrous fashion is almost poetic irony. I see it as a positive sign—that there is such a thing as natural justice, don't you see? That there is a God who cares about what men do."

"Yes," I agreed. "You as much as said so in your letter to him."

My companion nodded, pleased with himself—but then my response caused him to stop and blink several times. Whiskey tends to make men a bit slow.

"*Written him a letter?* Dear heaven, why on earth would I do such a thing?" Neilson Poe's eyes narrowed suspiciously, an expression I would never have seen in credulous Eddie.

"I found the missing teeth a nice touch," I continued. "It was obvious at a glance that the woman's teeth were pulled after death—but *how long* after death was the question. Aware of the practice of selling teeth to denturists, I confronted the mortician with my observation. In exchange for my silence, and a small stipend, he was able to tell me who bought them. You have a striking appearance if I may say so, Mr. Poe. Every bit as memorable as your second cousin."

Neilson Poe shook his head sadly. "One cannot trust anyone in America these days."

"I wouldn't go so far as all that," I replied. "When a man is bribed once, it is no great surprise that he is willing to be bribed twice."

"That is true. I had not thought of that."

Now it was Neilson Poe who took a considerable pause, and myself who broke it.

"Believe me, Mr. Poe, I do not blame you in the least, nor do I hold you responsible for his fate. Eddie was, as you say, a monster. A disease. He infected the world."

"*Infected the world.* By God you have a way with words, Doctor!"

"As I see it, sir, your only act was to confront your second cousin with his own infectious morbidity. It was not your fault that the truth drove him mad."

"Exactly so!" My companion nodded vigorously—but then for a second he stopped, aware of what he had just admitted to. Then came an almost imperceptible shrug as though to say: *What difference does it make now?*

"Tell me, Doctor, what would you think of a man who stole a loved one from you as a child, then corrupted and destroyed her?"

"I would hate him for it, for certain. I would wish to do him harm."

Neilson Poe nodded, with the look of a man whose mind is elsewhere.

It has been my experience that the urge to tell one's story is well nigh universal. Under conditions of relative safety a man will reveal the most ghastly things about himself, almost with pleasure. Neilson Poe was no exception—indeed, his case would present an excellent case study for *Scientific American*.

"It began when Edgar moved in with Aunt Maria Clemm. At the

time he was one more burden in a troubled home. Cousin George—consumptive, coughing, and drinking himself to death. My great-aunt in bed, paralyzed and demented. My great-uncle, dying.

"Then there was little Virginia. Dear little Virginia. I had been her protector, don't you see, almost from her birth. I shall forever regret that I could not have been with her twenty-four hours a day. I shall always regret that Edgar could.

"My Virginia was seven when he moved in. A rosy little girl in gingham and pigtails. Edgar was twenty. Her big cousin played with her. He helped her with her sums. She called him *Buddie*—is that not the limit?

"She grew helpless in her affection for him, and remained so to the last day of her little life.

"Dear little Virginia was too young to see what I could see—that which would appear, for profit, in his dreadful stories. All those haunted dreams of incest come to life. His worship of the infantile. His morbid craving for the abnormal and the grotesque. Oh, it was all perfectly apparent, right from the start.

"Just think of it, Doctor: the ward of a rich man, having managed to get himself disowned, sponging off this pathetic group! As an alternative to any concession to duty, don't you see, it was not for Edgar to show obedience to his stepfather, or secure a paying job. Edgar was too important for any of it.

"I watched it happen, sir. My own father helped him publish his verse in *The Yankee*. I saw what he was, yet I could do nothing. I saw with my own eyes as he made love to Mary Newman, and I heard him propose to Mary Devereaux—dear God, little Virginia delivered love notes between them!

"Then, most grotesque of all, came the marriage.

"Edgar had recently returned from army duties. His stepfather was recently dead, immune to begging letters forever. Where was Edgar to turn now? Where to sink his proboscis and suck out a living while remaining so haughtily above life itself?

"Heaven knows when Eddie and Aunt Maria dreamed up this dreadful alliance, between a man of twenty-six and a girl barely thirteen—and first cousins, to boot. I suspect it was earlier than any of us can stomach.

"And what of Aunt Maria, her own mother? How could she consent to a match between little Virginia and a man of Eddie's age and dissipated habits? Would not any alternative be an improvement over life in an incestuous hive? To a husband who would contribute not even his company—unless he were ill, or in the throes of overindulgence?

"Not for Aunt Maria. Where my aunt was concerned, Edgar was the prince of poetry. His sensitivity, his talent, his poetic affectations had blinded her to everything else. The only person in that house who was genuinely in love with anyone was Aunt Maria.

"Edgar had a way with women, don't you see? He could subject them to his will.

"When it came to begging for money on his behalf, nobody could outdo Aunt Maria. Only editors, it seems, found the strength to resist her pleas—and even they shed tears over it.

"And what are we to think of my little Virginia, sir? Hostage for life, to a parasite who called himself a poet.

"To be sure, sir, at the wedding there was no white dress for little Virginia, no veil, not a penny spent so that she might experience a momentary, fragile glory as a bride.

"And who was to give Virginia away? Why Aunt Maria Clemm, of course—dear, long-suffering Aunt Maria! To this day, when I lay eyes on the woman I want to wring her wretched neck.

"Is my tale grotesque enough for you, sir? Does it not make your skin crawl as though with lice? Well, count on Edgar to exploit it again and again—tale after tale about incestuous brides, women buried alive in tombs, suffering amputation, wasting away . . .

"Yet who was the sufferer? Who inspired tears of pity? Why, Edgar Poe, of course. No matter what misery he brought down upon others, it was Edgar whose suffering mattered most." Neilson Poe grimaced at the sour taste of his whiskey.

"I sympathize with you utterly, Mr. Poe," I said. And yet it was not until the *Collected Tales* that you came to truly hate him. It was as though he had put between two covers all the cruelty and depravity he had visited upon poor little Virginia, into a single parcel, to be sold, for money.

"Why stop at that? Could he not have made a dollar or two by selling her blood-spattered handkerchiefs, swatches of her shroud, her bones and teeth? . . ."

Neilson Poe wept. "Stop. I beg you, stop. How did you know this?"

"Because in my own way I shared your sentiments. We have something in common, don't you see?"

Neilson Poe drained his glass, and wiped his gaunt cheek with his linen napkin. "You have seen through me at any rate, sir. You have cut me to the quick."

"So did your letter, sir. And the woman in the morgue. And when I saw the teeth I literally fainted dead away."

"I don't understand you, sir."

I took a large drink myself. As I might have mentioned, there are aspects to my tale that will not enhance my reputation.

"As I said, we have something in common, Mr. Poe," I said. "There were other clippings, you see. Eddie received other letters. I wrote them. I wrote them myself."

Dr. William Chivers returned to Baltimore. He resigned his position at Washington College Hospital, then moved to Richmond, Virginia, there to establish a modest private practice while writing his memoirs. At that time he became engaged to Mrs. Elmira Shelton. They remained engaged until his death.

Inspector Shadduck became Philadelphia's first police marshal, following the Act of Consolidation in 1854.

Finn Devlin fled north with Miss Genoux. There he joined the radical group known as the Fenian Brotherhood, whose aim was to take Canada hostage and thereby force England to grant independence to Ireland. In 1866, the Fenians launched a series of raids on Canadian territory. One was at Pigeon Hill, on the Quebec-Vermont border.

The Fenians plundered nearby St. Armand and Slab City, and, it was said, "insulted and abused" the population. On hearing that Canadian reinforcements were approaching, they began a disorganized retreat to the United States. The last two hundred stragglers were charged by a troop of cavalry, who managed to capture sixteen prisoners.

Finn Devlin was one of them. The last public words ever heard from him were, "Men of Ireland, I am ashamed of you."

Edgar Allan Poe returned to England, where he wrote under a variety of pseudonyms. Miss Genoux returned to France, and was never heard from again.